'A mixture of wonderful history, adventure and a heart-breaking love story; the world of fifteenth-century Venice and Constantinople is brought thrillingly to life'
Kate Mosse

'Fascinating historical mysteries and vivid colourful characters. It's a page-turner fast enough to make its own breeze'
Conn Iggulden

'A dramatic read from the very outset'
Simon Scarrow

'A gripping, epic tale set against a broad and breath-taking European canvas. Do not miss this compelling page-turner'
Alison Weir

'A fast-moving and superbly intelligent adventure, driven by the agony and triumph of empire, loyalty and revenge'
Jason Goodwin

'A grand, sweeping drama of the finest kind, miss this excellent book at your peril'
Ben Kane

## Also by James Heneage

*By Blood Divided*

### RISE OF EMPIRES SERIES

*The Walls of Byzantium*

*The Towers of Samarcand*

*The Lion of Mistra*

# JAMES HENEAGE

# A World On Fire

Quercus

First published in Great Britain in 2018
This edition published in 2019 by

Quercus Editions Ltd
Carmelite House
50 Victoria Embankment
London EC4Y 0DZ

An Hachette UK company

A CIP catalogue record for this book is available
from the British Library

PB ISBN 978 1 78648 020 0
EBOOK ISBN 978 1 78648 021 7

This book is a work of fiction. Names, characters,
places and events portrayed in it, while at times
based on historical figures and places, are the
product of the author's imagination.

10 9 8 7 6 5 4 3 2 1

Typeset by CC Book Production

Printed and bound in Great Britain by Clays Ltd, Elcograf S.p.A.

# ACKNOWLEDGEMENTS

This is my fifth novel and provides a good opportunity to mention two extraordinary editors who it has been my great pleasure to work with so far: Susan Watt and Cassie Browne. To both of you my deepest thanks.

To Xan, who is our Tzanis

# CONTENTS

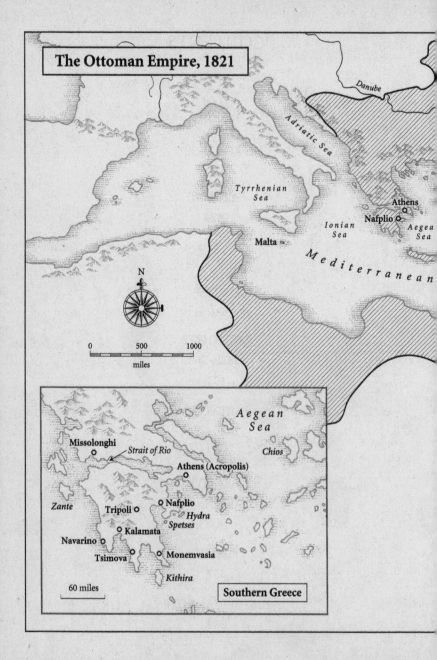

# The Ottoman Empire, 1821

Danube

*Adriatic Sea*

*Tyrrhenian Sea*

*Ionian Sea*

Malta

Athens

Nafplio

*Aegean Sea*

M e d i t e r r a n e a n

N

0        500        1000
miles

*Aegean Sea*

Missolonghi

*Strait of Rio*

*Chios*

Athens (Acropolis)

*Zante*

Tripoli

Nafplio

*Hydra*

*Spetses*

Kalamata

Navarino

Tsimova

Monemvasia

*Kithira*

60 miles

**Southern Greece**

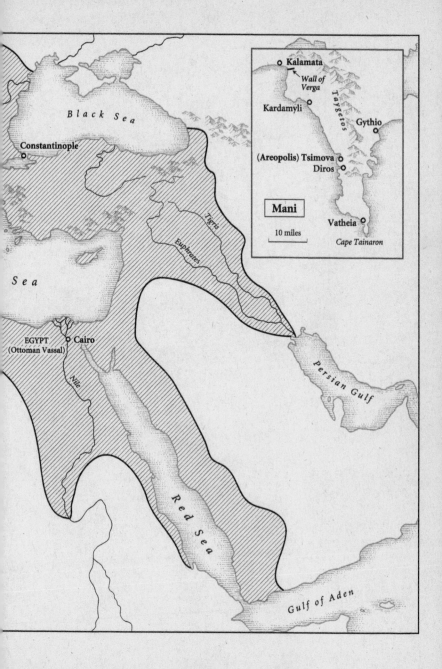

# PROLOGUE

## ISLAND OF CHIOS, 1822

There was no sound beyond the brush of water unrolling from the boat's sides to settle creases beyond. Nothing moved in the sea.

Up ahead, silent birds gyred over the beach and hills and the smoke that rose between. Hastings watched them as you might an unwelcome flag; their signal made him uneasy. He pushed hair from his eyes and leant forward a little.

There. In the water. Motionless. Seaweed?

*No.*

He lifted his hand to the sun, tilted his head back a little to be heard. 'Can you see those, Tombazis?'

He'd not spoken since they'd pulled away from the *Themistocles*, anchored outside the bay. Nor had the rowers who'd felt his unease grow with every pull. He pointed. 'There.'

'Ship debris?' Tombazis shrugged. His moustache had the wingspan of the birds, the same glide. 'I don't know.'

Hastings shook his head. 'On the beach too. And beyond.' He looked round. 'Everywhere, in fact.'

The boat had quickened and now the sound of running water

was beneath them. Hastings heard talk from the rowers and wished he'd learnt more Greek in the months he'd been here. He raised his head to a new smell, one he knew.

Then a cry.

He looked back to a man who'd pushed away his oar, saw what he saw: a hand clutching the paddle in the water, nothing beyond its wrist but blood. He heard Tombazis clamber over the benches behind him. They stood together.

'*Mother of God.*'

Most were women, children sometimes beside them. The blood moved as they did: red rafts holding them afloat. There were hundreds of bodies in the sea.

The boat drifted as though among islands. The rowers had stopped and were looking around them. The first bump sent a charge bow to stern and the men took up their oars and pulled hard, heads down. The boat lurched forward, parting bodies now.

As they approached the beach, sounds came out to them from the island. A dog barked and was answered by another. Birds screeched their alarm. The bow hit sand and Hastings jumped into the water, lifting his sword above his head. He heard Tombazis's splash behind him, then others. He waded his way to the shore, swaying from side to side.

The beach was littered with dead, some on the sand, some half in the sea with water lapping around them. Hastings knelt down next to a child whose eyes were fixed in a final glaze of horror. What had they seen? He looked around the beach, at the bodies strewn across it, big on top of small, arms stretched out in pointless supplication, white as lard. Gently, he closed the child's eyes and rose. He looked up into the hills to where a track ran up to a village. The way was scattered with bodies, dogs moving between them.

'We should go into the village,' he said. 'We need to know what has happened here.'

Tombazis grunted. 'I think we know, don't we?'

This much Hastings knew: Chios, an island only two miles from the Turkish mainland, had risen in revolt four months ago. No one had known why. The island was rich from trade with the Turks, its people the most agreeable in the Aegean. It had everything to lose from rebellion. Now it was a place of death.

He began to walk up the path, feeling the mid-morning sun on his neck, the heat of the packed earth beneath his soles, flies against his scalp. He marshalled his senses to ignore what lay around him. He summoned every drop of reserve passed through an English mother's milk.

A shot rang out and he turned. A sailor was standing over a dead dog. He watched him stoop to take something from its mouth. He looked away.

He reached the outskirts of the village and gazed up the steep, narrow street that divided it. It was choked with dead, their limbs spread in extravagant greeting. They might have been revellers soaked in wine. He saw a young girl slumped in a doorway, black circles of blood where once had been breasts. She held a stick in her hand, not thicker than her arms.

He felt a surge of anger stronger than any he'd felt since coming to this war. Sometimes it had been the incompetence, sometimes the greed, more often the random cruelty of those he'd come to help. He'd seen it from the Greeks, not yet the Turks.

'I want to find who did this,' he said quietly, turning to Tombazis. 'Now, while they're still here. It's happened recently.'

The Greek shook his head, his long hair brushing his neck. He had one palm resting on the gold pommels of two pistols

3

thrust into his waistband. 'No, we should go back to the ship. We can do nothing here, except get killed.'

'We must look for survivors. What about the hills?'

The dead littered the rising ground like cuttings, the smallest highest up. The children had run faster than their mothers. 'Give me your pistols. I'm going to look.'

Tombazis glanced up to where he pointed, then shrugged. He pulled the long barrels from his waistband and handed them over.

Hastings turned and began to walk up the hill, waving the flies from his face, head back and straight, not looking to left or right. He reached the summit and stopped, tucking the guns away. The land fell away into a deep valley with a river at the bottom with high banks. It was an absurdity of peace given what lay behind.

He realised it was the first time he'd been alone since joining the frigate *Themistocles*, the biggest ship in the fledgling Greek navy. He looked up into the intemperate sun, pinching sweat from the bridge of his nose and shaking it free. He undid the cloth from his neck and used it to dab his temples, then pulled his fingers through his hair. Suddenly, he was exhausted.

He walked down the other side of the hill, picking his path between the rocks and the hard, brown grass of late summer. He reached the small precipice of the riverbank and found a twisted tree clinging to its edge, its roots dug in like old fingers. He knelt and peered over. The river was the thinnest of trickles, brown and turgid. Further up he saw a dead animal stretched across it, legs in the air.

The first cry was very faint and he thought it part of the stream. He turned away and began to walk back up the hill. The second was more distinct: the cry of a child, coming from below.

*Below?*

He walked back to the edge of the bank and peered over the edge, his hand on the trunk of the tree. There was a big hole in the wall of earth, partially filled with dense shrub: placed there, not grown.

He swung himself over and slid down into the water, his sword hitting his thigh. He felt the cool seep through the leather of his boots and a momentary dizziness. He straightened and smacked the earth from his knees. He leant forward and drew aside the shrub.

After the sunshine, the dark seemed impenetrable. He blinked to adjust and heard something else: the shuffle of feet, the intake of many breaths. He drew his sword and cautiously entered.

'I'm not Turk,' he whispered in Greek, forcing calm into his voice. 'English. I have a ship.' Then louder. 'I'll not harm you.'

He saw something move in the darkness.

'So why have you drawn your sword? We are women and children.'

He heard a sound behind him. Tombazis. There was the strike of flint and the first splutter of pitch. Light flickered into the cave, revealing its contents in spasms. A woman stood facing him: tall, straight, about thirty, like him. The dress she wore had once been very fine, just as her hair had once been ordered. He stared into eyes full of contempt. She held a musket pointed at his heart.

Next to her stood a man, a little older perhaps, with a bandage around his eyes and circles of blood either side of his nose. Behind were people of all ages, some standing, some sitting on the ground. Most were women, with children beside them. All were staring at him from hollowed, starving eyes that

5

held more terror than he'd ever seen. He swallowed hard and sheathed his sword.

Slowly the woman lowered her musket. 'I am Manto Kavardis,' she said. 'Beside me is my factor, Panagiotis. His eyes were put out by the Turks. Behind are the people of my estate. We've not eaten for a week and would like to get off this island.'

Hastings saw movement at her knees. He looked down and saw, half-hidden among her skirts, a little girl with wide, staring eyes and her thumb in her mouth. He reached down and lifted her into his arms.

# PART ONE

# 1824

# CHAPTER ONE

## MANI, SOUTHERN TIP OF GREECE

Hara sat up in bed and listened to a storm louder than any she'd heard in this place of storms. Her head was pointed like a hunter's, nose high, every sense tuned to the drama. Lightning rimmed the shutters and the wind rattled them like shells in a net. The candles had blown out long ago.

Perhaps, she thought, the storms were fiercer here at the end of the world. Or perhaps it was because the old gods were much closer. After all, the mouth of Hades was only five miles away. Even the *pappas* said so.

This was the *boras,* coming straight down from Mount Elijah, roaring like a bull through its passes, blasting the stones to pieces at the coast. There was nothing to stop it in this barren land of the Mani: no trees, no riverbeds ... only rocks and the half-hidden, ancient remains that whispered of a better past.

And now there was just this wall between it and the bumps on her skin. She stroked her arms and shivered. She pulled the blanket up to her shoulders. At least the cisterns would fill.

She heard a banging on the trapdoor to the room below where

her brothers lived. Her bedroom was also a place of storage and she slept most nights half-drugged by the must of acorns.

Another banging. She rose from the bed and went to the trap-door and lifted it to her brother's face, lit by flickering candle.

'Ship,' said Christos, already turning. Below him, she could see her other brothers dressed and ready to go.

'Where?' she asked.

'Below Capo Grosso, going south.' He was already stepping down the ladder. 'The pappas is waiting with the mules.'

She nodded. Only the priest could calm them in this kind of weather. She dressed quickly and descended the ladder. She took a torch from Christos and followed him down to the bottom floor and out into the storm where the priest stood dripping beside the animals. His beard was a river of filth.

It was hard walking to the end of the world, to the mouth of hell. The wind bent them double and the rain scourged their heads and shoulders like flails, hurling little stones against their legs and salt into their eyes. Each of them pulled a mule, smacked by the pappas when the pulling wasn't enough.

By the time they reached the beach, the wind had risen to a savage, keening fury and they had to take shelter behind some rocks to fix the lanterns round the animals' necks, pulling the cords tight to secure them.

Christos said: 'Hara, go and look.'

She passed her mule to another and climbed to the top of the rock, then across others to the sea. She moved like an animal not wanting to be seen, her body low. She reached a jagged promontory and leant out as far as she dared, scanning the chaos for any sign of a ship. Like a cat.

Nothing.

But then she'd not expected to see anything. It was always

some other sense that told her where the ship was. She closed her eyes and concentrated. Yes. *There.*

A ship was out there and it was in danger, much danger. She knew it from some instinct denied her brothers and everyone else in the Mani. It was a talent she'd had for as long as she could remember, like diving deeper than any man she knew. It was why they let her go with them.

She waited a while to be sure, keeping her head level on the plinth of her shoulders, listening to every change in the wind. She blessed her short hair, cut to the scalp after the boy had come to seek marriage two months ago. She'd smeared herself with fish oil just to be sure. She'd not seen the boy again.

She turned and scrambled back to the beach. By now, others of the clan had joined and the longboat had been dragged down to the sea. The mules were tied together, lanterns lit. Their lights would resemble ships lying at anchor for any ship seeking sanctuary, drawing them onto the rocks.

'Well?'

Christos was peering at her from under his spattered hood. He was the eldest of her six brothers, twelve years older than she. He'd spent time as a prisoner of the Turks and still bore the scars. He frightened her sometimes.

'Something's out there,' she said. 'Big, and running before the storm. It might escape.'

Christos spoke to the man beside him. 'We'll go fast and wait behind the rocks. If it runs onto them, we'll be there.' He turned back to her. 'Will we make the rocks?'

She nodded. 'With God's grace.'

Then all was hurry. The men hauled the boat into the sea, straining to keep it level in the crashing surf, the oars banging against its sides like they wanted to escape. Hara pulled herself

11

up to the bow where she'd point to where they must go. She had the storm lantern held aloft, steadying it so that the candle stayed upright on its gimbal. She checked the ropes and grappling hooks beside her. A man shouted and she passed the lantern down to him.

They somehow got through the surf, rising and plunging as the sea battered the hull. Then the men got into their rhythm and Hara clung to the sides with both hands until one was needed to wipe salt from her eyes. She looked straight ahead, her frame as rigid as she could hold it, watching a sea she knew better than any man aboard.

'There!' She pointed.

It was closer than she'd imagined it would be, almost on the rocks. It had once been a fine schooner but its masts were stumps now, its sails in the water. There were men throwing themselves off, clinging onto whatever might become a raft. Their screams came and went on the wind. She could see a longboat half over the side, broken at the middle, two men clinging to it. A wave broke over it and they disappeared.

She turned to Christos seated at the stern, watching her. 'Faster,' she shouted. 'It's going down!'

Their boat had nine men and her aboard, with enough space left over for whatever they could take away in it. *Not much*, she thought, as the ship ahead veered onto its side. It must hit the rocks now, surely. *It must go down*. But at least she'd know where it was. She could dive later, in calmer seas.

They reached the rocks before the ship did, keeping their distance, working their way slowly around the jagged teeth, wary of sudden currents, of the dangers beneath. Suddenly the ship's stern reared up ahead of them. The windows of the master cabin were high above her, a light still on inside. She took hold of a grappling hook and swung it once above her head, launching it into the night. She felt it take hold and jerked it to be sure. Then she was in the air, swinging towards the ship with the rope coiled around a wrist to keep it in her hands. Her feet hit wet wood and she threw off a shoe for better purchase. She climbed, foot over foot, lurching from side to side with every plunge, hearing now the cries of the men above her.

She reached the cabin and pulled herself up to see inside. A man was trying to pull a heavy chest towards a window in the side. He wore a waistcoat and a white, high-collared shirt, too fine for a storm. He hadn't seen her.

A wave crashed over the ship and she nearly lost her hold. She looked down at the little boat dancing below, saw nine unsteady men looking up at her. She felt her heart quicken with the joy of it all. None of them could do what she was doing. *None.* She threw out a knee and levered herself into the cabin.

The man turned as she landed. He'd managed to lift the chest so that it was half-out of the window, balanced on its edge. She shook her head. *Don't.*

He stared at her, puzzled, like he'd seen her before. Then he lowered his shoulder and pushed. The chest disappeared. A wave crashed and the ship shuddered as it hit the rocks, sending her forwards. Then they were both on their knees, facing each other.

She gestured behind her. He nodded. She turned and scrambled to where the hook was still affixed. She climbed onto the rope and let herself down, fist over fist, glancing up to see if he followed her. They got to the boat just in time. The ship was breaking against the rocks, each explosion launching new parts into the sea.

She went to the bow and watched as the man was brought to

13

lie beside her. In moments he'd fallen asleep, despite the wind and the spray and the crash of the waves. She looked down at him. He looked about the same age as Christos but his face was not like any she'd seen before. His skin was pale, smooth, clean-shaven; his hair long but scissor-cut. It was a face built for conversation more than survival, but the jaw was strong. She watched him for a long time, fascinated, then she reached over to a blanket and lifted it up to his chin.

'Aristocrat.'

Christos was looking down with loathing. He turned and spat over the side. 'I suppose we can ransom him. Did you see anything in the cabin?'

She looked down again at the sleeping man. *A kind face.*

'No,' she said.

# CHAPTER TWO

## MANI

Prince Tzanis Comnenos woke up in hell. His head was on fire and he was blinded by flame.

He shielded his eyes and sat up, hearing the crackle of straw released. The sun disappeared behind stone, leaving only shafts of dusty light and a window bluer than the Virgin's veil. Perhaps he was in heaven.

He looked around, feeling the stiffness of a neck too long asleep. The room was small and square and had bare wooden floorboards with a trapdoor in the middle, a ring at one side to pull it up. Around the walls were sacks of grain and a crude ladder. The ceiling had thick beams across it and another trapdoor between. He heard birdsong outside.

He looked down at himself. Somebody had put new clothes on him, a tunic and short trousers. They were rough to the skin but mercifully clean. He examined his limbs and found them clean too. Someone had washed him.

He rose and went to the low window, feeling the heat now on his belly, and looked outside. He was at the top of a tower and beneath were other towers, each with a building and walled yard attached. Around them were fields, fringed by green cacti and flat stone walls, and beyond were mountains with snow at their tops. He couldn't see a single tree.

*The Mani.*

He sat on the floor and thought. What had Capodistrias told him about the Mani? It was the most violent place on earth, where clans were in perpetual feud, where every newborn son was a 'gun', every girl a disappointment. The mountains rang with musket shot and the people built towers to shoot down on their neighbours. He was at the top of one now.

Thank God he'd thrown the gold overboard. It was better lost than in the hands of the *kapitanos* who ruled this land. Well, almost lost: he'd taken a single coin from the casket before pushing it out. He'd put it in the pocket of his waistcoat. The waistcoat he was no longer wearing. *Gone.*

He thought of what else had happened last night. *Or was it a week ago?* He'd no idea. How long had he been asleep? He thought of the boy who'd suddenly appeared in the ship's cabin, who'd watched him throw the chest overboard, who'd saved him from that sinking ship.

He heard movement below, someone crossing the floor, climbing the ladder. He shifted himself round to face the trap-door, feeling ridiculous in his bare feet. Where were his clothes?

A cropped head appeared, then a hand pushed back the door until it fell with a crash. It was the boy carrying a tray with a jug and food. He climbed up into the room, ignoring Tzanis, and put the tray down and sat, back to the wall, knees drawn up to his chin, a column of light separating them. He watched as Tzanis leant forward and took some food.

As the prince ate, he examined what he could see through the dancing motes. The boy seemed to be wearing a knee-length tunic and the legs beneath were dark brown and hairless. Above the longest of necks, his face was a thing of astonishing beauty: two gigantic eyes, black-lashed and shoreless, set in a face of purest oval, gathered to a graceful end at nose and chin.

He finished and put the plate down. He stretched his legs into the sun, watching the motes scatter, enjoying the heat on his skin.

'Where am I?' he asked.

The boy didn't answer. The eyes blinked once, eyelashes brushing together like feathers.

Did they even speak the same language? He knew he was at the very bottom of Greece and they said it got wilder the closer you got to Africa. What was the name Capodistrias had given the Mani? Ah yes, *Kakavulia:* land of evil counsel. Not a single school, he'd said, and no law beyond the gun's. Just endless superstition.

'Is this tower where you live?' he tried again, pointing around. 'Is your father here?'

Still nothing, just the stare. He heard someone moving below, more shuffle than footstep. The ladder creaked and an older head appeared, one with sparse, wiry hair above shoulders clad in black. A priest.

The man climbed through and hauled himself to standing, one hand to a knee. He was middle-aged and had a grey beard that fell to his belly, a heavy crucifix on top. He clapped his hands together in a cloud of dust and wiped his palms on his bottom. He went over to the window and looked out, hands on his behind. He straightened and turned.

'Has she spoken to you yet?'

*She?* Tzanis glanced at the long neck, the hairless legs. *Of course.* He turned back.

17

'Not since the rescue. Was it last night?'

The priest nodded. 'Last night, yes. You were the only survivor.' He crossed himself, then lifted the crucifix to his lips. 'We must pray for their souls.'

Tzanis thought back to the crew. He'd not known a single one of them, not even their captain. He'd been Corsican: terse, businesslike and well-paid by Capodistrias. He would deliver Prince Tzanis and his gold to Corfu then go back to Ajaccio. The less he knew, the better for them all.

The priest sat down in the window, filling it entirely and blocking out most of its light. He scratched his beard with heavy, peasant fingers cracked by dirt.

'What are you?' he asked. 'Greek?'

'I am Russian.'

The priest studied him for some moments from beneath the matted tangle of his brow, his eyes small pools of suspicion. 'You don't look Russian. You look Greek.'

Did this man even know what Russian looked like? In truth, Tzanis was both Greek and Russian. His father, Prince Giorgios Comnenos, was directly descended from Greek emperors, but his mother was Russian. 'I can assure you that I am Russian. I am on my way to Corfu. To teach.'

The brows lifted a fraction. 'What do you teach?'

'English,' Tzanis said. 'There is demand for it there. The island is governed by the English.'

The priest nodded slowly. He looked around the room. 'What was on the ship?'

Tzanis glanced at the girl. Her face was impassive save for the smallest of frowns. 'I don't know,' he said. 'I was a passenger. The crew was from Corsica.'

Still the slow nodding. 'Corsica.' It was possible he'd never heard of Corsica either. It was possible he'd never been outside the Mani. 'Where did you sail from?'

Tzanis was growing impatient. 'From Odessa. Look, can you take a letter from me to whoever rules this place? I must take a boat to Corfu. I can pay.'

'Pay? How can you pay? You don't have anything.'

'By bill of exchange. Can you give me pen and paper?'

The priest frowned so deeply that his eyebrows almost met his cheeks. It occurred to Tzanis that he might not be able to write.

The man got slowly to his feet, gesturing to the girl who rose more quickly. How old was she? Eighteen?

The priest spoke without looking at him. 'I will take you to Prince Petrobey in Tsimova. He rules here in the Mani.'

A week later, they left as the first light of the sun exploded across a sky of seamless blue.

It was spring in the Mani and the road they took north was bordered by Jerusalem sage and broom in full flower. Beyond it, a tide of wild lavender swept up to small, terraced fields of thin wheat hemmed by tiny walls to shore up the precious soil. The walls marched up the mountains' skirts to die away among the boulders where cliffs rose suddenly, cloudy with cystus. Above them, the peaks of the great *Taygetos* reared up and marched into the distance, Mount Elijah's snowy top crowning them all. To their left was always the sea: an endless sheet of cool blue occasionally bumped by passing breeze. It was as if the storm had never happened.

There were just six of them: Tzanis, the girl, the priest and three mules. Around the animals' necks hung hollowed-out gourds that knocked together as they went. The girl walked in

19

front, the priest behind, and Tzanis, still dressed in his tunic, between.

He'd had a week to consider his predicament. He was in the Mani when he should be on Corfu handing over the Tzar's gold to Mavrocordatos, head of the Greek revolutionary government. Even now, he should be discussing Capodistrias's plan to unite Greece under a prince of the Comnenos line, linked to Russia by one, Orthodox communion. The gold was to be the first down payment and he'd lost it in the worst place on earth he could have chosen. And Petrobey?

'Father, can you tell me about the man we are to meet?' he asked.

'Our kapitano?' The priest wore his tall hat tipped back on his head. He walked with a stick. 'Born of a mermaid, they say.'

Tzanis heard a snort in front.

The priest stopped and spoke over him, pointing his stick. 'You shouldn't scoff. Not you. Why else his beauty?'

Tzanis knew something of Petrobey. He'd been the first to raise the standard of revolt in the little square of Tsimova three years ago. He'd done it too soon, but the rising had somehow survived, seeing off two Turkish armies sent to crush it. Now the revolution was in danger and needed the Tzar's money. But it had to be secret and it had to go to the right man. *Not Petrobey.*

The girl had stopped. She turned and looked past Tzanis to the priest. 'Is that in your gospel, pappas?' she asked. 'I don't remember you telling me that bit.'

Tzanis stared. Her solemn face had become a smile, slung like a hammock between her ears, crinkling her nose. He said, with some wonder: 'You talk.'

She turned away and the priest tugged at his mule. 'Talk?' he said after a few steps. 'And argue. She's more stubborn than this beast.' Tzanis heard the smack of his stick. 'Ask her brothers if she can talk.'

Tzanis moved closer to her mule. He glanced round, then said quietly: 'I owe you my life.' He paused. 'But perhaps you saw something?'

'I've not told anyone.'

Tzanis glanced behind him again. The priest was slowing and quite far from them now, bent forward on his stick because of the path's steepness. There were grunts with every step.

'Can it be salvaged?'

She shrugged, still looking ahead. 'Perhaps. By me.'

'You dive?'

'Deeper than any man. I am a mermaid.'

They were silent for a while and the birdsong seemed suddenly loud around them. He asked: 'What is your name?'

'Hara.'

'How old are you, Hara?'

'Eighteen, I think. That's what my brothers say.'

Her brothers. Tzanis thought back to what he'd seen of them. They hadn't looked like her at all.

'Who is your father?' he asked.

She didn't answer. She looked back to him. 'Was there coin in that chest?'

Tzanis thought about lying but he'd need this girl if he was to retrieve the Tzar's gold. 'Perhaps.'

He heard the rattle of rolling stones behind. The priest was catching them up; Tzanis fell back. A lizard darted between his feet, froze, then disappeared behind rocks in a flash of silver.

The priest said: 'When God made the world, he had a sack of stones left over and he dumped them all in the Mani.'

*

In the evening, they came to a village. At first, he didn't see it. The clustered towers seemed the same texture as the rocks beneath, shrugged into existence by some ancient, underground upheaval. He looked out to sea. The sunset had laid the water on its back, flattened it, beaten it to an uneven plate. Its calm beauty took his breath away.

The priest pointed up to the houses. 'We have come to Drialos, about half-way to Tsimova. We'll rest here the night.'

They saw no one as they approached, nor in the village square where black Maniot pigs rooted beneath the long shade of a carob tree, branches dangling with horny locust beans. They stopped and looked around in silence while the mules tossed flies from their eyes and the pigs ignored them. The priest hummed as he scanned the four corners of the square.

At last men began to appear from the shadows between the towers. They came out one by one: dark, lean, hewn beings with blue jowls and black, wary eyes. Their moustaches swept down in sword-swipes, bigger than he'd seen on the faces of Napoleon's Old Guard. They were dressed in baggy, pleated trousers that ended just below the knees. Over their shirts, they wore short *boleros* and their hair fell in thick, black waves to their shoulders. All of them were carrying muskets, longer even than the *jezails* of the Cossacks.

He glanced at the priest. 'Are they friendly?' he whispered.

'They are Petrobey's men.'

'Why are they here?'

The priest took off his hat and wiped his forehead with his sleeve. The evening was warm. He shrugged. 'To escort us to him, I suppose.'

Tzanis saw one of them go over and speak to Hara. 'Do they know her?'

The pappas grunted. 'Everyone in the Mani knows Hara.' The black hat waved and flies scattered. 'Some people say she is Petrobey's daughter.'

'Is she?'

'How should I know?'

The man gestured to Hara to follow him. Others came up to take their mules. The men led them to the tallest tower and remained outside as they stepped into a large, barrel-vaulted room, half-sunk below ground level, with a long table and chairs at its centre. On one wall, a range was tunnelled into the stone and had something cooking on it that smelt good. Grooved amphorae were stacked on one side and thorn faggots on the other. Ropes of onion and garlic hung from two small windows.

Above it all was the noise of birds. Tzanis looked up to see two nests amidst the beams. He watched the birds come and go for a moment.

'Swallows.'

He turned to see a man standing next to Hara, his hand on her shoulder. He was tall and dressed in a long, fur-lined gown in spite of the heat. Beneath it was an embroidered belt holding two pistols and a curved dagger. A necklace of gems hung around his neck above a rosary.

'I am Petrobey,' he said. 'And you are a Russian teacher from Odessa.' He gestured to the range. 'Are you hungry?'

Tzanis nodded. 'We've walked all day.'

'And she walks fast.' Petrobey nodded towards Hara. 'I have heard it said.'

Tzanis glanced from one to the other. If they shared the same blood, it wasn't obvious. Their beauties were quite different. Petrobey's was as hard as his landscape, Hara's held the promise of something finer.

Petrobey waved his hand and Hara left the room, closing the door behind her. He gestured to the chairs and they both sat. He reached for the wine.

Tzanis looked at the man before him. He was middle-aged and had a heavy moustache beneath a fine, hooked nose. His hair was long and tied at the back. His eyes were very blue. Not the eyes of an assassin.

Petrobey filled both glasses. 'You've got to know Hara. Did you know she can dive deeper than anyone? My family are said to come from mermaids. It's why they think she's my daughter.'

'And is she?'

Petrobey didn't answer. 'Her mother was my children's nurse. She died at her birth. She knew every herb in the Mani and how to use it, perhaps because she was a *tzinia*. Hara has her mother's gifts, and her beauty, though she does her best to hide it.' He drank. 'I don't think you're a teacher.'

'I'm surprised you're an expert,' said Tzanis. 'I'm told there are no schools in the Mani.'

Petrobey laughed. 'I plan to change that.'

*I plan to change that.* What had Capodistrias told him? That Petrobey had already signed himself as *generalissimo* of this revolution when he'd written to all the leaders of Europe? He was Napoleon reincarnated and the world didn't need another Napoleon.

Petrobey leant back in his chair and put his head to one side. 'I would say that you're a *phanariot* and in the service of the Tzar's Foreign Minister, Count Capodistrias. You speak to me as an equal. You can't help it.'

*Equal?* The presumption! He said: 'I don't know what a phanariot is.'

24

Petrobey looked surprised. 'Really? Well, let me enlighten you. A phanariot is a Greek nobleman whose family has lived in the Phanar district of Constantinople, where the Patriarch's palace is. Over the centuries, the phanariots have enriched themselves in the service of the Turkish Sultan, usually at the expense of their own people. They are, essentially, parasites.'

Tzanis considered this. In many ways, he'd liked to have been a phanariot, then his family might still be rich and expedient rather than poor and imperial. Then he'd not have the pressure to make a good marriage and wouldn't have to hear the constant complaint that he was leaving it too late. He was only twenty-nine, after all.

Petrobey had risen from his chair and was walking up and down, hands behind his back. 'I and the other kapitanos have won every victory in this revolution: Kalamata, Tripolitsa, Nafplio,' he ticked them off on his fingers. 'Only now do you phanariots arrive, when the battle's won. You know who the worst of your kind is?'

He shook his head.

'Mavrocordatos.'

*The very man I should be talking to.*

'He has set himself up at Nafplio as the head of a government without power or money. It will not lead Greece.'

Suddenly Tzanis felt less safe than he had that morning. Greece was fighting itself and this man and he were not on the same side. 'Where is he now?' he asked.

'He's gone to Missolonghi to help with the siege, God help it.' Suddenly he raised his hands. 'But my manners! What am I thinking of!' He clapped them and two women entered and walked over to the range. They lifted the cauldron off the fire and onto the ground. They filled two bowls and brought them over to the table. They bowed to Petrobey and left.

Tzanis savoured every mouthful. It was a mutton stew in a dark, russet sauce and he'd not tasted anything so good from the tables in St Petersburg. They ate in silence, the steam curling between them like queries. He could feel Petrobey's blue eyes on him all the while.

At last his host pushed away his bowl and put down his spoon. He dabbed his mustachios with his napkin and picked up the jug. 'What was on your ship?' he asked.

Tzanis put his hand over his glass. He needed to keep his head clear. 'I don't know. I was a passenger.'

Petrobey nodded, helping himself. 'You threw nothing into the sea before the ship hit the rocks?'

'Why would I do that?'

Petrobey shrugged. He stood and went over to the range. He took a chibouk pipe from an alcove and bent to light it from the charcoal. He came over to the table, plunged the mouthpiece into the bowl of water and offered it. Tzanis shook his head. Petrobey smoked on in silence, inhaling the smoke through his nose, twisting the stem in his mouth and wiping his eyes when they watered.

'We in the Mani are suspicious of visitors from Russia,' he continued. 'Its tzars have a habit of pretending to help while really wanting to rule. Fifty years ago, Catherine the Great sent the Orlov brothers to persuade us to rise against the Turks, except they turned out not to have any army. The Sultan sent the Albanians to punish us. We haven't forgotten.'

Tzanis shook his head. 'None of this matters to me. I am a teacher who needs to get to Corfu. Where can I take a boat from?'

Petrobey leant forward and tapped the pipe's embers out onto the tray. 'No boat is going to Corfu for many weeks and I can't spare an escort to take you overland.'

'Then I'll go alone.'

Petrobey laughed. 'Alone? You'd not make a mile. These are bad lands to travel in. No, you can stay in the Mani as my guest until we can find a boat to take you. You can earn your keep by teaching Hara.'

Tzanis considered this. 'What would I teach her?'

Petrobey pushed back his chair and stood up. He walked around the table and put his hand on Tzanis's shoulder. 'Teach her the wisdom of the phanariot,' he said. 'I'm sure you can manage that.'

After Tzanis had left, Petrobey sat for a while staring into his glass. Then he rose and went to the door. He opened it.

'Come in, Hara.'

He watched her enter. She looked more like her mother every year, more tzinia than warlord. But she had the nature of a *klepht*, like him, and he felt prouder of her every time they met. *When would he tell her?* When she'd had some education to add to her ripening beauty, when there'd be a clever match to make. Not before.

'You heard any of that?' he asked, sitting down and refilling his glass.

She stood in front of the table, rigid in her deference, eyes as wide as whenever he summoned her. 'No, Petrobey.'

He nodded the lie past. 'No, of course not.' He drank. 'Well, this Tzanis is going to teach you. Would you like that?'

She blinked twice beneath the tiniest of frowns. 'I . . . if it is your wish, lord.'

27

'It is my wish,' he said. 'You need some education.' He paused. 'I want you to befriend him.'

She stared straight ahead.

He leant back in his chair. 'I want to know who he is and why he is here. And I want to know what was on that ship.'

# CHAPTER THREE

## MANI

Petrobey had left by the time Tzanis was up and dressed.

From his window at the top of yet another tower, he could see that the village had filled again and the *rouga* was packed with people. A big loom had been dragged out and two black-clad women were already at work in the sunshine, their feet working the pedals. Over to one side he saw Hara talking to some men with guns.

Was she pupil or gaoler? *Or both?*

He tried the trapdoor, but it was bolted from below and there was no ladder to the one above. He sat on his bed and thought. He was certainly a prisoner, suspected by Petrobey of being what he was: in the service of the Tzar's Greek Foreign Minister. And his gaoler reminded him of someone he wanted to forget. Last night he'd dreamt of her.

He'd been in a village square and it was late summer. The Russian steppe stretched out to a wall of dust, fifty miles distant. Napoleon's army was coming and he'd been told to burn everything in its path. A girl stood next to her mother watching a Cossack set light to their roof. She turned her eyes to him. 'How will we live?'

'Do what you must.'

That's what he'd said as he'd turned his horse, not thinking of anything but getting away. *Do what you must.*

Then it was winter and she was standing in the snow in the same village, her hair cropped, a sign hanging from her neck, waiting for execution. She'd done what he'd said and it had turned her into a whore and a traitor.

Four words. In all that had happened afterwards, as he'd seen the *Grande Armee* snake its long way back to France, as he'd seen its frozen, starving stragglers sabred by his Cossacks, he'd thought of those four words. *Do what you must.*

He heard footsteps on the ladder. He heard the bolt drawn back and saw the trapdoor lifted. Hara pulled herself into the room. *The same hair.*

'Why am I locked in?' he asked.

She went over and sat in the window, her back to the view. She was dressed more as her gender this morning. She had a small cap on her head and wore a long-sleeved dalmatic above flowing *shalvaria* trousers. On her feet were slippers. She said: 'I am ready to be taught.'

'And I'm not ready to teach you. Why am I locked in? Where can I go?'

She tilted her head to one side in thought. Then she nodded. 'Nowhere without being murdered, it's true,' she said. 'So you can go where you want.'

He'd not expected this. Was she in charge of this village? He looked down at his bare knees: 'I can't leave the tower like this. I want proper clothes.'

'Your clothes will be brought to you.'

'And I need paper and pencil. I like to sketch.'

'I will bring them.'

By now most of his anger had been drawn by her endless, guileless acquiescence. He relaxed a little. 'So what am I to teach you?' he asked. 'Petrobey's instructions weren't specific.'

She placed her hands in her lap, fingers entwined, studying him from beneath her scrub of hair. 'Everything, I don't know. Like what *"specific"* means. Like how to read and write.' She paused. 'Like what the world looks like beyond the Mani.' She turned and went to the window. 'I want to know what happens behind those mountains.'

Tzanis's clothes were eventually delivered to him, clean and mended. Inside his waistcoat pocket was the gold coin.

On their first outing, he suggested they each take a sack to carry things in. They left in bright sunshine and she led him out of the village and up through carpets of flowers into the foothills beyond. They met a shepherd girl, a new-born lamb slung over her shoulders, four unblinking eyes fixed on them as they waited for her herd to pass, deafened by their bleating.

A little later he stopped in the middle of a field strewn with flowers amidst the stones: poppies, orchids, soapwort, pimpernel and a hundred others. 'Can you collect some stones of different sizes?' he asked. 'I've an idea.'

He walked on, glancing back to see her watching him, her head to one side as it often was. He thought of what she must see through those eyes: a man clumsy in this wilderness, a man whose talents held no meaning in this barren, beautiful land. He climbed over a wall and found himself in a field of little stones. He began to pick them up, looking for ones of the same shape and size. He put them in his sack. He sat down with his back against the wall and took paper from his pocket, then a pencil. He began to draw.

He thought about the girl below. She wasn't like anyone he'd ever met, but then the women he'd known were as distant from the land as migrating birds, moving from ballroom to ballroom on the breeze of court gossip. She was intelligent, he was sure. He might even be able to teach her enough to see through Petrobey's lies. *Yes, that might be something.*

But more importantly, she might be able to reach the gold.

It was late afternoon when they got back to the tower. He'd made three sketches and she'd picked herbs as well as stones. She explained each to him as they walked down, lifting them up for him to smell, telling him what they would cure, what they would flavour.

While she cooked downstairs, Tzanis knelt on the roof of the tower and created the world out of little stones. Its continents were vague – the unknown wastes of America, Africa and Asia vaguer still – but he made it with care. The sun was low in the sky when he called Hara up to inspect it, the tower's walls glowing with what they'd been storing since dawn, the village noise reduced to a murmur.

She came through the trapdoor carrying two plates of fried eggs, onions, garlic and lumps of pickled pork in oil. They sat on the wall to eat, their backs to the sun, and Hara studied the map in silence. When she'd finished eating, she set aside her plate and leant forward, her chin on her fist.

'What is it?' she asked.

'It's the world,' he said. 'God created it in seven days and it's taken me three hours. An achievement.'

She frowned. She'd not found this funny, just odd. She looked up. 'But it's just stones. Why is it the world?'

He put down his plate and looked up to find the moon and pointed to it. 'It's what the world would be like if you were looking down on it from up there.' He picked up a bigger, rounder stone he'd set to one side. 'Except that you'd only see part of it because the world is round, like the moon. Imagine it wrapped around this stone.'

Hara nodded slowly. 'So where is the Mani in this world?'

Tzanis picked up a stick he'd leant against the wall. He pointed to the Peloponnese. It was made out in blue stones, like the new Greek flag. It was a misshapen hand with three claws and a skinny wrist at the Isthmus of Corinth.

'The Mani is here, the southern-most tip of Europe.'

'Europe?'

He looked up at her. 'Have you ever been outside the Mani, Hara?' he asked gently.

She shook her head. 'No further than Tsimova.'

He smiled. 'Then we have a journey ahead of us.'


At first, Hara found the routine irksome. She missed her brothers and the scramble for shipwrecks, but Petrobey wanted her to learn and she would do her best. Anyway, she was curious about this man who'd lied about being a teacher. She liked to watch him sketch, as if the world could only exist through his pencil. He didn't seem bad or violent, just odd.

When he took an interest in something, she quite liked him. She enjoyed when he was explaining an idea and his whole face moved with his words and his eyes shone.

Every morning, she rose early, made coffee and took it up to his bedside, then climbed up to the roof to watch the sun rise, her long legs swinging over the side, listening to the birds waking up the world. He would come up an hour later, shaved

33

and wearing the waistcoat that was already showing the strain of too much sun and washing. She would greet him in English and read out the passage she'd learnt the night before from her book. Then they'd talk about the world, usually in Greek, but sometimes, more slowly, in English too.

The routine developed a rhythm, an order, which she hadn't had in her previous life. Surprisingly, she began to like it, especially the lessons on the tower's roof. In the evening they'd eat there, pulling up their food through the trapdoor in a basket to watch the sun set over the wide, unruffled sea, watching the moon rise like a silver fish above it.

One evening, she discovered what some flowers she'd picked for him were for.

'Greece was where everything began,' he said, laying yellow flowers on top of the blue stones, one by one. 'At first you were called Myceneans and you built a great trading empire.' He spread the flowers across the Peloponnese, out into the islands of the Aegean. 'One day I'll tell you about Helen of Troy.'

She watched him reach over to a second pile of flowers: blue. He put them on top of the yellow ones and spread them into Turkey, Sicily and Italy. 'Later, it was Athens that had an empire. Do you know of Athens?'

She shook her head.

'Well, it's a village now, with some ruins on a hill, but two thousand years ago it was a great city.'

'We have ruins here,' she said. 'Down in the south. I've seen them underwater. Who built them?'

'Kings. Their slaves.'

'Are there kings and slaves now?'

Tzanis seemed to think about this. Then he picked up purple, white and black flowers and spread them out in his open palm. 'Tomorrow I'll tell you about the greatest empire of them all: the Greek Empire, when great emperors ruled with wisdom and fairness.'

'Like Petrobey.'

'Is Petrobey wise?' he asked.

'Well, no one has ever enslaved the Mani.'

'That's true. But the Turks have enslaved the rest of Greece.'

'That's not what Petrobey says,' she said. 'The other Greeks have to pay them money, but they're free to do what they want.' She went on: 'He says the phanariots have traded for the Turks and become rich. He says they're the ones trying to enslave Greece but he won't let them.'

She felt some satisfaction from what she'd said. She wanted him to know that he couldn't fool her any more than he could Petrobey. She continued: 'You speak of these old empires as if they were your own. But Petrobey's right: you don't know this land.'

'And Petrobey does?' asked Tzanis. 'He knows the Mani, Hara, nothing else. He doesn't know about Greece when it was an example to the world. And he doesn't know about its future.' He paused. 'The world has moved beyond him. Greece needs to be a modern state with a modern system of government.'

'Why?'

'Because . . . because . . .' He looked down. He thought about Capodistrias leaning forward across his desk, saying what he was about to say again and again. 'Because it's best for the people.'

'Why?'

He looked up. 'Oh, Hara.'

\*

Later, as she lay looking through her window at a moon close enough to pinch, she thought about what he'd said. *Because it's best for the people.*

*This phanariot.*

She turned over and thought, for the first time, about her hair. Why had she cut it all off? Most Maniot girls put on the kerchief at eleven and didn't speak to a man until they were handed over as a bride. She must look ridiculous to one who'd seen the world.

*This phanariot.*

She looked up at the ceiling. He was up there in his bed dreaming of the life he'd left behind in St Petersburg, or whatever it was called . . . perhaps of the women he'd sketched in some palace garden. What must he think of her in her ignorance? What must he think of the pappas? *Of them all?*

She turned again. Why hadn't she told Petrobey about what she'd seen on the ship? She screwed her eyes shut. She'd never deceived Petrobey about *anything*. The very thought of it terrified her. Yet this phanariot, with his knowledge of what lay beyond the mountains, with all his ideas that she couldn't stop thinking about . . .

*No.*

# CHAPTER FOUR

## MANI

Prince Tzanis had been in the Mani for a month now and civilization had never seemed so far away. Nor had the Tzar's gold, sunk somewhere deep off Cape Tainaron. He knew that getting it was dependent on this girl, so he had to earn her allegiance.

But how? The *Comnenos* name meant nothing in this wilderness. He'd have to win her over by his knowledge.

The idea of the map had been inspired. It provided the canvas from which he could show off his mastery of the world, the brush-strokes of his glossy sophistication. But it would take time to have effect. Meanwhile, he got no word of what was happening elsewhere in Greece. Was Mavrocordatos still in Missolonghi?

Easter came as a relief, though the forty days of fasting brought temper to the village. The week before the festival, Tzanis had woken to a man ringing a bell in the square below.

'He's announcing a feud,' said Hara as she set his coffee down on the floor. 'Another man insulted his wife.'

'How so?' he asked, sitting up and taking the cup from her. She moved to the window and looked down into the square.

'He took her place in the church. It was deliberate. She'd turned her back on him in the square.'

Tzanis drank his coffee, as bitter as the day he'd arrived. He looked at her back, her feline grace smothered in rough tunic. 'That is absurd,' he said.

'Perhaps,' she said, turning. 'But someone will die for it. Then another, and another until they've had enough blood.' She sounded more critical than she might have a month ago.

They went up to the roof to eat their breakfast. There was still some of the night's chill in the air but no smell of fire, cooking being forbidden during the Lenten fast. Tzanis looked up into the early sun and closed his eyes, absorbing the warmth into a face still stiff with sleep. He felt alive in this place of sudden death.

'It always happens just before Easter,' she said, a plate of prickly pears balanced on her knee. 'People get hungry, they lose sense.'

They talked of other feuding families that morning. He showed her Italy on the map and told her the story of Romeo and Juliet and she listened in unblinking silence, her eyes never leaving his face.

On Easter Saturday they joined the Entombment procession from the church two hours before dawn and lit their candles from the pappas's at the turn of the new day, like everyone else. They slept deeply and awoke the next morning to the smell of lamb roasting over brushwood from the square below. By mid-morning, they were sitting at a long table with the rest of the village, gorging themselves on delicious meat, the smell of herbs and charcoal all around.

For a while, Tzanis felt part of things. No one cared if he was a phanariot or anything else. They'd just murdered Judas and drowned his memory in wine and he was an honoured guest. And Hara? She was certainly strange. He watched her biting great chunks of lamb from the bone and wiping juice from her chin. He pictured her in a St Petersburg drawing room.

She looked at him over her lamb. 'Why are you smiling?'

He shook his head. 'I—'

A shadow fell.

Hara's eldest brother stood over their table, blocking out the sun so that it took time for Tzanis to see who he was. Christos was swaying slightly and had wine on his shirt. He brought a hand to the table to steady himself.

'You bring shame on our family,' he said to Hara. 'You spend every day with this man . . . this *aristocrat.*'

'As Petrobey ordered,' said Hara calmly. She waved away a fly from her lamb. 'He is teaching me.'

'What is he teaching you?'

'To read, to write, to speak English.' She took another bite of lamb. 'Things I don't know.'

Christos grunted. 'Why would you need to learn English?'

'You learnt Turkish.'

Her brother scowled. 'I spent four years chained to a Turkish oar,' he said softly. He looked at Tzanis with unfocused hatred, still swaying. 'It wasn't a *choice.*'

Tzanis looked at him. Christos was a big man and he was drunk. 'Why are you here?' he asked quietly, closing his palm over a knife handle.

Christos was moving his head from side to side like he was afloat. He put both his hands on the table and leant forward, his breath too close to Tzanis. 'I came up to visit my sister, *phanariot.* Do you have any objection?'

'Well, you've seen her and she is well. Now you can leave.'

Christos stared at him. The tables around had fallen silent. He glanced down to where Tzanis held the knife. He began to shake his head and his hand moved slowly to his side.

Hara reached out. '*Christos,*' she whispered, taking his arm. 'These are Petrobey's orders. Will you defy them?'

Her brother's eyes were still on Tzanis, narrowed by loathing. He blinked twice and took a deep breath. 'I will not forget you, phanariot,' he said. 'Not ever.'

He turned and walked away.

At one minute past midnight, long after Tzanis had gone to bed, the still of the night was shattered by a single shot. Then a scream.

Hara came up through the trapdoor, candle in hand. Her short hair was on end and she was wearing a gown tied at the middle and nothing underneath. Her skin was the colour of honey in the flickering flame. She put the candle down and went over to the window.

'The feud has begun.'

There were people in the square below, none with torches, for the Easter moon was full. Everyone was talking at once.

He rose and joined her. He stood behind her and smelt the must of her hair, the good scent of her sleep. He moved away. 'What will happen now?' he asked.

She shrugged. 'The dead man's brothers will let their beards grow long, not cutting them until they are avenged. His mother and sisters will howl their dirges all day and all night. We won't sleep.'

She was right. The lamentations were called *miroloyia*, she told him: words of destiny. The women sang them without pause and nobody in the village slept. He thought himself going

40

mad, loathing this orgy of misery and superstition. He hated the cloves of garlic hung at doors, the crosses made with lamp-black on the lintels to fend off the *makryna*. Hara told him that the man's blood would remain until a wooden cross was driven into the place he'd fallen, that he'd be a werewolf until then, eating dough from the kneading troughs by night. *What nonsense.*

He had to escape, but how? He'd need Hara to do it.

One morning he brought up the subject of the gold.

'We should go and find it before someone else does,' he said, sipping his coffee on the wall of the tower. Two months had passed and the same dirge was rising from below. 'And I need to get away from this village.'

She wiped pear-juice from her chin with her sleeve. He noticed that she'd tried to calm her hair, as she often did these days. She even had shoes on her feet. She shook her head: 'No one will find it. It's too deep.'

'But we should try at least.'

She thought for a while, watching him beneath a little frown. Then she surprised him. 'All right. We'll go.'

They left a month afterwards, taking the same road south that they'd come by what seemed an age ago. This time the grass by the side was yellow and the land breathed heat, as if the *makryna* lived beneath.

As evening fell, they met a family on the road and knew they'd reached the sea. The man had salt encrusted in his whiskers and was carrying a sack over his shoulder. Some distance behind were his wife and daughter, barefoot and bent beneath wicker baskets. They wore straw hats over hair stiff with brine. The man nodded as Tzanis passed. *'Yassou, koumbare.'*

As they neared Cape Tainaron, the ground became ever more

41

strewn with ancient remains: broken columns carved with dedications, steps cut deep into rocks, chariot wheels grooved into the stones. They passed women doing their washing in ancient cisterns. They found a coin with an old god on it and he fell asleep watching the moon's reflection in its face.

The next morning, they found a fisherman who hired them his boat and they set off for the rocks where Tzanis's ship had foundered. They passed the cave of a hermit who lived off the alms of passing sailors and gave him the coin. For luck.

But no luck came to them. All day she dived while he sat, sketching and planning his escape. He'd choose the right moment, then overpower her. He'd put her ashore and sail off. He wouldn't hurt her.

By late afternoon, she was tired. She hauled herself onto the boat and leant back, watching him.

She held out her hand. 'Can I see?'

He passed the sketch to her. She looked up at the shoreline, to what he'd drawn, then back.

'Do you want to draw me?'

He looked at her as he might one of his models in St Petersburg. Quite often they'd been prostitutes, laid out like banquets on their cushions: plump, teasing. But she was the opposite. There was no artifice in the way she draped her long, brown limbs over the bench, no coyness in the eyes that looked into his.

He laid the paper to one side. 'No,' he said. 'I'll try diving while you rest.'

'You? You'll never get deep enough.'

He pulled off his shirt and took the deepest of breaths and dived into the water. It was colder than he'd imagined and grew

42

colder as he went deeper. When he could hold his breath no longer, he rose.

He broke surface to a sea bubbling with jellyfish. He thrashed about with his arms but there were too many; the pain from their stings was beyond enduring. He saw the boat coming towards him, the oars moving quickly, not quickly enough. Then she was helping him over the side, driving off the jellyfish with an oar.

'Why did you come up in the middle of them?' she asked. 'They can kill you.'

He was in too much pain to reply, lying in the bottom of the boat, clutching himself, his eyes closed.

'Lie still.'

She began to massage his limbs: first his shoulders and arms, then his legs. She was rubbing some liquid into his skin that she took from the fisherman's bailing bucket beside her. It was soothing but it stank.

'What is it?' he asked, as the first burning began to subside.

'It doesn't matter. Lie still.'

She was strong but she was gentle. When she'd finished, she went over to the side and dropped a fishing line over and in minutes had caught two fish. She covered him with their cool scales, their oil. At long last, lulled by her caress, he fell asleep and dreamt of a village on the steppe.

He awoke with a start. It was evening and the sun was a quivering fireball over the sea. He watched her leaning over the side, dipping her finger in the water. He saw her stand and hold it up to the wind, her head to one side.

'I'm going to put the sail up,' she said over her shoulder. 'There's a little wind.'

He pushed himself up. 'What about the gold?'

43

'Another day. You need to get home.'

*Home? Where was home?*

He watched her sit and gather the sail into her lap, then pull it up the mast in quick jerks, tying it off at the cleat. He heard the sound of water against the boat's side. They were moving.

He sank back painfully on his elbows, shedding fish-skin as he went. The smell from his body was overwhelming. He looked over to a shore trembling in the evening haze, vague terraces climbing to mountains tipped by flecks of orange cloud. In the west he saw wraiths of islands in the distance, skimming gulls nearer-to, a turtle floating languidly, then skulling down to the blue-green depths. He saw the water suddenly erupt and dolphins flung themselves out like careless acrobats. They disappeared beneath the surface, then emerged either side of the boat, shaking off splinters of silver, running beside them with fire on their backs.

He thought: this, *here*, was the heart of Greece, or its soul. It was what had been here long before the feuds or the towers or the superstition, before the Turks. In spite of everything, he felt part of it.

*This, perhaps, is home.*

He turned back to her. She was watching him, not with pity but something else. He looked away.

'In all this time, you haven't said anything about yourself,' she said, 'except that you're a teacher. Petrobey thinks you're a soldier. Are you?'

He still felt weak and there might be some comfort in honesty. After all, she'd kept his secret. 'I was a soldier once,' he said. 'I fought against Napoleon.'

'Who Petrobey admires.'

Tzanis nodded. 'Yes, well he would. They are two of a kind.'

'Do you have a wife?'

He was surprised by the question. 'No. Why do you want to know?'

'Because a man of your age in the Mani would have a wife and many children by now.'

He thought back to St Petersburg, to endless balls in palaces where his mother would point out another heiress. It had always been about money. He smiled. *As elusive as what lies beneath us.*

'Why do you think Petrobey wanted me to teach you?' he asked.

She frowned and turned away. She untied the rope from the cleat and tightened the sail. 'I don't know,' she said. 'He must have had a good reason.'

'I think you do know.'

She shrugged. 'It could be many reasons. Perhaps he just wants you to have company.' She scratched her chin. 'Am I good company?'

'Of course, but it's not meant for me. Petrobey will want you to marry someone important to him.' He felt a bump below as a dolphin knocked the boat's side. He remembered the story that she had told him one morning. 'You can't always cut all your hair off and cover yourself in fish oil.'

She nodded slowly. 'I suppose I should be pleased that he cares.' A little frown appeared as she considered this further. 'Why do you think he cares?'

'Perhaps because you really are his daughter,' said Tzanis. 'Perhaps because you are extraordinary.'

'Because I can dive?'

'No. Because you're beautiful, Hara.' He leant forward. 'Whatever you do to your hair, you are beautiful.'

She looked at him in astonishment and pleasure. 'Do you think so?'

He looked away. Three hours ago, she'd gutted fish to squeeze oils over his swollen body, now she was blushing without trying to conceal it. She was as guileless and extraordinary as the women of St Petersburg were artificial and ordinary.

'It doesn't matter what I think,' he said quickly. 'You are being prepared for a marriage you don't want. But if you take me away from the Mani, now, in this boat, you can escape it. You can go to Nafplio or further north or anywhere you wish.' He paused. 'You can go beyond the mountains.'

'No.'

It was as firm as anything she'd said to him. He was taken aback by her certainty. For a moment he thought of overwhelming her, but he was in no state to – even if he could bring himself to try.

'I have already done what I should not have,' she said quietly. 'I've kept your secret. It's enough. What's that?'

He sat up to see what she was pointing to. Close to the horizon were sails. It was a ship, big and going north. Was it coming towards them?

'A schooner, I'd say,' he said, leaning forward. 'We'll not escape if it wants to chase us. But why would it bother? We're fishing.'

'Without nets.'

They watched it in silence. There was no doubt that it was coming towards them, though whether it meant to stop was anyone's guess.

She asked: 'Can you see its flag yet?'

He rose and came to stand next to her. The pain from his

46

stings was lessening all the time. He lifted a hand to his eyes. 'Turk,' he said. He looked towards the shore. 'Can we swim?'

She shook her head. 'You'd not make it.'

'You could.'

She glanced at him. 'Me? Why would I go? I've got to guard you.'

There was a boom from across the water and smoke rose from the ship's side. A splash.

'It's too late anyway,' she said. 'They've seen us. And they'll row quicker than I can swim. They'll want information.'

*And me*, he thought. How long would he stand up to Turkish torture? He'd heard they made no allowance for rank. He glanced back at the shore. *Too far.*

They waited for what seemed like a long time for the ship to close the distance between them. Hara was silent for most of it, but when night fell and the dolphins left and the ship was nearly on top of them, he felt her hand come into his.

She said: 'If we escape this, take me with you.'

Then her hand went. He stretched out a finger, but it was gone.

Shouts came from above and he looked up. There were torches all along the ship's rail and, beneath them, turbans, moustaches and the glint of scimitar. A ladder was being lowered over the side He looked back to her. 'Remember, you're a simple peasant girl who knows nothing.'

She looked up at him. 'Isn't it the truth?'

He reached into his waistcoat pocket and brought out the gold sovereign. 'Take this,' he said, putting it in her hand. 'Keep it and hide it. Tell no one what you know, ever.'

He climbed the ladder and dropped down onto the deck, Hara just behind him. He looked around. They were surrounded by men in white pantaloons, all staring, their brown chests shining beneath torches. Some wore turbans, some a single pigtail, some were bald. He heard a curse in French. A tall man was pushing his way through, elbowing his way past the crew as if they were cattle. He came to the front. He was wearing a uniform Tzanis had seen before.

'*Salauds*,' he said, pulling his green topcoat together, his thumbs hooked around its eagle buttons, epaulettes swinging. He swept the hair from his eyes and brushed his sleeves with quick, angry movements. He was perhaps ten years older than Tzanis and had a face made hard by war. His skin was burnt and scarred, his moustache yellow from smoking, his nose flat to his face. His eyes were blue but distant, closed forever to emotion. They'd seen too much death for emotion.

He glanced at Hara, then spoke to Tzanis. 'You are not a fisherman.'

'No,' he replied. 'I am a teacher from Russia. I was shipwrecked on my way to Corfu and I've been recovering in the Mani. I was fishing.'

The Frenchman's eyes held no clue as to whether he believed this or not. They passed to Hara and looked her up and down. 'And this?'

'She has been looking after me.'

The man nodded slowly, his eyes still on her. 'I expect she has.'

Tzanis glanced at Hara. She was staring down at her feet. 'Will you put us ashore?' he asked.

'Without introductions? I'd not hear of it.' The man turned his gaze from Hara. 'I am Colonel Joseph Anthelme Sève, in the service of Prince Muhammed Ali, Khedive of Egypt and the Sudan.'

Tzanis thought fast. Egypt was a vassal of the Ottoman Empire but neutral. It had a modern army and navy trained by the French. He felt some relief. 'I am Tzanis Valitski, teacher of languages in Odessa.' He bowed like one unused to it.

'And why are you going to Corfu, teacher?'

'Because there's no call for language teaching in Odessa. A man must make a living.'

'Indeed he must,' said Sève. He glanced to Hara, then back. 'So why do you want to go ashore? I am going north. I can take you as far as Navarino. You can take a ship to Corfu from there.'

Tzanis considered this. He could leave the Mani, get to wherever Mavrocordatos now was. He could explain about the gold. But what about Hara? He asked: 'And the girl?'

Sève appraised Hara once more. 'She can come too. She can look after us both.'

Tzanis shook his head. 'No. She must be put ashore. This is her home.'

'No?' Sève's eyes were glaciers as they returned to Tzanis. 'You forget yourself, teacher,' he said quietly. 'You are my guest and the Mani is currently in revolt against my master's sovereign.'

Tzanis looked back to Hara. She was following their exchange with quick movements of her head, like watching a shuttlecock. Now she rested her eyes on him. 'What is he saying?'

'Hara,' he said in Greek. 'We are on a ship from Egypt and this man is in the service of its ruler. He is taking us to Navarino.'

She looked astonished. 'Navarino? Where is that? I don't want to go to Navarino.'

'You don't have any choice. He won't put you ashore.'

'Why not? What would he want with me?'

*What?* Tzanis felt the same fear he'd felt twelve years ago in a village on the steppe. *Do what you must.* He lowered his voice.

'If you swim to the shore, they'd not catch you in the dark. It's me they want.'

But Colonel Sève had signalled for two men to take her arms. He went up to her and lifted her chin with his finger. He spoke in Greek. 'You'll not swim anywhere.' He took a knife from his belt and turned to Tzanis. 'Now, I would like to know who you really are, teacher. And I will cut a piece from this face every time you lie to me.' He lifted the point to Hara's cheek. 'What is your real name?'

Hara stood completely still, her eyes wider than Tzanis had ever seen them. They were more angry than frightened.

'I am Prince Tzanis Comnenos,' he said quietly.

Hara stared at him in disbelief, her mouth open a little. Her teacher was something else entirely.

Sève lowered the knife. 'Good. Now we are properly acquainted.' He put the blade in his belt. 'Take her away.' He turned to Tzanis. 'You will come to my cabin.'

Tzanis stayed long enough to see Hara taken into a forecabin. He turned and followed Sève to another at the stern. It was a big, low room lit by wall sconces and a squat chandelier, a cot in one corner and a round table and chairs in the centre. On the table were food and wine.

'Sit, eat, drink,' said the Colonel, waving his hand. 'I imagine you've been living off acorns or whatever muck they eat down here.'

Tzanis sat. 'They've treated me well. The girl in particular.'

The Frenchman drank for a while in silence, studying Tzanis with his ice-cold eyes. He put down his glass, took out a cheroot and struck a match on the side of the table.

'So, prince, why have you come to Greece?' he asked, lighting the cheroot.

'To join the revolution,' said Tzanis. 'But I was waylaid in the Mani. Is it over yet?'

Sève leant forward and took a chicken leg from the plate, his cold eyes never leaving him. 'Far from over,' he said. 'Very far.'

Tzanis watched him eat and smoke at the same time, biting off meat and exhaling through his nose as he swallowed.

'The Greeks think it's over because they've won some battles, but their enemy was not a serious one.' He found gristle and leant over to spit it to the floor. 'Now they fight between themselves.' He examined both sides of the chicken bone for more meat, then drank his wine in one gulp and poured more, not offering any to Tzanis. 'Let's see: is it the north against the Peloponnese, or the kapitanos against the government? I've lost count.' He paused and drank. 'Whatever it is, they'll not withstand what's coming.'

*What's coming?*

Sève picked meat from his teeth with his fingernail and flicked it away. 'They've an army of bandits with obsolete muskets and a navy of fishing boats. Unless the Great Powers join their cause, they're finished. And the Great Powers won't do that because they're terrified about what might replace the Ottoman Empire.'

It might have been said by Capodistrias, sat behind his desk at the Tzar's Foreign Ministry. 'Isn't Egypt neutral in this war?' he asked.

Sève drank more wine and dabbed each side of his moustache with his fingers. 'Indeed. We're here to do a survey of the archipelago.'

*Or a reconnaissance.* He felt Sève's reptilian gaze on him again.

'Where was your ship lost?' asked the Colonel. 'Could you find the place again?'

Tzanis felt unease. Why did this man care where the ship had been lost?

'In fact,' continued the Frenchman, 'were you looking for it when we picked you up?'

This was dangerous. 'We were returning from a fishing trip,' he said quietly. 'As I told you.'

Sève glanced down at Tzanis's bare arms. 'Yet your body has been stung by jellyfish. Were you trying to catch the fish in the water?'

'I was swimming. I was hot.'

Sève nodded slowly, his eyes not moving. Both of them were weighing the lies of the other. He sat back in his chair. 'Tell me about the girl.'

How could he make Hara irrelevant? 'She is a simple peasant who was teaching me how to sail,' he said.

'Who also happens to be pretty. I like her.'

Tzanis frowned. 'You are an officer,' he said quietly. 'That should mean something.'

'How would you know?' asked Sève, his head to one side. 'Unless of course, you were one yourself. Perhaps we met at Borodino? Or perhaps at that unpleasant crossing of the Berezina? It was cold that night, wasn't it?'

Tzanis said nothing.

'I thought so.' Sève leant forward and stubbed his cheroot out amidst the chicken bones. 'You know, I think that, for us French, the retreat from Moscow left not much space for . . . *meaning* . . . except, perhaps, what it means to survive.'

Tzanis looked away. He thought of a village on the steppe and a young girl looking at him with the same innocent eyes as Hara's. *How will we live?*

The Colonel rose and stretched. 'Don't worry. I'll drop her off

somewhere, after you've shown me where the ship went down.'
He turned and walked out.

Tzanis didn't leave the cabin for two days. He saw neither Colonel Sève nor Hara, although he heard the Frenchman often enough. His food was brought in by two crewmen, one with a musket pointed over the other's shoulder.

On the first night, a strong easterly carried the ship swiftly over to the Messinian peninsula and up its west coast. Tzanis was woken shortly after dawn to the sound of an anchor chain on the run. The noise was brief which meant the water was shallow. He rose from the cot, went over to the window and drew back the curtain an inch. They were in a wide bay with tall hills all around. He could see a fort on top of one and the flash of metal from its ramparts. It flew the blue cross of the revolution. They'd come to Navarino.

He spent the day lying on his cot, thinking of how he might escape. Even if he could get out of the cabin, how would he get to Hara? Or should he trust the Frenchman to drop her off, regardless of what Tzanis did? No, he'd have to try to reach her. Without him, she'd not even be on this ship.

On the second night, he heard the creak of a small boat being lowered over the side and the sound of muffled oars as it rowed away. He heard it return three hours later and whispers in French. A reconnaissance had been made of Navarino Bay and he'd heard it all. He lay on his back and stared up at the cabin ceiling to think. There was no conceivable way he'd be allowed to live. He knew too much.

He looked around the cabin, lit only by moonlight filtered through curtains. The chandelier glowed like something more precious than it was. He got up and climbed onto the table.

*There.* A glass shard: sharp at its point. He broke it off and slipped it into his boot.

He heard sounds outside the door. He got down as quietly as he could and tiptoed back to the cot and lay down facing the door. Just in time. There was the sound of a key turned. He opened one eye a fraction.

Sève was standing in the doorway, watching him.

The next morning, he took his chance.

When the two men came in with his breakfast, he was waiting beside the door. He grabbed the musket barrel and kicked the first in the stomach, sending the tray spinning into the room. Then he pushed past and ran out onto the deck.

It was crowded with men assembled for prayers. The way to Hara's cabin was blocked but he had to try. He lowered his head and charged. They were too many. He was pinned down, then dragged across the deck to where Sève was standing next to an opening in the ship's side, watching a man come up from the tender. The Colonel glanced at him, shaking his head. 'Really.' He looked back out to sea. 'Now you'll have to stay tied up until we've returned to Cape Tainaron and you've shown me what I want.'

Rope was brought and he was tied at the wrists and ankles. He glanced at the gap in the ship's side. It was wide enough, his only chance. He tensed his body then threw himself towards it. Men tried to grab his ankles but he rolled past them and out into air. He hit the water and sank fast, his ears exploding. He landed on the bottom in a cloud of sand. He'd been right about the chain: the bay was not deep. He forced himself to stay calm.

He dragged his boot along the sand, again and again, digging in the heel. He felt it come loose, then off. Quickly he trapped it with his toe. He saw the shard peeping out and swung his body round so that his hands could take it. He grasped it and began to saw.

His lungs were beginning to ache and black spots appeared before his eyes. His hands were cut and stinging. He sawed harder, faster.

*There.*

One rope had severed, one more to go. Then his hands were free. He crouched down and kicked himself off the bottom, his ankles still joined, up, up, his lungs bursting and his ears bursting and the sun bursting through the water to meet him, *so close . . .*

*There!* He broke the surface as his mouth gasped for air that had never tasted so good, never felt so good against his cheek. He opened his eyes to see men at the ship's rail looking out. There were more getting into the tender, coming out to make sure he was dead. He turned and saw rocks. He'd swim to them and hide. He dived again.

When he got to the rocks, he pulled himself up and wiped the sea from his face. He looked back.

The boat was coming towards him.

# PART TWO

# 1825–26

# CHAPTER FIVE

## BOSTON, MASSACHUSETTS

In Boston, Massachusetts, the Brattle Street Unitarian Church was full to bursting on the evening Samuel Gridley Howe passed by looking for distraction.

Distraction was what he needed. Just before Christmas, he'd graduated top of his class in medicine at Harvard University and celebrated his engagement to Fleur Armitage. On New Year's Day, she'd told him she was moving to the other side of America.

The evening had a stillness that threatened thunder. He heard the caw of crows and looked up to see a cannon ball still lodged in the church tower. The cost of revolution was everywhere in Boston, as if they'd done it alone. He heard a rumble in the distance and turned up his collar.

He looked at the billboard.

MR EDWARD EVERETT, SENIOR LECTURER AT HARVARD UNIVERSITY, WILL ADDRESS THE SUBJECT OF INDEPENDENCE FOR THE GREEK PEOPLE AT SEVEN O'CLOCK.

He took out his watch. That was in three minutes' time. He was on his way to drink himself to oblivion down at the docks and, for once, the rights of man could wait. Why was he even considering going in? The first flecks of rain hit his forehead.

He walked up the steps and peered around the open door. The pulpit was an enormous piece of wood fashioned for oratory. He looked at the congregation: most middle-aged and respectable and in need of oratory. The lecture would be a heady mix of massacre, rape and enslavement, all reassuringly distant. There would be thrill, guilt and a collection at the end.

At the back sat the students, most of them disciples of Everett, most able to recite Byron by heart. He'd read Byron to Fleur once, in the days when he'd liked him. His eyes came to rest on someone more interesting: a man dressed in dirty clothes with a bandage around his eyes, seated alone. He had a stick clenched between his knees that he leant on, his fingers interlinked over its pommel, his unshaven chin propped. He sat very still. There were empty spaces either side, the only ones in the church. Howe went over and sat next to him.

He heard footsteps behind and Everett hurried past carrying a sheaf of notes. When he reached the pulpit, he took its steps two at a time. The shuffle of paper was the only sound in the church. His lifted his spectacles to his nose.

'Pericles,' he said. 'Solon, *Aristotle* . . .'

*Oh no.*

He glanced at the door, now shut. He'd hoped this might be more than another lecture on mankind's debt to Greece. After all, Everett was supposed to be an original thinker, even to have the ear of the President.

Everett had raised his voice and his finger. 'You will ask me what we Americans, safe in our new democracy, should have to do with this faraway place where democracy began?' He was pointing left, centre, right, then up to heaven. 'So I will tell you.'

*Yes, you will.* He rose to leave.

'Wait.' A hand had caught his. The voice wasn't American.

He glanced at the bandaged face beside him. It was raised a little, as if the man had just caught his own smell. The grip tightened. 'Wait.'

Howe looked down. The claw would not easily give up its prey. He settled slowly back into his seat.

'Think of Ancient Athens . . .' The speech wore on and the grip lessened, then went. Howe considered escape but he had the sense that something interesting was about to happen.

It was when Everett had paused to drink water that Howe's neighbour rose to his feet. He was taller than he'd expected and held himself straight. He banged his stick on the wooden floor, three rifle-shots that echoed through the church.

*'Stop this nonsense!'*

Three hundred heads turned in surprise. Everett peered over his spectacles, glass poised mid-air. He took time to identify the interruption, then his eyes came to rest on the blind man. 'Excuse me?'

'I am from Greece,' said the man, 'the only person in this hall who knows what is happening there. Three months ago, I was on Chios.'

Everett, leant forward, hands to the pulpit edge. 'Where the massacre took place?'

The audience had switched its allegiance now, all heads turned to the back.

The man continued. 'What happened on Chios will tell you everything you need to know about the Greek Revolution. The Turks may have committed the crime, but it was the Greeks who led them to do it.'

Edward Everett wanted his audience back. 'What are you

61

talking about?' he thundered, banging the pulpit with his fist. 'The people of Chios were innocent!'

'Yes, they were,' agreed the man. 'I was one of them. We didn't want to rebel. We were forced to by people sent to our island.'

'What are you saying, sir?' cried Everett, now shaking his head at the enormity of the claim. 'That other *Greeks* bear responsibility for the massacre? That is preposterous!'

'And yet it's true. You are raising money for arms to fight a war that cannot be won.' The man turned to the congregation. 'Spend your money on food and medicine. They're what will be needed.'

Everett was beckoning to men in the front row who now rose and came back towards where Howe was sitting. They took the man by the arms and dragged him to the door of the church. He was still shouting.

'Do not be misled! Do not give him your money for arms!'

He was pushed through just as another peal of thunder shook the roof. The two men shut the door and stood in front of it. There was an embarrassed silence. Howe rose from the pew and walked to the door. He stepped between the men and opened it. Outside, he looked both ways down the street. The stranger had disappeared.

It began to rain so he did up his coat and stepped down to the street. He headed for the docks.

It was three hours later when he returned to the church. He'd sat alone in a tavern, drinking something he knew would make him ill, thinking mostly about what had happened. The blind Greek had managed to dislodge Fleur from his mind, bringing back thoughts that had pre-dated her. He'd felt again the heady

62

promise of a life beyond the comfortable, medical marriage. It had seemed doubly intoxicating with the bourbon.

Now he felt sober and oddly alert. Perhaps it was the soft, insistent rain that had forced the dam of his collar. He sneezed.

The Greek was sitting on the church steps, sheltered from the rain by the porch roof. His back was resting against a pillar with his stick against his knees. Howe hesitated. He suspected that any conversation with this man would change his life, but then his life had already been changed. *Perhaps some symmetry might serve*. He walked over and sat down across from him, his back to another pillar.

'Where did you go?'

The man looked up. 'Not far. I am blind.'

Howe's eyes travelled over his body. He was gaunt beneath his clothes. 'Who is looking after you?' he asked.

They both knew the answer to that. Even in good, God-fearing America, it was better to be leprous than blind. Beyond family and the kindness of strangers, there was nowhere to go. The land of the free was blind to the blind.

Howe looked out into the night. There were candles flickering through the smeared windows of the house opposite. He saw cosy domesticity through the rain and, for a moment, thought of what he'd lost with Fleur. *Cosy*. He turned back. 'May I know your name, sir?'

'You may,' said the man. He stretched out his hand. 'I am Panagiotis Persides, once factor to the Kavardis family on the island of Chios.'

Howe leant forward and shook the hand. 'Samuel Gridley Howe at your service. And your story?'

The man scratched his bandage first one side, then the other. He asked: 'What do you know of mastic?'

'Mastic? Nothing.'

'It is a gum. It comes from a small tree that grows only on the island of Chios. It does many things but, above all, it sweetens the breath of the Sultan's harem. So the Turks have always cherished the island where it grows. We paid few taxes and built schools and were happy. And we made sure we got on well with the Turks because the island is only two miles from their mainland.' He paused. 'Then the revolution came to us.'

'How did it come?'

Panagiotis rubbed his chin. 'From the island of Samos. They had always been jealous of our wealth. Men from there landed on Chios and attacked the Turks, who shut themselves up in their fort. A week later, the Turk navy arrived and the Samians fled. Then the slaughter began.' He shook his head slowly. 'The Turks brought over fanatics and brigands from the mainland to do their killing. For two months, they slaughtered women, children, monks, nuns. Anything that could move.'

Howe was shocked. 'And your master?'

'He was one of the first to die: hung from the city wall.'

He thought back to Everett's outrage. 'Did no one send help?'

'Help? Our leaders in Nafplio were just pleased to see the Turk navy somewhere else.'

'What about the other islands?'

Panagiotis scoffed. 'Do you know what help the other islands gave us? When my mistress had brought us all up to the north to be evacuated, when we'd escaped death a hundred times, when we were *starving*, they demanded payment to take us off the island. We had nothing to give them, so they left us there.'

'So how did you leave?'

'An Englishman came,' said Panagiotis, 'a brave Englishman called Hastings. He took us away.'

'Was that when you lost your sight?'

He scratched again. 'The Turks caught me foraging for food. They wanted to know where we were hidden.' He paused. 'But I would never betray my mistress.'

Howe stared at him. A woman walked by, stopped and looked, then hurried on. He felt a sudden surge of pity. 'Your mistress,' he said. 'She sounds extraordinary.'

Panagiotis scratched his temple again. The filthy bandage must be itching and that, at least, was something Howe could help with. 'I will tell you how extraordinary Manto Kavardis is: after the Turks came, the other landowners fled, but she stayed. She went to the Governor and threatened to go to Constantinople herself if the slaughter continued. It worked for a while. The killing stopped. But then they sent over a madman from the mainland: Kanaris. He blew up the Turk flagship, killing their admiral. After that, there was no stopping the massacre.' He paused. 'And do you know what she did then? She gathered everyone from the villages and led them right across the island to the north. Where Captain Hastings found us.'

The man lapsed into silence, his head sunk into his chest. The bell above them chimed the hour and the rain fell outside the porch and the candles in the windows opposite went out one by one and the world seemed much darker and more dangerous than it had that morning. Much colder, too. Howe drew his coat tighter around him.

He thought of what he'd heard: a world so distant from what he and Fleur had planned. He recognised old thoughts that had been with him for some time. Had Fleur sensed them too? Was that why she'd left?

Panagiotis let forth a deep sigh. 'Chios was more than a massacre,' he said softly. 'It was a sign. We saw then a hatred we'd never seen before. And we saw what would happen when this war was lost. The selfish factions: merchants, phanariots, intellectuals ... all the vultures would fly away and leave the people to their fate.'

'Why will the war be lost?'

'Because the Ottoman Empire is big and we are small. Because they have howitzers and we don't. Because the Greek leaders hate each other more than they do the Turks.' He nodded towards the church. 'And your money? It will be spent on guns that will just delay the end and make it even bloodier.' He pointed at him. 'That's when doctors will be needed.'

Howe looked at the ground. He felt the same prick of guilt that he'd felt in his *political* days, in his life before Fleur. *A calling.*

'The people of Greece are good,' continued the man across from him, 'and they deserve leaders who care about more than themselves. Like Manto. She is their only hope.' He paused again. 'Why don't you go and help?'

'Me? No. *No.*'

'But you care.'

Howe was startled. 'Why do you say that?'

'Because you came into the church. Because you left and came back, smelling of drink. I think you are restless.'

'My life has hardly begun,' said Howe quietly. 'I've just qualified as a doctor.'

'So why not be a proper doctor in Greece where you'll be needed?' He scratched. 'You have a calling.'

*A calling.* 'But I don't know anything about Greece, or its war.'

'Manto knows everything. I'll send you to her. Before the war, she was mistress not just of Chios, but of the world. After the massacre she hid herself away. She lived alone with her Turk servants and saw nobody.'

He gathered his stick and got up slowly, pushing himself to his feet. He took out a letter. 'If you do go, give this to her. I've been waiting for someone to take it.'

'And if I don't?'

'Then give it to someone who will.' He turned.

'Where are you going?'

'That,' said Panagiotis, 'is not your business. You'd like to help me but you can't. You can't bring back my eyes.'

He began to walk away.

'Wait.' Suddenly, Howe didn't want this man to leave. 'Let me at least look at them.'

'You can't,' said the man over his shoulder, still walking. 'They're on Chios.'

# CHAPTER SIX

## ISLAND OF KITHIRA

The ship that took Samuel Gridley Howe to Greece was the *Virginia-Anne*, a decommissioned navy frigate that had served in the war against the British of 1812. She'd managed eight knots across the Atlantic and, according to Captain Abrahams, was the fastest ship in the new American Navy.

But the Greek vessel was fast too. It was heading straight for them and had the wind behind her. They had just passed Cape Tainaron.

'What can she want?' Abrahams had lowered his telescope to the bib of his beard and was peering over the side. He was tall and entirely white of hair and beard. Only his face, red and veined by weather, suggested the flow of blood. 'She's no more than a mile away. She must see our stripes.'

Howe looked up at the 24-starred flag snapping in the breeze, as big and obvious as the country it stood for. 'They'll have seen it.'

Abrahams raised the telescope to his eye again. 'But they're flying the Greek flag. And those are eighteen-pounders she's bearing. We'll have to stop.'

Howe frowned. He was in a hurry to get to Nafplio and they'd been beating to windward for a week now.

The captain moved away, leaving the deck to Howe. Despite the approaching ship, he still felt the exhilaration he'd felt two months ago when he'd come aboard as the first buds had appeared on the Boston trees. Since then, with nothing but waves and soaring, diving, spouting creatures to distract him, he'd had time to think. He'd come to realise the inevitability of what he'd done. Fleur and he had been moving apart well before she'd put a continent between them. Her destiny was to be settled while his was less certain.

He heard noise above and saw men scrambling up the nets. One by one, the great sails were hauled up as the ship came about, rocking gently in the swell under a sun strong enough to peel its New England timbers.

Captain Abrahams climbed up to the aft-deck and joined him at the rail. They watched the ship approach in silence. It was also a frigate with two decks of guns, but it was a merchant ship adapted for war.

'The *Themistocles*,' said Abrahams. 'I've seen her before in these waters. She's out of Hydra and her owner is one Tombazis, a merchant from the island.'

'Who's turned from trading, it seems,' said Howe. 'That ship has seen some action.'

That much was obvious. Its sails were torn, its rigging loose and there were holes in its sides. Some of the gun ports had lost their hatches. A cannon boomed.

'She means to escort us,' said the captain. 'What the deuce can she want? We're neutral!'

The ship was changing course, not heading for Nafplio. Howe glanced ahead, pointing. 'What is that island?'

'Kithira. One of the Ionians. It's governed by the British.'

'Well, they want us to follow them there.'

It took two hours to reach Kithira and another to drop anchor and be rowed ashore. They were met on the quayside by a tall, straight-backed man, older than Howe, with red hair and thick sideburns. Beside him was a smaller Greek.

The redhead stepped forward and performed an awkward bow that went no further than his neck. 'I am Captain Frank Abney Hastings of the *Themistocles*,' he said. He wore a blue naval jacket with high collar and held a hat to his hip. He turned his whole body, hat as well. 'And this is Captain Tombazis, who speaks no English. You will want to know why we've escorted you into Kithira.'

Abrahams was still angry. 'We do, sir, aye. This is an American vessel.'

'And a fast one, I'd wager. But there is an Egyptian fleet behind you that you'd not outrun with this wind. You can be grateful for our interception.'

Howe was staring at the Englishman. Surely this was the man who'd rescued Manto and her factor from Chios. There couldn't be two of them. 'An *Egyptian* fleet you say, sir?'

Hastings nodded like he was pecking. 'Egyptian and out of Alexandria. I dare say the biggest fleet seen in these waters since Napoleon: over a hundred ships. Ten of them of the line.'

'And where is it headed?'

'Probably Nafplio. It carries the army of Ibrahim Pasha, son of the Khedive of Egypt. He means to invade Greece.'

'My God.'

'We have been trying to keep it at Crete.' The Englishman shifted his hat to the other side of him as if it was a parade drill.

'But it broke through our blockade yesterday. We were eight against a hundred.'

'So what do we do?' asked Abrahams.

'You lie with us here until the fleet passes, then you go on your way. What is your destination?'

'Nafplio.'

'Ah. Well, that may not be possible if Ibrahim is making for there too. Unless, of course, you'd like to add your ship to our fleet?' Hastings glanced at the ships at anchor. 'You have guns, I see.'

'The United States are neutral in this war, sir,' replied Abrahams sternly, 'as is Great Britain, if I recall.'

Hastings nodded. 'Indeed, sir, but I am retired from His Majesty's navy.'

*Retired?* Howe studied the Englishman. He could be no more than early thirties. Why was he retired? He smiled. 'Well, shall we take a drink, sir? It sounds like we may have some time together on this island.'

They walked up empty, narrow streets between mean houses with small shuttered windows of no glass. It was stiflingly hot and they went in silence. Howe looked up at the rest of the town, climbing in heat waves up to a shabby castle flying the British flag.

They found a tavern with a terrace and sat beneath a jacaranda tree looking out at the view. They were served sour wine from a jug with slices of lemon floating on its surface. A sullen boy brought it to them and left quickly without speaking. It was midday and Captain Hastings loosened his collar, then his jacket. The white shirt beneath had once been fine but was now frayed and mottled with sweat.

Howe studied him. There was something bizarre about the man, despite their shared language. Perhaps it was the short, clipped sentences, perhaps the restless energy. It might have been the high eyebrows that made everything a surprise. He seemed a vessel of trammelled purpose, quick to action and perhaps to take offence.

Howe poured for them both. 'To friendship between our two countries.' He smiled, raising his glass. 'Can we agree it was an unneccessary war?'

Hastings look surprised. 'Against Napoleon? Certainly not, sir!'

'No, no. Between our nations. British and American people are of the same stock, we are natural allies. Why should we ever fight?'

'You were rebels against your king, sir,' said Hastings, 'then you were supporting the French. We cannot forget that.'

Howe put down his glass and looked out to the sea. It was empty of any fleet. He glanced at the Englishman. He'd hoped for some entertainment after dull Captain Abrahams, but this was unpromising. 'But you no longer serve your king, sir,' he said. 'You seem awful young to be retired.'

Hastings looked hard at the jug. 'I had a disagreement with a senior officer,' he said quietly. 'I resigned my commission.'

This was more encouraging. 'Disagreement?'

'I challenged him to a duel.'

Howe threw back his head and laughed. 'A duel? Now that is something!'

Hastings got up. He looked thunderous. 'It is no joke, sir.'

'No, no, of course it isn't.' Howe half-rose. 'Please sit down. Look, I'm sorry. Please.' His arms were spread in entreaty. 'Please.'

Hastings sat down slowly. His face was a sea of red beached by sideburns. A drop of sweat fell into his wine.

Howe leant forward, his hands flat to the table. He spoke confidentially. 'Well sir, I myself am here because of a duel, you might say. A woman rejected me so completely that she moved to the other side of America.'

Hastings grunted. He drank some wine, parting the lemon pieces with his finger, one eye still on Howe.

'So we're both free from authority,' continued Howe, 'in a way.' He leant back to examine his companion. Was it the Greeks who'd made this Englishman so brittle? He'd have to be more careful. *Or more direct?*

'The fact is,' he said at last, 'you're a big reason I'm here at all, Captain Hastings. If you'll permit it, I'd like to hear of what happened to you on Chios.'

The Englishman's face darkened. 'Chios? It was a slaughter-house. That's all.'

'But you brought a woman away, and her factor and many of her workers. On the *Themistocles*. Three years ago.'

Hastings was still wary. 'I did my duty, sir. So did Captain Tombazis and his crew.' He wiped his forehead with his sleeve. 'How do you know all this?'

'Because I met the factor in Boston three months ago. He is blind.'

'Panagiotis?' Hastings nodded. 'Yes, that is possible. He was brave.'

'As was his mistress Manto Kavardis, it seems. Where is she now?' He patted his chest. 'I have his letter for her.'

Captain Hastings tilted his glass so that the lemon slices bumped its side. He looked into it. 'She is in Nafplio.'

'Panagiotis told me that she is a great woman.'

Hastings looked up. 'She is.'

'Can you tell me more?'

'She was married to a rich man on Chios, executed by the Turks. The family had trading interests around the world and she spent much of her time abroad. They say she is the best connected person in Greece.'

'But now she's a recluse?'

'She lives alone and sees no one, except me when I come back from the sea, and then only sometimes. I can take your letter to her. But she won't see you.'

They lapsed into silence and Howe looked out over the bay where their two ships were being towed towards a hidden inlet. He felt deflated.

'Can they win this thing, the Greeks?' he asked quietly.

Hastings smacked a fly against a sideburn and looked down at his hand. 'The government has no army, just what the kapitanos sometimes bring.'

'But I've heard of volunteers coming from all over Europe to fight for it.'

'And you'll see them in Nafplio, if you ever get there.' Hastings shook the fly from his hand. 'They're pathetic creatures now, half-starving, destitute. No one wants them. What the government needs is outside help, from the Great Powers. Manto could help with that, if she could be persuaded.'

The two men were silent for a while, Howe wondering how much he himself might be wanted by the Greeks. At least he was a doctor, and a good one. He looked around the little terrace. It was deserted save for a cat that watched them from the comfort of a cushioned chair. It was the fattest thing he'd seen on the island so far. He looked back to Hastings.

'But they want you,' he said. 'How so?'

Hastings took no offence this time. 'I can train guns,' he said, 'which they can't. But they don't like advice.'

Howe wondered how this man's advice might be given. 'Such as?'

'Such as mounting cannon in the proper way, such as not torturing their prisoners, such as not paying the crew *before* they set sail.' The man shook his head slowly. 'The list is long.'

'But at least they have a navy. Can it win?'

For the first time, the captain looked enthused. This was something he'd given thought to. 'With the right ships, yes.'

'And what would those be?'

'Why, steam, of course.'

Howe thought of what he knew about steamships. He'd seen a version two years ago in Boston harbour, an ungainly affair with paddle-wheels at its sides and a tall funnel in its middle. He'd watched it do an awkward turn around Massachusetts Bay, then explode. He remembered the laughter up and down the quay.

'Does it work?'

'Certainly,' said Hastings. 'Imagine us off Crete, unable to stop the Egyptians because the wind was in the wrong place. Imagine us, instead, coming up to them and pouring shot into their sides, then moving to fire again. *Imagine!*'

The Englishman's face had become animated, creating new channels for his sweat. He wiped each cheek with his sleeve. 'A single steamship, properly commanded, can beat them, yes.'

'Properly commanded by you, I daresay,' said Howe, smiling. 'Where would you build it?'

'London.'

'And what does your Admiralty say?'

Hastings scowled. 'The Admiralty is full of old men.'

'So they won't give you any support.' Howe looked out to a

calm sea, empty of armada. It was a vision of peace yet he felt foreboding all around him. He said: 'But if Ibrahim Pasha's army is as formidable as you say, and the Greeks as divided, do you have time to build a steamship?'

Again they fell silent. He heard Hastings sip his wine, the creak of his chair as he leant back. 'That may depend on where that fleet is headed for.'

They heard a young voice behind them. It was the boy who'd served them.

'Navarino,' it said.

# CHAPTER SEVEN

## ISLAND OF KITHIRA

It was not a boy, but Hara who'd stepped out from the shadow of the doorway. She'd watched the two men talk for an hour and overheard most of what they'd said. It was time for her to speak.

Since coming to the island a year ago, she'd not much wanted to speak. It wasn't just the silence of these strange people who lived across the water from her home. It wasn't even the ghosts from Hades that were said to stalk it. It was the memory of what a Frenchman had said before he'd pushed her into the sea.

'I'm afraid Prince Tzanis is dead.'

Colonel Sève had left her alone in her cabin for the journey to and from Navarino, only bringing her out when they'd neared Cape Tainaron. She'd been brought onto the deck, a guard prodding her from behind, to find him leant over the side.

'Jellyfish,' he'd said in Greek. 'More than I've ever seen.' He'd waved. 'In every direction.'

She'd already decided to be what Tzanis had suggested: *a simple peasant girl who knows nothing.* Above all, she mustn't be searched. She still had the coin in her pocket.

'Perhaps the same ones that attacked poor Prince Tzanis.'

77

Sève had turned and looked at her speculatively. 'Is that possible, do you think?'

The questions had gone on for a while and she'd done nothing but stare at him. At length, he'd grown bored.

'Throw her to the jellyfish,' he'd said, turning back to the sea. 'Shoot her if she comes up.'

She'd landed amidst the jellyfish but plunged through them to a level deeper than anyone would have expected. She'd risen, unscathed, too far for them to shoot at, let alone see. Then she'd begun her long swim to the nearest shore.

Kithira had suited her mood. It was even more desolate than the Mani, a rugged landscape of mountain and ravine thrown up where two seas collided. It was a land blasted by storm where only pirates felt safe, hiding their *trattas* and *caiques* among the cliffs and creeks of the coast, far from the population who'd long ago moved inland to escape.

It also suited her predicament. The island was unmoored from its brothers: neither Ionian nor Aegean, Greek nor English. It was like her: alone, abandoned, half-educated and scared. But at least it was a place to hide and think of what to do next.

First, she'd had to master her fear. What the pappas had said about the island's ghosts had seemed real enough when she'd gazed across the straits from Cape Tainaron. From the beach she'd swum to, shrouded in swirling mist, it seemed certain. But the first sun had broken through and she'd remembered what Tzanis had told her: superstition was a man-made thing, invented by those with power to keep those without it cowed. It was to be challenged. *And you, Hara, have the courage to do it.*

She'd told him she'd wanted to go beyond the mountains. Now, in a way, she was beyond them. But how was she to live?

She couldn't go back to the Mani, that much was certain. That was where superstition lurked and where an unwanted marriage someday lay in wait. She'd disobeyed Petrobey and got Tzanis killed. She could never return.

So she'd had to make a living somehow on this island. She knew how to do two things: dive and collect herbs. She dived first. Many ships docked at Kithira, either to escape pirates or weather, and they needed their rudders cleared, hulls de-fouled, anchors freed. But as the *meltemi* season passed, they got fewer, and the nights got colder under her blanket on the beach.

So she'd turned to herbs. The only tavern in Kithira Town sold nothing but roasted goat and she saw that the English garrison avoided it. So she collected herbs to make the goat taste better to entice the English to come. The landlord gave her a roof over her head.

Every night in the tavern attic, she'd take out the coin and polish it slowly. She'd stare down at its golden face and wish she knew who the woman was. *Who Prince Tzanis was.*

As the months passed, she grew restless. She had to move on, but where to, and how? She needed to know more of the world before answering those questions. So she took to loitering at the tavern's tables, at its open windows, to hear the gossip of the English garrison. Despite her half-grasp of their language, she learnt that the Greeks had won the first part of their revolution but were now fighting among themselves.

Then one day, she learnt of Armageddon.

The two men who sat at the table were very different. One was a tall English naval officer with red hair and sideburns who sat very straight with his jaw out. The other was a dark, handsome man, more at his ease, perhaps ten years his junior. He'd come all the way from America where Tzanis had told her the people were truly free. They'd been talking about steamships and a huge Egyptian fleet on its way to somewhere they didn't know.

But she did.

'Navarino,' she'd said.

Captain Hastings was the first to turn to her. 'I'm sorry?'

'Navarino,' she'd repeated. 'The ships go to Navarino.'

'What . . . how do you know this?'

'I was on the Frenchman ship. It went to Navarino. To look.'

The American had risen. She looked at him properly now and saw a face that was open and might be honest. Only its eyes were surprising. There was something restive in them, quite at odds with the rest of his demeanor. He held out his hand. 'Samuel Gridley Howe.' He gestured for her to sit. She sat.

'What is your name?' asked Hastings.

'Hara.'

'Why were you on the Frenchman's ship, Hara?'

She'd told them everything about a fishing trip that had ended in capture and a detour to Navarino. In her broken English, she'd told them about Colonel Anthelme Sève and his silent, night-time foray into Navarino Bay. But she'd told them nothing about anyone called Prince Tzanis Comnenos, whose gold sovereign she turned in her pocket as she spoke.

At the end, they looked at her in amazement. Captain Hastings was the first to speak. He said: 'We are indebted to you, ma'am.'

'Indebted?'

'We owe you for what you have told us.'

'Then take me with you.'

And so it happened. They waited another day to check that Ibrahim Pasha hadn't changed his mind, made their farewells to Captain Abrahams, then set sail for Nafplio. With a brisk *levante* in their sails, they made good time.

They sailed on the *Themistocles*, the crew of which had been too long at sea. When Hara found their stares too much to bear, she went to join Hastings and Howe in the cabin. She found them bent over a drawing of a boat with a chimney between its sails.

They looked up as she entered.

'May I stay in here?' she asked.

Hastings glanced through the open door, then nodded. 'Of course.'

She curled herself up by the window while they talked. She didn't understand much of what they said but she liked watching them. She liked the way they listened to each other, how they nodded, how they found things to agree on. It was so different from the Mani. *Yassou, koumbare.*

After a while, her curiosity got the better of her and she got up.

Hastings was talking about the Battle of Trafalgar. 'I was a midshipman on the *Neptune*,' he was saying. He saw her next to him and switched to Greek. 'Not much older than you, I imagine.'

'Lord Nelson,' she said, remembering what Tzanis had told her. 'He won.'

Hastings nodded. 'With his band of brothers, yes.'

She looked at him, then Howe. 'Like you?'

Howe laughed. He glanced at Hastings. 'Like we might hope to be. One day.'

She remembered what she'd overheard at the tavern. 'With Manto Kavardis, and me. I can dive.' She looked down at the drawing. 'What is it?'

Then they talked about what steam could do and how it could win this war. She listened to every word and thought of another who might have been a brother too. Had he lived.

'Gold,' she said suddenly. 'Can steam bring gold up from the sea?'

Hastings looked surprised. 'Yes, quite possibly. What do you know about sunken gold?'

She looked away towards a sun that had just crept into the window frame, turning everything in the cabin amber. She remembered another sunset in another boat. *I'm afraid Prince Tzanis is dead.* She said: 'A man told me. A teacher.' She rose and went to the door. She turned. 'He's dead now. And I've forgotten it.'

# CHAPTER EIGHT

## NAFPLIO

They dropped anchor at Nafplio as the sun set over a blood-red sea. Captain Hastings walked them through the darkening town to his lodgings and Hara fell asleep in a bed more comfortable than she thought even Petrobey might own, the gold sovereign pressed to her heart.

She awoke to sunshine and noise. She rose and went to the window, the coin still in her hand. She looked out over a sea of orange tiles broken only by towers with bells at their tops. She'd never seen so many tiles. Below her was a square busy with people selling every kind of food and men and women in strange costumes that seemed too tight for the heat. Some carried parasols that they twirled above them.

She watched it all for a while, listening to the promise of sellers, the laughter of buyers. It didn't seem that anyone was much preoccupied by invasion, but then perhaps they didn't know. She looked down at the coin. She pressed her thumb to the woman's face, then traced the strange script around its edges. *What would he have wanted her to do?*

There was a knock at her door and an old woman entered.

She carried clothes. 'For you,' she said without looking up. She left.

Hara went over to examine what she'd brought, placing the coin on the dressing table. There was a dress like the ones she'd seen in the square, cut low at the front. There was a petticoat too, shoes and a hat. She put everything on except the hat and stood in front of the long mirror, turning to left and right, lifting the skirts in her fingers. She looked ridiculous. *Her hair.* She looked around her for a brush. There: on the table. She sat and brushed it in front of another mirror. *Better.*

She heard the sound of a door opening behind her, then a cough.

'I'm sorry. I should have knocked.'

In the mirror was Captain Hastings, dressed in cut-away coat, breeches and stockings. He came over and stood behind her, his hands on the back of her chair. He leant forward a little. 'Much better.'

Was he mocking her? The face above the notched collar had the same arrangement as at the tavern, the voice clipped but kind. She thought of Howe offering her the chair. Was everyone beyond the mountains so kind? *No.* Colonel Sève wasn't kind.

She looked back to herself. Her hair was calmer now and she looked, she supposed, a little less strange.

'Is that yours?'

He was pointing at the coin. She picked it up quickly. 'Yes,' she said. 'Mine.'

He was frowning. 'I've not seen one before: a Russian dollar with Empress Catherine's head on it. I didn't think they still existed. How did you come by it?'

She rose quickly and put it in a pocket.

Captain Hastings watched her. Then he turned and walked

over to the window, his hands behind his back. He stood there for some time, looking at whatever was happening in the square below. He went over to the table and picked up her hat. 'There is someone I have to deliver a letter to,' he said. 'I'd like you to meet her. Come.' He walked over to the door. 'And bring the coin.'

Until Nafplio, Tsimova was the biggest town Hara had visited. With its two churches and many towers, Petrobey's capital had seemed vast. But what she saw from the rim of her bonnet left her breathless. She was grateful for Hasting's arm.

They walked out into a square thronged with people of every nationality. There were serious men in frock coats, silly women in gowns, fierce *kelphts* in skirts with pistols in their belts, unsteady sailors and Albanians in pantaloons and slippers. On one side stood a ruined mosque with a broken minaret and tiles missing from its dome. Wretched men sat on its steps in ragged uniforms that once must have been fine.

They pushed their way through to a side street where the sun was blocked by tall houses with shutters, each painted a different colour. Most had the new flag of Greece draped from a balcony.

They came to a big house set back from the others with a front garden and gate to the street. Its shutters were closed and there was no flag anywhere in sight. Above the gate was a winged lion with its paw over an open book. She remembered Tzanis telling her Nafplio had been Venetian once; they'd built a fort there. She looked up and saw ramparts and the zigzag of steps down to the town. *There.*

They walked up to the door and knocked. It was opened by a Turk of middle age dressed in a white *thoub* with two children behind him. She stared at him. *A Turk?*

But Hastings stepped forward and took the man's hand in both of his. 'Mustafa. Are you well?'

The Turk bowed and raised a palm to his heart. A string of amber prayer beads, tied to his wrist, rattled with the movement. 'Allah is merciful.'

'And your family?' A boy of perhaps Hara's age had appeared behind. 'Suleiman. You grow more like your father every day.'

'I am blessed,' said the boy, also bowing.

Hastings took a letter from his pocket. 'Is she upstairs? I have a letter for her. From America.'

Mustafa's eyes had moved to Hara.

'Ah, yes,' said Hastings. 'This girl has something she'll wish to see. May she come up too?'

Mustafa's gaze turned to something like surprise. For a moment, she saw what he saw: a small, Greek peasant girl pretending to be a lady from Paris. She felt herself flush with embarrassment.

'I will ask.'

They walked into a hall with a wide central staircase and rich hangings on the walls. It was filled with children who parted before them in silence. They stood at the bottom of the stairs while Mustafa went up. After a while, he returned and led them up to a broad landing with a single door. Mustafa opened it and stood to one side.

'Please,' he said.

The room was large and stuffy and smelt of lilacs. A woman was standing at a shuttered window, looking out through its cracks. She wore a long black dress of some expensive material. She turned.

'Captain Hastings,' she said in English, 'back from the sea at last. It is a relief to see you safe.'

He lifted the letter and placed it on a table. 'From America, ma'am.'

She looked at it for a moment. Her eyes moved to Hara and returned with a question.

'Greek,' he said. 'Picked up at Kithira. Interesting story.'

Hara met the woman's gaze. She was perhaps the same age as the English captain but no taller than herself, though she seemed so with her straight back and head held high. Her face was lightly lined and had beauty in it, but one stretched by pain. Her long hair was ordered but dull. Her eyes were in another place.

'Well?' the woman asked, in Greek.

Hara could feel sweat at her hairline and wanted to take off her bonnet. Then she remembered the unkempt hair beneath. 'I have told my story,' she said quietly, relieved to be speaking her language again. 'I was fishing in the Mani. I was picked up by the Frenchman and taken to Navarino. I went to Kithira and the captain brought me here.'

The woman nodded. She looked at Hastings again.

'She has something you should see, ma'am,' he said. 'A coin.'

Hara frowned. 'It is mine. It was given to me.'

'I'm sure,' said the woman. Her eyes travelled down Hara's dress and back to her face. They had the first hint of interest in them. 'We've not been introduced. I am Manto Kavardis.' She held out a hand.

Hara waited a moment, then took it. 'Hara.'

Manto's head had moved to one side. She was looking at her as if puzzled by something, almost as if she'd seen something unexpected in a mirror.

'Can I see the coin, Hara?'

She shook her head. 'I promised not.'

'Promised? Who did you promise?'

He'd been very clear. *Keep it and hide it. Tell no one what you know.* But there was something about this woman that made

Hara want to confide in her, something warm and familiar in her eyes that was not in her bearing.

Manto turned to Hastings. 'Why is this coin interesting?'

'It is the Tzar's gold, ma'am,' he said. 'But it has the image of the Empress Catherine on it.'

'Indeed?' Her eyes travelled back to Hara. 'Catherine the Great's gold found in the Mani. Who gave it to you?'

Hara didn't answer. She imagined the coin in her pocket: heavy, close.

'It might be leftover from the Orlov time,' said Hastings. 'That would explain it.'

'Or it might not.' Manto's gaze stayed on Hara. 'In which case, it might be important.' She came over and lifted Hara's chin gently and looked straight into her eyes. 'Can I see it, please?'

It was now, this close, that Hara saw how different this woman's eyes were to her poise. For all her calm beauty, there was pain in them, and loss. Need too.

Manto leant forward. 'Hara,' she whispered. 'You are dressed in a dress that isn't yours and you're in Nafplio where you know no one.' She paused. 'Would you like to go back to the Mani?'

Hara shook her head.

'So you need help and I can help you.' Manto smiled. 'Now, show me the coin.'

Hara put her hand in her pocket and closed it around the coin. What Manto said was true: she had to survive. And her instinct was telling her to trust this woman. *He will never know because he is dead.*

She took out the coin and passed it to her.

Manto looked at it for a long time, turning it over in her hand. 'Who gave it to you?'

Hara decided. 'I will tell you,' she said, 'but only if you help me.'

Manto looked back to her, some surprise in her eyes. 'And how do you think I should help you, Hara?'

'Teach me. The man who gave me the coin gave me some learning. I need more.'

Manto looked back to the coin and nodded slowly. She seemed to think for a long time. 'Why not,' she said at last, looking up. 'Why not?'

Through her window blinds Manto Kavardis watched Hastings leave. The English captain with his stiff neck was one of only two people she trusted in this town, the other being the Turk with the prayer beads who'd shown him in. She'd given Mustafa and his family shelter from the massacre after Nafplio had fallen. Now he wouldn't let anyone past her front door.

*Except this girl.* This girl, who was even now being shown around her new home, this girl, with her strange hair and interesting coin. For all their differences in class, education and age, she'd seemed familiar. Manto had not wanted her to leave.

She turned and looked around the room: her world. On good days, she read. More often, though, she'd sit and fight with her past. Her memory was as ruthless as it was cunning. It crept into her dreams by stealth: getting over the wall when the sentries were asleep, hunting her through the hills with its dogs. Sometimes it came in sudden flashes: her husband swinging from a rope outside the citadel; her factor Panagiotis returning to the cave with sockets for his eyes; the girl who chose to run . . . *Yes, that had been the hardest:* the girl who'd been so hungry that she'd run from the cave. They'd heard the dogs first, then screams that had gone on too long. *She'd been about Hara's age.*

She went over to the table, sat down and examined the coin. Then she picked up the letter. For a long time, she remained quite still, looking down on the louvred sunlight that striped it. She knew who it was from and what it would say. It would be the plea of an honest man whom she'd abandoned. It would be a reminder of *duty*. She preferred to leave duty to Hastings, who still had a taste for it.

She turned it over and saw stains on the parchment. Blood? She pulled it open and read. It wasn't long.

*Lady,*

*I am in America now. I wish I could tell you about its great cities and plains and rivers, but I can't see them. What I can tell you is that its air smells better than Chios in the spring. I wish you could smell it. It is the smell of freedom.*

*I pray you have forgiven me for leaving, but in truth you had already left. You saved our lives, then shut yourself away. Was it the horror of what you'd seen? Or was it that you'd lost your faith in humanity? I think it was both. I left without saying what I should have said, so I will say it now.*

*Lady, trust the people, as they trusted you. When the rich all fled Chios, you stayed behind and led the people to freedom. They were right to trust you then, and they will be right to trust you now. They never wanted this revolution and it will be they who suffer most when it is lost, as they always do.*

*You know that the only way to win is to bring help from outside Greece. Only you can do that.*

*Your ever faithful servant,*
*Panagiotis Persides.*

She read it again, then closed her eyes, for once dropping her guard to memory, for once letting it in. She remembered the gathering of silent people, the hushing of children, the anxious looks up towards the fire beyond the hills. She remembered the ancient paths taken through the mountains at night, each holding onto the one in front. She remembered the first, distant howls of the dogs, the cries of children who'd heard them too. She remembered sharing out the last of the food, and the hunger that was with them every moment when it was gone, shutting out every other thought. She remembered reaching the last village before the coast and seeing the bodies piled in its streets, right down to the beach, to the sea.

*Then Hastings.*

She put her palms to her eyes. When had she last cried? Not for a long, long time.

She looked away. He was right. This war was too big for the Greeks. They needed help from those who'd already won their revolutions, from those who had money: America, France ... England.

*But Russia?*

She looked over to the coin still on the table. She picked it up and looked at it. *This belongs to the Tzar,* the Tzar who is supposed to be neutral in this conflict.

# CHAPTER NINE

## NAFPLIO

Captain Hastings left Manto Kavardis's house in search of male company. He generally preferred it, when it was sober. His was a world of science, and the sexes were quite clearly divided in that area. He'd go and find the American. He was male, a scientist and therefore sensible. And he'd seemed surprisingly interested in steam.

Manto was the exception, of course. She was rational, pragmatic. If only her intellect could be brought to bear for the cause. After all, she knew everyone important abroad. And what a fascinating story he'd just heard. Russian gold lost off the coast of the Mani, brought by a Greek prince, a *Comnenos*, no less. But who had his gold been *for*? The girl hadn't known. Nor had Manto.

He arrived at his house and let himself in. The American was sitting at the table looking through drawings of steam experiments. This was promising. But there was bad news to deliver first. He took off his hat and sat down.

'She won't see you, I'm afraid,' he said.

Howe looked up. 'You gave her the letter?'

Hastings nodded. 'And she was grateful.'

Howe looked beyond him. 'So where is Hara?'

He placed his hands on the table and studied them. This was the difficult part. 'Ah, yes, well. She stayed.'

Howe looked amazed. 'Stayed?'

'It turned out she had something Manto wanted. She exchanged it for a berth.'

Howe stared at him. 'What did she have?'

'Well, that I can't tell you, I'm afraid.' He shrugged. 'Anyway, she still refuses to see everyone else. Even Mavrocordatos is turned away.'

Howe shook his head. Then he looked down at the drawings in front of him. He smoothed the paper with his palm. 'On the ship, Hara called us a band of brothers. But it could just as well be sisters too. Your revolution needs Manto Kavardis.' He looked up. 'And perhaps I can help. After all, I am American.'

Hastings bridled. 'Your meaning?'

Howe lent forward. 'That I'm new to this, so I'm not part of any faction.' He paused. 'Will you try again?'

Later, after Hastings had left, Howe went out to eat. It was his first sight of Nafplio in daylight, and he was shocked. Everywhere there were Greeks in gaudy new uniforms passing wretched *philhellenes* sat in doorways. He gave a coin to one without legs who pushed himself around on a trolley and wore what was left of his uniform perched on the back of his head. He asked him where he'd lost his legs.

'Peta,' said the man, placing the coin carefully between his stumps. 'I am what's left of Steer's class of '21.'

'Peta?'

'A battle we lost.' The man straightened the hat on his head. 'Nine of us came from the *Akademie* in Munich to fight for the Greeks. At Peta they betrayed us.'

Howe sat down in the doorway's shade. 'Tell me.'

'It was three years ago,' said the man. He was unshaven and scabbed and smelt of his own fluids. 'Hundreds came from all over Europe with Byron in their pockets. The general somehow made us into a battalion and gave us some discipline. The rest of the army were *Souliotes* from Epirus commanded by two men who hated each other. At Peta, one of them made an agreement with the Turks and left the field with his men. The Turk cavalry attacked us from behind.' He leant out from the trolley and spat. 'My friends were all sabered and I lost my legs.'

A shadow fell. He glanced up to see that a group of philhellenes had gathered round to listen. Many were nodding.

He turned back to the man. 'So why don't you leave?'

'Leave?' he laughed bitterly. 'How can I leave without money?'

Howe looked around at them. 'But you're all educated men. Won't your families help you?'

'My family has disowned me,' said a man wearing only tattered breeches with a rope to hold them up. 'I'm not wanted in France any more than in Greece.'

Howe rose. He felt in his pocket and brought out what coin he had. 'Here,' he said, giving it to the man in the trolley. 'Share this between you. I am a doctor. Tomorrow you will find me here with my bag. I will help those I can.'

It was on the third day of Howe's outdoor surgery that Mustafa came. Word had got round that an American doctor was dispensing free care and philhellenes from all over Nafplio were queuing to receive it. Howe was bent over two orange crates that served as an examining couch.

Mustafa announced himself by the rattle of amber as he approached.

'There is a queue,' said Howe without looking up.

'I don't come for medicine,' came the deep voice. 'I come from Manto Kavardis.'

Howe glanced up to see a tall, hooded figure at the end of the makeshift bed with a string of prayer beads in his hands. 'Please wait.' He tightened a bandage and patted the arm. He gestured to the man in the trolley who sat with loaves in his lap. 'Take some bread. One piece.' He turned to Mustafa. 'So she's decided to see me after all?'

The Turk shook his head. 'No. But she wishes to help. She has heard what you are doing.'

Howe turned to wash his hands in a bowl of water perched on another crate. He picked up a towel and dried them. 'How has she heard?'

Mustafa waited a moment before replying. 'You have a friend in Captain Hastings.'

He was surprised by how happy this news made him. He asked: 'How does she want to help?'

'There is an empty building in the town that was once a *madrassah* for those of my religion. She would equip it as a hospital for you to work in.'

Howe folded the towel. 'That is a generous offer. Why could she not have made it herself?'

'My mistress has withdrawn from the world,' he said. 'She prefers to conduct her business through me.'

Mustafa lowered his hood and Howe looked into a quiet, noble face fringed by a well-tended beard of silky grey. He could

95

imagine such a face denying access at Manto's door with infinite politeness. He nodded.

'Then you may tell her that I accept her offer.' He paused. 'But she should know it will not be Greeks who I'll be helping but the poor wretches you see in this line.'

Mustafa dipped his head. 'It is what she hopes for.'

It took two weeks to fit out the hospital. Beds were brought in from the islands and medicine from British Corfu, all paid for with Manto's gold.

Hastings came to help, Mustafa too. The Englishman couldn't help but take command and they deferred to him as good manners required, although, as Howe tried to explain, a hospital was not entirely like a ship. But it worked, this curious trinity of British command, Yankee expertise and Turkish calm. It brought forth a hospital.

In a month they were open and the wards were instantly full – the kitchens too, for some men came just to be fed. Howe spent his days cleaning old wounds, amputating what had gone bad, re-setting what hadn't. He worked until he could work no more, then slept-walked his way back to his lodgings. He'd not felt so fulfilled in years.

For staff, he'd recruited a Greek doctor and four nurses, but volunteers were plentiful. The hospital had caught the imagination of the town. One morning, he found someone he knew waiting in his office.

'Hara.'

He didn't recognise her at first. She stood before his desk, her back quite straight and her hands folded to her front like she was in church. She was dressed entirely in black but the design was subtle and expensive. She seemed taller.

'It is Manto's,' she said in English, as he stared. 'I am living with her.'

Howe walked over to his desk. 'I'd heard,' he said. 'That is quite a change.'

Hara sat. 'Is my English better?'

'Impressively so.' He sat down. 'How did you manage it?'

She shrugged slightly. 'She seems to like me. Perhaps I remind her of someone.' She smiled. 'Anyway, I am here now. I want to help you.'

'Help me?'

'Be part of things. I know something of medicinal herbs and I have healing hands.' She showed her palms to him. 'I learn quickly.'

That much was obvious. He was finding her demeanor difficult to believe. On Kithira, she'd seemed part-animal. He asked: 'Does Manto know you've come?'

She nodded. 'She sent me.'


So Hara came to the hospital every day and learnt as fast as she'd promised. Her natural intelligence allowed her to absorb everything Howe taught her, while her instinct did the rest. Soon she was performing basic surgery. For the first time in his life, Howe bore witness to hands that truly healed.

Then, not long afterwards, Manto herself paid a visit. She arrived in a dress identical to the one that Hara wore every day. It was after dark and Howe was working to the light of an oil lamp suspended high above his desk. When the door opened, it flickered in the draught. He didn't look up.

'Hara,' he said, rubbing his eyes with his fingertips as he leant back in his chair, 'did our mysterious benefactor ever teach you to add up? My accounts are a scandal.'

She sat down and watched him for a minute in silence. His loose cravat gave him a rakish air and he wore a strange instrument around his neck.

'I doubt she'd notice,' she said.

Howe swore as his knees met the top of his desk. He was rubbing them as he rose, his stethoscope askew.

'Manto.'

She looked unearthly in the lamplight, like someone had painted her from a sepia palate. She held herself very straight and still: a facsimile of someone who'd sat there not long ago. The resemblance was uncanny.

'I thought . . .'

'You thought I was Hara, which is a compliment.' Her English bore almost no accent and had the precision of one used to transacting business. She opened a fan and began to cool herself.

Howe heard voices come and go outside the room. He glanced at the door.

'Mustafa is out there,' she said. 'No one will disturb us.' She looked straight at him. 'Why did you come to Greece, Dr Howe?'

He sat down again, closing the accounts ledger and putting it to one side. He'd asked himself that question so many times and always came up with different answers. This time he said: 'You are part of the reason, I guess. I wanted to meet the woman who could change the world.'

She smiled thinly. 'Well, now you have. Not very impressive, I'm afraid.' Her eyes stayed on his: still formal, but with a hint of challenge. He thought they held some curiosity, but it might have been the light. She tucked a stray hair behind her ear. 'I wish to come and work in your hospital.'

'My hospital? It's yours.'

'Which you run. Very well, I understand.' She looked down at her hands. 'I wish to come every day and help for a few hours. Will that be agreeable?'

Howe nodded. 'Of course. May I ask why?'

'For my own reasons. Perhaps to see how you are spending my money.'

'Ah, the accounts. Well . . .'

'I don't care about the accounts. I am interested in how you work.'

He found himself pleased. 'Then I shall be delighted. You can join Hara.'

She shook her head. 'No. I will work at different times to her. But we will be dressed the same and both wear masks.'

This was curious but hardly his business. He spread his hands. 'As you wish. Of course.'

So Manto came to work at the hospital. To the patients, and Howe sometimes, she and Hara were the same: one continuous, masked, competent presence, always in black. It was uncanny how they seemed to have merged.

She seemed happy to take the more menial tasks: cleaning, making beds, preparing food. She hardly spoke to the patients and turned away when spoken to. It was as if she'd brought her reclusiveness with her to the ward. Howe found himself watching her more and more.

One evening he found her again in his office. She was sitting in the same chair, dressed in the same black dress. She had her mask in her lap. He sat down across from her.

'Tell me about my factor,' she said. 'You met him and he gave you a letter.'

Howe thought back to a rainy night in Boston. 'He was keen

for me to meet you,' he said. 'He said you're the only one who can win this war for the Greeks.'

She shook her head. 'He exaggerates. The Great Powers have a treaty to sign. That is what will win this war.'

'But someone has to persuade them to sign it. He was very clear that it could only be you.'

He stared at her and her eyes came back to his and didn't move away. They were tiny points of light surrounded by darkness, perhaps too tired to move. When had she last slept? He felt suddenly desperate to know more of this woman.

'Tell me about Chios,' he said.

Her eyes stayed on his. 'Why?'

'Because you must think about it all the time. Because it is part of you.'

She nodded slowly and looked down. 'You're right.' She drew a deep breath. 'It was a vision of hell not meant to be seen in this life. Whatever's painted on church walls doesn't get near to it.' She shook her head slowly. 'I never realised there was so much hate in the world.'

'But you survived it and were the reason others did too.'

She looked up. 'Yes, but to what end? There have been many massacres in this war.'

'Which you've chosen to hide away from.'

She bridled. 'Rather than what? Once Chios had shown the way . . .' she trailed off, suddenly shutting her eyes. She looked down. They were silent for a while. He watched her struggle with something behind the curtain of her eyelashes. 'I never want to see anything like that again,' she said softly. 'Not ever. That is why I choose to hide away.'

'Yet Hara,' he said. 'You took her in. And now you are here.'

'In disguise,' she said. 'And Hara had something to give me.'

'What was that?'

She glanced at him. 'It's better that you don't know.'

'Why?' He paused. 'I've trusted you.'

She stared at him, weighing it up. 'Very well.' She nodded. 'A young Russian prince of Greek descent was shipwrecked off the coast of the Mani. The ship was carrying gold sent by the Tzar of Russia to help the revolution. Hara rescued him and looked after him while he recovered. The two of them went out to look for the gold but were picked up by a Frenchman in the service of the Khedive of Egypt who was reconnoitering for an invasion. Hara found her way here.'

'And the prince?'

'Dead, killed by the Frenchman.'

He nodded. 'Who was the gold for?'

'We don't know.' She reached into a pocket and put Hara's coin onto the table. It glowed in the lamplight. 'But the prince gave her this. It proves that it came from the Tzar.'

Howe stared down at the coin. 'And Russia is supposed to be neutral,' he murmured.

They sat in silence for a while, both thinking the same thought. At last he said: 'Such a coin . . .'

But she was rising. 'You are astute, Dr Howe. Such a coin could be useful. But Russia is only one of the three Great Powers. There is still Britain and France, whose king wants nothing to do with another revolution.' She smiled. 'It will take more than a coin.'

# PART THREE

# 1825–26

# CHAPTER TEN

## NAVARINO

Tzanis had stayed at Navarino far longer than he'd intended, persuaded by the man who'd rescued him from his rock. He was a young Swiss called Meyer and he'd untied Tzanis's ankles and rubbed them until some blood returned. Then he'd glanced back to where the tender was being hoisted up the side of Colonel Sève's frigate.

'Surveying,' he said, turning back. 'That's what they said as we passed. So why not stay and survey with them?'

Why indeed, when Hara was still aboard? But then the sound of an anchor rising. *Too late now.*

The Swiss had been dressed in a linen suit, thin-cut for the heat. He was not much older than Tzanis and hid his baldness beneath a straw hat the size of a plate. Tzanis told him some of his story as they were rowed to shore, a little more as they walked into the town. It was a hot day without wind and the doorways were filled with men in tattered uniforms, either drunk or asleep. There were dogs and flies everywhere. The place stank.

'The last of the Byron Brigade,' murmured Meyer, 'trying

to find a passage to Nafplio, then home. They've come from Missolonghi.'

They stopped to look. 'Is Mavrocordatos still there, do you know?'

Meyer removed his hat and wiped his brow with his sleeve. 'He left when Lord Byron died. Everyone left then. The siege was over, anyway.'

*Byron dead?* Tzanis had felt then the last gust of a hurricane that must have swept the world, but not the Mani.

'Why was Byron in Missolonghi?'

'A good question,' said Meyer. 'He arrived last winter and all the philhellenes flocked to join him and take his money. He'd already bought himself an army of 500 Souliotes who were running riot in the town. When the philhellenes weren't duelling, they were fighting the Souliotes. A drunkard called Parry arrived from London with cannon that didn't work, and Byron made him generalissimo. Then he went down with fever and died just after Easter.'

Tzanis looked at the dapper man. He wasn't made for war. 'And you?'

The Swiss started to walk again, fanning himself with his hat. 'I went there to set up a newspaper. I've been getting ink from Nafplio.'

'But you knew Byron?'

'And admired him. He spent his money generously, if not always wisely. And he faced down the Souliotes, eventually.' He paused. 'Most of all, he put Missolonghi into the mind of the world. He did more for Greece by dying than he ever did by living.'

They'd come to a big house with a Greek flag outside. They were shown into a room where two men were looking over a map on a table. One was the Greek garrison commander and the other a Frenchman called Clavier, also on his way to Missolonghi. Tzanis told them what he knew.

'Impossible,' said the garrison commander, looking him up and down. 'The Egyptians are neutral.'

'And Colonel Sève a traitor?' said Clavier. 'Never!'

'But,' asked Meyer, 'why wouldn't the Turks ask their Egyptian vassals for help? And we know Colonel Sève's been in the service of the Khedive. It's said he's built the army into a formidable force.'

'Perhaps, but Egypt is not at war with Greece.'

'Then why all the secrecy?' asked Tzanis. 'Why the reconnaissance at night? And why did they want to kill me?'

'I have no idea,' said Clavier, returning to his map.

Meyer had known things only a journalist would know, such as why Tzanis should not leave for Nafplio.

'There's no ship going there and the countryside is overrun by Kolokotronis's klephts,' he said. 'Better to stay here until the winter. It could be exciting if your invasion comes.'

Tzanis remembered that Kolokotronis had been the first kapitano to join Petrobey at the start of the revolution. He'd taken Tripoli and beaten the Turks when they'd come to take it back. He was a hero.

'But why should I have anything to fear from Kolokotronis?'

Meyer shook his head. 'You've much to learn,' he smiled. 'After beating the Turks, Kolokotronis took on the government. But he lost and Mavrocordatos locked him up in Nafplio. Now his klephts are wandering the hills murdering anyone who even hints of government connection. You'd never make it.'

'And Petrobey?'

'Sulking down in the Mani with his men,' said the Swiss. 'God help us if the Egyptians do come.'

Eventually, Meyer had grown bored of waiting for the invasion and took ship for Missolonghi, Clavier with him. It was rumoured that a second Turk army was coming down to besiege the town. A little later, Tzanis left too. Winter was not far off and the mountain passes would close. With any luck, the klephts would stay at home.

He was too angry to stay anyway. He'd written four letters to Capodistrias, each in code, and received nothing back. He'd written to Mavrocordatos too. Nothing. He'd been abandoned, cut adrift. He'd lost the Tzar's gold and no one wanted anything more to do with him.

He left before dawn. It was two hundred miles to Nafplio and he must get through the passes before the weather set in. But winter was early that year. A blast of ice swept in from the north and, on his first night out in the open, it began to snow. He awoke the next morning beneath a cloak stiff as wood.

He rose and set off but felt weaker with every pace. There was sweat on his brow despite the cold. Should he return to Navarino? *No.*

By midday, it had begun to snow again and he was exhausted. He left the road to sit down against a rock.

Afterwards, he'd wonder about divine intervention. What else had made the klephts pass by his rock, prod the snowdrift with a stick, step back when it stirred?

There'd been four of them: men of the mountains who knew every submerged track, every meagre store of food in this frozen landscape. They carried him to a village high in the mountains where smoke rose from chimneys. They took him into a house and laid him down to sleep.

This time he was not allowed to leave. He stayed in bed while the fever ran its long course and the winter winds roared outside. He knew nothing of the old woman who nursed him back to life, bringing thick soups to coax down his throat, furs when he shivered, snow for his sweats. He heard none of her muttering as she shuffled from fire to bedside to door. He never saw the amulet with its single eye laid on his chest.

He woke to find her lying beside him: big, warm and smelling of every animal except humanity.

'You almost lost your toes,' she said.

For the next few weeks she gave him proper food and gentle blows if he refused it. She gave him news as well. A vast army from Egypt had landed at Navarino with fearless giants who devoured everything sent to stop them with guns that spat flame and could burn down forests. But the government had released Kolokotronis from prison and he would soon drive them back.

One day her son came to visit. He stooped as he entered, removing his hat and stamping snow from his boots while she scolded him. He sat on a chair beside the bed.

'It's time to know who you are,' he said.

Tzanis felt too tired to lie. Anyway, Kolokotronis had been released so perhaps he was less of a suspect. 'I am a Greek from Russia,' he said. 'I have urgent business in Nafplio.'

'What business?'

'With Mavrocordatos.' He paused, watching the man's frown grow. He changed tack. 'How is the war? Is Kolokotronis beating them?'

The man looked down at the floor. 'Nothing can beat them,' he said quietly. 'It is Kolokotronis who is beaten.'

'Has he surrendered?'

The man looked up and stared at him. 'Surrender? Are you mad?'

'I meant . . .'

The man was shaking his head, his moustache sweeping his chin. 'No one will surrender. Not even when there's nothing left.' He thought for a moment, then rose. 'Are you well enough to walk?'

They left early the next morning beneath the first sun they'd seen in a week, packs on their backs and muskets longer than pikestaffs slung from their shoulders. They climbed up through passes, then down into a steep valley. They came to a wall of rock where pigeons sheltered among grasses in its cracks. They killed eight birds and filled bags with mushrooms and herbs that they knew where to find beneath the snow. It was mid-morning when they followed a path down into the foothills.

They came to terracing with a village below. They climbed down to the first house, whose charred beams reared up like some monstrous carcass, white with snow. They walked through ruins to more terraces where the olive trees were nothing but black stumps. At the bottom of each something lay scattered. At first he thought they were twigs.

He went over and knelt down. He picked up a bone and held it up, too shocked to speak. He felt the klepht leader kneel down beside him. 'It's a collarbone,' said the man. 'About my mother's size.'

When Tzanis could speak, it was in a whisper. 'Who . . . ?'

'Ibrahim. The price of our not surrendering. He was merciful at first.'

Tzanis stared at him. 'There's more?'

'Everywhere. He's killing everything that moves. Or enslaving it.'

Tzanis felt sick. 'Why did you bring me here?'

'Because you draw. You have paper and pencil in your pack.'

Tzanis looked around him. Everywhere were black stumps with bones around them. 'You want me to *draw* this?'

The klepht nodded. 'And take it to Mavrocordatos.'

When spring came and the passes opened again, Tzanis found it was too dangerous to leave. Ibrahim had sent his men back into the mountains to spread fire and terror. In every direction, smoke hazed the horizon as another village was set alight. Even with an escort, it was too dangerous to travel.

With summer came the news that Ibrahim's army had stopped its slaughter and was gathering in Tripoli to march on Nafplio. There was nothing more to destroy anyway. The harvest had been burnt to stubble and the population left behind would be too weak to trouble them.

Tzanis could at last set off. He chose the mountain route to Nafplio. It was little more than a track, bordered by scorched grass moved by snakes disturbed by his tread. In the villages, he found refuge, sometimes food, usually kindness. People were poor and frightened, but Christian too. He thought about his time in the Mani and a kindness he'd taken too much for granted.

After Tripoli, he came back to the road. The people here had yet to see an Egyptian but they knew what was coming and wanted to know what he'd seen. He watched them gather their children, then look to the horizon. He hated himself for the contagion he brought.

He was only forty miles from Nafplio when he met deserters from Kolokotronis's army: men who'd seen too much defeat. They were angry and humiliated and hungry and, by the time he saw them, it was too late. There was no point in running. He was half-starved and they had muskets, so he greeted them as he passed. Then they hit him.

And as he went down, he thought of how angry they'd be when they found all he was carrying was a sketch. As he hit the ground, he was praying they'd not take it.

# CHAPTER ELEVEN

## NAFPLIO

Howe was finding reasons to meet Manto in every part of the hospital – in corridors, by bedsides – anywhere. He got to know the routine of her day, the places she'd be at certain times. Because of the mask, it was her eyes he got to know best. With nothing else to help, they were inscrutable. But sometimes they would meet his. Sometimes they would stay.

A stranger was brought in with a beard that covered most of his face. He'd been found half-dead on the road, beaten by klephts who'd robbed him. Howe ordered him laid on a bed at the other end of the ward.

'Can you shave him?' he asked Hara as she passed. 'He won't know it's happening.'

'Who?'

Howe pointed to the man. 'Him. Over there.'

She glanced over to the bed. 'Of course. Will he live?'

'God willing.'

He watched her go over to prepare things, talking to the nurses through her mask as she tested the razor's sharpness. He heard her laugh. He saw her go to where the man lay as if in death, his half-naked body a landscape of bruises. He saw her stare down at him for a long time, every part of her completely still. He saw her body jerk as if electricity had passed through it. He saw her put out a hand to the bedstead. He wondered if she'd had some form of siezure.

'Hara?'

She didn't reply, didn't move.

He began to walk towards her. 'Hara?'

This time she turned and he saw that her cheeks were streaked with tears. But she was smiling too.

He stopped beside her. 'Do you know him?'

She looked back down. She nodded. 'I had thought him dead.'

Howe looked down at a man he'd never expected to meet. 'Well, let's make sure he's not,' he said quietly. 'Can you shave him?'

He went over to where he could watch without her knowing. He saw the infinite care with which she revealed his face bit by bit, as if every inch was precious beyond words. When it was finished, when she'd dried it and carefully folded the towel, he saw her lean forward, lower her mask and kiss him on the forehead. Then she straightened and put her head to one side to consider her work. He saw her smooth his hair with her palm, then nod. Once.

As she moved away, she stopped and looked down at the table beside his bed, then picked something up. It was a piece of paper.

That evening, Manto invited Howe to her house. He arrived with Hara to find Hastings already there. As Mustafa served them dinner, Manto made an announcement.

'I am going to London,' she said. 'I leave in a week.'

They were seated around a small table in her parlour and the windows were open for whatever breeze might come from the street. Hara was dressed in Manto's black because she'd just come from the hospital. She was fanning herself.

Howe felt shocked. He'd argued for it, but had not imagined it would ever happen. 'What has persuaded you?' he asked.

'This,' she said, putting Tzanis's sketch on the table. 'Hara brought it to me from the Prince's bedside. It was the only thing the klephts left on him.'

They all stared at the picture.

'Proof of what Ibrahim is doing,' she said quietly. She paused and looked around. 'And things have changed abroad. There is a new thing called popular feeling. Newspapers are fanning it and statesmen are having to react. I can help.'

'Byron's work,' said Hastings.

She nodded. 'And others. A Frenchman painted the Chios massacre and the French king now finds himself embarrassed to be building ships for Ibrahim Pasha.' She looked at Hara. 'I want to take your coin with me.'

Hara looked up, bewildered. 'It's not my coin. And he is alive.'

Manto nodded. 'Alive, but unable to talk. Do you know why I want to take it?'

Hara remained silent.

'Because the Russians will be in London. I have a friend in the ambassador's wife. She will tell the Tzar I have his coin.'

Howe interrupted. 'But will you be safe?'

'I will be going with her,' said Hastings.

Howe stared at him. 'What will you do there?'

Hastings smiled. 'I'll build a steamship.' He glanced at their hostess. 'Manto will speak to the Admiralty.'

Hara was frowning. 'Will one ship win us the war?' she asked.

Hastings drank some wine. 'A steamship might. I'd pit it against the whole of Ibrahim's navy, and the Sultan's. And we can build more.' He paused. 'Which brings us to the gold. You've told us it's too deep to dive for.'

Hara nodded. 'I tried.'

'But could you find it again if you had to? If some other way could be found to raise it?'

'Of course.'

'Good. Because when I return with the steamship, that's exactly what we'll do first: raise it.'

The Captain reached behind his chair and brought out drawings of a new engine that would use steam to drive air down into a diving suit. Howe watched as he explained it to her. There were few people who wore their genius so lightly as this stiff English captain. He would miss him.

He felt Manto's breath on his ear. 'I want you to take care of her,' she whispered, leaning in to him. 'And I want people to think I am still here.' She paused. 'It is why we have worn the same clothes, the same masks all this time.'

He turned to her. Her eyes were very close. 'Why is that important?'

'Because my success in London relies on attachment to no faction. If people knew that I'd gone, they'd draw their own conclusions. Hara's presence will make them think I am still here.'

After Manto had left, the hospital seemed little changed. After all, to most people in it, she was still there.

For Howe it had changed drastically, and in no way that was good. It seemed that some part of its purpose had gone with her, despite her presence having been mostly silent. He spent much time thinking back to their last meeting.

Meanwhile, Hara nursed Tzanis as if he was the only patient in the hospital. The klepht beating had been severe and his fever had returned. As he sweated his way through more sleep, she sat by his bedside, sponging his forehead. She always dressed in Manto's black and she always wore a mask.

Then, one evening, when his fever had nearly run its course, she left the hospital and didn't return.

# CHAPTER TWELVE

## NAFPLIO

As the summer passed him by, Tzanis had drifted in and out of consciousness, not knowing if he was dreaming or seeing. Sometimes there'd been a woman bent over him with long hair, as black as her dress. She'd worn a mask that covered her mouth and nose. But the eyes he thought he knew.

At last he woke one morning to the scent of cut lemons. A plate of them was being held beneath his nose by someone sitting on his bed.

'Can you hear me?'

The language was English but the accent new to him. He lifted his head to a young man with a clipped beard and even features, dressed in a white coat with bloodstains browning it in patches. Around his neck was what looked like an ear trumpet. Tzanis stared at the instrument.

The man glanced down. 'A stethoscope,' he said. He lifted it for inspection. 'New in from France. It told me you were still breathing.'

He looked around him. The room was full of sunlight and beds with men in them beneath clean sheets. In fact, the whole room shone with cleanliness. His eyes came to rest on his bed-side table where some coins had been left.

'Where am I?' he asked.

'You're in Nafplio.'

He felt an odd sensation on his face: breeze. He put his hand to his cheek. He'd been shaved. He shook his head and blinked again. He felt tired and hungry but otherwise well. There was an obvious question to ask before he fell back asleep. 'Why is an American doctor working in Nafplio?'

'Because he can help.' The man put out his hand. 'Samuel Gridley Howe.' They shook.

Howe gestured around him. 'As for this, a rich and good woman called Manto Kavardis has paid for it all.'

Tzanis remembered something. 'Has she been here?' he asked. 'At my bedside?'

'Manto?' Howe paused for a moment and looked down. 'It's possible, yes.'

'Would she have been dressed in black, worn a mask?'

'Yes.'

He glanced at the coins on the table beside him. She must have left them for him. He laid his head back on the pillow and closed his eyes. He felt overwhelmed by tiredness. 'Then I wasn't dreaming,'

He lay there for a while listening to the hum of the town out-side. He heard birdsong and wondered why he'd not marvelled at it before. *Alive.*

He thought of something. 'Did you find something on me? A sketch?'

The American nodded. He reached into his pocket. 'I have it here.'

Tzanis took it from him. He smoothed it against his knees

and studied it for some time. 'Is Mavrocordatos in Nafplio?' he asked.

'I believe so.'

'Can you get a message to him? That I would like an audience at the first opportunity?'

Three days later, he left the hospital against Howe's wishes. He'd sent three messages to Mavrocordatos, two of them written, and had at last received a reply. Prince Mavrocordatos had no knowledge of any Prince Comnenos and would have to be excused. He was too busy.

So he rose from his bed, dressed and walked out of the hospital and across the square to the government building. They tried to stop him, but mostly failed. Only at the minister's door was he held back by soldiers. He resorted to shouting.

It worked. The door opened and a small man came out. He peered at Tzanis though round spectacles and a face formed by topiary. Thick whiskers ran from ear to chin, and thicker eyebrows met above beady eyes and a beak-like nose. His hair was short and oiled and he wore a black frock coat with snow on each shoulder.

Tzanis shook himself free of the soldiers. 'Is that what it takes to meet you? Don't you know me?'

Mavrocordatos ran his eyes over him. 'I have no idea who you are.'

'I am Prince Tzanis Comnenos. We were to meet. On Corfu.'

He looked surprised. 'Corfu? Why?' He shook his head and turned. 'You had better come in.'

The office was full of boxes and correspondence piled on tables. Its owner seemed to be in the process either of arrival or departure. He went to sit down at the largest table and immediately disappeared behind paper. 'What is this about Corfu?'

'I was to deliver something to you there a year ago. Sent by my master, Capodistrias.'

The minister looked up and blinked, only his eyes above the paper. 'Capodistrias? What was it?'

Tzanis stared at him. Was this an act? A thought came to him. If this man knew nothing of the meeting, was he ever *meant* to get to Corfu? He thought of Sève.

'A message,' he said slowly, thinking fast. He paused. 'But it's outdated. We had intelligence of Egypt's invasion.'

Mavrocordatos looked amazed. 'You break into my office to tell me news I already know?' He was looking at Tzanis as if he was mad. He glanced at the door.

'Wait,' said Tzanis. 'I want to show you something.'

He brought the folded sketch from his pocket, opened it and smoothed it out on the table.

Mavrocordatos stared at the picture. 'What is it?'

'Can't you see?' He jabbed it with his finger. 'It is the remains of women and children, tied to olive trees and burnt alive. It is what Ibrahim is doing to our country. I drew what I saw.'

The minister turned away. 'I had heard something.'

'So what will you do?'

Mavrocordatos looked back. 'What can I? I have no army and Kolokotronis has retreated into the mountains.'

'So recruit your own army. Get mercenaries from abroad.'

'How? I have no money.' Mavrocordatos got up and went over to the window. 'We had a loan from England but it's all been spent on new uniforms.' He gestured to the square below. 'The Egyptians will soon be here and the town is in carnival.' He went back to his desk and sat down. He took off his spectacles and rubbed his eyes. 'This revolution can only be won by the intervention of the Great Powers.'

'And how are the Great Powers to be persuaded?'

'By Manto Kavardis, if she'd only do it.' He looked up. 'But she chooses to work at her hospital instead.' He rose. 'I am sorry, Prince, but the best thing you can do is go back to wherever you came from. Otherwise you'll end up among the wretches she cares for.'

# CHAPTER THIRTEEN

## MISSOLONGHI

Meyer's newspaper had the headline streaked across its front page: 'TURKS LAY SIEGE TO MISSOLONGHI'.

It was in English, of course, to suit the citizenry of the Great Powers. Byron's death had caused fascination for a village built on a swamp, which their leaders seemed indifferent to. The *Ellinika Chronika* was there to keep it going.

Hara sat on Missolonghi's wall with the newspaper in her lap and looked out at the islands stretched across the mouth of the lagoon. It was evening and the dying sun was setting fire to the water. *Like Greek fire.* Had Tzanis taught her about Greek fire? Or was it Manto? Or Mustafa on the long walk from Nafplio? Was it really six weeks ago that they'd come here, only days before the Turks?

A breeze came in from the sea and she felt her hair move against her neck. She wondered how much it had grown back. She thought of his hair, spread against the pure whiteness of a pillow, tangled, matted with filth like the beard that had hidden most of his face. When she'd gone over to shave him, she'd not recognised him at first. Then she'd had to hold onto the bedpost to stop from fainting. He'd been asleep but she'd woken him just enough to bring water to his lips, watching his thin, scabbed neck swallow the liquid, watching his eyes open for an instant to look into hers, the small frown after he'd closed them again. She'd rested his head back on the pillow so gently it had hardly creased. Then she'd looked away, blinded by her joy.

The shaving had taken an age. She'd wanted it to, oblivious to everything else in the room but his face, revealed bit by bit, like an icon, like the world he'd once shown her in stones. It was the face she'd first seen asleep in a boat, come back to her from the dead. *How we've changed, both of us.*

Was that why she'd fled?

There was a more obvious reason: that she'd betrayed him, given Manto his coin. But she'd also seen what this war had done to them both. They'd fallen and risen in equal measure, yet were not equals. They could never be equals and they could never be together.

She turned towards the setting sun, shielding her eyes. The sound of digging could just be heard from the plain. The Turks must have started their siege lines. At least it wasn't the Egyptian army out there.

She rose, folded the paper and walked down the steps to the town, nodding at the few she passed in the street. It was quiet tonight. People had seen the size of the Turk army, whispered it from ear to ear, then stayed indoors. Did their fear reach outside walls? She hoped not.

She came to the hospital, a two-storey building in the square. She stopped and looked up at the sign above the door, put up by Mustafa. She entered the building and went up to the ward that had views over the lagoon. She saw her two nurses approach between the beds, Eleni and Maria. One was a fisherman's wife, the other young, pretty and single, both with kindness in their bones. They'd learnt quickly, become her friends.

'We've given them herbs and most are asleep,' whispered Maria, looking around. She was carrying a little bowl with leaves in it: valerian, passionflower and poppy. They'd picked them in the hills above the plain with one eye out for the advancing Turks, then laid them out in many attics to dry. It hadn't altered the town's smell, but at least the hospital was fragrant.

Hara looked around the ward. 'Good.' She smiled. 'Now for some teaching. Today, tourniquets.'

She led them into a little office at the end of the ward with big glass windows where she'd prepared diagrams on a blackboard. She noticed something nailed above the window: garlic cloves to keep out the evil eye. She went over to it and turned. 'Eleni,' she said, 'we've talked about this. We use garlic for indigestion, remember?'

She wondered sometimes how they saw her. She'd come to Missolonghi with Manto's money and a servant called Mustafa. She'd rented a building and, within a week, turned it into a hospital with beds, sheets and medicine. She supposed they might think her rich, not from a place where superstition was in every stone.

'So,' she said, 'tourniquets.'

It was intoxicating, this teaching. For her, learning had begun with a dress tried on, jewellery pinned, a tidying of her hair in front of a long mirror, all before the first lesson had even begun. It had occurred to her, early on, that Manto might be making her into a version of herself. She'd had a husband, she knew, but no children. Perhaps she'd found something in her that she'd missed.

The tourniquet was tightened and the knot secured. The

lesson was over and the nurses were leaving for their homes. Hara would watch over the patients that night, sleeping in the little office where a cot had been erected. She took off her sheet and lay down on it, staring up at the ceiling, smelling its new paint. She turned onto her side. It was hot and there was no breeze from the lagoon. Thank God she no longer had to wear those tight dresses. They weren't made for Greece. Or her.

She turned back to the ceiling. She heard the snores of the men outside in the ward, the occasional shout of someone who'd rather not dream. She drifted into sleep. The questions that swirled in her mind became a storm out at sea with a ship driven onto rocks, a light still shining in its stern cabin. She saw a rope thrown up to it.

She awoke to lightning. She could see the windows of the ward lit up, the flashes almost continuous, thunder too. Some of the men had risen and were standing at the windows. No one was speaking.

She rose and went to join them.

'The Turk fleet,' said a man.

'But who is it firing at?'

She didn't wait for the answer. She walked out of the ward and down into the square. She went up to the walls and found Meyer there, a man more likely to know than anyone.

He turned to her. 'The Turks must have intercepted something coming in,' he shouted. 'Probably Admiral Miaoulis with supplies.'

They looked out in silence. The cannonade went on for a while. When it petered out, dawn was breaking.

'Something's coming through,' said Meyer, pointing. 'Look at that.'

At first she didn't see it, then she did. Above the mist spread out across the sea, was a small, single-deck frigate flying the flag of the Mani.

'My God,' she whispered, recognising the ship. '*My God.*'

'Who'd have thought?' Meyer glanced at her. 'Perhaps they're attacking us.'

The ship was more visible now. It limped at such an angle that one side was almost underwater. Only a single mast remained unbroken and its sails were shredded, smoking. Already craft were leaving the shore to help it.

'I should go down,' she said. 'There'll be wounded.'

Meyer nodded. 'And a story to tell. I'll come with you.'

She turned for the steps. 'First, we'll need to bring things from the hospital.'

They picked up the two nurses, Mustafa, stretchers, bandages and medicine. It all took time and when they reached the quay it was lined with people. Hara pushed her way to the front.

A small boat had left the ship and its rowers were working hard. A man was standing at the front urging them on. He kept glancing up at the quay.

It was Christos, eldest of her bothers.

She took Eleni's arm to steady herself. 'Can you manage the wounded?'

'Are you all right?'

'Yes . . . yes, of course. I'll take Mustafa back and prepare for surgery.'

They went back to the hospital. When they got to her office, she ushered Mustafa in and closed the door. She sat down on her bed and put her head in her hands.

Mustafa stood in front of the door. He emanated calm. 'Who is on the ship?' he asked quietly.

'I thought I'd left it all behind,' she said softly. She looked up. 'His name is Christos and he is my brother.'

'And why is that so bad?'

She looked away. 'I don't know. I just have a feeling something is going to happen.'

Mustafa sat down. He took her hand. 'Then he mustn't know you are here. You can wear a mask, as you did in Nafplio.'

'But he'll know my voice.'

He smiled. 'It is very different to what it was, I can assure you.'

After preparing for surgery, they sat and waited. She was more nervous than she'd been in months.

There was the squeak of cartwheels outside and shouts. Doors were flung open downstairs and footsteps came from the stairs. She rose and put on a mask and lifted it to her eyes. She took a deep breath.

Four men came into the ward carrying a stretcher, one of them Christos. She followed them in, then signalled for it to be put down. She knelt beside the wounded man: *Níkos*, one of the clan. His white shirt was a mess of blood and wood splinter. His eyes were closed and his jaw set. He was in agony.

She glanced up at Maria. 'Get the oregano and turmeric mix,' she said, her voice as muffled as she could make it. She turned to Christos. 'How many have you got?'

'Just two,' said Christos. 'Wood splinters. The other's not so bad.'

She nodded, looking down. 'Take this man into the next room. I'll need you to hold him down.'

Christos came to the hospital every day to visit the two men in the ward; Hara was always warned before he arrived and busied herself. Meanwhile the Turkish fleet sat outside the bay and its army sat on the plain.

More hot weather arrived without warning and temperatures rose in the ward. The garrison spent its days shirtless under a relentless sun, raising the walls even higher. The two wounded Maniots left the hospital to join them.

It was on an especially hot morning that she watched Christos chiselling stone in the square below. Suddenly, she was blinded. Something hung from his neck had caught the sun. She leant forward, her nose between the blinds. It was unmistakable: a gold coin. *How?*

She sat back and considered the possibilities. The obvious one was that Tzanis's gold had been found. But if it was too deep for her to get to, who else could have done it? Certainly not Christos.

She rose, left the office and walked down to where Mustafa kept guard by the front door. 'Mustafa, please go and find Christos,' she said. 'Ask him to come here, this evening at sundown. I'll be in my office.'

She spent the hour before he came making her office perfectly dark, hanging blankets anywhere light might enter. When Mustafa knocked on her door, she was lying on her bed dressed in her black dress.

'Come in.'

She heard the door open, saw her brother's silhouette against the light of the ward. She heard the door close behind him.

'I have a bad headache. Please sit.'

She heard him sit. She imagined him on the little chair, elbows on his knees, big hands together. She had the advantage. *Good.*

'I wanted to speak to you,' she said, her voice muffled by the wet muslin she'd draped across her face. 'Your men, are they well enough to work, do you think? Nikos still has stitches in.'

She heard him shift on his chair. In the Mani, no woman would dare ask what she'd just asked.

'He's needed. Nikos is strong.'

'Of course. But bring him back if any of the stitches break, please.'

No answer.

She said: 'It's a great thing Petrobey has done, sending you to Missolonghi. The other kapitanos only think of themselves.'

From the corner of her eye she watched Christos look round the room, his big head moving from side to side. She could hear his breathing and remembered him bent over oars. She saw a glimmer of moonlight enter the room. A corner of one of the blankets had come free from the window.

'There's something else,' she said quickly. She breathed in. 'I saw the coin hung from your neck. It looked like gold.' She paused. 'Was it a gift from your wife?'

She heard him move again. She knew the sound. Her brother wanted to be somewhere other than a dark room with a curious woman. She saw him rise.

'Wait. Christos. Please.'

Her veil fell away as she sat up. At the same time, the blanket came down from the window. He stared at her.

'Christos . . .'

He was shaking his head and blinking at the same time, unsure what he was looking at. '*Hara?*'

She swung her legs off the bed and sat on its edge, back straight. She rose and went to the windows and pulled off the blankets, one by one. Then she turned to face him. 'It's a long story,' she said. 'And I'll tell it to you, in time. But first I need to ask you something. Something important, Christos.'

She was aware of what her voice must sound like to him. 'I need to know about the coin around your neck. Where did you get it?'

'The shipwreck,' he said. 'The one the Russian was in. The man you ran off with.'

'I didn't,' she paused. 'I'll explain later. Just tell me where exactly you found it. Please.'

He was staring at her with a strange look in his eyes. 'I told you. It was in the shipwreck. The remains we found of the stern cabin.'

*Of course.* Tzanis must have dropped a coin before throwing the chest overboard. She felt some relief.

'You went diving? Was it the only one you found?'

He nodded.

'And what did you do with it? After you found it?'

'I took it to Petrobey. He said it was the Tzar of Russia's gold.'

Her mind was racing. She needed time to think. She tried to move toward the door but he took her wrist.

'Wait,' he said. 'I have questions too.' In the moonlight, his face was hard to read. He seemed confused as much as angry. He asked: 'Why did you run off with the Russian?'

'I didn't run off with him,' she said. 'We went out on a boat and got taken by pirates. I went to Kithira, then Nafplio. I haven't seen him since the boat.'

'Why were you on a boat at all?'

'I was teaching him to sail. He taught me, I him. It was the arrangement.' She paused. 'I survived. I would have thought you'd be pleased, brother.'

'*Brother.* I don't think so. Sit down on the bed.'

131

She sat down and rubbed her wrist. The moonlight made everything seem dream-like in the room: the desk, the windows, his long hair that was more like a mane. She heard a cough from outside.

Christos glanced through the window into the ward, then back. His voice had fallen. 'Petrobey wants you back in the Mani,' he said. 'We've been sent out to find you.'

'My brothers?'

He nodded. 'All to different places. And we're not your brothers. Petrobey's claimed you.'

*Claimed?* She wasn't his property. And she wasn't going to be married off for an alliance like some brood mare. 'I don't belong to Petrobey or anyone else,' she said quietly.

Christos shook his head. 'I'm taking you back with me.'

Suddenly she felt angry. He'd barely acknowledged her when she'd been his sister, now he thought to command her. 'Don't be ridiculous,' she said. 'Even if you could persuade me, you'd never get past the Turks. The town is surrounded, cut off.'

'We'll go after the siege has finished.'

She shook her head slowly. Had he always been this brutish? 'Christos,' she said quietly, 'I've changed. I'm different to what I was in the Mani. I don't belong there any more.'

He shrugged. 'I don't care about that. Petrobey wants you back, that's all.'

She leant forward. 'Why does he want me back?'

'To dive for the gold. You know where it is, and you dive deeper than any man.'

She looked away. So Petrobey knew of the Tzar's gold. He'd seen that at least one of the Great Powers wanted to be involved in Greece's war, so he'd switched allegiance to the party they'd align themselves to. There was one person who needed to know all this. He was in Nafplio.

She turned back to him, nodding slowly. She rose. 'Well, you have a siege to fight, and I a hospital to run. We both have to survive before going anywhere.'

He remained seated, not trying to stop her as she moved to the door. She opened it and stepped aside. He got up and walked through it without looking at her. He stopped outside and turned.

'I'll be watching you.'

She stood there for some time with her eyes closed, listening to his footsteps on the wooden floor, then the stairs, to the rapid beat of her heart. She hugged herself. Suddenly, she felt very alone. How could she get a message to Tzanis? How could she get it through the Turkish lines?

There was a way. But could she ask it of him?

# CHAPTER FOURTEEN

## NAFPLIO

Tzanis stared at the coins on the table. They were all he had left from what Manto had put on his bedside table and he'd stacked them to seem more. The tavern he sat in was next to Nafplio's quay and its menu suited those without means. He'd just eaten a meal of salted starfish, onion and maize bread. There was no money for wine. He'd written to St Petersburg for funds but they'd not be with him for Christmas. He had a single lace handkerchief left to sell.

He wished he had something the Greeks needed. He had an illustrious name and some skill at arms, but there were many soldiers in Greece, and a surprising number of princes too. The war was lost anyway. Ibrahim had taken most of the Peloponnese and news had just come that the Turks were besieging Missolonghi again. When his money arrived, he'd take the first ship back to Odessa, or anywhere that wasn't Greece. There was nothing left for him here.

A shadow spread across his table and he looked up. A tall man was standing there, his face hidden beneath a hood, his hands hidden in wide sleeves. He was perfectly still.

'Can I help you?'

'You are Prince Tzanis Comnenos?' The voice was deep, but quiet. It spoke in Greek but the speaker was not Greek. He was from somewhere further east.

Tzanis had not used his title whilst in Nafplio, except to procure credit. He was wary. 'Who are you?'

'My name is Mustafa,' said the man. 'I am a Turk.'

'Then you are brave. What do you want?'

'May I sit?'

Tzanis gestured to the chair across from him. 'By all means. This is a tavern.'

The man released his hands from his sleeves and sat, keeping his hood in place. Tzanis had caught sight of a beard, trimmed to a point. That, and his voice, said that this was a cultured man, perhaps a merchant. He held fine prayer beads in one hand, perhaps amber. 'I have a message for you.'

'A letter?'

The man shook his head. 'To be delivered by speech. From my mistress in Missolonghi. You know her. Hara.'

Tzanis sat quite still. So she'd survived. But why had she gone to Missolonghi? 'How did you get out?' he asked.

'I am a Turk. The town is besieged by Turks.' The man moved no part of his body when he spoke. His voice was calm, assured. He had managed servants before he'd become one himself. 'She has set up a hospital there.'

Tzanis thought of the eyes he'd looked into when he'd awoken in Nafplio's hospital. *Hers*. He glanced around. The tavern was empty but for them. He leant forward. 'So what is her message?' he asked quietly.

Mustafa brought his head to within inches of Tzanis's. A waft of sandalwood stroked the air between them and he heard the

135

rattle of prayer beads. His breath was clean. 'My mistress says this.' He closed his eyes and lifted his head slightly.

*'I was at your bedside, I shaved you. I left because you'd asked me to keep the coin, but I gave it away. I gave it to Manto Kavardis who has taken it to London. Now I have learnt that Petrobey knows about the gold too. Christos is here, sent by Petrobey to take me back to the Mani after the siege. He wants me to dive for the gold. Please send Mustafa back with your instructions and whatever medicine the hospital can spare, especially laudanum.'*

Mustafa opened his eyes. 'That was my mistress's message.'

Tzanis stared at him in disbelief. If this was Hara's voice, then she'd changed beyond measure. 'She dictated that to you?'

He nodded.

'Then she has changed.'

'A great deal,' said Mustafa softly. 'She has been taught by Manto Kavardis whom I also serve. She said I was to take you to Manto's house to bathe and eat, and give you money, if you needed it. My family is there.' He gathered his hands on the table. He was composed, awaiting command. Like a genie.

Tzanis glanced down at the scraps on his plate. There were so many questions to ask but he was sitting in rags with only salted starfish in his belly. He said: 'Thank you, I'd like that very much.'

He rose and walked into the town beside Mustafa. As they approached the square, they almost collided with Mavrocordatos and his secretary. The minister blinked up at him through his spectacles, then bowed.

They watched him go. 'He knows you,' murmured the Turk.

Tzanis shook his head. 'He'd never heard of me until recently, yet I was supposed to meet him on Corfu. It's a mystery.'

They walked on, Tzanis considering Hara's new voice. 'So Manto educated her?' He felt a little hurt. Hadn't that been his role?

'Every day,' said Mustafa. 'Like her daughter.'

'Has she grown her hair?'

Mustafa glanced at him. 'She has.'

Tzanis thought about a Hara with long hair, with education, with money. Had Manto *adopted* her?

They came to the house and went in. Mustafa greeted his wife, then his children each in turn. Suleiman he greeted last and held longest.

The next hours were as a dream. He'd not properly bathed or fed since the Mani and he'd not felt truly clean clothes against his skin since Meyer's in Missolonghi. He ate a meal of roast chicken and drank Santorini wine, then lay in a bath with rose petals floating on its surface. He closed his eyes and fell asleep.

When he awoke, he was in bed and it was morning. The bed was big and soft and faced long, shuttered windows through which sunlight peeped in bright, silver bands. He wondered if it was Manto's. *Or Hara's?*

He lay there for a long time, his hands behind his head, staring up at the ceiling and listening to the town outside, enjoying the lightest of breezes that came in from the sea. Nafplio seemed happier today.

He had new information he needed to consider. Hara had gone to Missolonghi because she'd told Manto about the gold. Petrobey seemed to know about it and to have sent Christos to bring her home. Christos was as violent and proud as every other man in the Mani and perhaps felt something for Hara, if the scene at Easter had meant anything. So she was in danger, not just from the siege. And much of it was his fault.

He rose from the bed. What to do? First, there was the medicine. Mustafa could carry only so much. Should someone else go with him?

He was frowning as he put on a fine linen shirt. *Should it be me?*

No, he'd done enough for this cause and been treated abominably, like every other fool. He'd wait for his money to come, then leave. He'd go back to Russia and marry well.

There was a knock on the door and Suleiman came in. He carried a tray with food and a newspaper. Tzanis took the newspaper and read Meyer's prose, enriched by a dead poet. He looked up. Suleiman stood there, silent and waiting, and there was no mistaking his sadness. His father would leave tomorrow to take medicine to people supposed to be his enemies. Tzanis felt a deep shame rise up inside him.

He folded the paper and put it to one side. He rose. 'Please tell your father I will leave with him tomorrow. I will ask Hara to send him back to you once he's seen me through the Turkish lines.'

Mustafa was at the hospital, collecting medicine to take back to Missolonghi. He stood next to Howe looking out of the office window, watching pandemonium at the government building opposite. Wagons were being loaded and smoke rose from rooms where things were being burnt. People were running everywhere with boxes.

'Evacuation isn't pretty,' said Howe. 'What are we being told?'

Mustafa spoke low enough for the ward not to hear. 'That Ibrahim Pasha is three days' march away and his scouts have been seen in the villages. I saw them on my way here.'

'Is your family ready to leave?'

Mustafa nodded. Manto had left instructions for them to be evacuated should the Egyptians come. There was a ship, there was money and soon there'd be Egyptians. But he wouldn't be going with them.

Howe glanced at the long, serious face with its trimmed beard, its sharp, clever eyes. 'They'll go in good time, I promise you. They'll go somewhere safe to wait for you. London, perhaps. Then America.'

He looked back out over the town's tiles, shiny and unmoored in the autumn drizzle. They said it happened in Venice too after rain: a roofscape on the move. Both cities carried salt in their air, the bitter taste of melancholy. 'You are a brave man,' he said. 'You must love Manto very much.'

'Yes, and I am worried about her.'

Howe looked at him. 'Worried? Why?'

The Turk paused before he spoke. 'I have learnt that it was Mavrocordatos who Prince Tzanis was bringing the gold to. But the minister knew nothing about it.'

Howe frowned. 'So who was it really for?'

'Well, that is the question. Could it be that Colonel Sève was *meant* to intercept Prince Tzanis on behalf of Ibrahim Pasha of Egypt, whom he serves?' Mustafa reached into his thoub and brought out some bound papers. He handed them to Howe. 'I found these in my mistress's desk after she left.'

Howe took the papers. On their front was written 'The Greek Plan' in English. He looked up.

'It is a report from the British government,' explained Mustafa. 'It describes a secret agreement, drawn up forty years ago between Russia and Austria, to destroy the Turkish Empire and restore a Christian empire with its capital in Constantinople, as it once was. I believe it could be happening again, but this time the Tzar's agreement is with Egypt. They mean to divide the Ottoman Empire between them.'

Howe stared at him. 'Are you serious?'

Mustafa spread his hands. 'It is an explanation.'

Howe shook his head slowly. 'But if that's true,' he whispered, 'it means the Tzar is not supporting the revolution, but its destroyer.' He shook his head. 'It could lead to a world war.'

Mustafa nodded. 'The Russians will not want it known and my mistress has taken a coin with the Empress Catherine's head on it to London, where they are.'

Howe was silent for a while, absorbing the enormity of what he'd just heard. He shook his head. 'She means to blackmail the Tzar.'

Mustafa glanced at him. 'Perhaps.' He turned. 'Forgive me, Dr Howe, but I have seen you with my mistress. I think you care for her. Would you perhaps consider going with my family to London?'

# CHAPTER FIFTEEN

## THE ROAD TO MISSOLONGHI

Two days later, Tzanis and Mustafa walked side by side ahead of a mule laden with medicines, food and weapons. They stayed well clear of the Egyptian army, passing charred villages left to dogs and cats, no one there to keep the peace between them. They didn't speak much at first, preferring the solace of thought or prayer.

After a week of walking, they came to orchards with blackened stumps. Mustafa stopped and stared, shaking his head slowly. 'Ibrahim Pasha is a fool,' he said. 'He doesn't know the Greeks.' He took the pigskin from his neck, pulled out its cork and offered it to Tzanis. 'Please drink.'

Tzanis drank, tilting back his head and squeezing a stream of water onto the back of his throat. He passed back the skin and wiped his chin. 'They say olive trees are difficult to burn.'

Mustafa nodded. 'They're stubborn, like the men who plant them. If you burn a Greek's olive tree, you burn him. They won't forget this.'

They continued on their way, passing mile after mile of destruction. When they thought it safe, they returned to the road. Tzanis tried to keep pace with the Turk's enormous strides.

'You've never told me about your past, Mustafa,' he said, putting his hand on his shoulder. 'And can we walk slower?'

Mustafa slowed his pace. 'My past? I come from a family of merchants who have traded out of Nafplio for generations, mainly with the islands. We did business with the Kavardis family of Chios, so I knew Manto. We had a good life in Nafplio, side by side with the Greeks. We prayed in our mosque, they in their church. We were at peace.'

Tzanis took his shoulder again.

'Forgive me,' said Mustafa, stopping and turning. 'When the revolution began, the Turks reinforced the town and the Greeks remained at peace. They'd been happy under Turkish rule.'

'Then the town fell.'

Mustafa nodded. 'The garrison was starving and Kolokotronis promised to spare everyone: soldiers, merchants, servants ... everyone. But his men remembered Chios and there was no mercy.'

Tzanis said: 'And Manto saved you.'

'She came in with the first soldiers. She knew what was going to happen. She tried to stop it but was able to save only my family. She gave us sanctuary.' He paused. 'All except Fatima.'

'Fatima?'

'She was my wife, mother to my children. I lost her in the chaos.'

Tzanis looked down. 'I'm sorry.'

'There is no need. Her children were saved and that is all that would have mattered to her.' He waved away a fly. 'Then Manto shut herself away. She'd seen too much horror, too much evil. She'd lost faith in humanity.'

'Until Hara came.'

He was quiet for a while. Then he said: 'Hara was an angel, sent down from Allah. I knew it the moment I opened the door to her. She was the only person who could save her.'

'And your mistress gave her an education.'

Mustafa glanced at him. 'To add to the one she'd already been given. I don't think her first teacher realised how grateful she was.'

Tzanis nodded slowly. He looked at the prayer beads still strung between Mustafa's fingers. 'Were those your father's?'

'The *Misbaha*? Yes, they were my father's and his before him.' He looked down at them. 'One day they will be Suleiman's, Allah willing.' He held them up so that the amber shone in the sunshine. 'Ninety-nine beads, one for every one of God's names.'

They walked on in silence, passing destruction that seemed never-ending. At last Mustafa cleared his throat in the manner of one approaching a difficult subject.

'I would like to talk about the gold, if you will permit it,' he said at last. 'The gold that was lost off the Mani.'

'What of it?'

'Who was it meant for, do you think?'

Tzanis glanced at him. 'Well, not Mavrocordatos, certainly.'

'So who?'

He thought for a while. He decided on trust. 'Colonel Sève was expecting to intercept me,' he said carefully. 'But on whose behalf?' He felt a faint tremor in the ground beneath him. 'What is that?'

They stared down the road. There were riders approaching, not far away, under a cloud of dust. They stopped and pulled muskets from the back of the mule.

143

Tzanis looked around and pointed. 'Those rocks over there. We'll ambush them. How many do we have loaded?'

'Six muskets, six pistols,' said Mustafa, passing three of each to Tzanis. He took powder horns and ammunition pouches from the mule then slapped it on the rump. 'Wha!'

The animal sprang off and the two men went over to the rocks and hid behind them, laying the muskets and pistols on the ground between them. The sound of hooves was closer now, men's shouts too.

'Do you shoot well?' asked Tzanis.

Mustafa was calm. 'Tolerably. And you?'

'Tolerably.' He peeped over the rock. The riders were very close. *'Now!'*

They rose together, took aim and fired. Two Sudanese lancers left their saddles. The horses behind reared, shrieking and turning.

They picked up muskets and fired again. Two more Sudanese fell. Mustafa shot better than tolerably.

'There aren't many of them!' shouted Tzanis, bringing his third musket into the aim. 'I count ten!'

Two more fell to the ground. Men were yelling, trying to turn their horses, hitting each other with their lances. It was chaos.

'Now the pistols!' They picked them up and ran round the rock to face the remaining Egyptians. They fired at point blank range. It was enough. The last two lancers turned their horses and fled. Eight riderless horses followed them.

One of the soldiers was groaning, his hand pressed to a red stain spreading across his belly. Mustafa walked over, picked up a lance and plunged it into his neck. The man jerked twice, then lay still.

'He deserved worse,' he said quietly. He looked round. 'We must find the mule.'

They split up, each searching a different side of the road. It was a land of fields that spread out to terraces of olive groves rising to hills. Mustafa followed a path that ran between low walls towards some trees.

He saw a thin plume of smoke rising above a wall among the trees. He walked forward slowly. It was a monastery. Its gates were open but no sound came from within. Birds circled above, big things. He stopped, and looked around. Nothing. He listened. Just the sound of buzzing. *Was that bees?*

He felt unease. Where were the Christian monks? He raised his pistol and approached, step by step. He came to the gates and went through them. He was in a courtyard with a church at its centre, steps leading up to it. In front of the church was a well, also raised on steps. Every part of the enclosure was covered with bodies. They were piled on the ground, on the steps, between the open doors of the church. They were all women and young children with hideous wounds. The ground was slick with their blood, the air above thick with flies. To one side was a row of beehives, all smashed.

He saw movement from the corner of his eye. The mule. It had its head in someone's lap, someone who was stroking its neck, someone wearing the uniform of Napoleon.

Mustafa raised his pistol.

'That would be foolish,' said Colonel Sève. 'Look behind you.'

He glanced over his shoulder. Two Sudanese troopers were standing in the gates, muskets at the aim. He lowered the pistol.

Sève bent towards the mule, stroking its nose. 'I assume this is yours? Medical supplies for Missolonghi.' He looked at him. 'And you, a Turk.'

Mustafa remained silent.

Sève glanced around him, as if noticing the slaughter for the first time. 'A Turk should be pleased by this,' he said. 'So many dead infidels.'

'Are you responsible for it?'

'Me? Not directly, no. I wasn't here when it happened.' He looked back. 'But indirectly? The men were under my command so, I suppose, yes.' His hand moved to his moustache and he shrugged. 'It happens in war.'

Mustafa was escorted into Tripoli on the horse of the soldier he'd speared. It was a fine Arab creature whose talents were wasted in the mountains of Greece. It had been Sève's theme as they'd ridden through the wasteland.

'Cavalry is squandered on this enemy,' he'd complained, looking around. 'They shoot at you from behind rocks, then run away. We can't decide this thing until we bring them to battle, but they won't come.' The Frenchman sounded petulant, like a child who'd had his toy removed.

Mustafa was thinking about Tzanis. There was no sign of him. Perhaps he'd managed to escape. He asked: 'Is it wise to burn their livelihood?'

Sève shrugged. 'They surrender or starve. Either way, the Khedive has loyal subjects waiting to take their place.'

They rode through Tripoli's ruined gates into a town empty of citizens. It had once been the Turk's capital in the Peloponnese but when it had fallen to Kolokotronis at the start of the war, all its inhabitants had been massacred. Now it was a military encampment with barracks, stables and armoury. Everywhere, soldiers drilled and the air was filled with French commands.

146

They rode into the central square and dismounted in front of a big, severe building.

'Ibrahim Pasha's headquarters,' explained Sève. 'You'll not be comfortable, I'm afraid.'

He led him inside and down steep steps to a long, low corridor with cells either side, sconced torches between. Beyond the bars were skeletal creatures slumped against walls, some chained. The air stank of human decay.

He was shown into a cell with a single occupant sitting amidst black straw. His hair and beard were tangled with filth and he was dressed in the last remnants of French uniform.

'Let me introduce you to my fellow countryman,' said Sève as he closed the door and stepped back for it to be locked. 'Colonel Clavier was in Missolonghi.' He turned and walked away, running his hand down the bars as he passed. He was whistling.

Mustafa watched him go. He looked around the cell, saw scratches on the walls from men who'd counted out the days of their misery. His eyes came back to Clavier. His legs were bare beneath the knees. They were black and swollen from bruising, covered in little cuts.

Clavier looked up. 'What is a Turk doing in an Egyptian prison?'

'I might ask the same of a Frenchman,' replied Mustafa. 'Have you been tortured?'

Clavier nodded.

'How did you get here?'

'I left Missolonghi before the Turks came.' He stopped and broke into a frenzy of coughing, his head between his knees, his shoulders heaving. Mustafa waited as he combed the spittle from his beard. Tiny spots of colour had appeared in his cheeks

147

from the exertion. 'I came south, hoping to get to the Mani. I ran into an Egyptian foraging party.'

They fell into silence. Clavier tried to stretch out his legs, his face tightened by pain. 'If only I'd listened.'

'Listened to who?'

'The Russian prince, or Greek . . . whatever he was. He warned me about Sève. In Navarino.'

'Prince Tzanis?'

'Yes, him.' He scratched his knee and inspected the blood on his fingers. 'There are men like Sève still in Missolonghi,' he said, 'men loyal only to the memory of Napoleon. He told me so himself.' He shook his head. 'Did you know my government builds ships for the Egyptians?' He coughed again, great spasms that shook his whole body. He recovered and wiped his lips with his hand. 'The *hypocrisy*.'

Mustafa nodded slowly. 'Hypocrisy is what keeps the Great Powers great.'

They heard footsteps approaching. Two men stopped outside their cell – Turks, not Egyptians. One of them pointed at Mustafa, speaking in his language.

'You come.'

Clavier took hold of his ankle. 'Just tell them whatever they want to know. This is not your fight.'

Mustafa put his hand into his pocket and brought out the prayer beads. 'It may be too late for that.' He leant over. 'Please, take these. If you survive this, give them to my son. He is called Suleiman and he is in Nafplio.'

Clavier took the beads and quickly hid them beneath his rags. The cell door swung open and Mustafa was pulled outside. As he was escorted down the corridor, he looked straight ahead, his head held high. They mounted the staircase and went through a door into a hall with high windows and big doors at the end. The sunlight was blinding.

The doors opened and he was pushed into a long audience chamber with crude pictures of Turks in ceremonial dress: former Pashas. At the other end was a big chair on a dais. On it sat a big man with a beard that covered much of a pock-marked face. He had dark, intelligent eyes above a hooked nose. He wore a scarlet, embroidered jacket and black silk pantaloons. A jewelled scimitar lay across his lap and beside him stood a tall chibouk, smoking. Beside the chibouk stood Colonel Sève.

The man gestured. 'Come forward.'

Mustafa felt the two soldiers release their grip. He walked forward unsteadily.

'Closer.'

He came to within a few feet and stopped.

The man leant forward and peered at him. 'What is a Turk doing in the service of the Greeks?' he asked.

Mustafa breathed deeply. 'What makes you believe I am in their service?'

'Well, you were taking medicine to Missolonghi and you killed eight of my men. Enough, I'd have thought.' He paused, putting his finger to his lips. 'You are not a servant, you shoot too straight. What are you?'

Mustafa remained silent.

'Do you know who I am?'

No answer.

'I am Ibrahim Pasha, son of the Khedive of Egypt, conqueror of Greece. What Darius the Persian couldn't do, I will soon achieve.' He took a long pull of his chibouk and leant back into his cushions. 'What I want to know now,' he said through the smoke, 'is who was with you.'

He stayed silent. At least they hadn't caught Tzanis.

'I can torture it out of you, or you can tell me,' continued the Pasha. 'Colonel Sève would prefer the first.'

Mustafa looked away.

Ibrahim Pasha raised a hand and the Colonel came forward and struck Mustafa on the back of his legs. He fell to his knees.

Ibrahim leant forward again. 'Colonel Sève wants me to hand you over to the two men behind you. They are Turks like you and think you are a traitor.'

He lifted the mouthpiece of the chibouk to his lips and smoked for a while. He lowered it and wiped his eyes with his sleeve. 'Let me help you. Your companion was a Russian prince with an interesting story about sunken gold. You only have to nod if I am right.'

Mustafa was forcing calm into his mind despite his racing heart. He was trying to picture his children. *There, waiting, praying to Allah for his return.* He turned his gaze to the man on the throne.

'No,' he said.

A week later, Tzanis reached the coast. He'd hardly slept, so he came tired to the village of Rio where the straits were at their narrowest. It was late afternoon and the fishermen were preparing their boats for the evening catch. Tzanis found one who'd take him across. Halfway there, he hit him on the head with the boat hook. It wasn't hard enough to kill him, just knock him out. 'I'm sorry,' he murmured as he tied and gagged him.

He sailed through the night, guided by the stars, and at dawn saw the ships of the Turkish fleet and turned for the shore. Two hours later, he brought the boat into the wind and dropped its sail, then spread nets over the side. To anyone watching, he was a fisherman out of Missolonghi. He stripped down to his underclothes and slipped into the water, pausing only to cut the rope binding the fisherman's wrists. He swam to the shore and edged his way along the coast, swimming from rock to rock until he was near the entrance to the lagoon. There were two Turkish caiques guarding it, both with cannon at their bows. He'd have to wait for nightfall.

When it was dark, he entered the lagoon. He swam as quietly as he could, guided by the lights of the town. The distance was greater than he'd thought and some he covered floating on his back, looking up at a night strewn with jewels. As he neared the walls, he heard something he'd not expected.

He lifted his head from the water. *Yes*. A fiddle and bouzouki and the beat of tambour. Laughter too. There was celebration in Missolonghi.

# CHAPTER SIXTEEN

## MISSOLONGHI

The cooking had begun the week before. There'd been only enough dough for two wedding breads but Hara had embroidered each with lovers' knots and roses, adding almonds for fertility. She'd made Maria's wedding dress herself, including a secret pocket to hold things against the evil eye. She'd pleated her hair and tied the wedding kerchief over her head so that her face was haloed by gold. Last night, she'd even joined the married women at the groom's house to prepare the nuptial bed, turning each rug in the four directions of the cross before sprinkling it with flowers. She'd led the wedding preparations as she'd led the hospital: with quiet efficiency. She was determined for Maria and Dhimitrios to feel joy on their big day. Joy was needed in Missolonghi.

Dysentery was the issue. It had crept out of the lagoon to sneak through the streets and under doors and into open, snoring mouths. It had taken hold of bodies and shaken them like dolls, emptying them of everything except fever. Hara's ward had doubled, with mattresses laid between the beds. Volunteers had come in to help, summoned by a young woman difficult to resist. It had been how Maria and Dhimitrios had met.

Most of the town was in the square, dancing and singing and clinking their glasses to the happy couple. Hara sat next to Meyer and watched a long line of dancers wind its way past. It was the most ancient of wedding dances, the *peloponisios:* three paces to the right, two to the left, then a dipping step back before the line snaked forward again. Men and women, joined at the shoulder, sang alternate stanzas of sad klephtic songs, heads flung backwards, eyes closed.

'I heard the Turks shouting their congratulations,' said Meyer, biting into a grape.

The Turks had inched their trenches forward to within a hundred yards of the walls. They'd made a dozen assaults, but been repelled every time. What damage their cannon had done had been repaired each night by the citizens.

'We need supplies,' said Meyer. 'Admiral Miaoulis should be on his way with food.'

'And medicine, I hope. Especially laudanum.'

'You've still not heard from Mustafa?'

She shook her head, suddenly sombre. 'It's been too long. Something must have happened. I know he would have tried to return.'

But had Tzanis come with him? Had he even been in Nafplio for Mustafa to bring? Or had he left like all the other phil-hellenes? There weren't many in Missolonghi now, just a few Germans and three Frenchmen who'd somehow slipped into the town yesterday and kept themselves apart. She looked around to see if they were there and met Christos's eye. There he was, as always, sitting where she couldn't fail to see him.

Meyer looked to where she looked. 'Does he bother you?'

'Not really.' She sighed. 'How does he think I'll escape? Will I swim out?'

She'd considered it once. After all, she could hold her breath long enough to swim under a dozen ships of the line. But that would mean leaving her patients.

She looked at the couple, sitting on their thrones in their seaweed crowns like sea-gods. In better times they'd have had orange-blossom in their hair, but painted seaweed would have to do for tonight. She heard the scrape of bone as the last kid was carved, its eyes saved for the groom. There'd not be more than a mouthful each, but it was a feast and that was the important thing. Her eyes travelled to General Botsaris in his full Souliote best: bolero, skirts and slippers. He nodded to her. The celebration had been her idea and it was working. For perhaps the first time there was friendship between the town's factions.

Except for the Frenchmen. Where were they?

Botsaris was walking towards her. He picked up a chair and set it down, nodding to Meyer. He wore his long hair cropped at the front like the klephts. He put a pipe between his teeth and bent down to strike a match on the stone.

Meyer asked: 'When do you think Ibrahim will be here?'

Botsaris inhaled, coughed and sat up straight, patting his chest. 'When he's taken Nafplio,' he said. 'There'll be only us after that.' He glanced at Hara. 'Except for the Mani, of course.'

*The Mani.* The name now filled her with dread. What would Petrobey do to her for failing him?

'So we must finish this siege before they come,' he continued, wiping his moustache. 'We must break out. A sortie.' He pointed at Hara with his pipe. 'Perhaps you should lead it.'

He was only half-joking. Since Hara had come to Missolonghi, there'd been something new in the air. The men felt it, the women and children too. They felt pride in this town of theirs that had held out against the Turks.

She smiled. 'We need medicine. I'd lead anything to get that.'

'Admiral Miaoulis will come,' said Botsaris. 'You'll see.'


It was the shots that woke Tzanis. He sat up and rubbed his eyes, smelling the salt on his hands, tasting it in his mouth. He'd been so deeply asleep that he felt disoriented, a little drunk. He got to his feet and shook his head. He looked down the wall. He couldn't see a single sentry.

He walked along to the city gate that had once led out to a jetty, now destroyed. He banged on it but heard nothing beyond wedding music and shooting. He sat back and wondered what to do. Easiest would be to go back to sleep but he was cold. He was worried too. This was the sea wall and the Turkish fleet was outside the lagoon. *Where were the sentries?*

He saw a light far out on the water. Phosphorescence? Or was it a boat? There it was again. A signal? He stood and looked along the ramparts. A flame, waved twice. *Yes, a signal.*

He looked out to sea again. The moon was behind cloud and he could see nothing, not even the black mass of the islands. But he could hear something. He turned his head. Yes, there it was: the sound of water moved by oar. A boat was approaching, more than one.

He looked up at the wall. It was too high to climb but only just. He ran to the next bastion, diving to the ground whenever the moon emerged. The beach was narrow here and there was a boat on it. He went to the stern and pushed, hearing the suck of sand as the keel released. He got it to the wall then climbed onto the bow and jumped for the rampart. On the third try he

155

managed to pull himself up. He crouched down and looked out to the lagoon.

He could see them now: at least five long caiques filled with Turks. They must have heard the celebrations and taken their chance. But where were the sentries? He looked along the wall and saw a body. *There.*

He ran to the steps, then down and into the town. The streets were empty and the sound of revelry came and went. The square was crammed with people of every age, some spilling out. They stared at this half-naked man who pushed through them shouting something they couldn't hear.

He reached the steps of the church and fought his way to the top. There were two Souliotes there, each with a musket.

'Not inside the church,' said one, stepping in front of him. 'Not tonight.'

Tzanis was breathing hard, hands to his knees. 'Is your gun loaded?'

'No more shooting. General's orders.'

He snatched the man's gun, turned and fired a shot. A thousand heads swung round. He pointed. 'The Turks are attacking the sea wall!'

There was a moment's pause then everyone started shouting at once. Tzanis watched the bridegroom lean over to kiss his bride, then rise. He saw Botsaris draw his sword.

He ran down the steps, still with the musket, and joined the exodus, breaking off into a side-street. He heard someone behind and glanced round. It was Botsaris. He slowed to let him catch up.

'Here,' said the General, thrusting a pistol at him. He drew a long dagger from his waist. 'This as well. Where are the sentries?'

'All dead,' said Tzanis.

The wall lay ahead, lit by a moon suddenly free of cloud. They got to the steps and took them two at a time, Tzanis leading. He looked over the ramparts. The beach was full of Turks, some still in the boats. Ladders were being passed over heads. A face beneath looked up at him, surprised. He aimed and fired.

He looked along the wall. Men from the town were streaming onto it now, fired with moonshine, screaming their klepht battle cries. The Turks turned in panic, some of the boats already pulling away from the sand. Men waded into the water to reach them, throwing their muskets aside. There was fighting on the caiques. He saw a man in a different uniform trying to board. *French.*

Tzanis jumped down to the sand and ran forward, pushing aside triumphant Greeks to get to the sea. He waded in, ignoring the men around him. The man was struggling with someone who didn't want him to board. He reached him and pulled him back into the water. He turned him round and saw the same uniform he'd seen another Frenchman wear. He put the knife to his throat.

'Are you one of Sève's men?'

The man stared back at him. He was defiant. 'I am the Emperor's man,' he yelled. *'Vive l'empereur!'*

Tzanis pressed the blade to his kneck, saw a thin trace of blood escape into the sea. 'Your emperor lost,' he said, 'and so have you. Where is Sève?'

'On his way with an army that will wipe this miserable town from the face of the earth,' hissed the man. 'You will all die here.'

He closed his eyes as he slit the man's throat, then pushed him away. Suddenly, he felt unimaginably tired.

He turned and waded from the sea, seeing nothing but blood. He climbed onto the wall and walked to where it was empty. He sat down with his back to the rampart and closed his eyes, listening to the sounds of victory. He'd seen what it looked like before: men dancing with severed heads on bayonets, scalps on the tips of their swords. He'd not watch it now.

Then the noise subsided. He opened his eyes and turned his head. People were parting to let someone through, lowering their bayonets and stepping back. A Souliote took something from his sword and hid it quickly behind him. The wall fell silent.

A soldier was coming. He wore a coat too big for him and carried a plate in one hand and a glass in the other. He had long black hair. He drew closer and Tzanis saw that he was not a soldier.

*Hara.*

She came up and stopped, looking down. Beneath the military coat, she was wearing a long white dress. She wore slippers embroidered with gold. He stared up at her.

It was her hair that was most arresting. He'd remembered something unruly, but now there were waves cascading to her shoulders. The face they framed was more beautiful than he remembered, and had something else he'd not seen before. He felt suddenly bereft.

She knelt down, placed the plate on the ground and handed him the glass. 'Moonshine,' she said. 'It might help.' She rose and took the jacket from her shoulders. 'And I've brought you something to wear.'

He leant forward while she put the jacket over him. He drank and put down the glass, then picked up the plate.

'Roast kid,' she said, sitting down beside him, her back to the wall. 'The last in town. Not much, I'm afraid.'

He turned to her. 'Mustafa,' he said. 'Is he here?'

She lowered her head to her knees and was silent for a long time. 'I had hoped you'd know where he was.'

'He came with me. We were attacked. We had to split up.'

She stayed like that for a while, perfectly still. Then she let out the deepest of sighs and looked at him. 'Well, at least you're here. We needed a hero.'

They stared at each other for a while, neither of them speaking, each thinking of a good man that should be sitting with them. The noise was moving away, leaving to celebrate something more than a wedding now. A distant fiddle started up again, playing a tune one might dance to. The moon went in and came out to pour milk into Hara's hair, turning it white. Tzanis looked away. He saw the bridegroom's seaweed crown lying on the ground. He picked it up, turning it in his hand.

'Tell me about the siege.'

'There's little to tell,' she said, bringing her knees to her chest, hugging them. 'The Turks came and dug their trenches and made some assaults but we've always driven them back. They won't win unless they starve us into surrendering. But the Egyptians are coming.'

'Yes, they are. With Sève.' He paused. 'Your message said Christos was here.'

She nodded. 'It turns out he's not my brother, after all. I am Petrobey's daughter and he wants me back.'

He looked at her. 'And he knows about the gold. How?'

'They found a coin in the shipwreck that tells its own story. Who were you taking it to?'

'Mavrocordatos,' he said. 'But he didn't know anything about it.' He shook his head, too tired to consider it now. 'Why did you run away from Nafplio?'

She turned to him. 'Because I betrayed you. I gave your coin to Manto. I'm sorry.'

He rested his head back against the wall and closed his eyes again. It was all too bewildering. He said: 'You've changed a great deal, Hara.'

'Yes, I've changed,' she said. 'I'm frightened now. I never was before.'

There was a flash from out at sea, then another, then the roll of cannon fire. Her hand slipped into his as it had in the boat. This time it stayed there.

'Admiral Miaoulis,' she whispered. 'At last.'

# CHAPTER SEVENTEEN

## MISSOLONGHI

Winter closed in on Missolonghi with doom-laden skies and no word of relief. The Turks stopped their attacks and their fleet's blockade couldn't prevent Admiral Maioulis coming back with supplies. But everyone knew it wouldn't last, that the Egyptians were on their way with howitzers. The Turks were merely waiting for them.

Christmas arrived with a light fluttering of snow. In the hospital, it was cold. Firewood had long since run out, both for heat and cooking. Not that the latter mattered – there'd be no roast kid because the Admiral had brought only corn flour to the town. Hara set Eleni and Maria to making sweet Christ's bread, with laurel leaves for each arm of the cross.

The hospital was full again, not just with soldiers but children too. At the start of the siege, many had been sent to the island of Kalamos in the lagoon for their safety. Now they'd come back to their parents, and those without were the ones that Hara took in. Orphans should have been unpopular in this overcrowded, hungry town, but they weren't. They reminded people of their humanity. They were *hope* in this place without much.

161

On Christmas Eve, Hara took them out to sing *kalanda*, leading them through the snow herself to each doorstep. They finished in the square, standing beneath the only tree left standing, inside a circle made by candles. There, they sang for the whole town.

*In this blessed hour, Christ is born, as the new moon.*

Later, she went to the Church of Ayios Spiridhon to hear the pappas chant the ancient verses of St Basil, men at the front, women and children behind, watching each new arrival light a candle and bow to kiss the icon of the Nativity. There were few sentries left on the wall. The Turks might not respect a wedding, but they'd not disturb the celebration of Christ's birth.

When the service was over, Hara turned for the door. Christos was standing outside it in the falling snow, accepting congratulations for his name-day, his men around him. Not many pressed gifts into his hand, for the Maniots were not liked in Missolonghi. They were brave but they were surly, and they stuck together, refusing to obey anyone but Christos.

'*Chrónia pollá,*' she said as she approached him, her hood pulled up against the snow. She'd said it on the same day for most of the thirty-one years of his life, but as a sister. Now she was something else. She tried to move on but he took her arm.

'You should come and celebrate it with us,' he said quietly. His eyes travelled down her long furred coat to her little leather boots, all Manto's. They came back to her face. 'With your clan.'

She forced a smile. 'Thank you, but I'm needed at the hospital. I have to feed the children.'

'Let others do that. Come with us. We've got drink.'

'No,' she said.

His face hardened. 'Do you no longer respect your family?'

'You're not my family, Christos,' she said quietly, looking him straight in the eyes. 'You told me so yourself.'

He leant forward so that his face was very close to hers. 'No,' he whispered, 'you're Petrobey's family.' He paused to scowl round at the people who'd stopped. They moved on and he turned back. 'And I'm taking you back to him after this siege.'

She tried to pull away. 'You're hurting me.'

'Leave her alone.'

Tzanis had come up.

Christos straightened. 'This is not your business, aristocrat.'

'Missolonghi is my business and Hara is needed at its hospital. Let her go.'

Some Souliotes stood behind Tzanis, men of his company. He looked after them, even dressed like them these days. He was the only outsider they'd ever respected, other than Byron, whose bodyguard they'd been.

There was a shout. Botsaris was pushing his way through, the priest behind him, still in his robes. By now, the church porch was a gathering of silent spectators, all waiting to see what would happen next. Christos let go of Hara's wrist.

'What is this?' Botsaris looked from one to the other. 'Prince Tzanis, please explain.'

'We were just congratulating Christos on his name day,' he said. 'And Hara is going back to the hospital.'

Botsaris looked at them both again, then grunted. 'Well, you're blocking the porch. Move on and let people through.'

Later, in the hospital, Hara thought about the encounter with Christos. Part of her was dismayed by it, most of her pleased. It had led to Tzanis's intervention, after all, one of the few times he'd shown any inclination to do so. So far in this siege, he'd kept his distance. Whenever he'd had free time, she'd seen him sitting on the walls: alone, sketching. *Always sketching.*

She'd told him she was frightened. It was partly true. There was some small fear of Christos and his men, of what would happen should the town fall, but her greater fear was that whatever bond existed between them in the Mani had disappeared. *Why?* Was it just this bloody, relentless war?

She rose and put on her coat. She passed a mirror and stopped. She looked at herself, the first time in weeks. Her face was pale and drawn and its bones were sharp in the candlelight. Most of her rations had gone to the children, who were always hungry. She had black circles around her eyes and her hair was dull and tangled. She had aged.

She found a brush and tried to tame her hair. She pinched her cheeks and rubbed her lips. She blinked her eyes to bring some light to them. She even slapped herself.

She went to the door and opened it silently, crossed the ward and went down the stairs, barred by moonlight. She'd only be gone an hour. She came out into the square and crossed it, to where he lodged with men from his company. She hoped he wasn't on watch at the wall.

A Souliote was asleep just inside the door. She shook him awake. 'Your captain,' she whispered. 'Is he here?'

'Upstairs,' said the man, already turning over, 'in the attic.'

Another time, she'd have been met with suspicion, but the men were tired and most rules had disappeared with the siege. She tiptoed up the stairs, cursing every creak. At the top was a ladder up to a trapdoor with a rope hanging from it. She went up and pushed it open with her head, holding onto the rope. She looked in. There was a table, chair and single bed, lit by a skylight with the moon in it. Against the wall was a musket and sword still in its belt. On the table was a pile of sketches. There was a shape in the bed.

164

She climbed into the room, closing the hatch behind her, remembering she'd done this once in a tower to bring him food. She went over to the wall and sat on the floor with her back to it, her head level with his. She looked into his sleeping face.

'Tzanis,' she whispered.

His eyes opened at once and looked straight into hers. She noticed his long, knotted hair and the stubble on his cheeks and chin. It suited him to be a little Souliote. He looked bewildered. 'Hara?' He sat up and she saw he was fully clothed. 'What are you doing here?'

'I want to talk,' she said. 'Like we used to. You've been avoiding me.'

He pushed his hand through his hair and blinked twice. He swung his legs over the side of the bed to face her, rubbing his face. 'This is a siege, Hara,' he said.

'Yet you sketch every moment you have free,' she said, glancing over to the table. 'You could talk to me instead.'

He studied her in silence for a while. 'What would we talk about?' he asked.

She felt the sharp prick of despair. *What? What?* She looked around the room, then back. 'Well, your gold for one thing. If I'm to play a part in bringing it up, I have a right to know what it all means.'

'Can you bring it up?' he asked. 'I thought it was too deep.'

'There may be a way: the steamship Captain Hastings is building in London. We can use its engines to pump air down into a suit. He told me so.'

Tzanis leant back on the bed, his eyes still on her. 'Why did Manto take the coin with her, do you think?'

'To persuade the Russians to sign the treaty. She's going to embarrass them into helping Greece.'

Tzanis nodded slowly. 'Except the Russians haven't signed,' he said. 'Why not?'

She didn't reply because she had no idea.

'I don't know either,' he said. 'But I do know I should find that gold. If I survive this siege, if Hastings gets his steamship, I should go and find it.'

'*I*? You mean *we*, surely.'

'It will be dangerous.'

'As Missolonghi isn't?'

He paused. 'It's a different kind of danger.' He looked at the moon, still framed by the window, still bright. He spoke up to it. 'Have you ever wondered why Colonel Sève was where he was?' he asked quietly.

'To reconnoitre Navarino Bay,' she said.

'Yes, but think of the chances of him finding us exactly where he did.' He looked at her. 'Unless, of course, he was *looking* for us.'

'Because he knew about the gold?'

Tzanis rose to his elbows. 'Think back to what he said that night. He certainly knew *something*.'

'But how would he have known?'

They both fell into silence.

He asked: 'What about Christos?'

'I can handle Christos,' she said.

'Is he in love with you, do you think?'

She was startled by the question. She thought back to the Easter feast when he'd arrived so unexpectedly. She'd thought him her brother then. 'Would it matter if he was?' she asked.

He looked away. 'No . . . I suppose it might just complicate things.'

She stared at him, hoping for more.

There were shots outside, coming from the land wall, then sounds coming from downstairs, curses and the clink of steel. He rose and picked up his musket and sword. 'I must go,' he said.

She watched him climb through the trapdoor and down the ladder, watched until his last hair disappeared. She listened to the clatter of boots on the stairs, then shouts from outside as men gathered in the square. There were more shots.

She rose and went to the window to watch him cross the square. She turned and caught sight of the sketches piled on the table. They'd be endless views of the town and its lagoon. She went over to the table and looked down. The top sketch had a figure in the foreground, one who was sitting, reading a book. She bent forward.

*Her.*

She put the sketch to one side and looked at the next. Again, it was a town scene with her in the foreground, this time looking out to sea. She looked at the next, then the next. She was in all of them.

New Year came and went without the usual round of fortune-telling. No one wanted to know what lay ahead. A dense sea-fog settled over the town and it became a place of astonishing stillness, of ghosts and sudden apparitions, of birds that shrieked out of nowhere.

On the morning of Epiphany, when the priests went from house to house with basil dipped in holy water, Tzanis was making his way across the square to the morning briefing. He felt dizzy, ungrounded by the fog, his eyes stinging from the salt it carried, his coat held tight to him over his Souliote skirts. He didn't see the man until too late.

167

'Wah!' said Christos, stepping back, his hand to his stomach.

Tzanis could smell the drink on his breath even from a distance. He watched him sway as he straightened. Two other shapes came out of the fog and stopped. Other Maniots.

'I'm late for Botsaris's briefing,' he said. 'Let me pass.'

'You knock a man over and expect to pass?' said Christos. 'Where are your aristocrat manners?'

Tzanis took a deep breath. 'I apologise. Now let me pass.'

Christos came up close. 'I've been wanting to talk to you,' he said. 'She was seen entering your house on Christmas Eve.' He stepped even closer, his breath reeking. 'What happened that night, aristocrat?'

Tzanis's hand hovered over his sword. 'That is my business, not yours. Now, get out of my way.'

Christos's lips were trembling with muddled fury. 'Know this,' he whispered, raising a finger. 'When this siege is over, she's coming back to the Mani. And in the meantime, I'm watching you, day and night.' He stepped aside.

Tzanis was still angry as he walked into the briefing room to find a dozen men gathered around a map, listening to Botsaris. Meyer looked up as he closed the door. He beckoned to him, finger to his lips.

'You're late,' he whispered. 'There's been a theft. Last night, from the central warehouse.'

'The moonshine?'

Meyer nodded. 'And food. Botsaris wants the town searched.'

'Oh God.'

The Swiss man turned. 'Are you all right?'

Tzanis had no doubt who'd done it, but if the Maniots' house was the only one searched, Christos would know it was because of him. The Mani honour meant he'd not rest until Tzanis was dead.

168

Botsaris was pointing at the town map, dividing it up into search areas. It would take men from the walls, men from their rest. It would shatter their painstakingly evolved unity. It couldn't happen.

'It was the Maniots,' he said.

Botsaris stopped talking and turned. They all stared at him.

'I met Christos in the square just now and he was drunk; so were his men. You should search their house first without telling anyone. Just settle it with them quietly.'

Botsaris was shaking his head. 'There's no question of that. They must be made an example of. Hanged.'

Tzanis walked over to the table. It was certainly tempting. 'No,' he said.

'But their greed means less for everyone else.'

'So we give them less next time, and the time after. That way, no one knows.'

'And why is that so important?'

Tzanis looked at Meyer. 'Tell them,' he said.

Meyer came forward to the table. He took the paper from beneath his arm and put it down on the table. The headline roared up at them: 'GREECE UNITED IN DEFENCE OF MISSOLONGHI!'

He pointed to it. 'In the eyes of the world, we are Greece: you with your guns, me with my newspaper, Hara with her hospital. We're all trying to show that not only can the Greeks hold Missolonghi, they can do it united.' He paused, lowered his voice, looked around. 'Otherwise, why would anyone believe the Greeks *deserve* their independence?'

Tzanis turned to Botsaris. 'So that's why no mention of this must go outside these walls,' he said quietly.

It was hard to accept, but it was true. Missolonghi was the eye of the Greek storm, the centre around which chaos prevailed. It, at least, had to remain united.

After the meeting, Tzanis was called to the walls, where they stood to action until evening. There'd been rumours of an attack but it had never materialised. In the evening, he returned to the hospital to find Hara in her office, safe. *Thank God.*

He sat down heavily. 'Christos and his men broke into the stores last night. Has he been here?'

She didn't look alarmed or even surprised. 'He came last night,' she said. 'He told me what he'd done. He wanted me to celebrate with him. He was drunk.'

'Oh God.'

'After he left, I went down to the basement.' She paused, then rose. 'I want to show you something.' She went to the door. 'Come.'

She led the way down, the air getting colder as they descended. At the bottom, they came to a narrow corridor with a floor of beaten earth. They followed it into a low room. She lifted the candle to show him black brick walls, shiny with damp.

'It used to be a factory, I think,' she said, looking round, her voice very loud in the space although she was whispering. She led him into a second room, then a third, no doors between them. 'This is where we'll send the children during the bombardment,' she said as she walked. 'We can bring beds down and everything else we need. Now look at this.'

She knelt next to the open mouth of a big tunnel about a foot above the ground. She put the candle inside and patted its wall. The sound echoed into the distance.

'Where does it go?' he whispered.

'Into the lagoon. It must have been how they got rid of their waste.'

'How do you know it goes there?'

She looked up at him. 'Because I've been down it. It's dry for most of the way, then underwater to the end.'

'Can it be swum?'

'By me, yes.'

He looked into the tunnel, smelling the salt and decay. It would not be the town's escape route. He looked back at her. 'No one must know about this.'

She nodded and rose. 'We should go back.' She gave him the candle. 'You lead.'

He took a few paces, then stopped. He turned to face her. In the light of the candle, she looked up at him with wide, unblinking eyes above hollowed cheeks.

'Hara,' he said softly. He paused, looking into the flame. 'On the ship, after I'd escaped . . .' His voice trailed off.

'Did he rape me?' she asked. 'No.'

He felt a flood of relief. They were silent for a long time, staring at each other. He started to turn but she took his hand. 'Wait. Would you sketch me, Tzanis?' she whispered. 'On my own? Just once?'

They heard footsteps. A light was approaching.

Christos came in with a candle. His eyes were heavy but he didn't appear drunk. He looked from one to the other of them, saw their joined hands.

'So this is where you meet.'

Hara took her hand away. 'This is where we'll bring the patients and the children if the town's bombarded, Christos. You can help us with beds if you like.'

Christos stared at Hara. 'Our house was searched this morning.'

'She didn't betray you,' said Tzanis. 'I did. I smelt the drink on you in the square.'

Christos turned slowly to him. '*You* betrayed us?'

'They were going to search the whole town.'

Christos pulled a pistol from his belt. He cocked it and aimed it straight at Tzanis's head. His whole arm was shaking. 'So now I will kill you, aristocrat,' he whispered. 'As I should have long ago.'

Hara stepped in front of Tzanis. 'If you kill him, you'll have to kill me too,' she said calmly. 'Because if you don't, I'll tell them what you've done. They might choose to overlook the theft, but murder? I don't think so. You'll hang and Petrobey won't get his daughter back.'

For a long moment, Christos held his pistol in the aim, his eyes on Tzanis's. Then, very slowly, he lowered his arm. Silence.

He took a step forwards. 'Do you know how a feud starts in the Mani, aristocrat?' he asked. 'First, the village is told.' He began to walk across the room, then back, his candle lifted above him, his head thrown back. 'I, Christos Koudourakis, of the village of Vatheia, swear to kill Prince Tzanis Comnenos. I will not shave, eat meat or change my clothes until the deed is done.' He stopped in front of Tzanis and held up his palm. 'This I swear.' He raised the candle. 'What's that?'

He was pointing at the tunnel's mouth.

'It's a drain,' said Hara. 'Where the waste used to go.'

'Into the lagoon?'

She nodded. 'But it can't be reached. I've tried.'

Christos went over and peered into the tunnel, lifting his light to see the curving brickwork. 'And you think I'll believe that?'

# CHAPTER EIGHTEEN

## LONDON

Unbeknown to her, Manto had arrived in London on exactly the day that Tzanis had come to Missolonghi. It was a day of cloud and drizzle and the teeming city seemed darker than she'd remembered it. She wondered again how a people of such narrow horizon could aspire to rule the world.

She took a house at a smart address and at once threw herself into society. She found every drawing room abuzz with Byron's last days in Greece, many with Meyer's newspaper spread out on the table. Everyone wanted to hear about Chios, to press her hand for her poor, *dear* husband, to learn whether Missolonghi would stand. She was fêted and she was busy.

It suited her to be busy. It diverted her from thinking about Hara. In the small hours of the night, she lay awake and missed her like she missed the all-absorbing light of Greece. She thought, perhaps, they were the same.

As a distraction, she'd occasionally think of Howe instead, and found it surprisingly comforting. He was not much older than Hara, yet he had a command more subtle, more effective perhaps, than even Hastings'. She'd felt it at the hospital, felt his scrutiny when he'd thought her unaware. She'd liked it then and liked it now. It made her feel warm in her English bed; desired. She'd not felt that since before her marriage.

The British ruling classes she found less desirable, more stupid, than she'd remembered them. Despite the sympathy, they were uneasy about another revolution so soon after the French. They couldn't see that they were in the midst of one much bigger that would change their world forever. Only a month after she'd arrived, the first steam-powered engine had carried coal from Darlington to the coast. Hastings had been right.

After a time, she realised her charm was having little effect. Whatever the English thought, their government had little appetite for involvement in Greece. Only Foreign Secretary Canning supported it, but then he was an ardent Philhellene. So she was surprised when she learnt that the Foreign Ministers of France and Russia were in London to discuss it, and that Nesselrode had arrived from St Petersburg with an old friend.

The week after Christmas, she was waiting for that friend in her carriage outside Apsley House, watching the morning sun draw the mist from the frost of Hyde Park. She wore a fur hat, coat and muffler and sat beneath blankets. There were more on the seat beside her.

After an hour, she saw the gates open and a man in a tall hat ride out into the park next to a carriage with a single woman in it. She saw them stop and the man bend over to talk to her. Then he tipped his hat and rode off.

Manto let him ride away a distance before leaning forward to her driver. 'Please take me alongside that carriage,' she said.

The woman looked up as she approached, shielding her eyes from the sun. She smiled. 'Manto, I'd heard you were in London.'

She drew up beside her. 'And cold waiting for you.' She patted the seat next to her. 'I have rugs and a spare muffler. And there's coffee somewhere, though it won't be hot.'

The other woman rose and got down from her carriage. She spoke to her driver and climbed in, pulling rugs up to her waist. She leant over for the kiss and put her hands into the same muffler. 'Manto Kavardis: always warm,' she said. 'You bring Greece with you.'

Manto squeezed her hands. She looked out at the man in the hat, now distant. 'And what were you doing with Wellington? Was the old goat as lecherous as ever?'

Princess Dorothea von Lieven was wife to the Tzar's ambassador to London. She was about forty, quite small and had the brittle attraction of quick wit and ambitious temperament. If Manto knew powerful men, Princess Lieven had them in her pocket, sometimes her bed. She had dazzled a generation of Europe's statesmen and made her advice more sought after than her husband's. She was friends with King George of England and Charles of France, and rumoured to be lover to both Palmerston and Metternich. The two women had been friends since their first meeting in St Petersburg.

'You know I won't tell you that,' she said. 'But I wasn't horizontal.'

Manto laughed. The carriage moved away down the gravel path that led into the park. It was busy with riders.

'Not a place for anonymity,' said Lieven, looking round. She took out a fan that was a riot of *chinoiserie* and held it up. 'I'd heard you'd become a hermit.'

Manto nodded. 'I saw things that made me not like the world.'

The Princess turned to her. 'Was Chios so very terrible?'

She was silent for a moment. 'It showed me how little it takes for us to go back to what we really are,' she said, shaking her head. 'We are savages, Dorothea, for all our sophistication.'

Lieven leant in. 'No, we're not. Not you and I, anyway. We've proved it before and will do so again.' She paused. 'Now, what do you want?'

Manto withdrew one hand from the muffler. She reached into a small bag beside her and brought out the coin. She placed it on the muffler. Catherine the Great's head flashed up at them in the sunshine. 'A chest full of these was lost off the coast of the Mani nearly two years ago,' she said. 'They were a gift from the Tzar for the Greek Revolution. The Tzar who is supposed to be strictly neutral.'

Princess Lieven stared down at the coin. She didn't seem especially shocked. 'But the Tzar's sympathies have been well known,' she said. 'Why else is Nesselrode in London? The Great Powers are considering a treaty.'

'A *protocol*,' said Manto, 'which we both know is very far from a treaty. And it is the Russians who are dragging their feet.'

Lieven looked up at her friend. 'And you hope to quicken things with this? It is just a coin, Manto.'

'One of many. The rest can be brought up.' She paused. 'And the man who brought them survived the shipwreck.'

The Princess's eyebrows lifted a fraction. 'And he is?'

'Prince Tzanis Comnenos.'

Lieven nodded. 'I remember him. He was handsome, charming and poor. A good draughtsman, I recall. The Comnenos were once emperors of Byzantium but their very name prevented them from working for the Turks, like all the other phanariots, so the family was forced to make good marriages in the Russian court. His father married for love so Tzanis was in need of a rich bride. They say he fought well in the war with Napoleon.'

The Princess took her hands from the muffler and picked up the coin and looked at it for a long time. Then she put it down and looked away. They were silent for a while, the horses' hooves loud on the gravel. She looked over. 'I'm afraid you are too late, Manto,' she said quietly. 'I was in St Petersburg for a reason. The Tzar is dead.'

Manto stared at her. 'Dead? How?'

'Of some marsh fever. He was in the Crimea.'

'So who is the new one?'

'Ah, well, that is being decided at this very moment,' said the Princess. 'But it's likely to be his brother Nicholas who is not fond of revolutions.'

Manto sat back in her seat. 'Which is the message Nesslerode has brought with him to London,' she murmured.

The Princess nodded. 'And I'm afraid the French king is of the same mind.'

Manto looked back to her. 'You mentioned Prince Tzanis drawing well,' she said. 'Well, I've seen one of his sketches. It is of a massacre: people of every age tied to olive trees, then burnt alive.' She paused. 'Dorothea, Ibrahim Pasha is destroying my country.'

The Princess held her gaze. 'And the statesmen don't care,' she said. 'Or most of them, anyway. Capodistrias cared enough to send the Comnenos prince but he was replaced by Nesslerode.' She looked away. 'You said that Prince Tzanis recorded this massacre? He must have changed.'

Manto thought of Hara. 'Well, he is loved. That can change you.'

The Princess nodded. 'That will sadden the women of St Petersburg. Who by?'

'By an ordinary girl who might be the true spirit of Greece, or what's left of it. It was she who restored my faith.'

Lieven turned to her. 'And does he love her in return?'

Manto looked away. 'I don't know.'

They lapsed into another silence, both thinking of something that had passed them by, for all their privilege. They were approaching the northern gate of the park where the Princess's carriage was waiting for them. She lowered her fan and gathered the rugs. She took Manto's hand and turned to her.

'What matters now is the French king. If he can be persuaded to listen to his conscience, then the Tzar might do the same. You should go to Paris, Manto.'

# CHAPTER NINETEEN

## MISSOLONGHI

A month after Hara had shown Tzanis the tunnel out of it, the Egyptians came to Missolonghi. Their opening salvo was fired as the first winter sunlight broke the horizon, the command given in French. It took the roof off the headquarters building.

Inside the hospital, Hara looked out of the window with her hand to her mouth, her ears ringing. 'What was *that*?'

'Howitzers,' said a voice behind, 'firing explosive shells. We need to get down to the cellars.'

The shelling went on for three days. A never-ending earthquake had struck Missolonghi and its citizens went underground, if they could, while their houses collapsed above them. Sleep was banished, food ejected, and blood ran from eyes, ears and nose. Children screamed, then stopped, unable to hear themselves above the noise. By the end of it, Missolonghi was in ruins.

The hospital was hit on the second day. Hara had put a white flag high above the building. No sooner was it raised than the Egyptian artillery directed its fire there. The first shell brought down the flag, the second a section of the roof.

She moved the ward down to the cellar, the children helping.

It became a scene plucked from hell: the wounded lying side by side on the ground in bloody bandages, the floor slick with blood. There was too much noise to hear their pain. She worked without stopping, without sleeping, her white robe tided with gore. When the bombardment finished, she collapsed where she stood. Tzanis came and carried her up to the cot in her office and laid her down to sleep.

He didn't linger. He ran to join his Souliotes on the land wall and found them tense, expectant. He went from man to man, talking to them, checking their ammunition, asking about wives and children. He reminded them of why they were there.

Then.

*'Allahu Akbar!'*

The Egyptians didn't rush the walls as the Turks had done. They came forward in disciplined ranks, pausing to fire volleys. There were French officers behind, ready to cut down any that ran away. The Souliotes poured fire into their ranks but still they came on, muskets levelled, bayonets fixed. Only at the last moment, did they charge.

The fighting was fierce. The Egyptians were small but they were tough, and they fought together.

'Close up!' shouted Tzanis. The Souliotes were unused to discipline, yet Tzanis had trained them well. They closed ranks, making a second wall to breach. Bit by bit, they drove the Egyptians back, the Frenchmen behind pushing and cursing and cutting down those who tried to flee. Then even the Frenchmen turned.

'Hold!' shouted Tzanis. 'Don't pursue. It's what they want!'

The Souliotes held, hurling insults in a language their enemy wouldn't understand. Tzanis found Botsaris by his side. He was holding a bloodied sword and had a bandage on his arm. He was shaking his head.

'Byron would've never believed it,' he said. 'The Souliotes obeying an order.'

'You are a Souliote,' said Tzanis, wiping his sword.

'And I don't obey orders.' The General glanced at him, smiling. 'Except yours, sometimes.'

The Egyptians made two more assaults and were beaten back each time with heavy casualties. Tzanis had told his men to aim for the French officers. By the third assault, the officers had decided to stay behind. There was no fourth.

Tzanis could barely stand. He left a third of his company on the wall and took the rest back to find what was left of their house. They walked through streets of rubble, charred brickwork and smoking beams. There were people lifting the dead onto stretchers, gathering their limbs, whispering prayers and crossing themselves. The wounded cried out for water but there was never enough. Children sat in broken doorways and stared out at the scene. Dust was everywhere, faces thick with it, turning hair, eyes white. Tzanis raised his head. *Almonds.* Was this the new smell of death?

He found Meyer staring at what was left of the warehouse.

'It collapsed during the assault,' he said. 'Half the food is gone.'

They watched the smoking timbers for a while in silence. Another wall went down, sending up a cloud of dust.

Meyer turned to him. 'Will he attack again?'

'I doubt it. Now he'll starve us out.'

Tzanis was right. No further assaults were made. The two Muslim armies sat behind their siege lines and waited. In the town, rations were halved, then halved again. There'd be no further supply with the Egyptian fleet now outside the lagoon. First to be killed were the horses and mules. There weren't many and their meat lasted only two days. Then it was the turn of the dogs, cats and finally the rats, caught in traps since the cats were no longer among them.

Hara fed her patients seaweed after that, collected every night from the rocks outside the sea walls. They began to get ulcers, scurvy, and their joints swelled. They grew weak and listless, too weak to talk. It was the same everywhere in the town. People sat in the rubble of their houses, staring out, too feeble to move.

Hara moved her patients back upstairs to where they could at least breathe air. She set the orphans to cleaning out the cellars and, when it was done, prepared new beds there for them. Upstairs was full.

She herself was more tired than she'd ever been, thinner too. She suffered from the same lethargy that affected every citizen of Missolonghi. She worked automatically, saying no more than the essential, biting and clawing herself to stay awake, forcing her exhausted mind anywhere but her constant, gnawing hunger. She found herself drawn to her mirror again and again, fascinated to see how a person wastes away, examining every symptom as if it were another's.

She was lying on her cot in the dark when Tzanis came to visit. It was the middle of the night and he closed the door so silently that she didn't know he was there. When she heard his cough, she turned. He was sitting watching her. She could only see his shadow, hunched against the cold and the effort of banishing hunger.

She held out her arm. 'Can we at least hold hands?' she whispered. 'For friendship? Is it dark enough?'

She heard the rustle of his sleeve as he reached out. They stayed like that for a while.

'Where's God in all this, Tzanis?' she asked after a while. 'The people are praying hard enough. What does it take?'

He didn't answer beyond pressing her palm.

'You never really explained where He fits into your new world,' she went on. 'Perhaps He doesn't.'

'I don't want to talk about God,' he said quietly. He started coughing again, a low, rasping sound that moved his shoulders. 'It's nothing, just the dust.'

'There's water on the table.'

He let go her hand and she heard him drink in great gulps. He set down the jug and wiped his mouth with his sleeve. He lit the candle, melting wax to fix it to the plate. 'How are the children?' he asked.

'Hungry, like everyone else. They eat seaweed now.'

He grimaced. 'Seaweed? Is there nothing else on the rocks?'

'Nothing that's not too deep.'

'But you could dive for it. If I helped you?'

She considered this. 'Perhaps. But what about the Turks? They're patrolling every inch of the lagoon.'

'The Turks are the Turks. We can evade them.'

She sat up slowly, brushing crumbs from the bed. 'When?'

'Tomorrow night. We could go when it's a little darker.' He paused. 'My Souliotes have guard of the sea wall.'

She got up from the cot. 'I need to think about it.' She moved to the door. 'I'm going down to check on the children.'

They left the ward and went down the stairs to the hall, then to the cellar. A draught came that made their candle flicker, but at least the smell of death had been scrubbed away. They came into the second of the rooms that was now the orphans' dormitory, six beds against each wall. She walked between them with the candle held high, Tzanis following.

They came to the last bed where a little girl lay clutching a felt lamb to her breast like it might be taken from her. Her eyes were wide open.

Hara sat down on the bed. She put her hand on the child's forehead and stroked her hair. 'Can't you sleep, Kanta?' she whispered. 'Was it a dream?'

Kanta nodded slowly. Her eyes stared up into Hara's, big and full of uncertainty. Gently, Hara prised the lamb from her grasp and looked into its button eyes, their noses touching. 'Is lamb afraid?' She glanced back. 'Not with you here. What is its name?'

'Sophia. She's a girl.' The voice was small and solemn.

'Sophia. *Wisdom*.' Hara nodded. She turned back to the little girl. 'Like you, looking after Sophia so well. To make her unafraid.'

She handed the lamb back to the child, leant forward and kissed her brow. She sat with her until her eyes closed once more in sleep.

After, they went back up to the hall, Tzanis leading with the candle. He hadn't spoken at all while they'd been in the cellar. Now he stopped and turned. He started to say something but she leant forward and put her finger to his mouth. Then she kissed him. It was brief, but it was on the lips. She looked up at him. 'Now it's your turn to sleep.'

They met the next evening where they'd agreed: beneath the bastion named for Alexander at one end of the sea wall. The moon appeared briefly and he could see she was wearing seal pelts tied to her body with cord: one around her breasts, the other round her hips. She held up a canvas bag. 'For whatever we catch.'

A flare went up over the lagoon, washing the water red. There were scores of small vessels, all watching for signs of Greek escape.

She led him along the rocks to a place where they could drop into the water. They did it as silently as they could, but its cold took Tzanis's breath away. They edged along the rocks, ducking their heads into the water every time a flare went up. At last they were far enough out.

'Here,' she whispered. 'Give me the knife.'

She put it between her teeth and plunged into the water. There was no splash, hardly a ripple. Tzanis pressed himself to the rock and looked out to sea. The boats were calling out to one another. Another flare went up. In its light, he saw something new. An enormous man-of-war was coming into the lagoon, towing barges behind it. Its decks were crowded with men.

Hara broke the surface. She had handfuls of shellfish that she emptied into the bag. She looked around and took the knife from her mouth. '*My God*. Should we go back?'

He shook his head. 'No, let's get what we came for. It will be a distraction.'

She dived again as he watched the slow ballet of vessels moving to station. The man-of-war seemed to be heading for the last island still in Greek hands: Klisova.

'No more,' he said, as she came up for a sixth time, tying the sack shut. 'They'll get indigestion.'

She turned to the scene in the lagoon. Under more flares, they could see barges being pulled alongside the man-of-war.

'They're going to try and take Klisova,' said Tzanis. 'Probably at first light.'

185

She glanced along the shoreline. 'With an audience,' she said. 'Look.'

Further down they could see some of the smaller vessels tying up to the rocks.

'We'll have to find another way back,' he said.

She looked at him. 'There's only one,' she said. 'The tunnel.'

'Do you even know where it is? You said it was impossible for any but you.'

'We don't have any choice.'

She turned from the rock and began to swim towards the centre of the lagoon, her stokes so gentle that the sea barely parted. He followed her. The lagoon was much emptier now, most of the smaller craft having gone to the side to watch the attack. But the clouds were getting fewer. There was no need for flares any more.

She stopped, looked over to the town and began to swim towards it, the black seal pelt part of the sea's texture. The moon came out and stayed out. Surely they must be seen now? He heard shouts from the shoreline. A shot rang out.

'Come on!' she said, kicking. 'We're nearly there.'

They swam as fast as they were able, no longer caring whether they were seen or heard. Tzanis heard a musket ball part the air above him.

She stopped. 'Here!' she shouted, turning, treading water. Another flare took to the sky. 'Take the deepest breath you've ever taken and follow me.'

She plunged down, giving one enormous kick before she disappeared. He drew air into his lungs and dived. The lagoon was murky by day, by night it was impenetrable. There was nothing but the deepest black. He went deeper and his ears felt they might blow apart. Then he touched sand. He turned around. No Hara. He looked up. *Nothing.*

He felt a pinch and turned. She took his hand and pulled him into the tunnel. They swam uphill in total darkness, following the slope of the seabed. His lungs were aching, his eyeballs too. They must be there soon. He was going to pass out. He had to open his mouth. *Yes!*

They were there. The sudden air on his face, the first gulp for breath; these were things he'd never forget. He lay against the side of the tunnel with his eyes closed, Hara next to him.

'We did it,' she said, turning her head to him. 'You've still got the sack?'

He nodded, unable to speak.

'Good,' she said. 'Then let's go and give it to them. You lead.'

They crept up the tunnel in darkness, using their elbows and knees. It was slow and painful but at last his fingers closed round the entrance and he pulled himself out, helping Hara through behind him. They leant against the wall and closed their eyes, heads down.

*Footsteps.*

They looked up and saw shadows lengthen into the room. Tzanis slowly reached into the sack and brought out the knife. *Christos.*

It wasn't Christos. The feet were bare and young and stood side by side beneath candles. They were a line of thin children, some with small animals in their hands. They were staring at the little sack, now in Hara's hand.

# CHAPTER TWENTY

## MISSOLONGHI

It was dawn and the children were feasting on as many shellfish as they were allowed. While they ate, they watched a small triumph played out in the bay.

The man-of-war's target had been the island of Klisova, as Tzanis had predicted. The Turkish general himself had led the attack, but his men had got stuck in the mud and were cut down. By mid-afternoon, it was the turn of the Egyptians. 3,000 of them were towed into the shallows and jumped from the barges into the same mud that had held the Turks. Half their number died where they landed, cursed by French officers who'd stayed on the barges.

It wouldn't alter the town's fate, and few had the energy to watch. Hunger stalked every street, hiding among the rubble and broken timbers, waiting at every corner, in every shadow, its fangs drawn. It preyed with its companion madness and they were merciless. Human bonds were their targets, the ties that bind. They severed them and got between, setting mother against daughter, father against son. At least there was no longer a newspaper to record it all.

*

Late one afternoon, Tzanis and Hara were summoned by Botsaris to attend an urgent council of war. A message had come from Ibrahim Pasha offering terms for surrender. When they arrived, all the factions' leaders were there: Thracians, Macedonians, men from Epirus, Thessaly and Crete. Christos would speak for the Maniots. Hara would speak for those that couldn't fight.

The room was hollowed by the silence of hunger as much as expectation. All eyes were on Meyer, who stood next to Botsaris reading a piece of paper.

Botsaris raised his hand for silence.

'The terms come from Colonel Sève who advises Ibrahim,' he said. 'They are in French which I cannot read.' He turned. 'Meyer, please.'

The Swiss looked up from the letter. 'If we surrender the town, they will let us live,' he said, 'soldiers as well.'

'Sold into slavery,' said the Thracian.

Botsaris nodded. 'Or converted to Islam.'

'It's not even a question,' said the Macedonian. 'We fight until we die.'

Botsaris turned to him. '*You* fight, Goran, because you can. But what of the people in this town who can't: the women, the old, the children? Might they not want to live?'

Tzanis was watching Hara, knowing it was she who'd have to speak for them. He leant over the map, pointing to the long spit of land that Missolonghi stood on. 'There is another way,' he said. 'We break out.' He pointed to the plain. 'Here.'

'Who breaks out?' asked Botsaris.

'Everyone who wants to, led by the strongest among us.'

'Even the women and children? We'd be cut down,' said the Thacian.

'And if we don't surrender, we'll starve. Which is best?' Tzanis

189

paused. 'We'll have surprise on our side. We'll get everyone through the gate and into the ditch, then rush their lines. It's not what they'll be expecting.'

There was silence around the table as people considered the plan. Tzanis pointed to the mountains beyond the plain. 'It could work if we coordinate with Georgios Karaiskakis, if we can get a message to him to attack at the same time.'

Botsaris nodded slowly. 'We've already tried,' he said. 'The messenger didn't get through the Turk lines.'

'So we need another,' said Tzanis, 'someone who speaks Turkish.' He looked at Christos. 'Weren't you a galley slave for the Turks once?' he asked. 'Surely you speak their tongue?'

'My Turkish hasn't been used for many years.'

'Nevertheless, it would serve,' said Hara. 'I remember it was good enough to fool merchants in the Mani.'

Christos glanced at her, then his eyes came to Botsaris. 'No,' he said.

There was some low murmuring around the table. Was the Maniot a coward?

Christos sensed it. He looked from face to face, saw the contempt. He glanced back to Tzanis, then Hara, knowing he was trapped. He nodded slowly. 'I'll go tonight.' He looked at Tzanis. 'Then I'll come back.'

After the meeting, as Tzanis and Hara were leaving, Meyer came up them. He whispered, 'stay behind.'

They waited for everyone to go. When they were alone, Meyer brought Sève's message from his pocket. 'There was more,' he said. He looked at Tzanis. 'Addressed to you.' He proffered the letter.

'Read it,' said Tzanis.

190

Meyer glanced at Hara. 'I . . .'

'Read it.'

Meyer hesitated for a minute, then put on his spectacles and lifted the piece of paper.

'*My Dear Prince Tzanis. I would be surprised if you agreed to surrender. My guess is that you will try to break out. Or perhaps you'll go alone, leaving the girl to her fate, as you did on my ship.*'

Meyer looked up. 'There's more, but I really don't think . . .'

Tzanis was staring at the ground, his fists clenched. 'Go on reading,' he said. 'Please.'

The Swiss glanced again at Hara, then looked down.

'*I hope you have enjoyed her as much as I did before I threw her off the ship. But you'll want to know how I knew you were both in Missolonghi. The Turk told me after you abandoned him too, though I'll admit we had to torture him hard to get it. Too hard, I am afraid, for he died. I send you his only possession.*'

By now, Hara was gently sobbing, her head moving from side to side. She turned to Tzanis who was still staring at the floor. 'He lied about what happened on the ship,' she whispered. 'He never touched me.' She moved towards him, then stopped. 'And if he lied about that . . .' She reached out her hand.

But Tzanis didn't take it. He raised his head and stared at Meyer. 'Where is it?'

Meyer reached into his pocket and brought out a little sack and placed it on the table. Tzanis lifted it and turned it upside down.

Onto the table rattled a string of prayer beads. They were made of amber.

Afterwards, Hara and Tzanis didn't return to the hospital. Instead, they walked in silence to what was left of the church.

It was deserted and half of its roof lay on the floor. Winter sunshine blinded them as they sat down against a wall.

Tzanis glanced up, closing his eyes to the glare. Neither of them spoke for a long time. Eventually he turned to her: 'I know he lied about you,' he said quietly. 'But I don't think he lied about Mustafa.'

She nodded, not looking at him. 'Nor do I.'

They lapsed back into silence, both thinking of a man too honourable for this world.

'His family must never know how he died,' said Tzanis.

'Nor Manto.'

He nodded. 'I will write to her with a better version. Christos can take it.'

'He won't take anything from you.'

'He'll think it's from Botsaris.'

She nodded. 'He can't read anyway.'

Tzanis turned to her. He took her hand. 'I'd like to draw you. Now, here.' He reached into his coat and brought out his sketch-book and some charcoal. He moved round to face her. 'Sit still.' He began to draw.

She composed herself, raising her chin. They sat there, surrounded by sunbeams and dancing dust, the scrape of charcoal the only sound in the church.

'Do you think the breakout will work?' she murmured, not moving her head.

He leant forward and blew carbon from the paper. 'Some might make it. It's better than the alternative.'

A bat flitted past. 'You know I can't leave the hospital, don't you?'

He looked up. 'You don't have to. You can escape through the tunnel.'

'And my patients? How will they get away?' She shook her head. 'I won't leave without them, you know that.' She rose and patted dust from her legs. 'I should go.' She met his eyes. 'I'll come back here later.'

She turned and walked out of the church and he stared after her, the sketch still in his lap. She'd not asked to see it.

He looked down. It was good, perhaps the best he'd done. He tore it off and put it to one side. Now the letter to Manto.

It felt like an age had passed by the time he'd finished. The night was splashed by phosphorescence, the moon moving through it like a coracle. He closed his eyes. Was there any point to it all? If only Byron was still among them to write a poem. He opened them and looked back down at the sketch. An idea had formed.

*Perhaps.*

Later, when Hara returned to the church, Tzanis wasn't there. She sat down against the wall and looked up through the roof to the sky. She closed her eyes. In too few days, they'd be parted, probably forever. There were so many things she wanted to tell him.

She heard movement. She turned and saw a shadow in the doorway. She rose, giddy with relief. 'You came back.'

He stepped into the light. 'I went to deliver the letter.'

'Can I see the sketch?'

He shook his head. 'I've sent it to Manto.'

She was bewildered. 'Why?'

'Because I want her to remember you.' He paused. 'I'll draw another, but not now.'

He took her hand and led her to where the moonlight shone through the roof to make a dream world of silver and shadow, a world unconnected to the terrible one outside. He took off her cloak and spread it between the broken beams, sweeping aside the dust with his palm. He laid her down and knelt beside her. He leant forward and began to unbutton the front of her dress. Her heart was beating so hard she worried he'd fumble, but he went on until he'd opened it. He looked down, then kissed her there. She felt his tears warm against her skin.

She took his head in her hands and lifted his lips to hers. She drew away, his face still in her hands. She saw tears streaking his cheeks, knew who they were for. 'I love you, Tzanis,' she said. 'I always have.'

She lay back and looked up at him, her hand still to his face, her eyes wide. In this moonlit world, anything seemed possible, even a future. She watched him tilt his head so that he could kiss the hand. She closed her eyes and his lips moved to her eyelids and kissed them so lightly it might have been a breeze. Then they met her mouth and stayed there and she forgot everything but the soft press of his lips.

She felt his hand on her thigh, the soft scratch of silk lifted.

'In a church?' she whispered into his ear.

'I don't think God is still in Missolonghi,' he said. 'He left long ago.'

At first, Tzanis thought it was thunder that woke them. He sat up. The ground was shaking beneath them.

'Those are shells,' he said, turning to her. 'We should go.'

She rose and pulled on her dress and threw her coat over her shoulders. 'Why would they shell us now?'

'Their answer to ours,' he said, tugging on his boots. 'Come.'

He held out his hand and she took it. He led her out of the church and through streets towards the square, explosions all around them. As they approached, a huge one flung them onto their backs. She looked up from the ground, spitting dust from her lips.

'My God,' she whispered. 'The hospital.'

They got up together. Ahead of them, the upper floor of the hospital was ablaze.

He was already ahead of her. He ran into the hall, shouting up to the ward. But the stairs were alight, a wall of fire at their top. He turned to her. 'Give me your cloak!'

She gave it to him. He went over to the water barrel and plunged it in, then draped it over his head. He ran to the stairs, then up. At the top, the heat from the fire threw him back. He heard screams beyond: children's. He bent double and prepared to charge, but there was an almighty roar and the ground before him gave way, engulfing the flames in a cloud of debris. The floor of the ward was collapsing, taking the walls down with it. It seemed to go on forever, more and more masonry and timber falling in an enormous plume of dust. When it was over, he was standing on the edge of an abyss, a sea of rubble below.

The bombardment stopped suddenly. He heard a cry. He looked down to see Hara scrambling over the rubble on her knees, tearing stones free with her hands. He ran back down the stairs to help her. He looked ahead and saw a felt animal held aloft by an arm seen only to the elbow. There was blood on it.

He crawled forward and started pulling stones away. She joined him and they worked as if their own child lay beneath, choking in the dust, in their rage. They exposed a neck, then a face. Hara stopped and put two fingers to the child's skin.

She sat back on her ankles and shook her head. 'Dead,' she said. She prised the lamb from Kanta's grasp and looked at it.

She brought it to her forehead and closed her eyes. 'Sophia too.'

The breakout was fixed for a night when the moon would be half. The few days before were to be spent deciding who went and who stayed, in making bridges to cross the Turk ditch, in packing gunpowder into the houses where people had decided to die.

The women changed into men's clothing and picked out the very darkest cloth for their families. They burnt cork to blacken their faces and hair. Some learnt how to use weapons, even taught their children. The remaining food was distributed, laudanum too, to keep the youngest quiet. All was done with silent purpose.

When the night arrived, Tzanis was summoned to Botsaris who was dressed, like Tzanis, as a Souliote warrior beneath a black cloak, two huge pistols thrust into his front.

'We've heard at last from Karaiskakis. He will attack at midnight. His signal will be shots from the hills. When we hear them, we go.'

Tzanis asked: 'Has Christos returned then?'

The general shook his head. 'No. The message was passed over the walls.'

'So it could be a trap.'

Botsaris shrugged. 'I'm not sure we have the leisure to worry.' He moved to the map on the table. 'We'll split into three parties,' he said, 'each with a thousand soldiers and twice that many women and children. We'll leave by the gate and spread out along the ditch until we hear Karaiskakis's shots. Then we go. You will lead the centre party. You'll have Meyer with you, and his family.'

*

When the evening of departure arrived, Hara helped Tzanis dress in his blackest clothes, to wrap his scabbard in hessian, to blacken his cheeks. She sang quietly as she worked: some ancient Mani dirge that meant nothing to him. She herself had dressed as she might have done for a wrecking expedition, her hair tied up as if short again. The last sight he'd have of her would be not Manto's creation but her own.

As he got up to go, he bent down and kissed her on her forehead. 'Thank you,' he said, his voice almost steady, 'for showing me how to live.'

'So far,' she said, looking up. She reached up to hold his face and press his lips with hers. '*So far.*'

He said: 'I will break out tonight and you will swim down the tunnel to the lagoon. Go to the place where you dived for shellfish. Wait there until I come.'

In the square, Meyer and his Souliotes were waiting for him in front of a long column of silent women and children. He saw the three Maniots near the front. He turned to the man behind him. 'I want those men watched.'

He took his place at the head. He felt a breeze and glanced up to see big clouds climbing over the horizon, gathering to come their way. *Good.* They moved off through the ruined streets, watched from shattered doorways by old people who crossed themselves as they passed.

When they got to the wall, he stopped. 'Tell everyone to sit down quietly and wait for the signal to move into the ditch. We'll go when the next cloud covers the moon.' He looked up at the sky. 'Open the gate.'

It was opened just the width of a single man. The column rose and went through it, soldiers then civilians, some carrying bridges. It took some time and, miraculously, the moon stayed hidden until they were all in the ditch. He took his place next to Meyer.

'It seems quiet,' whispered the Swiss, two nervous eyes looking out from his blackened face. His wife and child were crouched beside him.

The moon emerged and Tzanis could see the glint of cannon ahead, not more than a hundred paces distant, no soldiers around them. He heard one sentry call to another. It seemed unbelievable that it might work.

They stayed like that, watching and waiting, praying for the only sound to come from the hills. Midnight came and went and none had been heard. There were whispers down the line.

'Should we go?' whispered Meyer. 'We can't stay here much longer.'

The moon came out from behind cloud. A shot rang out, but from the ditch.

'Go!' shouted a voice and a great wave of people rose all along the ditch. *'Go!'*

*'Go!'* yelled Tzanis to the men around him. He rose and scrambled forward, Meyer by his side, his wife behind him.

A flare went up in front of them. In its light, he saw lines of soldiers behind the guns, the front ones kneeling to aim. It was a trap.

Meyer grabbed his arm. 'Do we go back?'

Tzanis looked around him. The ground was swarming with people running forwards, shouting too fiercely to hear any order.

The first volley came from both cannon and musket, a thunderclap so loud that it stunned before it murdered. A storm of lead tore into them, carving wide paths. Heads and limbs scattered, blood showered the earth.

Tzanis turned. He saw Meyer kneeling on the ground, trying to shield his wife and child from the horror. He glanced back to where a second line of enemy was kneeling to take aim. He threw himself to the ground.

This time it was just musket fire, but the effect was the same. Those that weren't hit tripped on the bodies, hampered by the children they carried. It was chaos.

Tzanis rose and looked back to the enemy lines. They were no more than fifty paces away, but the ranks were parting to let something through.

*Oh no.*

Rows of calvary.

There was no choice. He had to get to them before they charged, to stop some of the horsemen from doing their work. He turned back to Meyer. He was frozen in shock, looking to where he looked, seeing what he saw. He ran over to him, took hold of his shoulder. He shook him. 'You have to move!' he yelled. *'NOW!'*

Then he started to run towards the enemy, but their lancers were moving as well and people ahead were already turning to flee. He pushed his way through as the first line broke into a trot, lowering its weapons, gathering pace.

He drew his sword.

Hara heard the crash of the first volley. She was crouched in the ruins of a house near the rubble of the hospital, ready to help any who might need her, ready to make her final escape if they didn't.

But a volley could mean only one thing: the enemy had been expecting them. Christos had betrayed them. Tzanis would be charging into a trap. And he'd be at the front.

She heard more volleys, one after another, and screams. The gates had opened and people were streaming back into the town. A woman ran into the square, pulling a boy behind her.

Hara blocked her way. 'What happened?'

'They were waiting for us,' the woman cried, looking around wildly. 'We stood no chance.'

'Did Karaiskakis attack from the hills?'

'No one came!'

'Were you with Prince Comnenos?'

The woman nodded. 'The last I saw of him he was fighting the Egyptians.'

'You didn't see him fall?'

The child had begun to wail. The woman picked him up and lifted him to her hip. She ran on. More people were flooding into the square. Hara tried to stop one, then another, but they all ran past her. Dozens of flares were in the sky and the world was crimson. The shooting outside was continuous now.

*The woman hadn't seen him fall.* So he might have got through. She must get to where they'd planned to meet. She turned back to the hospital, then threw herself to the ground. The three Maniots were running towards it. She'd have to wait.

The first Turks were entering the square: big men with tall hats and curved swords. They fanned out, cutting women and children down where they stood. They were drawing closer to where she lay. She heard an explosion, then another. The houses were being blown up.

She got up and ran towards the hospital, stumbling through the debris, passing a Turk pulling rings from the fingers of an old woman lying in her blood. He lunged at her but she kicked him away.

She got to the stairs to the cellars and ran down. At the

bottom it was almost dark and she had to feel her way through the rubble. She heard shouts behind and glanced back to see the flicker of a torch. The Turks were following her.

She staggered forward, her arms held out like she was blind. She came to a wall and felt along it until she found the hole. *Thank God.*

She climbed in and pushed herself along, using her nails, her elbows. She heard shouts behind and froze, pressing herself to the side. Would they see her?

But the torch went away. She moved forward again, using her palms now. The air was getting colder and the smell of salt stronger. At last her fingers touched water. She pushed herself into it and began to swim, keeping her head down. She would soon be in the lagoon.

Her head hit something soft and she nearly choked with the shock. She brought her hands up and they closed around a face. She felt a moustache, an unshaven chin. *One of the Maniots.* She tried to get round but there were two of them, joined in desperate embrace as they'd try to escape. Their corpses were blocking the tunnel. She tried to pull them free but they'd not part,

She had no choice: she had to turn. But it was further back than forwards and she'd be swimming uphill. Her lungs were aching and her temples throbbing. She swam on, on. Surely it hadn't been this far?

Then air. She crawled out of the water, gasping and coughing. She lay on her back and stared into the darkness, shivering with cold.

She crawled up the tunnel inch by inch, hearing the slap of water behind her, remembering when she'd made this journey with someone who she'd not meet that night after all. She closed her eyes against the thought.

She felt the air change as she reached the mouth. She stopped and listened. She could hear faint sounds above, nothing more. She edged forward until she could see into the room. It was dark but empty. Slowly, she climbed out of the tunnel.

A match struck beside her and she saw the glint of gold against a chest.

# PART FOUR

# 1826–27

# CHAPTER TWENTY-ONE

## ENGLAND

Howe sailed into Plymouth Sound on a windy day in spring with his ears ringing. He was on HMS *Neptune*, a British 60-gun frigate that had brought him and Mustafa's family all the way from Malta.

It was not when he'd wanted to arrive but they'd been prevented from leaving Nafplio by an Egyptian blockade of the port. Only in the autumn, when Ibrahim Pasha had finally been stopped outside the town and his navy had lifted its blockade, had they been able to get away.

Captain Calthorpe, who stood next to him on the poop deck, was the cause of his discomfort.

'I know her,' he shouted, pointing out at a passing ship, the smoke from its salute wafting past. 'She's bound for the Americas.'

For a moment Howe felt a yearning. 'Boston?'

'Other end. The *Beagle* goes to Patagonia.'

His shouting was only one reason Howe was eager to part with Calthorpe.

Another was the man's loathing for Greece, where he'd never

been. It had been first expressed as they'd sat down for dinner on their way out of Valetta.

'Bloody brigand country.'

Howe had had some warning. The day before, he'd handed over Mavrocordatos's letter to the admiral of the Mediterranean fleet at Malta, with its request to give the bearer all assistance in his journey to London. 'You can go with Calthorpe in the *Neptune*,' the admiral had said. 'I'm not sure where he stands on Greece, though.'

Badly, it turned out, and it was all to do with money.

'Two thousand pounds!' the captain had thundered as the officers took their seats. 'The prospectus a pack of lies! Damned thieving country!'

Howe, placed next to him, bore the full gale. Calthorpe had invested his savings in the second Greek loan, floated a year ago by Messrs Ricardo Bank on the London Stock Exchange. The bond's value had since fallen by half.

'I blame Byron,' he'd said, helping himself to soup. 'Damned poet's death put the spooks up people. Bad timing. Bad form.'

In one way, Howe was reassured. He was predisposed to dislike the British and Captain Calthorpe confirmed all the smug superiority of a race believing itself born to rule. Now he felt obliged to offer some defence of a place he'd come to love. 'Greece may yet prove bountiful,' he said quietly, 'after she has recovered from Ibrahim Pasha.'

Calthorpe shook his head. 'Enough to pay back my money?' He signalled for more wine, then jabbed the table. 'They're all scoundrels, sir. Look at the two deputies sent to get the loan. Wandering around London like damned peacocks. Disgusting!'

'But the loan has been spent on a navy, surely?' asked Howe.

An officer further down, red-faced and whiskered, intervened.

206

'On fine ships from America which the monkeys won't even be able to sail. Even a steamship, by gad! The thought of it!'

At Plymouth he was met by news that cast Calthorpe from his mind: Missolonghi had fallen.

Soon afterwards, he and Suleiman went ashore for more information, reading everything they could find. But it was an old copy of Meyer's newspaper, published months before the town's fall, that told them of something far worse.

Its front page was all about how Prince Tzanis Comnenos had come from nowhere to foil a surprise attack on the town. Not until page five was there any mention of a companion who'd not arrived with him. It didn't mention Mustafa by name, but they knew.

He wrote to Manto in London and waited two days for an answer, spending the time arranging passage to America for Mustafa's family. When no reply came, he took the overnight post to London. He found lodgings in Goodge Street, bathed and sent a message to the address she had given him. He went out to buy clothes and be shaved. He returned to find the messenger back on his doorstep.

The boy held out the letter. 'Gone to France.'

'France?'

'Paris in France,' said the boy.

Howe tipped the boy and wrote to Hastings. Two days later, he received a letter. Hastings was overjoyed to hear that he was in London and impatient to show him his ship. He begged him to visit the Greenland South Dock shipyard at Rotherhithe at his earliest convenience.

So there he was, an American doctor, afloat on the Thames, with the river flowing wide and bright through fields of cows and cowslips. It was a scene of tranquillity quite at odds with the smoky, gaudy squalour behind him. London was a place of reckless ambition, a swarm of cranes and scaffolding, of chimneys and slums. Its streets were full of wealth and poverty side by side because this was a triumphant, fraudulent version of democracy. He hated every part of it.

They were approaching the huge loop where the Isle of Dogs' mongrel head pushes the river south. Already the smoke of a thousand kilns and forges smudged the sky. They rounded a bend and he saw a vast floating dock with a man-of-war amidst scaffolding, men clustering its sides like termites. There were barrels of smoking pitch at every level, piles of ropes and planking and the sound of a thousand hammers hitting nails. Cannon were being jerked aloft on ropes.

'Greenland South Dockyard,' came a shout from the back, pointing to where a forest of masts crenellated a low wall. A Union Jack showed them the way in.

They came into the wind, lowered the sails and paddled their way through the gates to see rows of ships on slipways, some half-built. He saw a sloop on its own at one end with a funnel between its masts. A warehouse beside it had 'Daniel Brent Shipwrights' painted on its doors. As they approached, he saw a man standing astride the bowsprit with his hands behind his back.

Howe turned. 'Can you put me alongside?'

They could, and soon Howe was embracing Hastings next to the giant curve of a paddle housing. On its side was the ship's name in gold.

'*Karteria* is Greek for perseverence,' said Hastings, 'which is what's been required all these months. The Admiralty has not been helpful.'

Howe looked round at the polished decks, the gleaming brass. 'But she's magnificent, Hastings.'

'I'll show you around. But first your news.'

Howe told him what he knew, lastly about Mustafa. They stood in silence for a while.

'What of his family?' asked Hastings.

'They're on their way to America.'

'Good. There is opportunity there. And they'll be safe.' He took Howe's arm. 'Let me show you my ship.'

Howe let himself be led through every part of the *Karteria*. At last they came back on deck. Hastings pointed to a metal fire basket that sat at the centre. 'That's where we'll heat up the shot,' he said. 'Everything it hits will burn.'

Howe nodded, looking round. 'Will it all work?' he asked.

'Of course.' Hastings patted the casing by his side. 'The paddles will only be used to manoeuvre. Otherwise we'll go under sail.'

'But is there coal in Greece?'

'We'll ship it down from the north.'

Something had occurred to Howe. 'You keep saying "we",' he said.

Hastings turned to him. 'I'd like you as the ship's surgeon,' he said. 'A Yankee doctor gives the crew confidence.'

Howe looked away. He could think of nothing better than spending time with this strange Englishman who seemed to loathe slavery as much as he. But he had to do something first. 'I have to see Manto,' he said.

'Well, you've missed her. She's gone to Paris. She goes where the great men go and they've gone there.'

'She may be in danger.'

Hastings stared at him. 'How so?'

Then Howe told him what he knew. 'Which is why I need to find her before I can consider anything else.'

Hastings turned to face him. 'Of course, but we'll go together. The *Karteria* will be ready to sail in two weeks.'

# CHAPTER TWENTY-TWO

## PARIS

Manto Kavardis had learnt of Missolonghi's fall soon after she arrived in Paris. The news threw the city into mourning and her into black despair. She retired to her house and didn't come out.

Then came Tzanis's letter from Missolonghi, forwarded to her from London. It told her that Mustafa was dead and that Hara had remained in Missolonghi to the last. No doubt she'd been trapped in the town when it fell. The two people whom she'd truly loved had gone. All that remained was a sketch that she'd found folded inside the letter.

For two days she did nothing but sit staring at Hara's portrait. She took no visitors and no meals. She didn't sleep. She blamed herself for leaving and she blamed Howe for not looking after Hara as he'd promised.

Then, on the third day, she decided to act. She rose from her chair, summoned her maidservant and told her to look out a dress likely to appeal to the painting community. Wearing the most *bohème* of her wardrobe, she made her first call not to the *salons* of the Faubourg Saint-Honoré, but to Montmartre where the artists lived. And she took Tzanis's sketch with her. She had a plan.

Six weeks later, she was standing by the banks of the Seine, watching the *Karteria* steam upriver. The ship was late, having had to return twice to Rotherhithe for repairs, but the view was impressive, if dirty. Now the paddles had stopped and a cloud of black smoke still hung over the river.

Manto watched her glide slowly in to the quay. From the ship's masts hung bunting, the Greek and French flags side by side. Her tall funnel was entwined with flowers like a maypole. Her side was gleaming black and the giant paddle housing rose above it with the grace of a wave. '*Karteria*, Hellenic Navy' was emblazoned on it, in gold. A garlanded gangplank was being lowered, and either side of it stood Captain Hastings and Dr Howe.

She stepped onto the gangplank and Howe came down it to meet her halfway.

'You let her go to Missolonghi,' she said.

He looked surprised, a little shocked. 'There was nothing I could do to stop her.'

'You could have gone after her.'

'But I didn't know where she'd gone. Mustafa wasn't there to ask because he went with her.'

'And he is dead too.'

'We don't know that for certain.'

'Well, Prince Tzanis seems to know that. I have his letter.' She stared at him a while, then walked past him to Hastings. 'Welcome to Paris, captain,' she said.

Hastings glanced past her. He had overheard the exchange and took time to recover from his shock. He bowed. 'You are most welcome. Let me show you around.'

She went to the side and peered over on tiptoes. 'Well, I've seen the paddles. Ingenious.' She looked over to the riverbank. People were streaming in from every direction, leaning out over the rails to see better, climbing trees. She felt Howe come up behind her and moved away.

'Where can we talk?' she asked Hastings.

He led her into his cabin, Howe behind. It was equipped with new furniture of gleaming mahogany and brass and its walls were covered with pictures of Byron and Kolokotronis. There were maps with arrows on them and newspaper headlines in frames. The whole room was a message.

Manto took it all in, moving from image to image as if she was reviewing troops. 'Very clever,' she said at last. 'The people will be moved.' She turned. 'But it's the King that matters and he won't come and see this ship, just as he hasn't seen me.' She paused. 'But I have a plan.'

Howe spent his evening wondering whether he should follow Mustafa's family and go back to America. He'd been excited by Hastings' offer to join him on the *Karteria* but the rejection, the *anger*, of Manto had wounded him more than he might have expected. And the news of Mustafa's certain death had left him numb. As the night wore on, his mood turned to anger.

Just before midnight, he dressed and went down to the street and along it to where he knew Manto was staying. He had to knock three times before an old servant opened the door.

He waited in the hall while the man mounted a sweeping staircase, grumbling at every step. He heard him shuffle along the landing then knock on a door. He heard muffled conversation, then more shuffling.

'Come up, please.'

Howe climbed the staircase and followed the man to an open door where Manto stood in a red dressing gown. She looked smaller than she had on the ship.

'Why are you here?' she asked.

Through the door, he could see the servant moving from candle to candle to reveal a large room beneath a painted ceiling. A big bed stood at one end that didn't look as if it had been slept in.

'To talk to you, since you won't do it elsewhere.'

'And what makes you think I'll do it in the middle of the night in my bedroom?'

'I need five minutes.'

She stared at him a while, then spoke over her shoulder. 'Leave us.'

The man shuffled past and they waited until he'd descended the stairs. A door closed below. She moved to one side.

Inside, there were two sofas set either side of a low table on which a letter lay open. She sat down on one and gestured to the other. She picked up the letter. 'I have been re-reading Prince Tzanis's letter. It was sent from Missolonghi just before it fell.' Her voice was as flat as before. She looked up. 'Why did you let her go there?'

He shook his head. 'I told you. Tzanis was brought into the hospital. She nursed him, then left before he could know that she'd done it.' He paused. 'There was nothing I could do.'

'You could have spoken to Mustafa. He might have stopped her.'

Howe leant forward. 'He went *with* her, Manto. I didn't know for certain he'd died until you told me yesterday.'

She was silent for a while, studying her joined hands. 'She was too young to be at a siege,' she said softly. 'She was a child, really.'

'Perhaps, but she knew what she was doing.'

Manto looked up. 'What was she doing?'

Howe thought suddenly of Fleur. 'She was removing herself from an impossible situation,' he said quietly. He looked away. 'I saw her shave him while he was unconscious. I've never seen so much love.'

'So much that she had to *leave*?'

He nodded. 'Perhaps she knew that whatever education you'd given her . . .' he trailed off. 'She knew that what she wanted was impossible.'

They stared at each other for a long while. Then Manto slowly leant forwards and buried her head in her hands. He saw her shoulders move. She was crying.

He went to sit next to her. When he put his arm round her shoulder, she didn't resist. He drew her to him.

'The newspaper said there were men from the Mani there, sent by Petrobey,' he said gently. 'She may have escaped.'

Her thick hair was beneath him. He put his face to it and closed his eyes. The woman he'd known at Nafplio had vanished and in his arms was a fragile creature who loved someone who might have been a daughter.

He felt her head move beneath him. Her face came up and her eyes came to his.

'Will you stay with me tonight?' she asked.

# CHAPTER TWENTY-THREE

## PARIS

'Exactly as you predicted,' said Hastings as he strode into the room. He was waving a newspaper in the air.

Manto and Howe were sitting at breakfast in an orangery full of lemons, the table between them patterned by sunshine and foliage. A bird was pecking on the glass outside.

Hastings slapped the newspaper down between them and tapped it with his finger. 'There she is, although the drawing exaggerates the funnel.'

Manto drew it towards her and peered down. 'Very fine. Any mention of Toulon?'

'Ah yes.' He raised a finger. '"Why aren't the French making steamships instead of frigates? Why are they making anything for *Le Sanguinaire*?"'

'Sanguinaire?'

'Ibrahim Pasha. The tone is insurgent!'

Howe glanced at the headlines. Even upside down, they were insurgent.

Manto lifted her napkin from her lap and folded it. 'Have all the pamphlets gone out?'

Hastings nodded. 'No one will escape.'

An hour later, they saw for themselves. Striding up the Avenue Navarre, they passed by a dozen men and women with pamphlets, all draped in the new flag of Greece. It was so busy that people could hardly see what they were holding. It didn't much matter. Everyone knew where they were going.

They arrived at their destination to find it even more crowded with people, many waving the pamphlet above their heads.

'Good heavens,' said Manto, stopping. 'How do we get through?'

Hastings linked arms with Howe and pulled him to her front. 'Brute force, ma'am. Dr Howe?'

They ploughed forward, the sound of rebellion all around. They reached the building and entered a vast hall ringed with columns beneath a cupola. Waiting between two of them was Princess Lieven and a slim man in his late twenties. He was tall with fine features gathered round a narrow moustache. His hair was the hair of an artist.

'The King is on his way,' said the Princess, coming forward and kissing Manto on both cheeks. 'He is coming with Canning and Nesselrode.' She turned. 'You know Monsieur Delacroix, of course.'

The painter bowed to kiss Manto's hand, his hair enveloping her wrist. He straightened, then nodded to Hastings and Howe. 'All is ready,' he said in French. 'The people will not be let in until the King has seen it.'

'Most of Paris is here,' said Manto.

'Or at the Seine,' said the Princess.

The painter stepped forward and offered his arm to the captain. 'Please?'

They walked away arm in arm and Howe was left with the two women. Lieven leant in to Manto.

'I never asked,' she whispered, 'how you got the King to come.'

'He had to,' said Manto. 'It is a gift.'

The Princess shook her head. 'You'll supplant me.'

They heard commotion outside, the sound of boots marching on cobbles, an order shouted: '*Faire place au Roi!*' Manto went to the door and looked out. 'The King is here.' She came back and they formed a receiving line: the Princess, Manto and Howe. Delacroix would meet him inside.

They waited in silence, listening to the jeers outside, the occasional shout of a soldier. They heard wheels on stone, then men stamping to attention. More jeers.

Courtiers ran into the hall, spreading out in all directions to fuss. They checked behind columns and doors and through windows. They fanned themselves and wiped their faces with lace, all the time glancing to the noise outside.

Then the King walked in.

Charles was a tall man in his late sixties with a mountain of white hair and bushy sideburns almost as long as Hastings'. He looked wary, as a man might who'd lived through a revolution and seen a brother assassinated. He was dressed more simply than his courtiers, perhaps to deter any attempt on his own life.

Behind him came men in frock coats and high collars, the uniform of the international statesman, and behind them a gaggle of secretaries with quills poised. No one spoke above the noise still coming in from the street.

The King appeared unruffled. He approached the Princess, who sank into the deepest of curtseys.

'Princess Lieven,' he said in French, as he brought her up. 'Your husband is behind me but you are here. I didn't know you were anything to do with this.'

'It is my friend Manto Kavardis who has commissioned the work, majesty.' She gestured to Manto who was still deep in her curtsey. 'She will have the privilege of taking you in.'

The King turned to Manto. 'Then let us go.'

Howe waited for the statesmen to pass, recognising Canning and Nesselrode from the newspapers. He joined the secretaries behind.

At the end of the corridor were a pair of enormous doors that swung open as they approached. They walked into a tall room lit by sunlight streaming through a ceiling of latticed glass. It was empty of carpet or furniture of any kind. There were no pictures on its walls and nothing to divert attention from the single object covered by a red velvet drape. Monsieur Delacroix was standing in front of it, holding a golden rope. He bowed as the King entered.

Charles stopped. There was silence as he stepped forward and turned to consider the room. He grunted. 'Nothing to distract from your masterpiece, eh Delacroix?'

The painter seemed nervous. He'd painted for the revolution, yet a king was a king. 'It is the fastest painting I have ever completed, majesty,' he said. 'Two months since its commission.'

'But is it good?'

Delcaroix nodded. 'The best I have done.'

The King lifted his hands and sighed. 'Then we'd better see it. Show us, please.'

219

Delacroix turned and pulled the golden cord. The velvet drape fell away.

'Greece on the Ruins of Missolonghi,' he said.

Howe stared. The painting was huge and framed in heavy gilt. It depicted a young girl kneeling amidst ruins, her arms open in prayer, in entreaty. Behind her was a man in a yellow turban planting a flag. The girl was dressed in the blue of the Virgin and her chest was almost bare. She was someone he knew.

*Hara.*

He was oblivious to the room around him, to the courtiers and ministers and scribes who, had he known it, were as transfixed as he was. He didn't know that every eye, not just his, was drawn to the masterpiece and its simple, unavoidable message.

*Greece needs you.*

At last the King spoke. He seemed angry. 'Delacroix, you go too far. She is dressed as the *Virgin!*'

'She is dressed as the Greek peasant, majesty,' said the painter, looking up at his creation, suddenly braver. 'They wear blue too.'

'I think she speaks to us,' came an English voice from the side. Canning had stepped forward to stand beside the King, his hands behind his back. He was shorter, less hirsute, with small, clever features. 'I think she speaks to us as Christians, hence her clothes.' He turned to Delacroix. 'But she is beautiful. Where did you find such a model?'

Delacroix glanced at Manto. 'She came from a sketch,' he said. 'She was in Missolonghi when it fell.'

'Is she alive?' asked the King.

'We don't know,' said Manto.

'But she is Greece,' said Delacroix, 'so she is eternal.'

The King turned to a courtier who stood at his other side. 'And the people are here to see this?'

The man inclined his head. 'I doubt we could stop them, majesty, without revolution.' The man threw a glance at Manto. 'There have been pamphlets.'

Princess Lieven had come forward to stand in front of the King. She gestured to Hastings, who was standing to one side. 'Majesty, this is the man who has brought the steamship to Paris: Captain Hastings of the Hellenic Navy. The ship is called the *Karteria*.'

Hastings performed a stiff bow. He was dressed in his odd uniform and held his plumes tight to his side like a chicken.

The King seemed disinclined to stay longer. 'I have heard,' he said without enthusiasm. 'But you are probably needed in Greece, captain.' He turned to leave. 'Don't let us detain you too long on the Seine.'

Canning had smelt advantage. He said: 'In Britain, we believe steam to be the future, majesty. Our shipyards are turning to it. France will not wish to be left behind.'

But the King had seen the morning papers and wanted no further talk of shipyards. 'Yes, yes, we'll look into it.' He started to go. 'Thank you, gentlemen, thank you, Delacroix.'

# CHAPTER TWENTY-FOUR

## MANI

Hara had watched Missolonghi expire into the night and felt her soul go with it. From the boat's stern, she'd watched the flames grow, then become an orange glow on the horizon. The little town that had transfixed the world, that had given her own life brief meaning, had finally gone. Had Tzanis gone with it?

She'd been grateful to watch it alone – grateful, in fact, for Christos's complete silence since leading her up from the hospital basement. She'd heard the screams of children through her escort of French soldiers, the pleas of their mothers. She'd known they would stay with her for the rest of her life. Now she wanted silence.

They were sailing on a fast cutter flying the flag of Egypt, on their way, she assumed, to the Mani. Only when they'd left the lagoon, passing through the Egyptian fleet without hindrance, did she consider what that meant. She was going home. But she had changed and home hadn't.

She was still standing there as dawn rose over the mountains to ignite the sea. Christos was asleep at the bottom of the mast, oblivious to the beauty. But what of his shame? Was he oblivious to that? He'd betrayed her and possibly the town. *What of Petrobey's part in it all?* She'd know soon enough.

She put her face to the wind and felt the sting of salt on her cheeks, the whip of her hair. *That will have to come off.* It would be the first thing she'd do on arrival: cut off all her hair, perhaps use the fish oil again. She looked down at the sleeping man. Would it be him? The reward for bringing her back? She closed her eyes. *No. Please.*

They sailed into Limeni with the setting sun, dropping the sails as they approached the harbour entrance. They saw a man standing alone on the quay, watching them come in. It was too distant to see his expression.

But Petrobey was smiling as she came ashore. He took her hands in his and bent forward to kiss her and she felt his moustache tickle her cheeks like they used to when his scent had roamed around her like a familiar pet.

'Welcome home, daughter.'

*Daughter.* Had she always known it?

He led her up the road to his house, his fur-lined gown flapping behind. They went out onto the balcony where there was a table and chairs set beneath an umbrella. They sat and he poured wine for them both.

'You have changed,' he said, setting the glass down in front of her and leaning back. 'A new Hara.' He raised his glass.

They drank and she watched him over her glass. Did he seem nervous?

Her father gazed out to sea. 'How you must have dreaded this meeting,' he murmured. He looked back to her. 'But the Mani is your home. It can change as you have changed. You can bring light into the darkness.'

She looked at him. Was this the man she'd once been so in

223

awe of? He seemed smaller somehow, even slightly ridiculous in his fur. 'I don't want to be here,' she said. 'I was brought against my will.'

'Your *will*?' said her father. 'What about the greater cause?' He paused. 'I've accepted Mavrocordatos and his government, after all. It's why I sent the cannon to Missolonghi.'

'You did it because you know they're the only faction likely to win.' She paused. 'And you sent Christos to bring me home.'

He stared at her for a long while, perhaps as amazed as she was by this answer. He took a pipe from his sleeve and struck a match on the side of his chair. He smoked for a while, looking out to sea. Then he said: 'You should know that Prince Tzanis didn't come into Karaiskakis's camp with the other survivors after the breakout.'

'He made it to the Turk lines,' she said. 'He was seen fighting there.'

Petrobey nodded slowly. 'Perhaps, but he never made it to the camp.' He turned to her. 'Which means he probably died. If he'd been captured, he'd have been ransomed. Like others of his kind.'

She stared at him, wanting him to stop, wanting to block her ears. 'We don't know that,' she said simply.

He studied her a while. Then he leant forward and tried to put his hand over hers, but she moved it. 'You know it couldn't have worked,' he said quietly. 'He was a Comnenos prince and you . . .' He sat back and picked something from his teeth. 'Well, he had to make a good marriage.' He looked away. 'Strange things happen in sieges.'

'I'll not marry,' she said.

'And I'll not make you,' said Petrobey. 'I'll not make you do anything but stay here and help me build a better Mani.'

224

His tone was gentle, beguiling. Had he, perhaps, changed too? He was suddenly serious. 'Schools, Hara. We need schools if we're to let the light in. We need money too.'

So there it was. The gold. He'd finally got round to it. But then, why not? He was right: schools did need to be built and it would take money. But she needed to know something.

'How did Christos get me out of Missolonghi?' she asked.

Petrobey puffed for a time, blowing wraiths out into the bay. 'I will tell you the truth,' he answered at last. 'Some time ago, after I had sent out the brothers to find you, Colonel Sève came to visit me. He told me that you were in Missolonghi. He said that he'd tortured the information out of your Turkish servant. He also told me that he knew about the shipwreck and the gold. He made a proposal: he would let you survive Missolonghi so that you could take us to the gold, in exchange for half of it. I agreed.'

'So Christos went straight to Ibrahim that night.'

'Yes,' said Petrobey. 'Christos went to Ibrahim but then he went on to Karaiskakis and gave him the message. He's not a traitor.'

Hara stared at him. 'Didn't you ever wonder how Sève *knew* about the gold?'

'He told me that you'd told him when he picked you out of the sea with Prince Tzanis.'

'I didn't.'

'I know. That was when I realised that he'd meant to intercept the gold all along, that it was not destined for Greece, but for his master.' He paused. 'That is why I reneged on our agreement.' He paused. 'I am not a traitor either.'

Hara was shaking her head. She needed to know what he knew. To be sure. 'But why would the Tzar send gold to Ibrahim Pasha?'

'Because it has all happened before,' he replied. 'The Russian Empress Catherine, who they now call "the Great", thought to use the Mani to foment rebellion in Greece, then carve up the Ottoman Empire with the Austrians. Now Russia is doing the same with the Egyptians.' He paused. 'Last time it cost my grandfather his life.' He picked up his glass and stared at it for a while. He looked up. 'Now, some truth from you, please. Can you reach the gold?'

'No.' She shook her head. 'I tried when I went out with Prince Tzanis. It's too deep.'

'And why should I believe you?'

'Because we would have brought it up if it was possible.' She put her head to one side. 'And why wouldn't I want to now that you've told me how it would be spent?'

He watched her in silence then nodded and rose, his face shaded by the umbrella. 'Very well.' He picked dust from his sleeves. 'We must guard you.'

'Imprison me.'

'No, guard you. And rather better than you did Prince Tzanis.' He moved out into the sunlight and shielded his eyes from the sun. 'After all, Colonel Sève knows where you are.'

# CHAPTER TWENTY-FIVE

## MANI

Two months later, Hara was some way back to what she'd been before Tzanis. She wore a tunic and shorts and spent her days looking for herbs. Only her hair stayed as long as when he'd sketched it. If she was to be free from the threat of marriage, then she'd keep it.

But was she free? She lived in comfort in Petrobey's house in Tsimova and could walk, swim where she wanted. But she had guards always with her.

She found herself in a sort of limbo. She'd applied a tourniquet to memories of a man who was probably dead and avoided thought of the future because she had no control over it. She was numb.

As if to test the limits of her freedom, she'd ride to the far northern boundaries of the Mani for her herbs, to the place where Petrobey had built a wall. It was at Verga, just south of Kalamata, and it ran between the sea and the mountains. It was a low thing, with towers at intervals, just tall enough to shoot over. It had two thousand men behind it.

She didn't think it would offer much defence against

Ibrahim's cannon, but then, no one thought he'd come. What had the Mani to offer except stubborn soil and stubborn people?

One morning, she was gathering snakes instead of herbs. She would take their venom back to help their victims. The men behind her held forked sticks to trap them and sacks for putting them in. It was a slow business for the grass was still tall.

The shout came twice before they heard it. They stopped and stared down the hill. Someone was waving up at them.

'The Egyptians,' said the man behind her. 'They've come.'

The Mani, where the revolution had begun, where the Turks had never managed to rule, was, after all, to be conquered and Petrobey was to be humbled. Hara suspected that she had something to do with it.

They ran down to the wall to find ammunition being distributed, powder casks broken open: all done under the direction of one of Petrobey's sons, her half-brother now. He had his father's looks.

'Where are they, Giorgios?'

'In Kalamata. 15,000 under Colonel Sève's command. They'll be here tomorrow. You should go back.'

Hara ignored Giorgios, then her guards who wanted to remain as well and knew there was only so much obedience you could expect from Petrobey's daughter. She slept behind the wall that night and was shaken awake just as the first sun crested the mountains.

'They've arrived,' whispered a guard, crouching down beside her.

She threw back the blanket. 'Let me see.'

The guard knelt against the wall and she clambered onto his back. She peered over the top.

She saw a flash, then another as the sun's rays lit the gun

barrels, one by one. The cannon were pointing at them from behind sandbags, not far away. She saw the glint of bayonet between.

'They crept up in the night,' said the man below her. 'They must have marched fast.'

She shielded her eyes from the new sun. She saw others do the same along the wall. Someone was climbing out over the sandbags in front. He held up a white flag.

'Don't fire,' shouted Giorgios from further down. 'Pass it along!'

The man was walking towards them. He was slowly waving the flag.

'He's either brave or stupid,' said a man beside her, his musket in the aim.

'I know him,' said Hara. 'Lower your gun.'

He was familiar now: the rolling stride of the cavalryman, the limp from a former wound. In a minute she'd see his yellow moustache.

Sève stopped. He looked up and down the wall, down the barrels of a thousand muskets. He seemed calm.

'Who is your commander?' he yelled. 'Petrobey?'

Giorgios shouted his answer. 'I am his son. I speak for him.'

Sève lowered the flag so that it rested against his leg. 'But do you speak for your men?' he asked. He gestured behind him. 'What will you say to them when we start firing these cannon at your little wall?'

'That they fight for the Mani.'

Sève nodded. 'Well, that must be right, for they couldn't fight for the traitor Petrobey.'

There were whispers either side of her. What could he mean by this heresy? She watched Sève turn his head from left to right, so that his voice would reach everyone.

'How many of you saw his daughter sail in from Missolonghi? Why was she in an Egyptian ship?' He paused. 'In fact,' he shouted, 'why was she alive at all when everyone else sent from the Mani perished?'

The man beside glanced at her, then quickly looked away.

She watched Giorgios climb up onto the wall. 'What is your message, Colonel Sève?' he shouted. 'My men are not interested in Egyptian riddles.'

But they were. Hara could hear whispers close-to, murmurs further along. There was unease, questions being asked.

'My message is simple,' said the Colonel, still loud enough to be heard by all. 'Give us the girl and we'll go away. My master has no quarrel with the people of the Mani. Give us Hara and you won't hear our cannon.'

There was silence along the wall as the men took this in. They waited to hear how Giorgios would reply.

But Petrobey's son was extravagantly shaking his head, as if what he'd heard was beyond comprehension. 'You are addressing men of the Mani,' he shouted, 'the same who held the pass at Thermopylae against the Persians. You're wasting your breath!'

Sève interrupted. 'But didn't they all die at Thermopylae?' He paused. 'At least they had a cause. Your father and sister are not a cause. They're traitors.'

But Giorgios was no longer listening. He'd turned away and was climbing off the wall. He seized the musket from the man who'd helped him and fired it into the air. 'Go home!' he yelled, as he walked away.

The Epyptians didn't go home, but nor did they attack. Under the blaze of the summer sun, they sat behind their sandbags and

230

did nothing. Meanwhile the Maniots grew hot and whispered among themselves.

By evening, the whispers had given way to the silence of exhausted nerves. They'd waited all day, expecting any moment to see destruction hurtling towards them. But nothing had happened. And they couldn't lie down in case they were attacked.

Giorgios walked up and down the wall, calming nerves, pulling men off to feed and rest by turn. He'd not sleep at all that night.

He avoided Hara as did every other man, even her guards. She sat with her back to the wall hugging her knees, more miserable than she could ever remember. By the time the moon had risen, she'd made up her mind.

She waited until there was cloud before slipping over the wall. She used all the stealth she'd learnt luring ships onto rocks. She made no noise as she disappeared into the night.

She padded her way through the grass and stones, making sure every step was silent. She watched the shadow of the battery loom up ahead and heard the low murmur of the Egyptian army, smelt their cooking.

She heard a sound to her right and froze. The moon was still behind cloud but she thought she could see the shape of a man. She settled into a crouch and waited.

'Hara,' came the whisper.

'Christos?'

The shadow moved towards her. It stopped.

'What are you doing here?' she whispered.

'Stopping you. You have to come back.'

She shook her head. 'I brought them here,' she said. 'I can make them go away.'

'Do you believe that?'

She rose.

'Stop. Wait.' He edged closer. She could see him now. 'Just hear me.'

She glanced at the battery ahead then up at the moon, still behind cloud but not for long. She crouched again. 'Speak quickly.'

'I know why we need you now. I saw what you did in Missolonghi.'

'But if I stay they will attack.'

'And we will throw them back. As we always have.' He paused. 'Better, if you're among us.'

'But you heard the murmurs,' she said. 'The men think I'm a traitor.'

He shook his head. 'No. I spoke to them. They know what happened.' He looked down. 'I lost friends to bring you back, Hara. Their deaths can't be in vain.'

She stared at him through the darkness. Suddenly the moon came out and the world turned to silver. Slowly, she nodded.

'We'll have to crawl back,' he said.

They began to move, edging their way back, stopping to listen every few yards. Gradually they left behind Egyptian voices and began to hear Greek ones. When they were close enough to be heard, Christos stopped and whistled twice.

'We're coming in. Don't fire.'

He took her hand and they rose. 'Run,' he hissed, pushing her forward.

A single shot came from behind. She turned. Christos was on his knees.

'No!'

She ran back to find him now lying on his back. His eyes were open but he wasn't seeing. She looked down at his chest and saw the stain spreading from his heart. Another shot rang out behind, then the rattle of musketry from both sides.

*No!*

She heard shouts behind her. A hand grabbed her waist and lifted her in one movement. Then she was being carried back to the wall where men were leaning over to help her in. She was almost thrown up to them.

She heard Giorgios's voice behind her. 'I'm going back for Christos.'

The attack came an hour later. She was crouching next to Giorgios when the first cannon balls passed over their heads. She understood why Petrobey had built the wall so low.

The infantry advanced as they'd done at Missolonghi: in good order, kneeling and firing as they came. The Maniots shot at them and hundreds fell before they turned away. After three more attacks, they stopped.

It was as the evening meal was being passed around that Giorgios told her what she already knew.

'Christos was dead when I brought him back,' he said. 'We'll get his body back to Tsimova tomorrow.'

She stared down at her untouched food. She'd not spoken all day. 'I killed him.'

Giorgios shook his head. 'You were trying to save us.' He paused. 'Him as well.' He came and sat beside her. 'You'll go back with him. Petrobey wants you safe. We can hold them here.'

That night she didn't sleep. She lay awake and thought about a man she'd known all her life, yet hardly known. He'd been as dark and impenetrable as the Mani, yet he'd had his strange honour and he'd saved her life, perhaps twice. Now he was dead. *Because of her.*

She left before dawn with her guards. They each rode horses and Christos's body was carried on a mule. They didn't speak as they went.

Around mid-morning, as they were cresting the hills beyond Pigi, they saw three sails out at sea. They stopped.

Hara shielded her eyes. 'Those are big ships,' she said. 'Can you see a flag?'

They stared. The ships were moving quite fast under a full spread of sail because the *melteme* was blowing hard behind them. But there was nothing flying above their top gallants.

'They're not flying one,' she murmured. 'I wonder why not.'

Then she knew. She turned to her guards. 'I have to ride on,' she said, 'fast.' She turned her horse. 'One of you can come with me, the other stay with Christos.'

She kicked her horse. She heard hooves on the track behind. She kicked harder.

They rode fast but the track wound through the hills and they had to slow often for rocks. They lost sight of the sails. It wasn't until mid-afternoon that they entered Tsimova's little square. It was full of women preparing to receive the wounded from the front. They'd seen the ships pass an hour ago.

She sped on, her guard following. She rode down to Diros where she saw the ships again, this time anchored in the bay with small boats by their sides. She was shouting as she rode into the square.

'Come out, all of you! Bring something to fight with!'

And since their menfolk were up at the wall, it was the women who poured out into the square: mothers, daughters, sisters holding scythes and pitchforks and kitchen knives. Some had basket lids and pans for shields.

Hara stood up in her stirrups. 'The Egyptians are landing on the beach,' she shouted. 'They're trying to attack our men from behind!' She leant forward and took a pitchfork from an old woman, then brandished it. 'To the beach!'

She led them down just as the first of Sève's men were jumping from their boats. The Maniot women charged into the waves and met them in the shallows and slaughtered them to a man. Hara watched it all from the shore, her bodyguard forbidding her to join.

And when it was over, the women of Diros celebrated their victory by drinking their husbands' moonshine.

As had never happened before.

# CHAPTER TWENTY-SIX

## MANI

Christos's body was taken home to Vatheia and Hara went with it. Sève's beaten army had returned to Tripoli and there was nothing to remain for. She would go back and bury one brother and stay with the others. Where she was meant to be.

Once there, she took back her old room at the top of the tower and resumed life as it had been, determined to squeeze any other from her mind. She didn't read because there were no books. She didn't converse because there was no one to converse with. As summer turned to autumn and the rains came in on the cold, northern wind, she began to realise that this bleak land was where she belonged. It was part of her, a part she could never escape.

In time she started wrecking again. She would wake in the small hours to ride out to dying ships, coming back wet and frozen with whatever had been salvaged. It was what kept her feeling alive.

Then, one day, she was summoned back to Tsimova.

Petrobey greeted her at his gate and was as affable as ever. Was she comfortable? Had Christos been buried with proper ceremony? But she just nodded and smiled and wondered why he'd asked for her.

It was during lunch that he told her. 'There is a steamship on its way from Nafplio. Manto Kavardis is on it, with the Englishman Hastings and an American called Howe.'

Hara stared at him. She had soup in her lap that she gripped to keep her hands steady.

'I imagine they're coming to get the gold,' he continued, 'although you say it's too deep to get.' He leant forward and gently took the bowl from her grasp. She felt heat on her knee from where it had sat. 'Our victory at the Verga Wall has given new hope, but apart from the Mani, only Nafplio and the Acropolis still stand. We need another army and we need that gold.' He paused. 'Can the steamship bring it up?'

She continued to stare. He'd seemed smaller when they'd last met, but now it didn't seem to matter. 'Yes,' she said, 'it can.'

'And will you help?'

Hara looked at the ground. The world across the mountains, the one that no longer had him in it, was coming for her and all she wanted to do was run away. She looked up. 'Yes. But first I'd like to go back to Vatheia.'

A week later, on a night of shrieking wind that blasted the towers of Vatheia, she was woken by the crash of trapdoor on wood. She sat up.

'There might be a wreck,' said a brother, shielding his light from the draught.

She pushed her hair from her face and rubbed her eyes. 'How do you know it's there?'

'A boat has put out from Porto Kayo.'

Porto Kayo was the neighbouring clan's lair, but the seas were everyone's. If there was a ship out there, it belonged to whoever got there first. She said: 'I'll be down.'

The storm wasn't as fierce as the one when they'd found Tzanis. They reached the beach quite quickly and dragged the boat down. As they rode the waves, she wondered if it was really fierce enough to drive a ship onto the rocks. But the men from Porto Kayo had seen something.

From the prow, she peered out like a gargoyle. But there was no ship, no boat. Nothing.

Then a shout, carried to her on the wind, and a glimpse of light. She pointed.

'Over there!'

One side of oars lifted free of the waves while the others dug deep. The boat turned and teetered on a crest before plunging into the valley below, then up, up. There were rocks ahead and lights on them, moving. But there was no sign of any wreck. She heard movement behind her and a man came up to her side. He looked out beneath a hand spattered by rain.

'Where is she?'

She shrugged. 'Beyond the rocks? I can't see anything.'

'Perhaps all her lights are put out.'

'Perhaps.'

They approached the rocks and saw the boat from Porto Kayo hauled up between the boulders so that just its stern was in the water. There were men in it and more above on the rocks. Some had lanterns but it was hard to see what they were doing.

'Do you recognise anyone?' asked the man.

She shook her head. 'They're all hooded. Put me ashore and I'll look.'

It was the obvious thing to do. She was the one most likely

to jump without slipping, the one who'd get back if she needed to. It had always been her. He nodded and clambered back.

She felt the boat turn and stall as the rowers waited for the wave to take them in. When it came, she readied herself, muttering the usual prayer. It would take all the rowers' strength to pull the boat out at the last moment, all hers to jump.

They swept in on a bigger wave than she'd expected. The rocks came at her too fast and she jumped too late. Her hands met rock but they couldn't take hold. She was sucked away in the retreating wave, her leg scraping something sharp below. She found herself angry. *Have I forgotten how to do this?*

She rose on a wave and glanced behind to where the boat should be, but it was carried too far away. Another wave was coming. She'd try again.

She made a plane of herself to surf the wave, head down, arms stretched out to take hold. *Now!* She rode in over the rocks that lurked below, only straightening at the last moment.

*There.* She'd got a foothold but not yet a handhold. Her fingers scraped stone to find one, but her balance was off. She was falling back into the sea. She closed her eyes and took a breath.

Then, just as she was about to go under, a hand came out of the darkness and took her wrist. Suddenly she was in mid-air. She'd been lifted clean out of the sea and over the rocks.

She let out her breath and opened her eyes. A tall man was crouching over her in the driving rain, nodding, pleased. He had a moustache made yellow from smoking.

She spent most of the journey back cursing herself for getting captured by the same man twice. At least this time she knew what he wanted. She'd not do it, no matter what was offered.

They rowed for a long time, hugging the shoreline as close as was safe, nothing breaking the silence but grunts and wind and rain. They rounded a headland and came into a sheltered bay where the storm couldn't reach. The wind dropped, the waves fell and the rowers slowed their rhythm as a big ship loomed out of the darkness. It had no lights, not even a stern lantern, and no sound came from it. They came alongside a ladder and she climbed up. Two sailors lifted her silently onto the deck and escorted her to a cabin. Not a word had been spoken by anyone since she'd been snatched from the sea.

The cabin was lit by a solitary candelabra hung from a beam but its windows were shuttered tight to let no light escape. It was a grand affair with a dining table, tall chairs and a large cot suspended on gold ropes in the corner. Next to the bed was a copper bath with a pail beside it. Spread out on the table were clothes for a woman of her size.

She looked round at it all: the comfort available to her if she complied. Where was the place for when she didn't? It would be deep in the hold where the darkness was so complete that you couldn't see the rats when they bit you. She'd seen such places in the wrecks. She closed her eyes and hugged her wet arms. She shivered. *Be strong.*

There was a knock on the door. She turned and went over to it, knowing who it would be. She opened it. Colonel Sève was standing there, looking surprised.

'You don't like my clothes?' he asked, removing his cloak, shaking the rain from it and stepping in. 'Don't they fit?'

She walked back into the cabin and sat down at the table as he shut the door behind him.

'I won't wear them,' she said, 'any more than I will tell you where to find the gold. It's too deep, anyway.'

He came over and took an apple from the bowl. 'That's a pity,' he said, biting into the apple, examining it as he ate, turning it in the candlelight. 'But I think you will.'

She had joined her hands on the table to stop them from shaking. He was standing behind her, so close that she could smell his mix of wet clothes and old tobacco. He put his cold hand on her shoulder and she shivered.

He bent down. 'Have you any idea how famous you are, Hara?' he asked. 'Just like Byron.'

What was he talking about?

'In Paris,' he continued, 'they queue all day for a glimpse of you. I'm told people camp all night in the street, just to greet you in the morning.' He nodded. '*Hellas*, they call you.'

She glanced at him. Was he mad?

'In fact,' he said, straightening, 'I feel quite honoured to have you on board my ship. Which is why I gave you nice clothes, yet you spurn them.'

The grip on her shoulder had hardened. She felt his nails dig deep into her skin. She closed her eyes and bit her lip against the pain.

'A famous artist has used you as his inspiration for a painting that is transfixing the world. Did you not know this?'

She shook her head. His nails were going deeper but she'd not cry out.

A big swell came and his hand left to stop the fruitbowl sliding from the table. She felt blood on her shoulder.

He moved to the other side and sat down. He examined his nails, flicking away what might have been skin. He took out a kerchief and wiped the blood from his fingers, one by one. He looked up. 'I have asked Prince Tzanis about it,' he said. 'He imagines that the painter somehow saw his sketch of you.'

She reeled. For a moment she couldn't speak. She looked up. 'You . . . you've seen him?'

'Of course. Sometimes every day. He is my prisoner.'

She shook her head. She felt weak with longing for it to be true, but this man told so many lies. 'I don't believe you.'

'No?' He put a hand into his coat. 'Where is it? Ah yes.' He took out a piece of paper and unfolded it on the table, smoothing it with his palm. It was sketch of himself, unmistakably by Tzanis. 'A good likeness, don't you think?'

She stared at it. She felt giddy, breathless with joy. She picked up the sketch and gazed at it, running her fingers over the pencil lines, unable to stop herself. 'Where is he?' she whispered.

'I have him in Tripoli,' he said. 'He must be very bored, I'm afraid, which is why he finally agreed to draw me.'

Then it came to her. *Of course.* She looked up from the sketch, sickness pitting her stomach, hating this brutal, pitiless man. 'And you will kill him if I don't show you where the gold is.'

'Precisely.' He smiled. 'I will kill him and then I will kill you, the face of Greece.'

# CHAPTER TWENTY-SEVEN

## NAFPLIO

The *Karteria* had steamed into the bay of Nafplio like an auspicious comet, passing the islands of Hydra and Spetses, squabbling parents of the Greek navy. The ships in their harbours seemed suddenly obsolete.

It was a miracle that she steamed at all. The journey from Paris had been difficult. The giant paddles had compromised the ship's seaworthiness and crossing the Bay of Biscay had been a nightmare. They'd run out of coal and the wood they carried hadn't burned hot enough.

'We need coal,' Hastings had said as he and Howe sat over another game of chess. 'We'll have to put in at Malta.'

For Howe, playing chess with Hastings was what he'd come to rely on. In the early stages, Manto had stayed close to him, grateful for his strength. But as they drew closer to Greece, she seemed to change. Her warmth turned to civility and she no longer sought his comfort as she had that night.

At Malta, the admiral of the Mediterranean fleet gave them coal, and information too.

'I'm being replaced,' he said. 'Vice Admiral Sir Edward

Codrington is to take over the fleet next spring. He had the *Orion* at Trafalgar.'

Manto seemed unsurprised by the news. Later, over dinner, she told them why. 'I have been lobbying for him in London. He's exactly the man we want. He loves fighting, and there's not one atom of diplomacy in all his body. If ever there's to be a treaty, he's the one we want interpreting it.'

After Malta, Howe found her ever more remote, and more eccentric too. She changed into seaman's breeches and a smock and got Hastings to teach her the workings of the ship. She made herself one of the crew.

'They seem to like her,' said Hastings as they watched her on her knees, scrubbing a tunic. 'She even washes their clothes. Did you ever expect to see such a thing?'

Howe stayed silent. He'd remembered something from the hospital at Nafplio: how she'd taken on only the most menial tasks. She'd done it to merge into someone else who might do such things. He was starting to realise that it was happening again. Whether alive or dead, Hara was the missing part of her, and the missing part of Greece. She was its remembered essence.

*Hellas.*

And that left him outside, really.

She changed out of her smock as they came into Nafplio. Beneath the bunting and pennants, she stood between them at the rail as they watched the harbour come into view, crowded with every citizen of the town. They passed the Bourtzi fortress and answered its salute with one of their own. They swept past the mole and performed a pirouette beneath a circle of black smoke. The shore erupted in cheers.

First up the gangplank was Mavrocordatos, small and

bespectacled and sweating as he shook their hands. Behind came Kolokotronis and others of the government, unusually united in their eagerness to see the ship. The *Karteria* was the only evidence so far of the navy bought by the second English loan.

'The rest of the ships are on their way under Lord Cochrane,' explained Mavrocordatos, as they set off on a tour of the bay. 'We've hired him to win the war for us.'

'Expensively,' said Manto. 'I hope he's not too late.'

The minister mopped his brow. 'Ibrahim has been weakened by the Mani disaster. He's waiting for a new fleet from Alexandria. We need to turn the tide before it gets here.'

'Turn the tide where?' asked Hastings, who'd overheard.

'The Acropolis. It's still under siege. That would recapture the world's attention.' Mavrocordatos glanced at Manto. 'As happened in Paris, I hear.'

Howe watched her steel herself to ask the question. It came almost timidly. 'Is there news of her?'

The minister nodded. 'Why, yes. She's back in the Mani. With Petrobey.'

Manto closed her eyes and put her hand out to the rail, gripping it, her knuckles white. Her eyes were pure happiness when she opened them again.

'Then we must go there,' she said, 'today.'

'First we must take on coal,' said Hastings, 'and provisions. We're down to our last biscuit.'

'And there is someone in Nafplio who wants to meet you,' said Mavrocordatos. 'A messenger from Russia.'

The messenger had come from Princess Lieven. Like Mustafa, he'd memorised his message to stop it falling into the wrong hands. He stood facing them in the hall of Manto's house, dripping because Nafplio was under deluge. Manto was still smiling.

He spoke in French. 'The Princess asks me to tell you this. The Tzar has received the news from France. He accepts that the French and British now mean to intervene in Greece's affairs and that Russia may have to join them.' He paused. 'But the Princess believes he still plays for time, and time is not what the Greeks have.'

Manto frowned. 'So what does the Princess believe is needed to move the Tzar into signing the treaty?'

The messenger must be trusted, for he knew the answer to this. 'Something that lies at the bottom of the sea off the Mani,' he said quietly. 'Something that would prove an embarrassment to his Imperial Majesty, were it to be brought up.'

This time the *Karteria* sailed, rather than steamed, out of Nafplio. The point had been made to Ibrahim's spies and coal was too precious to waste.

Once past Spetses, they sped down the coast of the Peloponnese with everything spread, pausing briefly at Monemvasia to raise cheers from the battlements. They rounded Cape Maleas and picked up a brisk *garbino* that drove them due west to Cape Tainaron. They rounded it and turned north for Tsimova.

With all the sails up and nothing to do, Howe leant over the rail to watch the landscape go by. Above the razor peaks of the Taygetos, black clouds were gathering and all below cowered in their shadow. It was an iron-clad land of terraces and low walls climbing as far as there was soil to cultivate. He could just see villages among the foothills, little clusters of towers as bleak as the rocks they stood on. This was a place where man existed at nature's pleasure.

He felt someone arrive beside him. Manto took hold of his arm.

He looked at her. 'That is the first time you've touched me in weeks,' he said.

She held her hair to her temple. 'Really? I'm sorry.'

'Are we to be just friends?'

She said nothing for a while, seemingly absorbed by the view. At last she said: 'We are reaching the final scene of this tragedy, and everyone is crowding the stage to say their part.' She turned to him. 'Perhaps friendship better suits the moment.'

They were silent for a while.

He turned to her. 'He may not give her up, you realise.'

She looked at him as if the thought hadn't occurred to her. 'Why not?'

'He is her father. And you've never professed to trust him much.'

She frowned. 'Well, he'll have to.'

At last they came into the port of Limeni where Petrobey had welcomed Hara. They steamed into a harbour alive with shipping.

Petrobey was waiting on the quay, this time surrounded by the whole population, who'd come out to see the phenomenon. There was no cheering, no waving, just silence as the ship came in. This was the Mani after all. Manto went below to change into her most alluring dress. Petrobey would be charmed before he was threatened.

They made a turn before dropping anchor. 'So that he sees all our guns,' explained Hastings.

Petrobey needed no threat. He was all helpfulness. There was a spoonful of quince jam, and a coffee or thimbleful of ouzo as they entered his day room. He took the tray round himself.

But there was no Hara.

'She went home,' he explained with a shrug, putting the tray down. 'She went back to where she'd been raised. Before I claimed her.' He raised his ouzo. 'Long life.'

Manto sipped hers. She'd been very quiet. 'Where is her home?' she asked.

'Vatheia. Right down at the bottom. Where Prince Tzanis was shipwrecked.' He threw his head back for the ouzo, wiping his vast moustache with the back of his hand. 'Where they say the mouth of hell is.'

'We will go there.'

'Of course,' he smiled. 'But you'll find her changed. She's taken up wrecking again, I'm told.'

Howe watched Manto absorb this news. Her calm seemed precarious. 'But you're her father,' she said. 'You could stop her. It's dangerous.'

He shrugged again. 'Hara is Hara. She'll do what she wants.' He looked at her. 'But you're right about the danger. She nearly lost her life recently.'

Manto frowned. 'How so?'

'She went out with her old brothers to find a wreck that wasn't there. She got caught on some rocks and they thought they'd lost her. She was missing for two days.'

'Well, she will be coming back with us.'

He shrugged. 'Perhaps.' He took another glass of ouzo and emptied it. 'But only after she has brought up the gold. We need to talk about that.'

Which they did. At length. Petrobey was straightforward: he had rescued Hara from Missolonghi and reneged on his agreement with Sève, which had provoked an invasion of the Mani. And he'd kept their secret. He was owed something.

Just after midnight, they toasted their agreement in more ouzo. Then the three of them went back to the ship, where they'd sleep more easily than in Petrobey's home.

They left early the next morning with the first fishermen. This time no one watched, the Maniots preferring only brief sightings of the outside world. The wind was still with them and they'd rounded the cape by midday and anchored in Porto Kayo by mid-afternoon. There was no one there to greet them.

'Perhaps she didn't know when we were coming,' said Manto, looking out from the rail. She'd returned to her smock and trousers as Howe had expected her to.

They hired mules and rode the track to Vatheia, sailors walking behind with muskets, looking to left and right. They were strangers in this land.

Vatheia seemed empty at first. They left the mules and walked into the narrow streets without seeing a soul. Nor did they hear anything, except the low moan of the wind between the towers. It was a place of ghosts.

They came into a little square with a church on one side and a wretched tavern on the other, battered chairs outside. The houses between were shuttered and grass grew between their tiles.

'Hello?' called Hastings through cupped hand, turning to address all corners of the square. 'Is anyone here?'

A door opened and a small figure came out. She was dressed in a shawl that covered her head and shoulders. She looked at the ground.

Manto stepped forward. 'Hara?'

She didn't look up, just raised a hand. 'Don't come any closer, please. I'm not well.'

249

Manto stayed where she was. She watched her for a while, very still. 'Do you know why we're here?' she asked.

'To get the gold.'

Manto stared at her. Then she looked around. 'Where is everyone?'

'Gone to Porto Kayo,' said Hara, 'to look at your ship.'

'But we didn't pass anyone on the road.'

'They took a different one.'

Hastings went to stand beside Manto. 'Will you return to the ship with us?' he asked.

She nodded, keeping her head low. 'We should go now.'

She drew the shawl tight around her and walked past them to the street without looking up. They watched her in silence.

Hastings glanced at the other two, then shrugged. He went after her.

Howe came up to stand beside Manto. 'What's wrong, do you think?'

Manto was still staring after her. 'You heard. She's ill.'

Howe shook his head. 'I don't think so.'

Manto glanced at him. 'Well, Petrobey said she'd changed,' she said quietly. She went after them. Howe looked round the square again, then followed.

The road back was equally deserted. They rode their mules in silence, while Hara walked behind with the sailors, head always down. Manto kept glancing behind but she never looked up.

They reached Porto Kayo and found it almost deserted. The *Karteria*'s audience had come and gone, leaving only fishermen sat over their nets, indifferent to the wonder in their bay. Hastings led them down to the quay where a boat was waiting to take them over to the ship.

Hara didn't speak or even look at them as they were rowed

over. Only when they reached the deck did she say something. 'We should leave straight away, before the weather turns. My brothers will join us when we get there. I am too ill to dive, but they can.' She glanced quickly at Hastings. 'Can I have a cabin? I'd like to sleep.'

'Of course.' Hastings led her to his own, stopping at the opened door. 'I'll wake you when we need you.'

Howe watched her close the door behind her. He turned to Manto, who was staring at the door. 'Something isn't right,' he said.

Hastings came back to join them. He looked where they looked. 'She doesn't want to come back with us, but is afraid to say,' he said quietly. 'That's what it is.'

Manto said nothing.

Hastings gave his orders and the crew went about their duties, raising the anchor and dropping enough sail to get underway. They would go back around the cape before needing to wake Hara, then she'd direct them to where they needed to dive. He took Howe over to a chest and opened it. Inside was a brass helmet with a window in it lying on top of a folded canvas garment.

'A diving suit,' he said, lifting the helmet for Howe to look at. 'We'll use steam-powered bellows to drive air down this tube.' He picked up something long with his finger. 'And we use this one for exhaling. The wire is for signalling to the surface.'

'Who will be in it?' asked Howe, taking the helmet and turning it. He could see his face in the brass.

'I'll send one of the brothers down since they're coming to help. After all, they know these waters. All he has to do is fix ropes to the casket's handles. Then we can pull it up.'

It took four hours to round the Cape and only then did

Hastings wake Hara. She came on deck wearing the same shawl and stood at the wheel, telling him where to go. When they got there, he brought them into the wind and dropped the sails and the ship bucked and rolled in the choppy sea. Hara looked out towards the land.

'It's too rough to dive,' said Hastings. 'We should wait.'

'No,' she said. 'We should do it now.'

Manto went to stand next to them. She glanced at Hara. 'Why all the hurry?' she asked quietly.

Hara looked away. Long strands of hair whipped around her like loose threads. 'Because a storm is on its way.' A rogue wave threw spray over the side and she raised her hands to wipe her eyes. 'My brothers will get it if you can keep the ship steady.'

Manto looked back to Hastings. He shrugged and glanced around the sea. 'Under steam, I suppose we might, yes.'

Hara straightened. 'They're coming.'

They all looked out to see a boat rounding the headland. It was a wrecker's boat: long and low and sleek and built for speed. It came and went in the big sea.

Manto stared at it, frowning. 'Why exactly do we need your brothers, Hara?' she asked.

Hara lifted her shawl to her eyes. 'I told you,' she said through the cloth. 'It's deep and will be difficult with these waves. My brothers are used to it.'

Manto didn't reply. She continued watching the boat, which was making good progress through the waves. They could see the rowers now, bent over their oars, all hooded against the spray. They heard a shout.

'We should put the ladder down,' said Hastings. 'I'll do it.'

He walked off and they waited in silence. Manto was very still, watching the boat approach. She shook her head slowly. 'I don't like this.' She turned to Hara and took her arm. She forced her round. 'Why won't you look at us, Hara?' she asked softly.

The shawl opened and a pistol appeared, pointing to Manto's heart. Hara said: 'I'm sorry.'

Howe saw the dread in her eyes, the shaking arm, the knuckles white around the pommel. He stayed where he was.

Further along the ship, Hastings was shouting orders to the crew. There was the sound of a rope ladder knocking against wood as it was lowered.

Manto hadn't moved any part of her body below her head which she was slowly shaking. 'Why?' she whispered. '*Why?*'

'Because if I don't, Sève will kill him.'

'He's got Tzanis?'

Hara nodded. She raised her other hand to her eyes. She was crying softly. 'I'm sorry.'

'Do you know what this will mean?' asked Howe quietly. 'The gold will go to Alexandria and another fleet will come. With settlers this time.' He paused. 'He means to kill everyone, Hara. *Everyone.*'

'Stop!' she hissed. 'I know that.'

They heard the sounds of boots landing on the deck. Howe glanced across to see three hooded men being helped over the side. Hastings' back was turned to them. The tallest walked over and punched him hard. He fell to his knees and a barrel was put to his head.

Colonel Sève pulled back his hood and looked round. 'Stay where you are.' He turned to his men. 'Take the guns.' He saw Hara and beckoned. 'Bring them over here.'

Manto's eyes hadn't left Hara. There was more pain in them than Howe had ever seen. She hadn't moved.

Hara lowered her pistol and turned away. 'Go. Please.'

'Hara . . .'

*'Go!'*

Howe took Manto's arm and led her gently over to where Colonel Sève stood surrounded by his men. The Frenchman crouched down so that he was facing the kneeling Hastings. He put his barrel below his chin and lifted it. Their faces were very close.

'Now, Captain Hastings,' he said. 'Let us get this gold up.'

# CHAPTER TWENTY-EIGHT

## THE KARTERIA

The *Karteria* had been holed by a single shot, but it was a hole big enough to put your head through. Down below, Manto sat at an angle, an inkstand lying up-ended at her feet, spreading black across the teak. Only the lithograph was upright in her lap, held fast by her hands. Hara's face looked up at her from the ruins of Missolonghi, her hands open in supplication. *Help us.* It was a good copy of Delacroix's masterpiece.

She looked around the cabin. There were drawings of the ship pinned to every inch of its panelled walls. Her eyes came to rest on the one she'd always liked best: a sketch of the hull divided into watertight compartments. She looked out of the window. *Really?*

It was an hour ago that Colonel Sève had left on his ship, standing next to Hara at the stern to watch them sink. It wasn't only the gold he'd taken, but their masts and coal as well. He'd even taken the diving suit.

The door opened. Howe stood there holding onto the frame. 'We need your help,' he said.

She lowered the picture and looked at him. He was handsome,

this American, brave too. If there were more like him, America would become the greatest nation on earth. 'Are we taking to the boats?'

'Not if we can get moving.'

'But Colonel Sève took our masts and our coal.'

'Hastings says we can use wood.' He looked around the cabin. 'Every bit of furniture . . . we need it all for the furnace.' The ship gave another lurch. He looked out of the window. 'And a storm's getting up.'

'Well, she didn't lie about that, at least.'

Howe half-turned, then stopped. 'Will you ever be able to forgive her?'

She looked down at the picture. 'Will she ever forgive her-self?' she asked quietly. She put it to one side and rose. She glanced at the table. 'Shall we start with this?'

By the time they'd reduced it to kindling, the storm had risen to a pummelling fury. They carried the wood to the engine room where they found Hastings stripped to the waist, his face blackened by soot. He'd lit the furnace and had a pile of fuel beside him, some of it gilded. They could hear men shouting nearby.

'They're bailing!' Hastings shouted as they put down their piles. 'But once we get the engine going, we can turn on the pumps!'

Howe glanced at the wood. 'Is there enough to reach shore?'

Captain Hastings shook his head. 'We're not going to the shore,' he yelled. 'We're going to catch that ship and get our gold back.'

The storm was as violent as Hara had promised, but the wind helped the *Karteria* on her way. The ship rose and fell, carried by waves twice as tall as the funnel. More than once, they lifted her and almost put her on her side.

As night fell, a human chain formed from the engine room up to the stern cabins where bunks, washstands – anything that might burn – were being smashed into pieces. Manto, stripped to her petticoats, stood in the corridor between two marines, her arms torn and bleeding as she passed the wood. At one point Hastings stopped in front of her.

'Will we survive this?' she asked.

He glanced to left and right. 'Water's getting into the engine room,' he whispered. 'If it gets any higher, it'll put out the furnace.'

The wind reached its peak just after midnight when the world felt it might end. She heard the furnace hissing as water splashed into it. The men in the line heard it too. There was praying now among the grunts.

But then, just as the first hint of dawn came out of a blasted sky, the storm left as suddenly as it had come. The wind dropped and the sea fell enough for the ship's paddles to stay underwater. Hastings told Manto to go and sleep.

She awoke on the floor of his cabin beneath a coat that someone must have put over her. The ship had stopped and the world was still. She rose and went out to find thick fog had hidden most of it, only the furnace glowing through the murk. The crew were moving around like ghosts, some carrying cannon balls. She found Hastings and Howe on the upper deck, leaning against the only rail remaining.

Hastings raised a finger to his lips. 'Shhh.' He looked tired and dishevelled but was dressed in his uniform and had his hat on his head. He made room for her beside him. 'She's out there, I know it.'

'Where are we?' she asked.

'The very same question I was asking,' said Howe. 'He says we're somewhere on the way to Alexandria.'

'We held our course?'

Hastings shrugged. 'Apparently.'

She looked out. The fog was as dense as anything she'd seen. There were no sounds beyond the shouts of look-outs and some muffled banging below. 'Why have the paddles stopped?' she asked.

'The boiler again,' he said. 'It's being repaired.'

A midshipman waved to them. They went over to where he peered into the gloom.

'Did you see something?'

'I'm not sure, sir. I thought . . .'

Hastings turned to an officer. 'Load the guns. Red hot shells.' He tilted his head and closed his eyes. He was listening.

A flash came out of the gloom, then a muffled bang.

'Down!' he yelled, pulling Manto and Howe to the deck as a cannon ball sailed over. He sprang to his feet. *'Battle stations!'* He ran behind the huge 68-pounder and bent forwards over its barrel, his hands on his knees. He straightened and tapped the man beside him on the shoulder. 'If you please Mr Orr.'

The cannon roared and the boat shook from bow to stern. There were screams from across the water and the world turned orange.

'She's on fire,' said Hastings. He called to the poop deck. 'Get us closer if you please, Mr Greville.'

They edged their way towards where the orange was brightest. They could hear the crackle of burning wood. The fog thinned and the frigate lay before them in flames. There was a flag running up its mainmast. She was surrendering.

'Man the pumps, bring out the hoses!' shouted Hastings. 'We need her afloat!' The paddles stopped as steam was diverted. Soon water was spraying over the frigate's fore-deck.

'Let go the boats!'

In minutes the longboats were in the sea with crews ready to row. Hastings put on his hat and straightened it.

'I'm coming with you,' said Manto.

He began to shake his head, but she came up to him.

'Don't ever talk to me again of danger,' she said softly.

He stared at her for a moment, then nodded. They went over to the ladder and climbed over the side. Three of the boats were already out at sea, pulling men out of the water. They boarded theirs and went straight for the frigate. The fog was lifting.

They were helped on board, one by one, Manto behind Hastings. She straightened and looked around the steaming deck. It was strewn with dead bodies, mostly burnt, but there was no sign of Sève or any other Frenchman.

An Egyptian officer approached them. He seemed still in shock. He offered his sword and bowed. 'I have no alternative but to surrender. Your gun killed half my crew.'

Hastings took the sword. 'Where is Colonel Sève?'

'The Frenchmen all left as we passed Kithira. They were never coming all the way to Alexandria.'

A loud bang came from the *Karteria*. The hoses had stopped. A final burp of smoke issued from the funnel, then no more.

The Egyptian captain looked back. 'How will you take us back?'

'You will,' said Hastings. He looked up to the sky. 'We just need some wind.'

*

They got their wind and came into Nafplio on the Egyptian frigate, the *Karteria* in tow. They disembarked and made straight for Manto's house where new servants greeted them and showed them to food. They collapsed into chairs and sat there for a long time in silence, staring into the fire.

Manto was the first to speak. 'Where will he have taken her?'

'Probably Tripoli,' said Hastings. 'It's where he's based.'

'We must find her.'

'But will she want to be found?' he asked. 'And what do we do if we find her? She is, after all, a traitor.'

Manto shook her head . 'No, she is one of us. She was forced to do what she did.' She looked hard at him. 'And we got the gold back, didn't we?' She looked down at her hands. 'No one must know what she's done. Can you trust your crew?'

Hastings nodded. 'Certainly. I'll speak to them. But I don't think we can use the *Karteria* to search for her. As soon as we're seaworthy, Mavrocordatos will want us to go to Athens. And this time, you're not coming.'

She looked down at the picture in her lap, the only thing she'd brought from the *Karteria*. 'Nor will I want to. I'll stay here and look for her.'

# CHAPTER TWENTY-NINE

## TRIPOLI

In Tripoli, the barracks and parade grounds were emptier than when Tzanis had last seen them, the military hospital fuller. What remained of Ibrahim Pasha's army was being decimated by disease. It needed reinforcements badly.

Meanwhile, it confined itself to the easier business of murder and enslavement. More villages were burned, more people starved. More were led away as slaves.

Tzanis was housed in a small room without windows. He had a straw mattress, candle, bucket and nothing else. Once a day, stale bread and water were passed though a hatch in the door in exchange for the bucket. He'd seen nobody except Colonel Sève who he'd been forced to sketch.

'To show her you're alive,' the Colonel had explained, 'to give her hope, should we ever meet. Surely you'd want that?'

*Should we ever meet.* He'd assumed from that remark that Sève had some expectation of doing so, that Hara had somehow survived Missolonghi. But if so, what would she be now? A slave? *Whose slave?*

Some nights he woke screaming so loud that the guards had

to bang on the door. Memories came up through his dreams that he'd managed to banish by day: running across open ground with a thousand others, a flare going up to reveal rows of cavalry with their lances levelled, waiting to charge, waiting to ride them down.

*Meyer.*

He'd last seen his friend crouched over his wife and child, trying to shield them from the lancer riding towards them. He'd seen him lifted as the lance-point came through his shirt. He'd seen him pitch forward into the sand.

*A newspaper man from Lausanne.*

The fault lay with him, of that he was certain. He'd suggested the breakout. Meyer's death, his family's, everyone's . . . *all his fault.* It was just as Sève had said. No torture that he could devise would come close to such pain.

He now spent his days lying on the mattress, bathed in sweat, looking up at the ceiling. It could be morning or night, he had no idea. His life had become timeless and unending and he wanted so badly for it to end. *No more, please.*

Which was how Colonel Sève found him early one morning when the first chill of autumn reached into the cell. He entered and crouched down beside the bed, his face only inches away.

'I wanted to bring the news myself,' he whispered into his ear. 'Thanks to Hara, and you, of course, the gold is now on its way to Alexandria. As soon as it arrives, a new fleet will set sail to finally put an end to this miserable revolution.' He paused. 'I wanted to thank you in person.'

Then Sève sat back against the wall and told him everything that had happened. 'They're all dead,' he said. 'Manto, Hastings, the American. I saw them sink. And the gold is where it should be.' He dipped his head. 'And it's all thanks to you.' He pushed himself up from the wall. 'And with the gold, I don't need you any more. You'll die here.'

Tzanis didn't care where he died. There was only one thing he cared about. 'What have you done with her?'

Sève rose and went over to the door. He turned. 'Ah, that's the best part,' he said. 'I could have killed her, but I thought of something much better: setting her free. Just think of it – she'll be forced to wander the earth with the memory of what she's done always with her. Like Eve.' He laughed. 'And the irony is that she was meant to be the saviour of Greece.'

Hara left the village as the air was turning cold. The couple she'd stayed with had given her furs and a sack full of dried acorns and maize, threatening her with death if she refused it. They'd been kind to her, but then they didn't know what she'd done.

She had no idea where to go. Everywhere would be the same: full of starving people waiting for soldiers from Egypt to put them out of their misery. How long could she bear to take their charity?

At first, she went down to the plain, but she found the villages abandoned, only dogs left to pull meat from corpses, snapping at birds that came too near. In one she found piles of skulls, smallest at the top, and was seized with sudden rage, kicking and kicking until their pieces were scattered across the ground. Then she knelt and cried until she could cry no more.

When she found humans, she ran from them. They crept out from the olive groves onto the road: skeletons with skins on their backs and madness in their eyes. They pretended to be friends and called out to her but she saw their hunger and fled.

She went back into the mountains, climbing through thick forest towards a peak hidden by clouds. She found a stream that skipped through mossy rocks and stood in it with her spear, numb to the thighs, until she'd snatched four fish. She climbed up to a ledge just below the summit. That night, she dug a hole and lit a fire and cooked her fish.

She was finishing her third when she heard the fall of scree in the darkness. She'd dug deep enough for her fire not to be seen, so it must have been the smell. She picked up her spear and rose. She could hear breathing.

'Who's out there?'

A child emerged, her eyes fixed on the single fish that still hissed over the fire. Another came to stand beside her. Suddenly she thought of Kanta.

She lowered her spear. 'Would you like it?'

She went over to the fire and pulled the fish off and put it on a stone in front of the children. 'Wait until it cools.'

But the girls couldn't wait. They ripped it apart and blew on it and ate it in three mouthfuls.

A voice came from behind. 'Is there more?'

A woman emerged, not much older than Hara but bent with suffering. There were others behind her.

Hara reached down into her hole and brought out the sack. 'Just acorns now,' she said, opening and offering it. 'Who are you?'

They were three women. They came forward and sat on the ruins, scooping acorns from the sack and cramming them into their mouths with both hands. One of them glanced up. 'We came up here to escape the men.' She spat out a husk. 'They're eating people now.'

Hara shivered. *No.*

'It's true,' said another. 'Nowhere is safe.' She looked around into the night. 'Are you alone here?'

She nodded.

'We could come and join you. We have a musket.'

That was how it started: five of them at first, then ten, then twenty and more, all women and children, all desperate and scared and seeking the comfort of numbers. When the first snows came to the mountain top, they moved back down into the trees where the children could play, their voices drowned out by the rushing streams. They built huts for themselves and Hara taught them how to hunt. But she knew they'd not survive the winter there and would have to move on.

She led them further east, towards Corinth and the Isthmus where they'd be closer to what Nafplio still claimed to rule, to the sea where they'd find more fish. They moved through the mountains, avoiding the plain, often travelling through deep snow that glowed by the light of the moon. Sometimes she imagined herself as Manto, leading her exodus through the hills of Chios.

At length they came to the Isthmus and the ruins of an ancient wall that had once straddled it. They decided to stay there, to use its stones to build a new camp. There were more than fifty of them now, all women and children. They had five muskets between them, and two mules.

They built shelters for themselves but there was little to hunt in that winter landscape. So Hara took one of the mules and rode down to the coast to find fish. She took blankets and a musket and went alone. She wanted to think.

It was evening when she came down to where the sea gathered into a bay with a beach and a little church among the grasses behind. She dismounted and tied up the mule and tried the church door and found it open. She walked in to thick dust and a roof half open to a violet sky. She spread out a blanket and lay down on it, keeping her musket by her side, and looked up at the first stars. Despite the cold, she was soon asleep.

She awoke to whispers. She sat up very slowly and brought the musket into her lap. She could see the flicker of torches through the side window, moving round towards the entrance. She strained to listen. The voices were male.

Very slowly, she pointed the musket at the door and pulled back the lock. The torchlight disappeared, then came back to rim its frame. She heard more whispering, then the creak of old wood as the door was pushed open. She lifted the barrel into the aim and breathed in. *Is this how it ends?*

But the voice was English, and it was young. 'Don't shoot.'

A torch appeared, then the face of a boy. He had a large hat on his head: blue with gold trim like Captain Hastings had sometimes worn. He looked frightened but resolute.

'Don't shoot,' he said again, stepping into the church, his sword pointed. 'Lower your gun.'

'Lower your sword first,' said Hara, not moving. Two men had entered behind the boy. They wore red jackets with tall black hats with cockades and held muskets to their shoulders. The boy signalled and they lowered them.

'You speak English,' he said, slowly sheathing his sword. 'Who are you?'

Hara rose and breathed out slowly, still feeling her heart against her ribs. Hastings had told her that he'd once been one of these: a *midshipman*, a boy pretending to be a man. No wonder he was scared.

'Where is your ship?' she asked.

He glanced around the church, then up at the stars. He reminded her so much of Hastings, she wanted to touch him.

'We are anchored in the next bay. HMS *Cambrian*. We saw you come down.'

'And why should that be strange?'

'A woman,' he said awkwardly, looking down, 'alone in this country. It's not safe.'

She almost laughed but he was serious, this English boy. Just like Captain Hastings was serious. She smiled for the first time in weeks.

'Can you take me to your ship?' she asked. 'I'd like to talk to your captain.'

In Nafplio, Hara had heard talk of the *Cambrian*. She was a 40-gun frigate that had proved herself a friend to the Greeks, using her quiet, anchored presence to shift events to their advantage more than once. She'd heard of her captain too: Gawen Hamilton: a man with a reputation for even-handedness. He'd taken Turks on board after the fall of Nafplio to prevent them being massacred.

She'd almost forgotten God, but it did seem to her that He might have sent Captain Hamilton to her that night.

But Hamilton greeted her warily. 'Madam,' he said, closing the cabin door. Inside, was a wood-burner that crackled in the corner and put dancers on the wood panelling. He looked her up and down with curiosity. 'We have hot water. You may use my cabin to bathe and I will remove myself.'

She shook her head. 'Perhaps later, thank you.' She glanced around. The room was warm and ordered and smelt of wax. 'First I would like to know how things stand,' she said, looking back, 'with the war.'

He gestured for her to sit, then placed himself across from her. 'May I know your name?'

She'd already decided to lie. This man would know Manto and Hastings and they must never know where she was.

'I am called Eleni,' she said. 'I escaped from Kalamata when the Egyptians burnt down the town. I have brought women and children to a place near here. They are cold and starving. Can you help?'

The captain was looking at her closely. 'How can I help?'

'I need food, blankets – tents if you have them. But some news first: has the Egyptian fleet arrived?'

Hamilton leant back in his chair and put his hands behind his head. He was more handsome than Hastings, less formal too. 'From Alexandria?' he asked. 'Not yet, but it will. They say it's bringing colonists.'

Her stomach lurched. She'd hoped for some miracle. 'And Ibrahim Pasha?'

Hamilton shook his head. 'He is waiting for it and meanwhile still burning everything that stands.'

'And you cannot stop him?'

'Great Britain is neutral,' he said quietly. 'We do not take sides.'

'Yet you yourself have. In the past.'

He stared at her for a while. Then he leant forward. 'Very well, I'll tell you what I know,' he said. 'There is a protocol agreed between Great Britain, France and Russia. If it ever gets signed as a treaty, it will allow the Great Powers to intervene. But Russia is delaying and we are running out of time.'

She bathed and spent the night on the *Cambrian*, sleeping in sheets with the good smell of clean skin around her. She slept deeply and well.

In the morning, she found breakfast on the table and clothes laid out for her, more for warmth than style. She ate and dressed and found Captain Hamilton out on deck leaning over the rail with a telescope to his eye. The young midshipman was by his side.

'No sign of any klephts,' he said, looking round, 'but you'll still need a guard. I am loading the longboat with supplies and Mr Fisher here will accompany you back with some marines.' He dropped his voice. 'Are you sure you want to go? I can easily take you off.'

'I do,' she said. 'But might you come back with some seed?'

He smiled. 'So you mean to build something permanent.' He nodded. 'I'll see what I can manage.'

New Year came and the snows stopped and more arrived at the camp. Word had got round and people flocked to where they might find food and safety. They had to rebuild the walls to include more shelters.

At first, only women, children and the old were admitted – those deemed most innocent of crime. But as spring approached, Hara knew that men would be needed to lay out the fields. So some were allowed in, but only if they brought a mule or plough and left their weapons at the gate.

Hara was strict. People could stay if they worked as hard as their age allowed. There was building to do as well as hunting and growing. She herself became a teacher in the mornings, passing on what she'd learnt to rows of silent children. In the afternoon, she ran the hospital. Afterwards, as the evening settled its calm across the hills, she'd go out to stand among the fields, running her eyes down the long furrows, pregnant with wheat, potatoes, beans and whatever else the *Cambrian* had brought. She felt then a glimmer of the peace she'd felt in the Mani: the peace brought on by forgetting. *By surrender.*

Captain Hamilton was as good as his word. Once a month, he came to the bay with supplies bullied out of Nafplio's merchants or commandeered from foreign ships, though Hara sent others down to meet him. She couldn't risk someone recognising her; no one could know where she was.

When spring turned to summer and the fields began to show some growth, she received a message that the next delivery would be his last. He was being sent on a delicate mission and would be away until the year-end. He'd do what he could to find someone to replace him.

On the day of his last visit, she decided to go down to meet him. She wanted to thank him and find out who else might come in his place, for the harvest was still two months away. But as the party assembled to leave, she was called to the hospital. There was a baby to be delivered. She'd join them as soon as she'd brought it into the world.

It was afternoon when she left the camp on the one horse it owned. She rode fast through hills washed with broom and orchids and butterflies that danced in the breeze like wisps of silk. She saw wild poppies scattered like paint-spill, proof that the land still had blood in its veins. She thought of a place that would be knee-deep in them by now: behind mountains she'd once dreamed of going beyond.

She got her first glimpse of the sea as the sun began its descent over the mountains behind. She wound her way down through a long valley half in shadow and thought of the miracle of human kindness.

Her horse stopped suddenly, its ears horizontal. It was backing away from something. Was it a snake?

'What is it?' she whispered, patting its neck. She dismounted and looked down the path. Nothing. She turned. 'Did you hear something?'

She took a step forwards and strained to listen. *There.* She heard voices around the bend: whispers.

She turned again and rested her hand on her horse's nose, raising a finger to her lips. '*Shhh.*'

Very slowly, she led the horse back up the path until she found a tree to tie it to. Then, crouching low, she crept up the valley side and crawled along its top until she could see what lay beyond the bend.

The light was fading fast but she could see them. Behind every boulder was a man with a gun, waiting for the food to be brought up from the *Cambrian*. It was an ambush.

She rolled onto her back and closed her eyes. There was no other way down to the beach. Captain Hamilton would wait perhaps another hour, but then he'd assume she wasn't coming and her people would return with the food. The massacre would be too quick for the British to intervene. She cursed the klephts for their barbarity.

She rolled onto her front again and watched the path, willing it to stay empty, listening for the jangle of harness. Nothing. The falling night was as still as death: no breeze, no birds. *Nothing.*

For an hour she watched, then another and another. The moon slowly climbed up to join the stars and bathed everything in its soft silver and still the path remained empty. She felt her eyelids grow heavy and her head nod. She was tired from her ride, from bringing new life into this precarious world. She had to stay awake, but it was hard.

She woke suddenly and blinked up at the moon. She'd heard something. She turned over and crawled to where she could see. The klephts had grown restless. She saw one crawl from his rock to another, heard him whisper. She saw him point. Were they giving up?

No, they were too close to success for that. But they needed the cover of night, even one washed by moonlight. She watched them rise one by one and steal quietly down to the path, then along it towards the beach, every musket levelled. She waited a while, then followed them.

It wasn't far. The valley turned twice before the bay opened out before them, a semi-circle of sand rimmed by rocks, the little church behind. On the beach was a pile of boxes with men sitting on them, some with muskets in their laps. There was no sign of the mules.

And there was no ship in the bay.

Captain Hamilton had left, taking his marines with him, and his guns. The food on the beach was a banquet laid out for the klephts to take at their ease, with only a few, ill-armed men to protect it. It was all too easy. *But where were the mules?*

She watched the klephts spread themselves out behind the rocks circling the beach: shadows that moved without noise. She heard a night-call that might be an owl. She waited.

Still the sentries sat on the boxes with their muskets across their knees. *Why weren't they moving?*

Then one of them did. A man appeared from behind the pile of boxes, musket slung from his shoulder. He walked slowly, glancing around him from time to time.

She knew that walk.

# CHAPTER THIRTY

## NAFPLIO

It had taken months to get the *Karteria* ready to sail again after its tow back into Nafplio. Hastings had had to go as far as Hydra and Spetses for parts and while he was at it, had planned improvements. He re-plated the boilers and lifted the furnace. He redesigned the paddles and weighted the keel. Smaller masts were fitted but with bigger sails. Such was the curiosity, the crew had to take turns to stand guard. He and Howe spent every day there.

Meanwhile Manto brought the gold ashore and wrote to Princess Lieven, enclosing a single coin and the signed statement of Sève's Egyptian captain, now in captivity. Her letter went on a ship with a man she trusted to throw it overboard should he be intercepted. She expected her friend to act with caution, but there was no disguising her intent: to blackmail the new Tzar of Russia.

Through the winter nights, she locked her door, posted guards outside and lay awake thinking about what she'd done. Her letter would bring success or assassin. To stiffen her resolve, she would light a candle and bring out the picture of Hara.

There she was: Greece, hands held open amidst the ruins of Missolonghi; a daughter's hands held open to a parent. *Help me.* She'd have given every penny of her fortune, her very life, to help her. But where was she?

She recruited a band of klephts and sent them out to search the Peloponnese. They came back with stories of such horror that she could hardly bear to listen, but nothing more. So she sent them out again. And again.

New Year came and went without celebration. Greece was still not conquered but everyone knew that Ibrahim only waited for reinforcements to finish the task. And they would come soon.

She heard that Captain Hamilton was back in Nafplio and asked him to visit her. But his news was only of some refugee camp.

'It's been set up at the Isthmus,' he said. 'It holds thousands by now. I'm to get food from the merchants here but I'll need money.'

'You'll have all the money you need,' she said, only half-listening. 'Tell me about Athens.'

Hamilton examined his hands. 'I don't care to talk ill of a countryman, but Cochrane listens to no one but himself, Mavrocordatos has paid too much for a charlatan who'd not get a sloop if he still fought for his country. His plan is to relieve the Acropolis which the Turks are besieging,'

'Could you not help in some way?' she asked.

'I am in the service of the British Navy, ma'am,' he said stiffly. 'I do not have the luxury of taking sides, as Cochrane can.'

Eventually, the *Karteria* was ready for war and Manto climbed up to the Palmidi fortress to watch her and the *Cambrian* over the horizon. She was saying goodbye to three friends, sailing off on a plan none of them had faith in.

The disaster, when it came, was worse than even Hamilton's predictions. The Greek army was cut to pieces by the Turkish cavalry on the plain before Athens and the Acropolis surrendered to them. It was the bloodiest day the revolution had yet suffered and now only Nafplio and the Mani remained in rebel hands.

Then came even worse news: the Egyptian fleet had sailed from Alexandria. It hadn't waited for the gold.

Three days later, the *Karteria* limped back with one less mast and hundreds of wounded crowding its decks. Hastings and Howe spent the day getting the men ashore and it was evening by the time they came to Manto.

Hastings was shaking with rage as he threw his hat onto the table. 'It was lunacy,' he said, 'sheer madness. Cochrane is an arrogant fool.'

She listened to a story she'd heard too many times before. Someone had expected the Greeks to behave like a disciplined army on the open plain, but they'd fought as they always fought, so they'd been massacred. The two men's bloodstained clothes told of the horror.

She looked over to Hastings, now slumped in a chair. He looked exhausted and something else. His stare was endless. She went to sit next to him and took his hand in hers. It was the first time she'd done such a thing. 'Was it very terrible?' she asked softly.

He lowered his head and brought his fingers to the bridge of his nose, closing his eyes. For a shocked moment, she wondered if he was crying.

'I'd thought we'd seen the worst of it at Chios,' he said. He took a deep breath. 'This was different, but just as bad.'

She'd often wondered about Hastings and Chios, wondered if the English reserve had simply masked a trauma too deep to express. She rose. 'Well, I'm afraid I have more bad news,' she said. 'The fleet has sailed from Alexandria after all. It's on its way.'

Hastings stared at her. 'But we have the gold!'

She shrugged. 'It seems Ibrahim Pasha didn't wait for it. After all, he's so close to victory.'

They fell into a dismal silence, all looking at the floor.

She heard Howe clear his throat. 'So we need that treaty,' he said quietly. 'Is there any news?'

She turned. 'Captain Hamilton is summoned to the Crimea to meet the Tzar,' she said, 'so perhaps yes. He leaves tomorrow and I will speak to him before he goes.'

'And Hara?'

Manto rose and went over to him. 'None.' She sat down on his arm-rest. 'I've sent out one search party after another. Nothing.' She put her hand on his shoulder. 'Go and bathe, sleep if you can. There are fresh clothes in your room.'

An hour later, Howe was so deeply asleep that he knew nothing of the figure that crept through his window and sat in the chair facing the bed. He was oblivious to the person who watched him in complete silence, chin resting on folded hands, legs stretched out against the pain. He didn't wake up to the first or second whisper of his name. Only a gentle kick brought him back to life.

He stared into the darkness. 'Who are you?'

The figure brought its hands down to the arms of the chair. A breeze moved the curtain and moonlight entered the room.

'Tzanis.'

Howe sat up and leant over to the candle.

'Don't.' The voice was uneven, broken. 'You'll not like what you see.'

He heard a grunt as Tzanis shifted in his seat. Then half of his face emerged from the shadow. Howe had only seen it at the hospital, but this might have belonged to another man. It was cadaverous and there were deep scars on the cheeks and neck. Burns too.

'What has he *done* to you?' he whispered.

'Everything he did to Mustafa.' The voice was exhausted. 'He held me for a while then he set me free, which he knew would be worse. He had the gold so I was no longer a threat.' He leant forward and used his hands to shift his leg. 'He did the same to Hara. Have you found her?'

Howe shook his head. 'Manto has searched everywhere. Nothing.' He saw the head drop. 'What happened after you got away?'

Another cough and a hand came up to wipe something away. 'I came here. I've been in hiding.'

'Hiding? From what?'

Tzanis shifted again in his chair. Sitting was clearly painful. 'I came back to Nafplio to get money I'd requested from Russia. There was a letter instead from Princess Lieven, who I'd known in St Petersburg. She told me to leave Greece immediately because my life was in danger.' He paused. 'Why would she have said that, do you think?'

'Because you are the link to the gold. The Tzar is threatened.'

'But the gold is in Alexandria. The Tzar has nothing to fear.'

'No, it's here,' said Howe. 'In this house. We took it back. Hastings was right about steam.'

Tzanis closed his eyes, absorbing this new fact. 'Yet the fleet has sailed.'

277

'Because it had to. Ibrahim Pasha is a breath away from winning the war. He only needs more men.'

Tzanis stared at him. 'If we have the gold, Sève will be very angry he let me go.' He paused, looked away. 'Will the Tzar now be persuaded, do you think?'

Howe shrugged. 'Captain Hamilton of the *Cambrian* is summoned to the Crimea, so yes, perhaps. He is to visit Manto tomorrow morning before he leaves.'

They were silent for a while. The breeze rustled the branches of a tree outside the window and a faint smell of jasmine wafted into the room.

Howe swung his legs over the side of the bed. 'Look, I'll take you to the *Karteria*. It will be in dry dock for a while and guarded day and night. You'll be safe there until we can get you away.'

'And Hara?'

'Wherever she is,' he said quietly, 'it's somewhere we're not meant to find.'

They left Manto's house just before dawn, Tzanis heavily cloaked. He'd bathed and shaved and been given fresh clothes that hung from him like a scarecrow. He needed a stick to walk. They crossed the sleeping city to the shipyard, passed sentries and climbed the gangway onto the *Karteria*. Howe had brought blankets and a pillow. By the time the first rays of sunlight were creeping across the ship's deck, Tzanis was fast asleep in Hastings's cot.

He woke with a sense of dread that froze him as completely as if he'd dreamt again of the steppe. He looked up at the cabin ceiling and thought of all Howe had told him. If he was the link to the gold, then so was Hara. Neither of them was safe but at least he was warned. He had to find her.

He heard sounds from outside. He got up and lifted a curtain to see a mast being winched onto the ship. Men were waiting in a line to receive it, arms cupped, while others swabbed the deck. The *Karteria* would soon be ready to sail.

He went back to a chair and sat down. There was a map of Europe spread out across the table. He made a compass of his hand and measured the distance to the Crimea, thumb over finger, then again. *Not so far.*

He rose and went to where his cloak was hung. He put it on, pulling the hood far over his head. He found his stick and opened the cabin door and went out into bright sunshine. The men stopped their work to stare at him but he limped past, down the gangway and onto the quay. He left the shipyard and headed back towards Manto's house.

While waiting for Captain Hamilton to arrive, Manto had found hammer and nails, then a chair to stand on. She'd hung the lithograph of Hara above the door opposite her desk where she would see it every time she looked up from her work. She was looking at it when Hamilton entered the room, dressed for travel in high boots and a cloak.

He said: 'I come to say goodbye. I leave this evening.'

She rose from behind the desk. 'And your refugees?' She gestured to the chair. 'Please.'

He sat and put his hat on his knee. 'Your gold bought enough to last them another month, seed as well. It's late to plant but they might just make a crop.'

'What will they do while you're gone?'

Hamilton pulled his gloves from his fingers one by one. 'That's what I wanted to ask you. Might you be able to persuade Hastings to take over during my absence?'

'I'll ask him.'

There was a knock on the door and a servant entered. 'There is a man downstairs who wishes to see you, ma'am,' he said. 'Not Captain Hastings or Dr Howe.'

Manto frowned. 'Who is he?'

'He will not give his name. He is aware that Captain Hamilton is with you, ma'am. He wishes to speak to you both.'

She glanced at Hamilton who shrugged. 'Show him up,' she said.

Manto heard the slow footsteps on the stairs, the tap of the stick. Somehow, she knew they were Tzanis's and found herself apprehensive. She brought her hands together to stop them from trembling.

He entered the room in clothes she recognised. He was half the weight of Howe, and the coat's sleeves ended quite far from his skinny wrists. There were scars on his cheeks and neck and flecks of grey in his hair. Last time she'd seen him, he'd been young.

'Forgive me,' she said, recovering from her shock, stepping forward. 'I believe you may not know Captain Hamilton of the *Cambrian*.'

'We've not met,' said Tzanis, bowing stiffly. 'Honoured.'

She turned to Hamilton. 'Prince Tzanis Comnenos was ship-wrecked three years ago in the Mani, bringing Russian gold for our cause.'

'From Russian philhellenes,' nodded the captain. 'I imagine there are many.'

Tzanis glanced at Manto, then back. 'From the Tzar, actually,' he said quietly. 'Not this one, but the last. I was ordered to take it to Mavrocordatos in Corfu.'

Hamilton frowned. 'But Russia is neutral, sir. All three of the Great Powers are neutral.'

Neither Tzanis nor Manto said anything.

He turned from one to the other of them. 'Is it not so?'

Manto was looking hard at her desk. 'Nevertheless,' she said quietly. 'Tzar Alexander sent gold to a cause his country had sworn not to support.'

Tzanis looked around him. 'May I sit? I find standing uncomfortable.'

Manto gestured to a chair and he sat, his stick propped against his leg. He looked at Hamilton. 'I understand you're going to the Crimea, sir. I would consider it a service if you let it be known that the man who brought Russian gold to Greece still lives to tell the tale, that you've met him.' He paused. 'The Tzar will need to know this before making any decision on the treaty.'

Hamilton stared at him. 'Do you plan to threaten the Tzar?'

'As his brother once planned to have me killed, and as he does now. This time, I am forewarned.'

They were all silent.

Tzanis stretched out his leg slowly, his hand to his knee. 'Unless the Great Powers intervene now, captain, this war is lost. You know this and we know this.' He paused. 'We have tried other ways.'

Hamilton nodded slowly. 'Like your sketch that Manto told me about. I'd like to have seen what Delacroix made of it.'

'You can,' said Manto, pointing over their heads. 'It's up there; well, a copy anyway. Above the door.'

They looked round. It was so close, Tzanis wanted to touch it. He stared at it.

'But I know her,' said Hamilton, rising. 'She's the one at the refugee camp.'

'What refugee camp?'

'At the Isthmus. The one I have asked the *Karteria* to visit while I am away.'

'And she's working there?'

'She built it,' said Hamilton. 'She told me her name was Eleni.'

# CHAPTER THIRTY-ONE

## NAFPLIO

This time, what should have taken a month took a week. Manto opened her purse strings and the shipyards of Nafplio ground to a halt for all business but the *Karteria*'s. The price Manto exacted for her largesse was her own cabin. She intended to come with them and no argument would dissuade her.

'I've braved the Bay of Biscay and you've had me passing firewood in my nightclothes,' she said.

They were sitting in her cabin in armchairs that yesterday had furnished her drawing room, Hastings the less comfortable of the two. He blushed. 'Yes, but confound it, Manto . . .'

'Do you think I fear battle?'

'No, but . . .'

'Ah, then it's the cabin.' She waved towards the newly painted partition. 'It's only temporary and yours was too big.' She rose and straightened the picture of Hara that she'd hung above her cot. The space was a clutter of furniture and *objets* she'd brought from her house. She glanced at Hastings, who was staring at another cot propped against the side. 'For Hara,' she explained, walking over to it and straightening it too, 'when we've found her.'

It wasn't only her cabin. The mess room, where they would dine, had been fitted out with no expense spared. When Hastings had shaken his head in disbelief, she'd had none of it.

'One day we'll be the flagship of the Greek Navy,' she said. 'Would you have us embarrassed?'

They left Nafplio under steam, partly for the benefit of the spectators on the shore but more because there was no wind. The ship's thermometer rose inexorably and the air was scalding hot.

They paddled out of the bay and put in to the island of Hydra where a shipment of coal lay waiting for them. The rest of the Greek navy was at anchor there, nursing its wounds and casting an eye over the last stretch of water still in revolutionary hands.

Manto stood on deck looking out, her long hair gathered beneath a wide-brimmed hat. Hastings stood next to her with Howe on her other side. Tzanis, who she'd not spoken to since the meeting with Hamilton, stood a little away.

'They just sit there,' she murmured.

'Because they've not been paid,' said Hastings. 'The crews won't take to sea without three months in advance, the blackguards.'

'Do you blame them?' Tzanis had turned to address them, his elbow on the rail. 'When every party they might believe in has taken his share?'

Manto studied him. If she ever remembered him, it was as a young cavalry officer fought over by the women of St Petersburg. Now she saw someone thin, scarred and full of anger, not all of it for their Muslim enemy. 'You'd prefer Ibrahim Pasha then?' she asked mildly. 'Or the Sultan, perhaps?'

He looked at her as if she'd spoken another language. He pointed over to the ships. 'Those crews will know little difference. Revolution changes nothing.'

Howe bristled. 'That is cynical, sir,' he said. 'My country has managed it, why not here?'

Tzanis shook his head. 'Your country is not involved here.' He gestured to Hastings. 'But *his* country? What will it demand for its help?'

Hastings had turned from the rail to face him. 'What are you suggesting?'

'I'd have thought that was obvious. Every party is in it for their own gain.' Tzanis shook his head. 'At least Hara understands that now.'

Manto found her temper rising too. 'Are you so certain that you *know* what Hara understands?' she asked quietly. 'Or even what she wants?'

He stared at her.

'She betrayed this revolution to save your life,' she continued, her voice not quite even. 'She betrayed *herself*. I doubt even she knows what she understands or wants any more.'

She turned and walked away. Hastings patted the rail twice, then left too.

A day later, they rounded the Argolid peninsula and saw the only corner of Greece untouched by flame. The villages were intact, the fields golden with summer wheat. It was a vision of what might have been without the curse of Ibrahim Pasha. They shut down the engine and dropped their sails to catch a brisk northerly that would take them up the coast to the Isthmus. They kept close to shore, for Egyptian ships patrolled these waters, looking for fishing boats to sink.

Tzanis was on deck, leant over the rail, watching dolphins play in the ship's wake, taking turns to dart forward to bump its side. Further down, sailors were hanging over it roaring the odds over the sounds of the rigging.

He was thinking about seeing Hara again. He wished he was meeting her on his own. Hastings and Howe would have let him, he was sure, but Manto? She seemed to claim some sort of ownership over her. Her hostility was bewildering. He was glad she often kept to her cabin.

*Where the picture is.*

He watched a dolphin skip away from the side, then dive. He saw it rise with others, further out: perfect arcs of skin that shone in the sun. He saw something move beyond them and lifted his hand to shield his eyes. There, on the shore: people, hundreds of them crowding the beach, waving their hands, their shirts. He looked over to where Hastings was talking with Howe.

'Hastings!' He pointed. 'Do you see them?'

Hastings looked over. He turned and cupped a hand to his mouth. *'Come about!'*

The ship turned and men left the dolphins to race up the rigging. In four minutes the ship was rocking gently in the swell. Hastings had put on his hat.

Manto emerged from her cabin and walked over. 'Why have we stopped?'

Hastings had a telescope to his eye. He passed it to her. 'Women and children on the beach,' he said. 'They need our help.'

She asked: 'Can you fit them on board?'

'We'll have to.' He was already turning to issue orders. 'Man the longboats!' He looked back to Howe. 'Doctor, you'll accompany me if you please. There may be wounded.'

'And I?' asked Manto. 'There are women and children there.'

He nodded and turned to Tzanis. 'You'll stay, if you please.'

Tzanis looked out at the beach. There were people in the water now, wading through the surf towards them, shouting: women with children in their arms. He watched the four longboats lowered over the sides, then went below with the quartermaster to see to the food. It was dark and musty and it took time for them to find the barrels. Once others had taken them up, he sat down to catch his breath. A shaft of sunlight shone in from the hatch and he saw the outline of a trapdoor above. Hastings's cabin. *Or Manto's?*

He pushed and found it wasn't bolted. He rose and pushed harder and it opened enough for him to see inside. It was Manto's.

He hauled himself up and looked around. He saw the two cots side by side, one with a flower on its pillow. He saw Hara's picture above them. He went over and took it down, then sat on the cot and stared at it.

Close up, it was an extraordinary likeness, and true to his sketch. Delacroix had captured the beauty beneath the skin, the courage. He felt a shiver steal over him.

Then a sound. A key was turning in the door. It opened and Manto was there. She glanced around the cabin, taking in the open trap door, the picture in his lap. Her eyes came back to his.

'What are you doing?'

Tzanis laid the picture on the cot. 'I thought you'd gone ashore.'

'I'm more useful here,' she said, closing the door behind her and walking over to the cot. She picked up the picture, looked at it, then took it over to the table. She sat down, untied her hat and laid it over the picture.

They looked at each other for a long time. Outside, the familiar noises of the ship went on as usual: the creaks and shouts and screech of sea birds above. Inside, they were becalmed in silent, unchartered waters. At last Tzanis disturbed them.

'Why don't you trust me?'

She frowned slightly. A lock of hair fell across her temple and she tucked it away.

'Don't be absurd. If you mean what passed between us on deck . . .'

'No, I don't mean that. It's something else.' He spread his hands on his knees and looked down at them. 'You never had children,' he said. 'Did you and your husband not want them?'

She rose from her chair. 'I think you should leave.'

He studied her. Her eyes, always so assured, held something new in them.

'Tell me about Chios,' he said.

She looked up at the cabin beams and took a deep breath. She blinked twice and brought her eyes down to his. Then she sat down again. 'It was horrible,' she said quietly. 'As if someone had opened the gates of hell.'

'They killed your husband.'

She nodded.

'Did you love him?'

She paused before answering. Then she looked away. 'Of course.'

'Why "of course"?' he asked. 'Many wives don't. Especially where fortunes are concerned.'

She looked back. 'Which is what you were seeking in St Petersburg, as I recall.'

'Yet I came here.'

They stared at each other for what seemed an age.

'I will tell you what I think,' he said at last. 'I think that Hara is the daughter you could never have and I think you think me unworthy of her.' He was watching her intently. 'I think you remember me from St Petersburg.'

She looked at him. Another wisp of hair had fallen to her brow but she didn't notice.

'Well, you're wrong,' he said. 'I have changed. I love her.'

He got up and limped over to the table and removed her bonnet from the picture. He looked down at it for a while. Then he lifted it for her to see. 'Doesn't this prove it?' he asked. 'Delacroix only painted what I'd already drawn.'

They heard shouts outside. They felt a bump against the side and heard the sound of running feet.

'The longboats are back,' he said. 'We should go.'

Outside they found men lining the rail to bring people on board. Tzanis watched the first child lifted onto the deck: a girl no more than five who was nothing beneath her rags. In her hand she held a wooden dog on wheels.

He turned. 'Open the barrels,' he shouted. 'No more than three biscuits each, eaten slowly or they'll choke. Break open the water kegs.'

He and Manto worked side by side, giving comfort to the crew as well, many of whom were fathers. He looked around for Hastings. 'Where is the captain?'

'Still on shore, sir,' said an officer. 'There's news of an attack on the camp.'

He stopped what he was doing. 'An attack? Who by?'

'The women say they've seen klephts making their way over the hill,' said the officer. 'An ambush.'

*

289

Hastings's plan was a simple one. When they got to the Isthmus, they would hide the *Karteria* and take empty boxes onto the beach with straw dummies to guard them. They would wait until night when the klephts would tire of the ambush and steal onto the beach. Then they would steam into the bay and blow them to pieces.

But the plan needed one man to be on the beach to give the signal at exactly the right time.

'Me,' said Tzanis.

'But you're still . . .' Hastings floundered. 'Why not someone else?'

'Because,' he said, using his stick to rise, 'she might be there. Hamilton told her it would be his final drop and she might want to meet him in person. Someone has to tell her of the plan, and it should be me.'

Manto had kept silent throughout the exchange, watching him with an expression that gave no clue to her feelings. She kept to her cabin as the preparations were made.

They dropped anchor at midday behind a tall hill that hid them from the beach. They lowered the longboats while Tzanis and a dozen marines prepared to leave with the cargo. He was being helped over the side when he heard footsteps on the deck. He felt a hand on his arm and turned. It was Manto.

'Good luck,' she said.

By mid-afternoon, the boxes were stacked, the straw sentries in place and the marines hidden behind rocks to the side. The longboats had returned to the *Karteria*.

Tzanis sat on the beach and waited beneath the dead weight of the afternoon sun. As evening approached, he heard the bray of a donkey and looked up to see a long line of men, women and animals winding their way down to the beach. He narrowed his eyes to see better, shielding them with his hand, his mouth dry. There was no sign of Hara. He felt a wave of disappointment that emptied his stomach.

No matter. There was a plan to carry out. He met the group as they arrived and told them of it. They looked behind them anxiously, wondering if they were being watched even then. He told them to take the animals far away and hide themselves with the marines. He was left alone on the beach.

He waited, sitting on the boxes among the men of straw, his musket in his lap. He watched the sun go down over the mountains, heard the first cicadas erupt into chorus, smelt the evening scent of garlic and thyme steal in from the hills. Flies buzzed around him, then moths. He felt the first bite of a mosquito.

He stared up at the hills, watching their folds dissolve beneath the magenta rim of the horizon. He saw a single tree etched against it, standing like a spectator: head thrown back, arms stretched out to such beauty. He wished Hara were there to see it with him.

Night came suddenly. The horizon disappeared and the tree vanished with it. Soon, there was nothing but sound: everywhere and deafening. An army could steal up and not be heard. He turned his head to listen above the cicadas. *Nothing.*

Then a shadow. Black against black in the soft moonlight: low, furtive. Was that the sound of pebbles disturbed? Slowly, he stood up, his musket in his hand. He climbed down from the boxes, passing a sentry: back straight, head lolling against its shoulder. He reached the ground and stood motionless, peering into the night. *There.* A shadow moving, then another. They were coming.

Silently, he pulled the flare tube from his waistband, and took the toggle between his fingers. He waited until the shadows crept closer. Then he pulled.

There was a pop, a whoosh and the sky turned to crimson. The klephts were frozen in a wide semi-circle on the beach, their faces raised to the sky. He saw them turn to each other as the sound of the *Karteria*'s paddles came out of the night.

He turned and limped away as fast as he could go. As the first shell landed behind him, he threw himself to the ground. He heard the screams of klephts, then the shout of someone else, not male. A second flare went up and he turned his head. A figure was running towards him. He sat up. *No. Please.*

'*Go back!*'

But it was too late. The world exploded and he was flung back onto the sand. He tasted blood in his mouth, his nose, but his limbs seemed still with him. He shook his head and got to his elbows, then knees. As the smoke parted he saw a body on the ground, not far from him.

*Hara.*

Another explosion, then another: but further away now. The *Karteria*'s guns were following the klephts back into the hills. He saw his marines running after them across the beach, past her. He felt a wave of dizziness and fell onto his front. He began to crawl forward, muttering to himself, blinking through eyelashes clogged with sand.

*Closer, closer.*

Then he was beside the body. It was entirely still.

'Hara,' he whispered. '*No.*'

He choked back what was rising inside him. He knelt and put his arm under her head and lifted it gently onto his knees and looked down at her, but his eyes were still gritty with sand and smoke. He bent over and brought his ear to her chest. Was that her heart beating or his? *Too slow for his.* He felt a surge of hope.

Then a voice below him.

'Am I hurt?'

It was a choked sound, the gurgle of blood behind it.

'Don't speak,' he said.

She tried to turn her head. 'I can't see you. Hold me; I'm so cold. Please.'

He brought her closer in to him, felt the blood warm against his chest. There were explosions far, far away. He screwed his eyes shut against the tears, unable to look. He held her even tighter. 'You cannot die,' he whispered. 'Not now.'

# CHAPTER THIRTY-TWO

## THE ISTHMUS

Howe and Manto came ashore with the first boat and a bag full of opiates. They ran over to where Tzanis still knelt over Hara. Gently, Howe pulled him away and examined what he could see of Hara beneath the blood.

He turned to him. 'You should go,' he said gently.

Manto put her hand on his arm. She smiled at him for the second time. 'Go,' she said.

So Tzanis went and sat on the rocks and watched the lanterns brought, then a stretcher. In a trance, he saw a fire lit to boil water, instruments cauterised and laid out on a sheet. His eyes never left the huddle of people that knelt around her. At last one of them rose and came over to him.

'She will live,' said Howe with his doctor's eyes, preparing to give bad news. 'But she will never be the same.' He paused. 'Her face is bandaged.'

Tzanis wondered if he knew how little that mattered. He said: 'But she'll live.'

'We must get her back to the camp.'

'The camp? No, we must take her on board.'

Howe shook his head. He looked round at the men and women that circled the beach, all watching them. 'They'll not let her go.'

Three hours later, once the food had been strapped to the animals and Hara had been laid gently on a stretcher with something given to her for the pain, they set off for the camp.

The torchlit procession that wound its way back through the hills was a long one. First came Hara's stretcher with Tzanis on one side, Manto the other, Howe behind. Then came the beasts with the food, guarded by men from the camp. Last came the long line of new refugees. From the deck of the *Karteria*, it must have looked like some pagan burial.

They walked through the night and drew close to the camp as the morning sun broke over the hills. A man had been sent ahead to warn of their arrival and a multitude was waiting for them, silently lining the road: men, women and children, old and young. It nearly broke Tzanis's exhausted heart to see the bowed heads, the love, the reverence felt by that huge mass of people. Then, as the first light reached out across the camp, he saw what Hara had created: a city of tents, set out in ordered rows, with a hospital, dining pavilion, church. There was a low wall with fields beyond it, already golden with growth. It was a place of rebirth amidst a murdered landscape, a place of healing and hope. A sanctuary.

'*My God*,' whispered Manto beside him. 'Hara, what have you built?'

Manto and Tzanis stayed with Howe at the camp while Hastings went off to collect more food. They took turns by Hara's bedside, only leaving when Howe came in to change her bandages. For the first week, she didn't speak. When she finally did murmur, it was of nothing they could understand. The few words she'd spoken on the beach seemed to have been a brief moment of clarity, quickly swept away.

After a month, there was no change. The *Karteria* returned with more food and Tzanis went down to collect it. He passed a stranger on the road.

As soon as the newcomer set foot in the camp, he was introduced to Manto. After all, she'd paid for him to come.

'This is Dr Jenner from Geneva,' said Howe.

It was early morning and Manto was serving food. The day was already hot and the school tent open, with a queue forming for morning assembly. She handed the ladle to another and wiped her hands on her apron. 'Shall we talk under the tree?'

A big oak stood in the middle of the camp with a table beneath it. They sat down and Manto brought water, watching the Swiss doctor as she poured. He was a neat, bearded man tucked into a white linen suit, who wore glasses that magnified his eyes and a hat not wide enough to shade them. He carried a small bag and a cane, both with care.

'What can you do?' she asked, sitting.

'I haven't seen the patient,' said the man, placing his bag and cane on the table. 'But I'm told it's severe.'

'Very,' she said.

Dr Jenner drank some water. 'I would normally take skin from the upper thigh. It will never match perfectly but it will be better than what she has now.'

Manto nodded. 'Well, we just have today. Prince Tzanis will be back tomorrow.'

They began immediately and continued through the

afternoon, Jenner and Howe working side by side, Manto outside the tent, waiting. As the sun was setting, Howe came out.

'It's done,' he said, sitting down beside her. 'But we'll all have to lie to her.'

She looked at him. 'Tell me.'

'When she comes back to us, she mustn't know what she looks like. The shock might cause her to attack the stitching before it's done its work. We'll tell her that her eyes have had surgery and can't be exposed to the light.'

'So her whole face will remain bandaged?'

He nodded. 'For now.' Then he turned to her. 'Are you still sure Tzanis shouldn't be told?'

'No. Not yet.'

She rose and went into the tent where Jenner was drying his hands and talking quietly to the nurses. She walked over to the operating table. A lamp was suspended above and in its light she saw a face that was now a patchwork of skin, laid out like little fields, hedged by tiny stitching. Above it all, the bandage across her eyes seemed too white.

She looked down for a long time, feeling the shock reach every part of her body. She felt a presence by her side.

'It will improve as the skin grafts,' said Dr Jenner quietly. 'I will bandage her now.'

She nodded. 'Thank you. I'll do the first watch.'

Jenner left soon afterwards and Manto was left alone with Hara. Outside the tent, she heard the noise of supper being prepared: quietly, as if any noise would wake Hara from her sleep. She heard the camp's sounds give way to insects' and felt the human world drift away. She thought of what Tzanis had said to her on the *Karteria*. He'd been right about so much.

She looked down at the bandaged face, quite still. She closed her eyes and joined her hands. She did what she hadn't done for many years. She began to pray.

Summer gave way to autumn and the hills above the camp turned yellow around the black stumps of the olive trees. The nights grew longer and colder and people queued in their blankets for their breakfast. Hara slept most of the time and, when she woke, she was somewhere else.

Manto and Howe ran the camp with calm efficiency, training up the best of Hara's followers to take over should Hara not recover her senses. They did their best but they weren't Hara. The camp was a quieter place than it had been.

Meanwhile, Ibrahim Pasha waited in Tripoli for the reinforcements he needed from the new fleet. The refugees were grateful for the respite but knew it wouldn't last. When his new army marched out, it would be with them in a week.

Tzanis and Manto continued their vigil by Hara's bedside, coaxing whatever sense they could from her, wondering if she'd ever come back to them. Hastings came with supplies and news from the outside world, none of it good.

'Not a word,' he said, when Manto asked him about Hamilton. They were sitting with Howe and Tzanis under the oak tree. 'He went straight from the Crimea to Malta where Codrington's got the fleet. If it had been signed, he'd have stopped off in Nafplio to tell Mavrocordatos. It doesn't look encouraging.'

A cloud passed over the sun and a chill came in on the breeze. Tzanis rose. 'It's my turn to watch,' he said. 'I'll see you at dinner.'

He went into the tent and sat down beside Hara's sleeping body. He picked up the book he'd been reading last time: Homer's *Iliad*. He opened it and read while the wind gathered outside and the first rain hit the tent's sides. He fell asleep.

He woke to find a hand in his. He thought at first he was dreaming. He sat up and blinked and looked down at her. The bandaged face was turned towards him.

'I know who you are,' she said, squeezing his hand. 'I'd know you anywhere. Why can't I see you?'

He couldn't speak at first. Outside, he heard wind and the drip, drip of rain falling from canvas, the last of the storm that must have happened while he'd slept. He stared down at her.

A frown came to the only part of her face not bandaged. 'You are Tzanis, aren't you?'

'Yes, yes,' he said quickly. 'It's me.' He took her hand in both of his. He felt delirious with happiness, giddy with it. 'Thank God. *Thank God.*' He leant forward and kissed her fingers one by one.

'Why are my eyes bandaged?'

He rose and sat down on the bed, still holding her hand, feeling her thigh next to his. Her head followed him. 'Howe had to do something to your eyes,' he said. 'They can't be exposed to light. Not for a while.'

She nodded slowly. 'How long have I been here?'

'A long time.'

'And you've been with me all through it?'

He nodded. 'With Manto, yes. We've taken it in turns.'

She lapsed into silence, her head held very still. She was looking up at the tent's roof. 'I remember now,' she said softly. 'You were hurt too.' She turned her head towards him. 'Weren't you?'

He thought of Sève's torture, far worse than anything he'd suffered on the beach. But she'd never know about that. Not ever. He said: 'I'm better now.'

'How have you passed the time?'

He looked down at his book. He lifted it and put it into her hands, closing her fingers around it. 'Reading the *Iliad*, most recently. It's Manto's copy.'

He watched her run her fingers over the cover, the spine, then lift it to her nose.

'Leather. At least I still have that sense.' She paused. 'You used to read to me from it,' she said. 'On the tower. Do you remember?'

He smiled. 'I remember.'

'You told me about Helen, whose face launched a thousand ships.'

'Well, yours launched a steamship.' As soon as he'd said it, he wished he hadn't.

'Mine?' She lifted her fingers to her cheek. 'Bandaged,' she whispered, resting them there. 'I had a terrible dream. My face . . .'

He took her fingers before they could travel further. 'Your face is still beautiful,' he said softly, lowering her hand to her side, holding it there.

'So you'll sketch me again? When I'm better?'

He felt tears rising and closed his eyes. He couldn't speak.

'Tzanis?'

He swallowed. 'Yes, yes. When you're better. Soon.'

'Beneath the tree.'

He opened his eyes. 'The tree?'

'The big one, in the middle of the camp.' She turned her head to him. 'There was an oracle here once. She said Zeus spoke through its branches. She would sit on her tripod and listen to the wind in the tree. She was blind, like me.'

'You're not blind.'

'Nor am I an oracle. Otherwise I'd have seen what was coming.' She squeezed his hand. 'Or will. Like whether you'll stay.'

He nodded, took a deep breath, as silent as he could make it. 'I'll never leave you, Hara. Never again.'

The news that Hara had finally woken caused the camp to erupt in joy. People gathered near the tent, hoping she might emerge, but Howe sent them away to their work. Later, while Manto sat with her, Tzanis waited for some of them to return from the fields. Much of the winter crop had been washed away by autumn rains and he'd suggested ploughing new ground further away. They should have been back by now, but they were late.

As evening approached, he and Howe went out to look for them. The storm had passed but there was promise of more. Dark, bullying clouds blustered across the sky and leaves swirled around their feet. He felt joy but trepidation too. Hara was back to them but she wasn't safe. Sève would come with the army and she should not be there when he did.

He stopped and turned to Howe, who was lifting his collar to the wind. 'Now she's awake, will you take her bandages off?'

Howe glanced at him. 'Yes, I suppose so.'

'What will she be like?'

Howe turned to him. 'She'll never be what she was,' he said softly. 'But she'll improve.'

Another gust of wind swept up the valley, lifting the hair at his neck. He looked up at the sky and felt sudden dread steal over him. He took Howe's arm. 'If anything happens to me, anything at all, swear to me that you'll look after her.'

Howe frowned. 'Of course, but . . .'

'No, swear it.' He gripped harder. 'She cannot live alone in this world, not like that. Take her back to America.'

Howe nodded slowly. 'I swear it.'

Tzanis let go and they walked on, cresting the hill and coming

301

down to the new fields behind. They were empty. There were some trees to the side and Howe pointed to them. 'They might have taken shelter.'

They trudged around the fields, passing small piles of stones that the women had cleared. They came into the trees and it was suddenly dark. They heard whispers and stopped, peering into the gloom. There were shapes among the trees.

They stopped. 'We've found you,' said Tzanis. 'We can take you home.'

'Not quite yet.'

The voice was known to only one of them, the one who'd closed his eyes. Colonel Sève stepped out from the trees with two others behind him. They all had pistols aimed.

'Prince Tzanis will stay behind. The women can go with Dr Howe.'

The two men took Tzanis's arms as Colonel Sève came up to stand in front of him.

'This is the third time, isn't it?' he asked. He turned to Howe. 'The first time he escaped; the second, I let him go, which was foolish.' He shook his head. 'I thought I'd hurt him badly enough but I was wrong.' He stepped back and sighed.

Then he punched Tzanis hard in the stomach.

'I won't make that mistake again.'

The moment she'd heard Howe's voice calling Manto from the tent, Hara had known that Tzanis had gone.

For two hours she'd sat with Manto and held hands and talked of Nafplio days that were so distant they seemed to have happened to someone else. She'd listened to her quiet voice and remembered it filling her mind once. Then had come the sound of canvas parting.

302

Was his leaving to do with her? Was it to do with the strange voice he'd used when he'd talked to her, or that lie about eye surgery? She knew enough of medicine to know that no one had touched her eyes.

She sat up in the empty tent and swung her legs over the bed. She rose and felt her way over to the table she'd once used to brush her hair. It had a mirror on it. She found the chair and drew it back and sat down carefully. She lifted her fingers to the bandage and pushed. It was too tight, so she tried to lift it with her fingers. *There*. She could see.

Her heart stopped. The dream had not been a dream. She'd lost her face and here . . . *this* was its replacement. She wanted to wretch.

But there were sounds outside the tent: Manto's voice and Howe's, drawing near. She pulled down the bandage and went back to her bed and climbed into it. She'd just laid her head on the pillow when the tent opened.

Manto came over to her. 'We have to go,' she said. 'Now, on the *Karteria*.'

# PART FIVE

# AUTUMN 1827

# CHAPTER THIRTY-THREE

## NAVARINO

Hara offered no resistance when they carried her through the hills, then rowed her out to the *Karteria*. When they led her to Manto's cabin and put her to bed in her cot, she made no complaint. She would be compliant. For now.

Without Tzanis there, Manto was by her side constantly: sitting by day, sleeping by night. Since sight and movement were still denied her, Hara got to know her new home by sound. She listened to the creak and lap of sea voyage as she'd done once in the Mani. She thought of when she and Tzanis had last been together at sea, when she had stared at a sunset and known she was watched. *When she'd wanted to be watched.*

They swept south before a strong wind, passing the plains of Argos, the walled beauty of Monemvasia, then Cape Malea and the island of Kithira where she'd first met Hastings and Howe. She didn't ask to go on deck or even leave her bed. She'd made up her mind.

One morning, the engines stopped. She heard shouts outside and Manto left the cabin to investigate. When she returned, Hara could sense her excitement.

'It's the British fleet,' she said, sitting down and taking her hand. 'Or a squadron, at least. Admiral Codrington is on his way to Navarino. The treaty must have been signed.'

Hara set her mouth to a smile. 'That is the best of news.' She squeezed Manto's hand. 'Does Captain Hastings plan to go aboard?'

'We all do. Can I leave you for an hour?'

She listened to the business of departure through the cabin door. It was a day of sunshine and sudden squalls and the sounds came and went with the call of birds. At last all was quiet on the ship.

She sat up and untied the bandage, unwinding it from her head like a shroud. She folded it and put it onto the cot, old habits dying hard. She rose and walked to the wardrobe, found clothes to put on, sailor's clothes: loose, rope-belted. She went over to a table and gathered some coin into a pouch that she tied to her belt. She went over to the cabin door and opened it a fraction. The deck was clear. She slipped out.

No one on the ship saw her cross the deck and climb silently over the side. No one saw her slide into the water and dive below. If they had, they might have assumed she'd drowned, for she didn't resurface until she'd reached the shore.

Hastings came aboard Admiral Codrington's flagship to a ring of admiration, but not the admiral's. 'Welcome, sir,' said Codrington, stepping forward. He looked out at the steamship. 'Not pretty, is she?'

Manto was helped on deck by two officers. She was carrying something beneath her arm and was dressed to charm. 'Admiral Codrington,' she exclaimed, looking round. 'What a big ship! Is she new?'

The admiral bowed. He was a man in his fifties who'd been at sea since a boy. His face was a slab of rare beef cured by sun and wind across four oceans, his sideburns long and stiff with old salt. 'Two years from the shipyard, ma'am.' He didn't sound like someone commanding obsolescence. He grunted and gestured to Hastings. 'But here's the man. Steam indeed!'

Hastings was helping Howe aboard. The admiral bowed to him. 'I've heard much about you, sir. Honoured.'

Manto had taken hold of Codrington's arm. She nodded over to the shore. 'My country is being burnt alive, Sir Edward,' she said quietly. 'May we go below and discuss how it might be stopped?'

As they crossed the deck, she said as calmly as she was able: 'I hear that Captain Hamilton is returned from the Crimea.'

The admiral opened the door to his cabin and stepped aside. 'With a treaty,' he said. 'But not the one we want.'

She stepped into the cabin, seeing the gleam of new wood, new brass, the maps and charts stretched out on the mahogany table, the dividers resting from their march. She turned. 'But a treaty nonetheless.' She looked around at the panelled walls, the mantelpiece over the pretend fireplace. She went over to it and took the picture from her side and unwrapped it from its cloth. She propped Hara up on it.

'There,' she said, stepping back. She turned. 'Did you know this painting, sir?'

Codrington was standing between Hastings and Howe. 'I'd heard of it,' he said. 'They say it brought France to the treaty.'

Manto nodded. 'It did. But how was Russia persuaded, do you think?'

The admiral went over to a decanter and poured wine into four glasses. He sat down. 'No one knows.' He reached into

309

his jacket and brought out a parchment, rolled and sealed. He waved it. 'But this is the result: far from satisfactory, but all we have. It requires me to prevent the resupply of Ibrahim's army and dissuade him from further destruction, yet forbids me to use force.' He raised his glass. 'I give you politicians, damn all their eyes!'

Hastings had kept his glass on the table. 'But there must be some allowance, sir, surely?'

The admiral shook his head. 'Not without a clear casus belli,' he said. 'And I doubt Ibrahim will be stupid enough to give us one.'

Manto was staring up at the picture. 'And all the while, my country burns,' she murmured. 'I assume you know he means to kill everyone?' she asked quietly. 'His new fleet has brought settlers from Egypt and lies ready to take off Greek slaves. Greece will no longer be a Christian country.'

The admiral scowled. 'I am aware of it, ma'am. But I am in a difficult position. My squadron is to be joined by ones from France and Russia. Their governments are resolute: no force.'

'So you'll just sit there and watch it happen?'

Codrington coloured. 'Madam, you are unfair.'

Manto leant forward, pointing at the window. 'No, sir. What is unfair is what is being done to my people,' she pointed now at Hara, '*her* people.' She tapped the rolled-up parchment with her finger. 'And this piece of paper will do nothing to help them.'

'But what would you have me do?' he cried, exasperated. 'I serve the British government, not the Greek!'

'Nothing until provoked by a clear casus belli,' said Manto, sitting back. 'You said it yourself.' She paused, then gestured to Hastings. 'I believe you know the captain?'

Codrington nodded. 'A good man, one of honour.' He looked

at Hastings. 'You were treated disgracefully, sir. Should never have been allowed to leave the service.'

'But he did,' said Manto, her hand now on the admiral's arm. 'Which means that he is free to act.'

The admiral moved his arm. He frowned. 'Madam, I cannot listen to any more.'

Manto rose. 'Nor shall you, sir,' she said brightly. 'Not from me, anyway. I shall return to the *Karteria* and not trouble you further. You gentlemen will have much to discuss, like what might be taken for a casus belli.'

She moved to the door as the three men rose from the table.

Codrington gestured to the mantelpiece. 'Ma'am, your portrait.'

Manto turned and delivered her most dazzling smile. 'I shall leave her here,' she said. 'She can watch over you while you talk.'

# CHAPTER THIRTY-FOUR

## NAVARINO

It was early morning and already hot for October. Manto sat at the stern of the admiral's pinnace watching ten men pull her across to the shore, not one of whom was looking at her. Yesterday, she'd been a mature beauty in silks. Now she was a midshipman in high-collared blue cutaway, hair gathered beneath a short wig. It was not how they wanted their midshipmen to be.

She was sitting next to Captain Hamilton, and in front sat Admiral Codrington and Comte Henri de Rigny, admiral of the French squadron. He was a man of middle years and stout frame, ill-suited to the Mediterranean heat, particularly in the thick felt of his dress uniform. They were on their way to what promised to be a difficult meeting ashore.

Most embarrassing for the rowers had been their admiral's impotence in the face of clear mutiny. Manto had had herself rowed over to the pinnace while they'd waited for the admirals, then calmly placed herself at the stern. They'd watched Codrington come down from the *Asia*, stop and open his mouth, then close it again. Now he just sat there and glared to his front.

312

Manto looked back to the British squadron moving gently in the swell, its sides gleaming in the sunshine, its sails gathered in perfect order. Those ten ships had sat outside Navarino Bay for a fortnight now, waiting for the French and Russians to arrive. It would be an impressive force when they did.

It was still early but the sun dappled the water in swirls of spun gold. The sky was blue and infinite and she thought of someone who'd be blind to all this beauty, who'd disappeared. She'd returned last night to find an empty cot next to hers and a bandage rolled neatly on top of it. *At least she'd taken some money.*

She thought back to when Hastings and Howe had got back from the flagship. It had been late.

'She's gone,' she'd said, as soon as they'd entered the cabin.

Both men had stared at her.

'Swum ashore. I should have stayed.'

'We'll find her.'

'Of course.' She'd nodded, gathering her hands in her lap. She looked up. 'So what has Codrington decided to do?'

'As Lord Nelson did: turn a blind eye. But I'm not to leave 'til he's gone ashore tomorrow. So he won't have to witness it.'

'And did he know where Prince Tzanis might be?'

'The French have a base at Itea in the Gulf of Corinth. Howe will go ashore just short of the town. I will create a diversion while he looks for him. It might provoke them.'

'Our casus belli.' She'd risen then and gone to the window and looked across to the lights of the squadron, her hands behind her back. She'd turned. 'Do you have any midshipmen about my size?'

Now that midshipman was entering Navarino Bay, crowded with ships of all sizes and traffic going back and forth to the land. On the quay, she saw women and children disembarking. *Settlers.* She looked away.

They came ashore to a welcome of carpets and turbaned officials who bent to usher them up steps to a wide, flat piece of land where a gigantic tent sat. Beneath its awning stood a ring of men in different costumes: Egyptians and Turks, Frenchmen in much the same uniform as de Rigny's. At their centre was a cushioned divan where Ibrahim Pasha lay at his ease, a chibouk resting across his stomach. He wore a long, fur-lined coat above wide pantaloons and coiled slippers. He raised a hand, corded with rings, and boys ran in with chairs for the guests. They placed them in a semicircle, outside the awning.

He raised his hand again and two more boys ran in with giant paddles. They began to fan him.

The two admirals glanced up at the sun, then at each other. They sat down side by side, Manto standing behind. She looked along the faces opposite and her eyes came to Sève at one end of the line. He was frowning.

Ibrahim Pasha picked up his pipe and resumed smoking, watching them all from his small, restless eyes. He didn't offer them water.

'Admirals Codrington and de Rigny,' he said at last, 'we are assuredly blessed. But no Admiral Heyden?' He raised his plump hands in surprise. 'Where are the Russians on this fine day?'

Codrington was sitting very upright on his chair with his hat in his lap and his knees tight together. His face was already filmed with sweat. 'On their way, sir, as is Admiral de Rigny's squadron.' He produced a rolled parchment from his jacket and placed it on the table.

'Ah, the Treaty of London,' said Ibrahim, 'signed by all three Powers. Remind me of what it says.'

'It calls for an armistice,' said Codrington. 'You are to cease all land and sea operations while we mediate an end to the hostilities. Its terms have already been accepted by the Greeks.'

'But not the Sublime Porte.'

'His Majesty the Sultan will not be aware of the facts on the ground.'

'Oh, but he is,' said Ibrahim. He signalled for the boys to quicken their fanning and lay back. 'He is aware that I am on the point of putting down his rebellion, a rebellion against an established monarch. Is that not what you fought your war against Napoleon for? To end all rebellions?'

The admirals exchanged glances. De Rigny was very red now, and blinking. He had sweat coursing down his cheeks.

Ibrahim pointed out to sea. 'And does Lord Cochrane, who serves this rebellion, know about this treaty? I hear he is preparing to attack my fortress at Patras.'

Codrington loosened his collar. Small beads were bubbling on his forehead. 'He will be ordered to desist,' he said.

Ibrahim Pasha took a long pull of his chibouk and let out a string of perfect smoke rings, each smaller than the last. He watched them dissolve into the air, then waved them away.

'I have read your treaty,' he said, 'and it is very clear on one thing, at least: it requires you not to take sides, not to join the hostilities on any account.'

'It requires us to take all measures that circumstances suggest,' said Codrington, mopping his brow. 'Its exact words.'

'Yet not to join the hostilities, is it not so?'

De Rigny placed his hand on his neighbour's arm. 'It is so,' he said quietly.

Manto watched Ibrahim Pasha lift the chibouk to his lips and smoke on for a while, watching them. She glanced at de

Rigny, who was swaying slightly on his chair, his breath coming in pants. She glanced back to Colonel Sève whose frown was deeper than before.

'Your kings are forced by their people to be hypocrites,' Ibrahim continued from his shade. He pointed out to the bay. 'Did you know that there are ships out there that were built in Toulon?'

Codrington was now well aware of de Rigny's discomfort because the Frenchman was leaning against him. Any moment he might faint. He put his hand on his arm.

But Ibrahim was in no hurry. 'Who do you think benefits from us attacking each other?' he continued, his eyes on Codrington. 'I will tell you. The power that isn't here.' He paused and smoked. 'What you do now could result in Russia annexing large parts of the Ottoman Empire, even threatening India. What will your government say to that, do you think?' He paused. 'What will *history* say?' He shook his head. 'No wonder Heyden didn't come.'

Codrington put his free hand to his collar, stretching it while he turned his head to left and right. Manto saw a nerve twitching in his neck. Was it the heat or anger? He cleared his throat.

'Your highness will be aware that we are not men of politics,' he said. 'We have orders to stop you destroying Greece while we mediate. So we require you to desist from sending any more expeditions ashore, or allowing any ship to leave this lagoon.'

De Rigny emitted a low groan. He slumped further against Codrington's shoulder. The British admiral rose, helping his neighbour to his feet. He was trembling all over and Manto had no doubt now that it was anger. 'We will return to our ships,' he said quietly, already turning. 'If we do not hear from you by six o'clock this evening, we will assume we are at war.'

*

They were rowed back to the squadron in silence. They'd been publically humiliated by a chibouk-smoking barbarian and there was fury aboard. Manto sat next to Hamilton and counted the ships they passed. She made them over ninety, a colossal number.

Once there, Codrington took the steps up to his flagship two at a time, de Rigny behind him, helped by Hamilton. By the time Manto stepped onto the deck, he was almost at his cabin door.

'Sir,' she called after him, 'may I speak with you?'

Her voice echoed round the deck and Codrington froze in his stride. He turned. 'I beg your pardon?' he asked quietly.

She ignored Hamilton's warning look.

'If I may?'

Codrington adjusted his hat and breathed deeply. He turned and walked over to where she stood, bringing his face very close to hers. 'Madam, I require you to go into the cabin I have allocated to you on board this ship and rest. I will put you ashore when you are recovered.'

It was dark when Manto awoke to the knock on her cabin door. She was lying on her cot, fully clothed. She rose and went to the door, opening it. Colonel Sève was standing there beneath a light drizzle, water dripping from his hat. He was alone.

'May I come in?'

She hesitated a moment, then stepped aside. Someone had visited her while she'd slept and lit candles. Hara's picture looked out from the panel facing the door.

Sève entered and stopped. He was looking up. 'I hadn't seen it,' he murmured. 'It is good.'

He took off his hat, then cloak and hung them up as she closed the door. He looked around the room to check they were alone, then turned to her. 'I knew it was you,' he said. 'Such a face is not easily disguised.'

She walked past him and sat. 'What do you want? I have no wish to prolong this interview.'

He sat facing her. He shook raindrops from each of his coat cuffs and watched them fall to the carpet. She looked at a face hardened by war and encounters with nothing good in the world. She saw scars and old bruises and lines belonging to a man much older than he. She felt a little afraid.

'I come to make peace,' he said, looking up. 'You have won.'

She didn't move. He was a snake, a dangerous one.

'Ibrahim Pasha played that meeting as badly as he could have played it,' he said. 'Humiliating your enemy is never a good idea.' He paused. 'But I spoke to him afterwards. He has accepted the terms of the armistice. He will cease all operations by land and sea while he awaits further instructions. For his part, Codrington will stop Cochrane from attacking Patras. Then he will retire to Zante, leaving one frigate on station.'

'So why are you here?' she asked. 'I could have learnt all this from the admiral.'

Sève leant forward, his fingers joined, elbows on his knees. 'Because there is something missing from the British squadron,' he said quietly. 'Where is the *Karteria*?'

She didn't answer. She stared into eyes still fixed on hers. She would not be intimidated by this leathered reptile.

He looked slowly round the cabin. 'I know what you're doing, Manto Kavardis,' he said softly. 'I know that you're using your considerable charm to persuade Codrington to attack the combined fleets. But you've won, so what is the point?' He paused. 'I ask again: where is the *Karteria*?'

'Where is Prince Tzanis?'

The Colonel sat back. 'I have him safe somewhere,' he said.

'Why did you take him? You have your gold.'

'Except that we don't.'

So he knew. 'Why is the Prince so important?'

Colonel Sève studied his fingernails. 'Well, he is important to Hara and she is important to you.' He paused and looked up. 'And you are important to Hastings, whose steamship is missing.'

She stared at him.

'So,' he said, 'we could agree a trade: Prince Tzanis for the *Karteria* brought back. It seems fair.'

'Except that you're lying, Colonel Sève,' said Manto. 'You have no intention of ceasing operations. You have 25,000 men ashore preparing to march on Nafplio.' She paused. 'Then you will march on Constantinople.'

He laughed softly. 'You are mistaken, lady. Why would we attack our allies? We have their fleet sat next to ours.'

'Where you can blow it from the water.'

He shook his head. 'And why would we do that?'

'To bring Russia into the war, to split the Sultan's empire between the Tzar and your master, Ibrahim Pasha. What is he giving you for all this?'

They sat across from each other in silence, both knowing now what the other knew, both trying to gauge what more there might be.

'Prince Tzanis,' said Sève very quietly, 'is the gold's only link to the Tzar. I have him. Whatever the *Karteria* does, the Russians will not permit an engagement.'

'So why do you care where it's gone? And you're wrong anyway. Tzanis's story is known by Captain Hamilton, who brought the treaty from the Crimea. Will you kill him too?'

He stared at her, something between hatred and admiration in his eyes. He rose suddenly and gathered his cloak and hat from where they hung.

'Prince Tzanis,' he said, 'will now join the combined fleets. He will be tied over a gun port and if any allied ship opens fire, he will be the first to die.' He put his finger to his lip. 'As for the *Karteria* – I have a good idea where she's headed. There'll be a surprise waiting for her there.'

He walked to the door and turned. He glanced up at the picture of Hara, then back. 'Will you be the one to tell her?'

An hour later, two marines came to escort Manto to a boat that would take her to land. She had changed into a dress and was waiting for them with a small briefcase on her lap. They assumed she'd offer no resistance and marched ahead of her. They were wrong.

Halfway across the deck she turned, arriving at the admiral's door before they knew that she'd gone. She walked in without knocking.

Codrington was the first to see her. He was sitting at the end of a table with a napkin tucked into his collar, the ship's officers either side of him, one of whom was Hamilton. They were eating quail.

He put down his fork. 'Madam, this is too much.'

She felt her arms taken by wet hands as the marines came up behind her. She looked at Hamilton. 'Tell him he must listen to me.'

Hamilton was sitting very still. He looked at Codrington, then back to her. He nodded.

The admiral removed his napkin and rose. 'Leave us,' he said to the table, then to Hamilton: 'Not you.'

The officers got up and went, the marines with them. The three of them were left alone.

'You are a determined woman,' said the admiral, shutting the door, 'but I will not do what you want. I'll not be the one to provoke war with Russia. Everything Ibrahim said was true, damn him. The treaty is unenforceable. He can do what he wants.'

'And why is it unenforceable?' she asked quietly, taking a seat. 'You know why: because the men who agreed to it are caught between doing what is right and what is expedient.' She paused. 'But they don't have all the facts.'

'What do you mean?'

'I mean that there are things they don't know: things that would change their minds if they did.'

'What things?'

She turned to the man across from her. 'Captain Hamilton, what do you think made Tzar Nicholas change his mind and sign the treaty? The one that you brought from Russia?'

The captain was folding his napkin with care. He placed it by the side of his plate and looked up at Codrington. 'I believe it was the news that the gold sent by his brother, the last Tzar, had been found by parties who could prove its real destination,' he said carefully.

Codrington went to his seat and sat down. 'I don't understand,' he said.

Manto poured him some wine. 'Then let me help you.' She watched him drain the glass. 'There once was a Russian Empress called Catherine the Great who devised a plan to recreate the Roman Empire with Constantinople at its centre, Orthodox Christianity as its creed and Russia as its master, but it never came to pass. Half a century on, a new tzar thought he'd try again, using the revolution in Greece as his pretext. He came up with a plan to divide the Ottoman Empire between Russia and Egypt. But gold intended for Egypt got lost off the Mani coast. Now it's been found and the secret is no longer a secret. Instead, it has become embarrassing. And deadly.'

Codrington was very still. 'You can prove all this?'

Manto pushed the briefcase towards him. 'It is all in there: gold coins, signed confessions, maps . . . everything. I will leave them with you to read.' She rose. 'I will return to my cabin.'

She walked to the door and paused. She turned. 'I understand you have agreed to leave a single frigate on station while you retire the squadron to Zante. Might I suggest that Captain Hamilton's be that frigate?'

# CHAPTER THIRTY-FIVE

## ITEA

Tzanis woke to hot breath on his face that smelt of old wine. It was dark and a man was bent over him, dust in his hair, shaking him. He recognized him as one of Sève's men. They were to leave immediately for Navarino.

He rose and dressed, picking up stale bread from his supper. Soon he was riding hard, galloping away from the rising sun, every movement a torture of broken ribs.

They rode all day past villages and fields scorched by war. They passed starving people lying by the side of the road, too weak to beg. The day was hot by mid-morning, mist rising over the sea to their left, clinging to its surface in rolls of white.

They boarded a ferry at the straits, holding the horses against a current that made their world unstable. At Rio, they disembarked and rode south, passing more devastation, more death. It was late evening when they saw Navarino Bay stretched out below them. Tzanis reined in his horse.

'What is that?' he asked, one hand to his ribs, the other pointing to a vast muddle of tents and hovels that scattered the hillside.

'Refugees.' The Frenchman leant from his saddle and spat. 'We don't have time for them.'

Tzanis didn't move. 'Who is feeding them?'

The soldier shrugged. 'No one, most likely. They'll be dead or enslaved soon enough. The town's full of Egyptians waiting to take their place.'

Tzanis's escort took his rein and they rode on. He'd thought briefly of escape, but not seriously. Navarino was where he needed to be.

The *Karteria* hadn't needed to raise her sails once for her journey up to the Gulf of Corinth. A stiff northerly had driven her past Zante to arrive at its mouth in a day and a night. It was midday when they ran the gauntlet of the Rio straits, an hour before a barge crossed over with Tzanis aboard. Hastings and Howe wouldn't have seen him anyway; they were below-decks, looking at a map of Itea.

'Codrington's scouts say there are two ships in the bay,' said Hastings. 'Both Egyptian frigates. Good prizes.'

'And you'd take them on?' asked Howe. 'There's a fort guarding the entrance. It will have a battery.'

'And we'll have surprise,' said Hastings, 'and steam. Tomorrow evening, I'll put you ashore here, with a dozen marines. I want you to tackle the battery, then send up a flare.'

Howe nodded. 'And make for the town. Where might he be?'

The captain shrugged. 'Search any house that looks official. I'll do my best to distract them.'

They dropped anchor late the next afternoon in a little bay just short of Itea's and Howe was rowed ashore with his marines, all dressed in black, their faces smeared with burnt cork, their muskets cloaked with hessian. An hour later, the *Karteria* lit its furnace and moved slowly out of the bay.

Hastings surveyed his ship, silent in the gathering dusk. Between the poop and forecastle was a raised deck dividing two wells where the guns sat behind bulwarks, four to port, four to starboard, fore and aft. All were within reach of the furnace that would turn their shot red-hot, while also making steam to drive the paddles. The two engines, one for each paddle, had been his idea. It would improve the ship's manoeuvrability. His eyes travelled up the tall funnel. Would the engines let him down this time? *Please not.*

He looked further up to the pennants. The sun had just died, the wind with it, and that meant that he'd be able to manoeuvre and the two ships in Itea Bay wouldn't. The conditions were perfect. He would steam in, sink them, and steam out again before they even knew he was there. He smiled. Casus belli.

An officer came to stand beside him: Tombazis's eldest son. They stood in silence for a while before Hastings turned to him. 'You will make your father proud tonight. You'll be making history.'

A flare went up into the sky, the signal that Howe had silenced the battery in the fort. 'Full steam ahead, Mr Tombazis,' he said, 'if you please.'

The order was given and smoke belched from the funnel as the *Karteria*'s paddles started up. The ship moved forward and passed the hill with the now-silent battery at its top. It picked up speed as it swung round into the bay.

'Oh God.'

Hastings gripped the rail, leaning out. There were eleven ships in the bay, not two, and they were all drawn up in order of battle with their gun ports open. He saw several flashes at once and an explosion flung him across the deck. He felt the sudden lurch of something wounded, something crippled, beneath him. He got to his knees and crawled to look over the side.

One of the paddles had been blown clean from the ship's hull.

On board the *Cambrian*, all was quiet. The sea at the mouth of Navarino Bay was not deep and the frigate rode at anchor, hidden behind the island. Below deck, the crew were mostly asleep, lulled there by the gentle swell and a breeze that murmured through the rigging. Captain Hamilton was loved by his crew but never more so than tonight. He'd decreed that just he, and a few senior officers, would keep watch while they rested. It was typical of the man and they'd toasted him with the extra rum he'd issued.

He leant against the rail next to Manto, who'd been rowed over to the *Cambrian* before the squadron had left, no luggage except her picture of Hara, which now hung in her cabin. Both of them had been silent for a while now, lost in their own thoughts, both comfortable in a friendship born out of growing trust. It was two days since Codrington had taken the squadron to Zante, and three since Hastings had left for Itea. Both men would be there by now.

Manto glanced at the man next to her. '"There'll be a surprise waiting" for the *Karteria*, that's what he said.'

'He's bluffing. How could he know where Hastings was going?'

Manto considered this. 'But if it's a trap, if the *Karteria* is sunk . . .' she waved towards the bay, 'then all this . . .'

Hamilton leant towards her. 'Hastings has steam, remember,' he said quietly. 'If it's a trap, he can just put his paddles in reverse.'

She stared into the night, tightening her cloak against the

chill. She looked up at the island. They could see the glow of the fleet behind, and hear its sounds. The Turk and Egyptian crews were confident.

'What do you think he'll do?' she asked at last.

'Ibrahim Pasha? If there's provocation, I think he'll react.'

Manto shook her head. 'I'm not so sure. He has too much to lose by breaking the armistice.' She pointed. 'There's a refugee camp up in those hills that he's not touched since it's been there. He'd not have done that before.'

'True, but the treaty forbids Codrington to use force and Ibrahim knows that.'

'But why would he take such a risk?'

He looked at her. 'Because he is Ibrahim Pasha. Because he has absolute power. Because he has a temper.'

Howe was standing on the ramparts of the fort, entirely still. Behind him, the marines were tying up the Turks who'd chosen to surrender. It had been an easy fight.

He was rigid with shock. He'd just watched the *Karteria* steam into the bay, into an ambush waiting for her.

Now she'd been hit. Her side had erupted in flame and one of her paddles was floating uselessly in the water. The ship was foundering, lurching like an old drunk. One more hit and she'd go down.

*Think.*

It was still a diversion. Hastings would die and most of the crew, *but it was still a diversion.* And somewhere in this town might be Tzanis, who he'd sworn to find. He turned to where the marines were standing looking up at him, waiting for orders.

'Leave them,' he said, 'follow me.'

They raced down the hill, skipping rocks, tripping over roots, skidding on scree. Below, the little town had come awake. At the top of a minaret, a man was shouting down to people looking up from their doors. Out in the bay, the boom of cannon was continuous, deafening.

They reached bushes and paused to catch their breath. There were more explosions from the bay, screams as well. Howe couldn't bear to look. But the man next to him had risen.

'Sir,' he said. 'You should see this.'

Howe got slowly to his feet. In the gathering dusk, the bay was a firework display of exploding magazines, of flaming masts and sails. There were ships ablaze, sinking, men clinging to spars. But not the *Karteria*. At the centre of this chaos, the steamship was turning in circles, driven by a single paddle, firing red hot shells from her huge guns as she went, setting fire to everything she hit.

'My God,' said Howe quietly, his face lit by the inferno, his head slowly moving from side to side. '*My God.*'

On his flagship *Asia*, anchored fifty miles to the west, Codrington was on deck because he couldn't sleep. His squadron had left Navarino for Zante two days ago. He'd stayed with it part of the way, then split off to take up station at the entrance to the Gulf of Corinth.

Five hours ago, he'd seen fire on the horizon. Now sleep was beyond him.

He was thinking of what he'd done. He'd acted with caution, but without it too. He'd sent a fast cutter after the *Karteria* with orders to stop her before she reached the bay. Then he'd placed the *Cambrian* to watch over the fleets in Navarino Bay. But he had little expectation that the cutter would catch up with Hastings, or that the *Cambrian* would do its duty.

He took off his hat and scratched the bald top of his head, still sunburnt from the meeting. He frowned. *The insolence.*

He saw a light out in the darkness, a ship's lantern. It was the longboat coming in from the shore. He went down the ladder to the ship's side, walking up and down as he waited for it, impatient for the news. He felt the bump far down the ship's side, heard feet running up the steps. A midshipman was standing in front of him, breathless, grinning.

'The *Karteria*, sir,' he said. 'She's sunk nine ships at Itea Bay.'

Dawn was breaking over the *Cambrian* and soon things would be back to normal. The first bell would sound, the crew would stumble grumbling onto the deck and the day's routine would begin. The night's watch would be over. Manto looked out at the mouth of the bay, as she had for the past eight hours. There was no sound or movement of any kind, just a low mist that clung to the water, faintly glowing in the first light of day. *Nothing.* She felt sick.

Hamilton straightened, yawned and stretched. He looked up. 'It will be light soon,' he said. 'I can't keep the crew below forever.' He turned to go.

She nodded. It had been one chance and it was nearly gone. She breathed in deeply to settle her nerves. She took one last look.

'What's that?'

Hamilton came back to the rail and peered out into the gloom. 'What's what?'

'I saw something, I'm sure of it,' she whispered. 'There, look.' She pointed.

He saw it: the very faintest outline of something moving

329

slowly through the mist, something very big. It might have been a ghost ship. He turned to her.

'I think we should go below,' he said. 'It's getting cold.'

Tzanis was locked inside a tiny cabin on the port side of Ibrahim Pasha's flagship, a 74-gun frigate fresh out of the shipyards at Toulon. It had a cot, a desk and a porthole not big enough to climb through. It smelt of unwashed humanity and worse. It was leaving the bay.

He'd come aboard six hours ago with Colonel Sève, hands tied behind his back, and been pushed painfully across the deck, laughter all around him. It had been crowded with slovenly sailors, loose ropes, unfastened rigging, empty buckets. The only men in uniform had been officers watching from the poop deck, half of them French.

He'd been taken to his cabin and given food and water. He had tried to sleep, tired from his ride, from the pain, but the banging and scraping from next-door had made it impossible. He'd heard tables moved, guns rolled across the floor, then more frenzy out on the decks. He'd heard French commands, the running of feet. The ship was being prepared for something.

He'd eventually passed into a fitful sleep, but not for long. He'd woken to the slamming of a door in the next cabin. He'd peered through the porthole from his cot and seen that it was nearly dawn. He'd felt the ship stir beneath him, heard the slap of wave against the hull. They were moving.

He'd heard voices and pressed his ear to the wall: *French*. One was raised.

'Nine ships sunk! Nine ships go to the bottom and you tell me to do *nothing*?'

'Majesty, it's a trap.' Colonel Sève had been trying to stay calm. 'It's what they want you to do.'

'And I shall do it! I'll blow that stinking, pig-shit steamer out of the water!'

Tzanis had sat up and shaken his head, still groggy from sleep. The *Karteria* had sunk nine ships. *Nine?*

'They'll be waiting for us,' he'd heard Sève say, still calm, 'even if we get past the frigate. Zante is across from the gulf and the British squadron is there. We'll be turned back.'

'Not if we go now. The wind is strong. We can beat them there. And the frigate won't see us.'

'It may choose not to see us and the wind is changing.' The Colonel had paused. 'Majesty, we have the army ashore, ready to march. Take Nafplio and you have Greece. We need the fleet intact for the next part, all of it.'

There'd been the slamming of a fist on the table that made the panel ring, his ear with it.

'It is my will!' the Pasha shouted. *'My will!'*

Now they were passing the island and there was no frigate to stop them. Soon they were fighting their way up to the gulf, the wind having changed as Sève had predicted. When they got there, Tzanis heard two shots fired across their bows, then more rage from the cabin next door. He felt the ship come about.

In a day they'd got back to where they'd started. Through the porthole, Tzanis could see Sphacteria Island again, this time beneath sunshine. And he could see something else. Three squadrons of fighting ships were lying at anchor just outside Navarino Bay: ships flying the flags of Britain, France and Russia.

# CHAPTER THIRTY-SIX

## NAVARINO

Howe surveyed the scene from his saddle. 'Sweet Lord,' he whispered.

It was the same horror that Tzanis had stopped for: thousands of people huddled in little groups, lying among tents or whatever shelter they'd assembled: too weak to move, the only sound one low moan of universal agony. He wondered how many of them were already dead.

'I'm going to stay here,' he said, dismounting. 'You go on.'

Hastings looked down at Navarino Bay, the island beyond. They'd ridden hard to get there so fast, leaving the *Karteria* docked in Itea Bay waiting for repair. He pointed. 'That's the *Cambrian* out there. I could get word to Hamilton to bring food ashore.'

But between them and the town was the Egyptian army's camp. Howe nodded to it. 'And get it past that?'

Hastings swung himself out of the saddle. 'Then I'll stay as well. We can look for Tzanis later.'

A woman was approaching them, picking her way slowly through the sea of people with a child in her arms. The child's belly was distended, its arm swinging like a pendulum.

They watched her come. 'Look at her dress,' murmured Hastings. 'What's a Turk doing up here?'

They saw people moving to make way for her, saw her stop to comfort them, the child in her arms not moving. She came on.

'It's Hara,' whispered Howe.

She came up and looked at each of them in turn. 'I'm glad to see you here,' she said, her voice muffled beneath the hijab. 'I'm in need of some help.'

They both stared at her.

She didn't lower the veil, but looked down at the child. 'She's just died. I was going to bury her but I don't have a spade.'

Howe took the little body into his arms. 'We'll do that.' He looked down at it for a while, then back. 'How long have you been here?'

'Not long. I heard what you did.'

'Do you know where Manto is?' asked Hastings.

'I saw her rowed over to the *Cambrian* before the British fleet sailed away.' She looked down at the body in Howe's arms. 'We should bury her.'

They left the next morning to buy food with the money they had, Hara going first to get them different clothes. They filled a cart with bread and pulled it up the hill to the camp, no one asking why three Turks were taking food to Greeks. The drama out in the bay was the thing to watch.

After distributing the food, they went to sit together at a place where they too could watch. But nothing happened. All day the two fleets stayed where they were: one in the bay, the other outside it. The only activity was in the army camp.

'They're getting ready to march on Nafplio,' said Hastings somberly, 'while Codrington just sits there.' He shook his head. 'After everything we did.'

They spent three agonising days watching nothing. Ibrahim's army marched out, but did not come their way. Nothing would happen to provoke the allied fleet.

Then, very slowly, something began to take shape in the bay. The Turkish and Egyptian fleets slowly manoeuvred themselves into an enormous horseshoe that stretched from the fort to the southern tip of Sphacteria Island. It was set out in three lines: the front with ships of the line and large frigates; the second with smaller frigates and corvettes; the third with the remaining vessels.

'That's clever,' said Hastings. He leant in to Howe and pointed. 'The smaller ships can fire through the gaps in the frontline, protected by the larger ones.' He shook his head. 'That's French cunning for you, damn them. The cheek of it, when they have their own squadron outside.'

Howe brought a telescope to his eye. 'And the smaller ships at each end, the ones facing frontwards?'

'Fireships, but they'll need wind.'

Howe lowered the telescope. 'So what does it mean?'

'What does it mean? "Enter the bay and be destroyed", that's what it means.' Hastings shook his head. 'Sève's played it well enough.'

On Ibrahim's flagship, Colonel Sève was looking out at the two Ottoman fleets rolling at anchor. It was a formidable sight.

He turned to Tzanis who stood next to him in chains. 'Codrington won't dare enter the bay – it'd be suicide – and he can't stay out there forever. There'll be winter storms on the way. He'll have to go back to Zante.' He gestured to the poop deck. 'And he knows that every ship in this bay has Frenchmen aboard. These aren't just *Egyptians* that he'd face if he came in.'

Tzanis was glad to be out of the cabin but the view was disturbing and the chains heavy. Worst of all were his ribs. He looked over to the town.

Sève followed his gaze. 'Yes, the army has marched,' he said. 'Codrington was too late.'

# CHAPTER THIRTY-SEVEN

## NAVARINO

Manto stood on the poop deck of the *Cambrian* watching Captain Hamilton being rowed back from Codrington's flagship. He looked unsettled.

Not so the weather. There was almost no breeze to disturb the mirror surface of the sea. The ships of the allied fleet hardly moved at their anchors.

He came aboard in a hurry and disappeared into his cabin to brief his officers. Twenty minutes later, he came out and joined her at the rail.

'Well?'

He leant forward and put his hands together as if in prayer, his thumbs joined and upright. 'Codrington's still talking to the two other admirals. It seems he's happy to wait.'

'Wait for what?'

'A change in the weather, new orders from Paris or St Petersburg, a casus belli. Take your pick.'

'What do they all mean?'

He was frowning hard down at the water. 'Different things. If the weather turns nasty, we'll have to go back to Zante. If the

Russians and French take fright, we might have to withdraw altogether.'

'And the casus belli?'

He shook his head. 'We've had that and it didn't work. Ibrahim turned back.'

They fell into silence. Through the gap between the island and headland they could see the huge crescent of the enemy fleets filling the bay. 'Well we can't go in there,' he said. 'We'd be blown to pieces.' He paused. 'And de Rigny would never fire on his own countrymen. The Egyptian fleet is full of them.'

Manto straightened. 'What's that?' She was pointing up at the hills where smoke was rising.

Hamilton raised the telescope to his eye. 'That's the refugee camp,' he said. 'It's on fire.'

On Ibrahim's flagship, complete silence had descended on the poop deck. Five telescopes were trained on the hills above the town.

'It's the refugee camp,' said a French officer.

Sève grabbed the telescope from him. He looked through it, then gave it back. He turned to the flag officer. 'Signal to the shore,' he said. 'Tell them to get up there and put that fire out.' He looked over to what he could see of the allied fleet through the entrance to the bay. 'Can de Rigny see us?'

Another officer replied. 'If not him, then another in his squadron, sir. Do you mean to send a message?'

'I do,' he said, turning. 'Message to de Rigny: "Fire not started by us". Is that clear?'

On the *Cambrian*, Manto had turned from the hill back to the *Asia*. The smoke was now a thick, grey smudge, spreading

337

further across the horizon by the minute. Admiral Codrington must have seen it by now.

Hamilton had his telescope trained on the masthead. 'Still no signal.'

'But Ibrahim's burning the refugee camp,' she cried. 'What more casus belli does he want?'

He lowered the telescope and turned to her. 'If it's him.'

'Of course it's him,' she retorted. 'It's what he's been doing for months. We must attack, surely.'

He gestured over to the crescent of ships in the bay. 'How exactly, Manto?' he asked quietly. 'By sailing into *that*?'

They watched two longboats leave the *Asia*'s side. The French and Russian admirals were rejoining their squadrons.

There was a shout from the yardarm. 'Signal running up the *Asia*, sir!'

He raised the telescope again, keeping his head very still. He kept it trained for an age, waiting to see what would join the admiral's pennant. At last he lowered it very slowly. 'Good God,' he whispered, staring ahead.

'What?' asked Manto.

He looked at her. 'We are to enter the bay.'

From the moment that the marine drummer summoned all hands to their battle stations, the deck of the *Cambrian* was a blur of running men. Galley fires were doused, hammocks rolled and lashed to the sides, slack netting rigged above to repel boarders and falling debris. Hamilton went down below to see to the removal of bulkheads and siting of cannon.

Manto was impressed and sometimes amused. The air was filled not just with the sounds of men, but animals too. She watched as cows, pigs, sheep and goats were dragged to the sides, then winched into boats. Cages were tossed from man to man.

'Why the hen coops?' she asked when Hamilton returned. 'Is it to stop them stealing our eggs?'

He was looking up, watching chains being taken up to secure the yards. He glanced at her. 'Splinters,' he said, not smiling. 'Much worse than musket balls.'

She felt shamed by her levity. She watched him stride off with his hands behind his back, glancing over to the *Asia* for any new message, stopping to receive reports while the deck whirled about him. After twenty minutes, everything was ready.

A stillness descended over the ship as men stood silently to their stations, the only sound the creak and whine of the anchor raised. He came back to her side.

'Cleared for action,' he said. He glanced at her, smiling. 'It's not just splinters, it's so we can see what's going on. Though after two broadsides, it's all smoke.'

She nodded slowly. Despite the smile, she could feel his unease in the air between them. She'd called for attack, but now that it might happen she wasn't so sure. 'Is this sensible?' she asked quietly. 'They have double our guns.'

He glanced at her. 'It's not the number that matters, it's how quickly they can be fired. Three times a minute was what won us Trafalgar.'

'But aren't there Frenchmen with them? Men who know what to do?'

'We'll see,' he murmured. 'We'll see.'

She marvelled at his calm. Was this how Great Britain ruled the waves? She thought of Hastings sinking all those ships. 'Can't I do something?' she asked.

He considered it, his finger to his lips. 'Actually, there is,' he said at last. 'It may surprise you that there are women on this ship. They're down on the orlop deck right now, helping the surgeon prepare. You could help them.'

She nodded, turned and walked over to the steps. Down on the middle deck, the gun crews were crouched by their guns, stripped to the waist with handkerchiefs bound round their heads and over their ears to deaden the noise. The powder monkeys knelt behind, waiting to fetch cartridges from the magazine. A man was throwing sand over the floor for the blood. No one wore shoes. No one spoke.

She kicked off her own shoes and lifted her skirts. She'd not disturb them with the sound of her heels. She smiled as she passed. 'God be with you.'

She descended to the lower deck. It was darker here, though what light there was shone through the gun ports and was magnified by the white-painted walls. She felt ridiculous in her long silks.

Down on the orlop deck, it was darker still, for they were below the waterline and there were no gun ports, only lanterns. She made her way back to the cockpit where the midshipmen's mess table had been taken over for the surgeon's slab. Knives and saws were lined up with baskets below for the discarded limbs. On the floor were old canvas sails to stop the blood soaking through the deck timbers. There were buckets of sand and water everywhere. The air was stifling and claustrophobic and smelt of vinegar.

Manto breathed deeply to steady herself. This part of the ship's preparation was shocking, but she could manage it, and she was pleased that Hamilton had known that. She looked at the surgeon. He was surrounded by women of all ages, all in their petticoats. He was staring at her.

340

Calmly, she stripped off her dress, folded it and laid it on the floor next to theirs. She stood before them in her underwear. 'What can I do?' she asked.

There was quiet throughout the Egytian and Turkish fleets too, so much so that the sound of the allied fleet's anchors rising carried quite clearly over the air. The deck of Ibrahim's flagship felt like a theatre waiting for the curtain to rise, uncertain what would happen next. Everyone was standing at the ship's rail except Colonel Sève, who was leaning against a mast smoking a cheroot.

'Which way do you think he'll go?' he asked Tzanis. 'In or out?'

Tzanis shifted his chains. His arms were aching almost as much as his ribs. Outside the bay, the allied fleet's sails were being raised but there didn't seem enough wind to go in any direction. He saw boats being rowed away full of animals.

'I'm no expert,' continued Sève, blowing smoke out to the view, 'but I'd say Admiral Codrington was preparing for battle. Can he be that mad?'

Tzanis remained silent.

'Anyway,' said the Colonel, walking over to the side and flicking the cheroot over, 'you'll be the first to know if he is.'

There was movement now on the ship's rail. Telescopes were being passed from hand to hand and men were pointing. Something was happening. He overheard whispers.

The allied fleet was moving. Infinitely slowly, with all sails spread to catch every breath of wind, it was moving into the bay.

The call to action was sounded. The ship's side was abandoned by men going to their stations, the French officers swearing and cuffing them on their way. Eventually it was done and all was silence again.

Sève broke it with a shout to the flag officer. 'Tell all ships to hold their fire. No one is to do anything at all without an order.'

The wait was nerve-twisting. The allied fleet had formed into two lines and was moving slower than a man might swim. But their progress was relentless, irreversible. The wind, such as it was, came from the south-west, blowing straight behind them.

'He'll be trapped in the bay,' said Sève. 'No way out.' He glanced at Tzanis. 'He'll be wishing he was on the *Karteria*, I'd hazard.'

The British squadron had passed the headland and were now entering the bay, the first of the French coming into view behind. Tzanis watched with a mix of admiration and horror. How would Codrington extricate his squadrons if he needed to?

A shout came from the poop deck. Admiral de Rigny was running up a signal from his flagship. Colonel Sève climbed up and went over to the senior naval officer. Another officer approached and handed over a small sheet of paper.

The officer read it, then glanced at Sève. He walked over to the Egyptian admiral and whispered in his ear. The admiral read the message for himself, then shook his head in disbelief.

Sève was watching it all. 'What is it?' he asked. 'What does de Rigny want?'

The officer turned to face him. 'Admiral de Rigny requires all Frenchmen to leave the Egyptian fleet. Immediately.'

Sève stared at him. 'I forbid it.'

'Admiral de Rigny is our senior officer, sir.'

'He is with the *enemy*!' hissed the Colonel. 'We serve Ibrahim Pasha!'

The officer was already turning away. He began issuing orders. 'Signal the fleet,' he called.

Sève went over to him, grabbed his arm and swung him

round. 'I forbid you to leave this ship,' he yelled, all composure gone. 'I *forbid* it!'

The officer shook him off as others appeared at his side. Sève looked around. It was already happening. Men were going below to inform the gun crews. He went from one man to the next, remonstrating, threatening. He was ignored, brushed aside. At one point, two men had to restrain him.

Tzanis looked out to the fleet. Boats were being lowered over the ships' sides to take off the French. Men in blue were running up from below to get to them, the officers pushing them on.

Sève was shouting and waving his hands at a group of officers. They moved away and he stared wildly around. His eyes came to rest on Tzanis. He jumped down to the main deck and strode over to him.

'It makes no difference,' he said, his face very close, his eyes wild. 'The only place for them to anchor is inside the crescent. They'll be blown to pieces.'

A man came up behind him. 'Sir, the last boat is ready to leave.'

'I am staying.'

'Sir, the Egyptian gunners are no match . . .'

Sève spun round. 'Didn't you hear me? *I am staying!*'

The man shrugged and turned. The last men clambered over the sides and rowed away. Silence fell across the deck.

Out in the bay, the *Asia* was moving majestically into position, her pennants streaming, her gun ports half-open, the rest following in two stately lines: the British, then the French, then the Russians. There was the sound of an anchor released and a brass band struck up from the quarter-deck. Tzanis watched more ships take their places: the *Albion*, the *Genoa*, the *Glasgow* – big veterans of Trafalgar.

Sève turned to him. 'I'm afraid Admiral Codrington has just signed your death warrant.' He made a signal. 'Take him below. Tie him to the side, the one facing the enemy.'

On the poop deck of the *Cambrian*, Manto was standing once again by Hamilton's side. He'd asked her twice to go back below, but she'd not moved. She was still dressed in her petticoats.

'Everything is prepared down there,' she said, 'and the women have left to help the powder monkeys. I'll go below once anything happens.'

But nothing did happen. Ship by ship, the allied fleet took up position inside the crescent, but they did nothing else. There was no sound but the shout of orders and the rattle of anchor chain.

She looked out to the entrance of the bay. The French squadron was passing the headland now.

Some British vessels had been detached to keep watch over the fireships at the end of the enemy line. She saw smoke rise from the deck of a Turkish corvette and heard the rattle of musketry. A small boat, sent out from the British side, was being fired upon.

Then it happened all at once. The British shot their muskets back and the marines from a French man-of-war unleashed their firearms. Then came the boom of cannon. The corvette had fired a broadside.

On every ship of the allied squadrons, the gun ports opened wide.

Hara was perched on the headland at a point where she could see the whole of the bay. She'd watched the allied ships sail in. She'd heard their anchors released and the band start up on the

*Asia*. Her heart was thumping so hard that she wondered that she heard anything at all.

Then came the sound of musket fire from the Turkish corvette and the boom of cannon. She saw the gun ports of the allied fleet open.

She looked back to Ibrahim's flagship. Its ports were opening too, but there was something between them. No . . . *someone*. A man had been lowered over the ship's side by chains attached to his wrists. *Tzanis*.

She got up and ran. It wasn't far to the headland's edge but she covered the distance in a tangle of leaps and slides, her hijab forgotten. She dived off into the waters below, holding her breath long enough to swim almost to the fleets. When she surfaced, she saw nothing but smoke, the continuous flash of cannon pulsing throughout. The sound was louder than anything she'd ever heard before: a continuous, deafening roar that pounded her temples, rampaged through her mind, numbed every sense. Objects were landing around her, most of them on fire. She dived again, as deep as her lungs allowed, and turned towards the Egyptian line. She swam through the murk, the sounds of battle far above, muffled, until she saw the dim outline of a keel ahead. She swam along its side, then another. But her lungs were bursting. She had to rise.

She came up to an ocean of blood. She burst through into foaming, crimson waves scattered with debris and men, dead and alive. She looked up at a vast ship's side with blood running down it. *Side?* There was nothing left of it but splintered, smoking holes through which men leapt, their mouths open to scream, nothing emerging above the continuous roar of cannon.

The broadsides were coming from only one direction now.

On her side, the guns were stopping one by one. Some ships were even closing their shattered gun ports, as if that would save them. She saw the one above lurch and a cannon roll into the sea.

She swam on, counting the ships as she passed. A body rose from the water before her: headless, blood rimming its neck. She pushed it aside and went on, diving whenever she saw missiles coming through the smoke.

Then she was there. If she'd counted correctly, this ship flew Ibrahim's flag, or did. She paused to look up at its side. It was shiny with blood, leaning at a giddy angle. It was sinking. She saw a black void where Tzanis had once hung.

In the cockpit of the *Cambrian*, Manto had her palms to her ears. She'd run down from the poop deck through an inferno of firing, bucking cannon. She'd fought her way through the smoke, been cursed by colliding powder monkeys, fallen flat to the timbers twice when the splinters had flown. She had never imagined such a noise possible.

She stumbled into the cockpit dazed and coughing, her hands to her ears. She was handed an apron as the first casualty was being lifted onto the operating table.

'Brandy and funnel!' the surgeon shouted over the din. 'Hold him down.'

The man's arm was smashed below the elbow and he was too shocked to scream. It wouldn't have been heard anyway. The sound was one, continuous roar and the walls shook with every discharge of cannon. She fetched the brandy and put the funnel to his lips. She tipped the cask until it ran down his chin. Two sailors, black with soot, stood either side of him, holding him down. She watched the saw brought from the heated water and put to his skin. She went to hold his feet. A jet of blood shot into the air and she felt it warm on her skin.

Not far away, Hara launched herself up to reach a hole just above the waterline. She hauled herself inside. It was a vision of hell. Through the dense, suffocating smoke, she saw glimpses of bodies strewn across the floor, some without heads or limbs, some still chained to guns that were no longer firing. She saw broken beams spattered with blood and flesh. The ceiling had fallen in and everywhere were little fires. The smell of cordite, gore and excrement was beyond bearing, as was the heat. She fell to her knees, gagging.

She heard a boom as another broadside hit them, the sound of rending wood. She threw herself forward as splinters missed her by inches. A cannon broke its ropes and careered across the deck, bouncing off struts until it crashed into the sea through the widening gash in the ship's side.

'Tzanis!'

Her eyes were streaming. She could see nothing but choking smoke. Why was she shouting? How could anyone have survived this carnage?

'Tzanis!'

A man emerged from the smoke, his face blackened, his hair burnt to the scalp. He saw her and staggered back, disappearing into the murk. For a moment, she thought she knew him.

She heard a shout and turned. She got a glimpse of a figure lying against the side of the ship, a figure with a chain at one wrist, not moving. She crawled forward, scrambling over bodies. Another broadside smashed into them and she flattened herself, feeling the hot wind sweep her back, its pressure assault her ears. She looked up and rubbed her eyes and shook her head. More smoke.

*Tzanis.*

She heard coughing. She hauled herself forwards, digging her nails into the wood. She came close enough to see, to be seen. She didn't care.

'Who are you?' he asked.

He was naked to the waist, spattered with blood, reaching out to whoever was there. She looked at his bloodied wrists. He'd somehow freed one from its manacle, but the other was still chained to the wood behind him. The ship lurched again, and she grabbed his chain, watching more of the deck slide underwater. Water was coming in fast, splashing over his legs. He would drown if he stayed there.

She looked around. A bar from a smashed gun port was lying on the floor. She picked it up.

'Hold still.'

She placed one end in the link closest to his wrist and tried to break it, but it was too strong. The ship lurched again and she fell against the side. Another cannon trundled into the sea, bodies rolling after it. They were going down. Fast.

She heard shouts from far above. She pushed herself up and turned to him.

'Wait.'

She staggered through the smoke to some broken steps. She saw a dead man lying at the bottom next to his severed arm, in its hand a wooden plug the size of his face. She looked around. *Which hole?*

She hauled herself up to the next deck. Twisted, burned bodies lay among broken cannon, some still loose. A man was shuffling around on his knees, begging no one alive for water.

She got up to the next level and found light coming through from above. She heard the sounds of running feet, shouts. She got to the steps and climbed them. She emerged, blinking, onto the main deck, now at an angle, the bodies heaped against the side. A man staggered past, glancing at her as he went, no horror in the look. She put her fingers to her face and felt thick soot.

She glanced around at the Egyptian fleet. Through the smoke, she could see nothing but burning hulks with small boats leaving them, hurrying to the shore with survivors. The allied ships were still firing and nothing was coming back. It was a massacre.

Then a voice she recognised. She saw Colonel Sève at the other end, helping to manhandle a boat over the side.

'Wait!'

Sève turned. His face was smeared with blood and soot, his uniform too. He said something to the other men, then left to walk towards her, pausing as the ship rocked to another explosion.

He came up to her. There was madness in his eyes. 'Fifteen attempts to surrender,' he shouted, '*fifteen.*'

'Give me the key.'

He seemed dazed. 'It's too late,' he said. 'You should leave.'

'Not without him.'

Sève shrugged. 'Then you'll die too.' He turned.

'Wait!' she shouted to his back. 'At least give me the key.'

'I don't have it,' he said.

She stared at him as he walked away. There was another lurch and groan of timbers. She looked over the side. How high would the water be now?

She turned and ran over to the hatch, then jumped to the

deck below, slipping as she landed. She heard a creak and the vessel lurched again. She saw water seeping through the planks around her, welling up through the boards.

She found the next hatch and lowered herself through. She held her breath and dived, pushing aside bloated corpses, limbs trailing blood. The ship was disintegrating around her and she was fighting her way past broken wood and bodies dancing like puppets. She looked around, no clue which way to go. She heard more groaning above, the muffled shriek of wood tearing itself apart. The whole ship was sinking on top of her. She was too late. She glimpsed the side: a hole, a way out. She kicked towards it. Closer, closer . . .

Then through.

# CHAPTER THIRTY-EIGHT

## THE REFUGEE CAMP ABOVE NAVARINO

It was two months since the Battle of Navarino had destroyed both the Turkish and Egyptian fleets and guaranteed eventual victory for the Greeks in their war for independence.

With no body to bury, they'd held a service for Tzanis on a hill overlooking the bay. The whole camp had come, but mostly for Hara. The week before, she'd brought food up from the town and sent ships off for more. She'd brought tents and set up a hospital and church. She'd done what she'd done at the camp at Corinth. She'd saved lives.

Of course she'd been helped by Hastings, Howe and Manto . . . Hamilton too. But they'd left most of it to her, knowing that only by such activity could she be diverted from her constant, overwhelming grief.

They'd left her alone, but watched her too.

She'd not put on the hijab again, nor any other mask. The only person she cared about was dead, and there'd be no other. In time, even the children stopped staring at her.

They'd told her about the battle. Hastings had watched it all from the hill set alight by Howe. 'They tried to surrender,' he'd said, 'but it was either not seen or ignored.'

The rest of Greece didn't care. The news of the victory was flashed from mountain to mountain and the whole of the Peloponnese erupted in bell-ringing joy. Ibrahim Pasha, on his way to Nafplio, heard it and paused. Then he turned back.

The allied ships stayed in the bay, preparing their prizes for tow. The *Karteria* was brought back and taken out of the water for repair. The few surviving Egyptian ships were sent back to Alexandria with the settlers. Codrington was recalled to London to explain his actions. Not everyone thought him a hero.

Hara concentrated on the camp. She brought help from Corinth and, with Howe, expanded the hospital to cope with the battle's many wounded. There'd be no distinction between races.

One morning, she was sitting with Howe on a bench outside the tent, enjoying the early sunshine. Both of them had their faces turned to it, eyes closed.

'Where is Manto?' she asked. 'I didn't see her at breakfast.'

Howe was silent for a while. 'Probably still in the tent.'

Hara opened her eyes. She looked at him. 'Yours?'

Howe smiled. 'We find comfort in each other,' he said quietly.

She nodded slowly. *Comfort*. She'd forgotten what that felt like. Guilt, on the other hand, was her constant familiar, beside her day and night, whispering in her ear: *you swam away*.

She wrenched her thoughts back. 'Will she go back to America with you?' she asked.

'No. Her place is in Greece and mine in Boston,' he said. 'I want to talk to the man who sent me here.' He smiled. 'He has much to answer for.'

'But it worked.'

He looked out to sea, where the allied squadrons rode at anchor: placid, powerful. 'Did it? Doesn't Greece just have new masters?'

They heard footsteps. Manto was approaching, wrapped in a shawl and holding something beneath it, something angled. She came up to them.

She spoke to Howe. 'Can I talk to her?'

He rose. 'Of course. I need to go anyway. Some new wounded have come in.'

They watched him go. 'Why are they so late coming in?' asked Manto. 'It's been two months now.'

Hara made room for her on the bench. 'Because we didn't have space before.'

Manto settled herself down. It was a day of cold, brittle sunshine and the air around them was misted with their breath. 'I'm returning to Nafplio,' she said. 'Is there any point in asking?'

Hara smiled. 'If I'll come? No.' She put her hand on Manto's arm. 'But thank you.'

Manto looked out for a long time before speaking again. Then she said: 'He's closer here, isn't he?'

Hara had not talked about him for weeks but she wanted to now. 'He seems to be, yes. I'm not sure I like it.'

Manto turned to her. 'There was nothing you could have done,' she said. 'The ship was sinking.'

She nodded slowly. It wasn't really the point. She said, 'I should be grateful, really.' She pointed to her face. 'How could he have loved *this*?'

Manto took her hand. 'It wouldn't have mattered.'

Hara turned to her. 'Not to him, perhaps, but to me?' She shook her head and looked down. 'Every glance . . .'

'You mustn't think like that. Look,' Manto opened her shawl.

'I have a present for you: a parting gift.' She lifted the picture and put it onto Hara's lap. 'I thought you might like it now.'

Hara stared down at herself. She'd not seen it before, not wanted to. She wasn't sure she wanted to now, but here it was. 'The face of Greece,' she murmured, tracing her fingers across its surface. She closed her eyes and shook her head. She felt the tears quickly breach her defences. Manto put her arm around her and pulled her in.

'Yes,' she whispered into her hair. 'As you were, and always will be. You are what brought us together: him, me, Howe, Hastings.' She paused. 'Turn it over.'

Slowly, Hara turned the picture over. There was a pencil sketch on the back. She remembered moonlight in a church, a cloak laid out for the only love she would ever make.

'It's what he sent me from Missolonghi,' said Manto quietly, 'what I gave to Delacroix. It was his idea.'

Hara hadn't known. She was pleased. 'Did he see what it became?'

Manto nodded. 'He stole into my cabin once just to be with it.'

Then she took Hara's head in her hands and kissed her on each of her cheeks. 'I will always love you, Hara,' she whispered, 'always.'

She rose. Then she walked away.

The tent flap opened and Howe emerged. He looked bewildered. 'There is someone here who wants to see you.'

She followed him in. He led her over to a bed.

The man's head was bandaged across his brow; the face below was a confusion of little scars above a beard. She stopped before she reached his bedside, too shocked to go on.

The man turned his head to her. 'You saw me on the ship,' he said, his voice broken but still calm. 'You didn't recognise me.'

'Mustafa.' She shook her head slowly as she came forward. '*How?*'

'Tortured, then enslaved. To Sève.'

She stared at him. She saw that his beard had become entirely white. He'd aged by twenty years. She sat down on the bed. She didn't know what to say.

'I saw Sève,' she said at last, looking down. 'On the deck. I went up there to get the key. He said he didn't have it.'

Mustafa shook his head. 'He didn't. I did.'

'What?'

'He gave it to me before the battle began,' he said quietly. 'I don't know why. Perhaps he was human after all.'

She felt her heartbeat quicken. 'Then . . .'

He was smiling now, the deep lines in his face parting like old curtains. She felt Howe's hand on her shoulder, felt his breath on her neck. He bent down to whisper into her ear.

'There is a man,' he said, 'over there, who needs shaving. You see, he can't do it himself. He can't see.'

# EPILOGUE

## BOSTON MASSACHUSETTS, FIVE YEARS LATER

It was a blustery day in Boston, Massachusetts, that promised rain. Samuel Gridley Howe looked up at the sky and opened his umbrella, thinking perhaps it might come soon. He was standing on the steps of the Perkins School for the Blind, waiting for the President of America to arrive.

Next to him stood Manto Kavardis, Greece's Ambassador to Washington, and next to her, Under-Secretary Panagiotis Persides, who himself was blind. If he'd been able to do such a thing, he might have exchanged glances with Howe. It was on a day like this, seven years before, that they'd met at a Unitarian church on Brattle Street.

All three of them wore black, for this was to be a day of mourning as well as celebration. Four years ago, Frank Abney Hastings had been killed in action. A wound he'd received at Aitoliko had seemed minor at first, but infection had set in. She still missed his stiff Englishness in this land of the relaxed.

She put a hand out to the rain and watched the first spots land on her glove. '"The Lafayette of the Greek Revolution"' she murmured, 'that's what they're calling you in Washington. Did you know that?' She nudged Howe with her elbow. 'Still, it got the President here.'

Howe turned to signal to Mustafa for another umbrella. 'No, you got him here, Manto,' he said. 'How much did you have to bribe him?'

She shook her head. 'I gave a small donation to his new party,' she said. 'That's all.'

Howe took the umbrella from Mustafa and passed it to Panagiotis. 'The Democrat Party,' he said. 'What America seems to have achieved but Greece can't. Why didn't Capodistrias give them a vote? It might have saved his life.'

Manto thought back to a good man who'd done his best as Greece's first president for four short years, only to be assassinated for his troubles. Not even Kolokotronis had been able to protect him.

The sound of wheels on gravel came to them through the rain as two carriages swept through the gates.

'Jackson will be in the first,' he said, as they moved together down the steps, 'royalty in the second.'

The carriage door opened and President Jackson stepped out, a wide hat clamped to his enormous mane of hair. He nodded to them. 'Manto, Samuel. I hope you're not wet?'

Howe held an umbrella over the President as they mounted the steps. Manto waited for the second carriage to open its door. She hardly noticed Mustafa arrive by her side.

Royalty sent its children into the rain first. She watched them handed down to the foot-plate and into the hands of Mustafa. She knew their names: Princess Kanta was four and Prince Christos three. She'd met Kanta as a baby.

'Manto.'

Childbirth had suited Hara well. It had filled her out in body and face. The scars and joins were less obvious than when she'd last seen her.

The two women embraced for a long time, before Manto turned to kiss the Prince on each cheek. She drew back, her hands on his arms. 'Are you *looking* at me, Tzanis?' she asked. 'Really?'

He nodded and smiled at the same time. 'It gets better every day. You're a blur, but you're there.'

The children were being shepherded up the steps by Mustafa. Manto linked arms with Hara and Tzanis and they followed them up.

'Both of us in black,' she said, squeezing Hara's arm. 'Like the old days.'

They arrived in the hall where a crowd was seated in two columns of chairs. They walked down between them, still arm in arm. 'When we unveiled you in Paris,' she whispered, leaning in, 'we only had one royalty. Hastings gets four.'

'Stop it, Manto,' hissed Hara. 'Has America made you republican?'

'It would be bad timing,' said Tzanis from the other side. 'I hear Greece is to have a German for king.'

'Invited by Kolokotronis,' nodded Manto. 'Who'd have thought?'

They'd arrived at the front where Howe and the President were standing either side of a bust covered by a velvet cloth. They went to stand beside Howe.

Manto looked over the audience. At the front sat the blind: men, women, girls and boys of all ages, with Colonel Perkins, who'd given the building, among them. Behind sat the staff: mainly Mustafa and his family. Howe was Director of the School but Mustafa would be responsible for running it. In the last rows were the rich of Boston: the men and women who'd joined Manto in paying for it. They looked as proud as they should be. The Perkins School for the Blind was the first of its kind.

President Jackson cleared his throat and the audience fell silent.

'Today we pay honour to an extraordinary band of people,' he said, 'all of whom are here, either alive or in sculpture.' He gestured to his side. 'Samuel Gridley Howe, Manto Kavardis, the Prince and Princess Comnenos,' he pointed to his front, 'and Mustafa. As unlikely a group to win a revolution as you might wish to meet.' He paused. 'And this man,' he turned and pulled a cord so that the bust of Hastings was freed of its cover, 'this man, who made up the last of this band, made the ultimate sacrifice of his life.'

Now the President turned and pointed to a picture that hung above the doors into the school.

'But he left us something to change the world,' he said. 'The *Karteria* was the first vessel to steam into battle and it changed the fate of Greece.' He paused again. 'And the world.'

Afterwards, when everyone had gone and Suleiman had taken Kanta and Christos to their beds, the five of them sat on chairs around the bust doing something that Hastings would never have permitted. They held hands. It had been Hara's idea.

She looked round at them. 'I think we should take him back to Greece,' she said quietly. 'Don't you?'

Manto nodded. 'There'll be statues of Kolokotronis and Petrobey in every square,' she said. 'Even Capodistrias, once they realise what he did.'

'And England won't honour him as it should,' said Tzanis.

360

'Where would you put him?' asked Howe.

Hara glanced at her husband. 'We have a place. In Tsimova, which is now called Areopolis.' She paused. 'In the Mani, where it all began.'

# HISTORICAL NOTE

Almost every town in Greece has a statue of a man with a flowing moustache and pistols in his belt. Every region has its hero or heroine who single-handedly won the Greek War of Independence. Every hint that not everything might have been heroic, or even Greek, is likely to be met with dismissal or worse.

Yet the truth about the Greek Revolution is that it was a messy, savage affair won as much outside, as inside, Greece and despite a Greek leadership that often spent as much time fighting itself as it did the Turks and Egyptians. This is in no way to deny the astonishing courage and sacrifice made by many, especially the ordinary Greek people.

The context of the war is as important as its events. After the final defeat of Napoleon in 1815, Europe's victorious monarchies determined there would be no more revolutions. Yet among the people of Europe, the mood was different. Romanticism was in the air and poets like Byron were stirring dreams of freedom for places like Italy and Greece still ruled by alien empires. There were new channels for people to express their will: not just in poetry, but through paintings, newspapers – even donations via the many Philhellene Committees set up across Europe and America. Greece became the subject of fascination for a

363

generation who'd received a classical education, read Byron and been denied visits to Italy during the Napoleonic years.

There were three main factions that fought the war on the Greek side: the traditional warlords like Theodoros Kolokotronis and Petrobey with their klepht armies (the klephts being the informal militia/bandits that had held sway over the Greek countryside during Ottoman rule); the Phanariots (the old Greek aristocracy, such as Alexandros Mavrokordatos and Ioannis Kapodistrias, who had either served the Ottoman Empire or lived abroad and now saw themselves with the hereditary entitlement to lead); and the merchant/trading families from the islands, especially those from Hydra and Spetses, whose merchant fleets became the basis for the revolutionary navy.

The war itself was a Greek tragedy played out in four parts.

In Part One, Petros Mavromichalis, Bey of the Mani (Petrobey), raised the standard of revolt against the Ottoman Empire in the little square of Tsimova, today's Areopolis. The Mani is the southernmost tip of Greece, a wild and lawless region that had never properly been subjugated by the Ottoman Empire in its 400-year rule. The Greek warlords and their klepht armies then roared out to take most of the Peloponnese while similar risings occurred in the north. They were well-timed. The main Ottoman army was away in Epirus dealing with another unruly vassal, Ali Pasha. The revolutionaries took Kalamata, then Tripolis and when the Ottoman army marched back, it was defeated by Kolokotronis at the Pass of Dervenakia.

Part Two saw these early victories largely thrown away as rival factions plunged the country into two civil wars. It was the

Phanariots (led by Mavrokordatos) that emerged victorious and they imprisoned their main rival Kolokotronis in the fortress of Palmidi above Nafplio, which then served as their capital.

Part Three opened in February 1825 with the invasion of the Peloponnese by Ibrahim Pasha. He was the son of Muhammed Ali, Khedive of Egypt, who'd modernised its government and army and made it almost independent of the Ottoman Empire. The Ottoman Sultan, Mahmud II, had offered him the Peloponnese as reward for putting down the revolution. Led by Colonel Anthelme Sève, the Egyptian army did its work with deadly efficiency. Despite Kolokotronis's release from prison, by the fall of Missolonghi in April 1826 (where Byron had succumbed to fever a year earlier), most of the Peloponnese was in Egyptian hands.

Part Four was brought about largely by Ibrahim Pasha's excesses. Faced with the Greeks' refusal to surrender, he resorted to genocide. The land was set on fire and the villages emptied for slaves, while Egyptian settlers were brought over to repopulate them. People abroad, already stirred by Byron and painters like Delacroix (who'd recorded the war's horrors in huge public masterpieces), were appalled. For perhaps the first time in history, public opinion demanded that *something should be done*.

The Treaty of London, drawn up between Britain, France and Russia in 1827, was the result, but it was as ambiguous as the Great Powers could make it. Their problems were twofold. How could they, as established monarchies, support insurrection against another of their kind? And if the ever-weakening Ottoman Empire were to fall apart, how would the spoils be divided between them without provoking a world war? The treaty stated that the Great Powers would mediate between the two sides and cut off supplies to Ibrahim's army in the Peloponnese, but forbade the use of force.

Luckily for the Greeks, the man to interpret it was not known for his diplomacy. He was Admiral Sir Edward Codrington, a veteran of Trafalgar, who immediately sailed the combined allied fleet to Navarino Bay in the western Peloponnese where the main Egyptian and Turkish navies lay. When it became clear that Ibrahim had no intention of stopping his genocide, Codrington ordered his twenty ships in to face a combined Turko/Egyptian fleet numbering over eighty vessels. Despite being so outnumbered, the skill and speed of the European gun crews completely destroyed the combined Ottoman fleets at the Battle of Navarino on October 20th 1827, the last naval engagement to be fought under sail. It was to take another five years of coercion and diplomacy, but Greece had won its revolution.

The war itself lasted eleven long years and almost destroyed the new country before it began. When independence was finally won in 1832, it was for an area that included just the Peloponnese and Attica (the strip of land north of the Isthmus of Corinth that includes Athens), with a population of only 800,000. But had it, in fact, been as much Europe's revolution as Greece's? There is a strong case for saying that what happened in Greece expressed a wider European stand against the reactionary politics of the post-Napoleonic order, that it led directly to the revolutions of 1830, 1848 and even 1917. That is why half of the main characters in this book come from outside Greece.

At its heart is Hara, a young girl from the wilds of the Mani peninsula who becomes swept up in events beyond her control. She is the essence of Greece and its unwitting face to the world (but not, in fact, Delacroix's subject for his masterpiece, 'Greece Expiring on the Ruins of Missolonghi').

Manto Kavardis is her Greek opposite. Part of a rich trading dynasty with contacts around the world, she is plunged into the greatest of the many atrocities committed by both sides during the war. Approximately 100,000 of the 120,000 inhabitants of the island of Chios were either slaughtered or enslaved in the spring of 1822, when the Turkish authorities brought convicts and fanatics over from the mainland to wreak their revenge. Delacroix painted it too.

In London, Manto meets Dorothea von Lieven (1785-1857), wife to the Tzar's ambassador to London and one of history's most intriguing women. She was instrumental in bringing Russia to the aid of Greece. London was then, as it is now, the centre for world finance. Its stock exchange had already tapped the Philhellenic mood by raising two loans for the Revolution, albeit on appalling terms. Both loans were largely misspent.

Prince Tzanis Comnenos is of the Phanariot class. Like many Greek exiles, he'd served the Russian Empire as soldier and diplomat but returned to Greece to fight for its cause.

Samuel Gridley Howe (1801-1876) was a great American abolitionist who also set up the world's first school for the blind in Boston, Massachusetts. He had a tempestuous marriage with Julia Ward, who wrote 'The Battle Hymn of the Republic'. Less well known were his adventures in Greece as a young man. His marvellous diaries show him to have been a good doctor and friend to Greece. Gratifyingly, there is a mysterious gap of a year in them, which has allowed me to imagine him going to London, something he almost certainly didn't do. He can be said to represent the many philhellenes who, as happened a century later in the Spanish Civil War, answered the call of freedom abroad. Most of these were young romantics, intoxicated by Byron, who were soon to be disenchanted by events on the ground.

Frank Abney Hastings (1794-1828) is revered in Greece, yet almost unknown in Britain. He was an English naval officer who'd resigned from the service after challenging a senior officer to a duel and joined the Greek Revolutionary Navy. He built the *Karteria*, the first steamship to fight in battle. He was killed in 1828 during a minor skirmish after Navarino. There is no monument to him at Areopolis as I suggest, but perhaps there should be.

Mustafa represents the many Turks who had made Greece their home during the four hundred years of Ottoman rule and were caught up in the wanton cruelty of the struggle. Entire Turkish populations in towns such as Tripoli were slaughtered in the violence of tit-for-tat, events that were to foreshadow the horror of Balkan ethnic cleansing in our own times.

Alexandros Mavrokordatos (1791-1865) was a member of one of the oldest Phanariot families who hastened back to join the Revolution in 1821. He became Greece's de facto leader and wrote its first constitution, looking to the British model for his inspiration.

If Mavrokordatos looked to Britain, his main rival, Theodoros Kolokotronis (1770-1843), looked to Russia for support. A former klepht, he became Greece's greatest warlord and was appointed overall commander of Greek forces in 1825, following Ibrahim Pasha's invasion. After the war he changed tack and became the main supporter of Kapodistrias's attempt to unify the country, then of its first king, Otto of Bavaria.

Count Ioannis Kapodistrias (1776-1831) was Greece's first president. A Phanariot, he had served Tzar Alexander I as Foreign Minister, but had not supported Russian intervention. In the four short years of his presidency, he laid the foundation for the Greek State. He was assassinated by one of Petrobey's sons in 1831.

Petros (Petrobey) Mavromichalis (1765-1848) was the main warlord of the Mani who first raised the standard of revolt in the square of Tsimova on March 21st 1821. Despite his son's murder of Kapodistrias, which he publicly disowned, he served King Otto's first government as a senator.

Lord Cochrane, 10th Earl of Dundonad (1775-1860), is one of history's most colourful characters. He was a daring naval commander in the Napoleonic War (nicknamed 'The Sea Wolf' by Napoleon), a radical politician and a mercenary commander of the revolutionary navies of Brazil and Chile before that of Greece.

Colonel Anthelme Sève (1788-1860) is the main demon of the book and this is certainly unfair. He was a veteran of the Napoleonic War who'd helped Muhammed Ali modernise the Egyptian Army and led the invasion of the Peloponnese. Nothing suggests that he was anything other than a good and professional soldier. He ended his life in Egypt, a convert to Islam, where he was known as Soliman Pasha al-Faransawi (or 'Suleyman Pasha the French'). His great-granddaughter was Queen Nazli of Egypt, mother of its last king, Farouk.

A central theme of the book is a secret shipment of gold sent by the Tzar of Russia to help the Greeks. This is pure fiction, but 'The Greek Plan', masterminded by Catherine the Great half a century before, was real. Its intention was to carve up the Ottoman Empire between Russia and Austria by stirring up revolt in the Mani. I have imagined a new version of this between Russia and Egypt. There is no evidence to suggest that it was even considered.